Crossing Hearts

Crossing Hearts

KIMBERLY KINCAID

Montlake
Romance

Text copyright © 2017 Kimberly Kincaid
All rights reserved.

Published by Montlake Romance, Seattle

www.apub.com

Amazon, the Amazon logo, and Montlake Romance are trademarks of Amazon.com, Inc., or its affiliates.

ISBN-13: 9781503941700
ISBN-10: 1503941701

Cover design by Damonza
Cover photography by Regina Wamba of MaeIDesign.com

Printed in the United States of America

*This book is dedicated to my husband, who taught me
exactly what's possible when someone believes in you
even more than you believe in yourself.
I write happily ever after because I know it by heart.
I love you.*

CHAPTER ONE

As far as Hunter Cross was concerned, life was only as good as it was simple. So the fact that he was about to fall a solid twelve feet from the hayloft where he'd been catching the bales his brother Owen had been tossing up from the ground meant Hunter was about to have a shit day of epic proportions.

"God dammit!" Adrenaline sent his heart slam dancing against his ribs, his breath jamming to his lungs as the last of his balance went on a complete walkabout and he tumbled over the hayloft's edge. Hunter vaguely heard Owen's voice, laced tight with panic as it burst up from the hard-packed dirt floor, and instinct flared in a split-second flash of saving his ass over protecting his arm. He thrust his hand blindly overhead from midair, his fingertips slapping over the splintered ledge of the floorboards and digging in hard for the mother of all Hail Mary saves.

Hunter's surge of relief lasted less than a breath before the force of the fall combined with his body weight, reverberating up his arm and sending a bolt of liquid-lightning pain into his shoulder like rusty razor wire.

"Ah!" The pain tore a direct path from his arm to his mouth, stunning him so completely that any other movement—hell, even *breathing*—felt impossible.

"Hunter! Hang on." The bale of hay in Owen's grasp thudded gracelessly to the barn floor, scattering dust motes and a string of swear words through the morning sunlight streaming in past the double-wide doors. Hunter forced himself to keep his grip on the edge of the hayloft despite the hell-hot burn burrowing deep into the spot between his neck and the back of his arm. His brother wasted zero movements clambering up the wooden ladder four feet to Hunter's right, and seconds later, Owen had hauled him back to the safety of the rough-hewn boards of the hayloft.

"Jesus, that was close." Owen sat back on the heels of his work-bruised Red Wings, gray eyes wide with concern. "You okay?"

"Yeah, I—" The pain pulsed out a steady stream of *change your tune, buddy*, giving Hunter no choice but to recant. "I think I might've tweaked something in my shoulder, is all."

"Tweaked something," Owen repeated, both his tone and his frown marking Hunter's statement for the dial-down it was, but come on. No reason to make a molehill into Mount McKinley just because he'd—

Another blast of pain ricocheted from the right side of Hunter's chest all the way to his glove-covered fingertips as he tried to lift his arm, and, okay, maybe "tweaked" was a bit of an understatement.

"You need to go get that looked at." Owen wasn't one to mince words, that was for damned sure, just like, normally, Hunter wasn't a pushback kind of guy. But between the unpredictable weather this year and soil compositions that had been more miss than hit for their corn and soybean crops so far, they were up to their belt loops trying to get in front of an already weak season.

"Last I checked, we run the family farm, not a quilting circle," Hunter said, sticking a smile to both his face and his answer. Yeah, his shoulder felt like ten miles of bad road in the rain right now, but if he took a breather every time an ache popped up, he'd be permanently parked on the seat of his Wranglers. Not to mention just as permanently miserable.

If Owen's expression was anything to go by, he remained unimpressed. "We do run the family farm, which is exactly why you should get that shoulder checked out. If you have an injury, a day's worth of work around here isn't gonna make your arm feel any better."

Hunter formed his response with care, taking direct aim at the path of least resistance. "Okay. I'll call Doc Sanders when we're done with these." He jutted his chin toward the fat stack of golden-brown hay bales below that still needed moving into the hayloft. "Maybe she can take a look this week."

"You'll call her now," Owen said, his concern blanking any rough edges the words might've otherwise carried. "You busted up that shoulder pretty good in high school, Hunt. No reason to go lookin' for trouble."

"Ah, that was a dog's age ago. Really, I'm cool. It doesn't even hurt that bad." Hunter rolled his shoulder beneath his sweat-damp T-shirt in an effort to maximize the no-big-deal factor. Of course, his muscles chose that exact moment to remind him exactly who was boss by cranking down hard enough to make his wince inevitable.

Owen lifted one dark-brown brow. "Go. I'll find Eli and get him to finish this. Lord knows he could stand some good, hard work, anyway."

Hunter's gut tensed right along with his shoulder at the disdain in Owen's voice at the mention of their younger brother. Not that Eli helped matters by doing as little as possible to skate by, especially now that they were behind the eight ball more than usual, but still. When Eli put his mind to it, he got his hands just as dirty as the rest of them.

"Cut him a break, O. He was up with the roosters." Literally. The last place Hunter had seen Eli was by the henhouse adjacent to the hay barn at o'dark-thirty this morning.

"Mmm. So was I, and so were you and Dad. It doesn't make him special, and it damn sure doesn't give him license to fuck around when there's work to be done. With the Watermelon Festival next Saturday, we're going to be up to our eyes in it this coming week."

Shit. How had Hunter blanked—even temporarily—on the annual town-wide festival that signified the official beginning of summer in Millhaven? The Watermelon Festival was one of the biggest local events in the Shenandoah Valley, and Cross Creek Farm always had a huge booth there, showcasing all the pre-summer bounty of a hopefully strong season to come.

"I'm going to head into town and see the doc," he said, hoping like hell that the swerve in topic would loosen some of Owen's annoyance with Eli. As well practiced as he was at playing referee between his brothers, the job was getting to be more tiresome than a fucking triathlon lately. "I'll see if she can't fix this up for me."

We have a winner. "Okay, yeah." Owen nodded, scrubbing a hand over his darkly stubbled chin. "Just do me a favor and check in when you get word, alright?"

Hunter pulled in a calm, cool breath, determined to smooth the corners of the conversation and his life back to status-quo territory once and for all. He hadn't even fallen all the way out of the hayloft, for pity's sake. "You're worse than Dad. An ice pack and a little ibuprofen, and I'll be right as rain."

Owen's chuckle was quick, but at least he let it out. "Uh-huh. Don't come back 'til the doc signs off on it, you hear me?"

"Yeah, yeah. I hear you. You pain in the ass."

Owen dropped himself back down the ladder to the barn floor, unclipping the two-way radio at his hip and putting out an all call to find Eli. Hunter sent up a small, silent prayer that his younger brother was reasonably busy somewhere on Cross Creek's 750 acres, a relieved breath pushing past his lips as Eli responded with a slow drawl.

With all systems go—at least for the moment—Hunter shucked his thick leather work gloves and kicked his boots into motion down the ladder and toward the main house. His father was the only one who had technically resided in the two-story Colonial ever since Eli had turned eighteen and moved to the apartment complex up the road a decade ago. But the house where Hunter and his brothers had grown up not only held the farm's business office, but it was the central hub for all four men during the course of any given workday.

Translation: while Hunter had his own cottage on the east side of their property and Owen lived in a matching residence to the west, the house in front of him and the farm around him would always be home.

Hunter's footsteps called out his presence on the whitewashed porch steps, then the molasses-colored floorboards of the main house as he made his way over the threshold. Other than to endure regular cleanings and necessary repairs, the main house hadn't changed in twenty-four years, mostly because his father refused to change it. The lace-edged curtains, the time-scuffed farm table in the kitchen with the worn pine benches to match, the hand-stitched quilts on every bed—they'd all been chosen with care by Hunter's mother.

Which, Hunter suspected, was exactly why his father had never had the heart to replace them, despite the time that had passed since breast cancer had stolen her from them at the age of only thirty-seven. It was sure as hell why Hunter never so much as mentioned updating the place.

Tobias Cross's life had been hard enough single-parenting three boys while running the biggest family-owned farm in the Shenandoah Valley. Just because Hunter and his brothers were adults now didn't mean he was going to throw a monkey into the wrench by broaching a subject that would break his old man's heart. Again.

Hunter leaned against the white enamel sink at the kitchen counter, his shoulder throbbing with every movement and every breath as he washed and dried his hands. Owen hadn't just been blowing smoke about Hunter's old injury, even if the emphasis was on *old*. The rotator cuff tear had been nasty, and even at the resilient age of seventeen, it had taken one reconstructive surgery, three doctors, and eight months of uncut determination to get him healed up right so he could get back to work on the farm.

He hadn't really given much thought to the freak-accident play that had ended his high school football career since he'd healed, although come to think of it, he *had* kind of been going through the Icy Hot a little faster than usual lately. Guess it wouldn't be the dumbest thing going to get Doc Sanders to take a look. With any luck at all, she'd green-light his shoulder real quick, and he could get back to the farm in time to start work on the corn in the north fields—and keep Owen and Eli from trying to knock each other's blocks off while he was at it.

Adjusting his ancient Cross Creek baseball cap against the glare of the mid-June sunlight, Hunter grabbed the keys to his equally ancient Ford F-250 and hit the road into town. "Town" was a bit relative in Millhaven, since the closest thing to a stoplight in the entire zip code was the flashing amber caution marker outside the fire station. But that was just the way Hunter liked it. Streamlined. Simple. No muss, no fuss, and definitely no stress.

Until he got through the nurse's Q and A about the reason for his visit and into Doc Sanders's exam room, anyway.

"Hunter Cross." The doctor lifted her sandy-blond-gray brows high enough to breach the wire rims of her glasses as she read the fresh notes on top of his patient file, and shit, this couldn't be good. "Nurse Kelley tells me you're having some discomfort in your right shoulder."

The paper on the exam table gave up a crinkle as he shifted his weight. "Yes, ma'am. A little."

"Can you rate the pain on a scale of one to ten for me, ten being the worst pain you've ever felt?"

For a second, Hunter was tempted to tell the doctor the worst pain he'd ever felt had nothing to do with bodily harm and everything to do with a smart, feisty redhead, but he swallowed the urge along with a healthy dose of *where the hell did that come from?* Busting up his shoulder might resurface a thought or two from back in the day, but diving into the past so wasn't his thing. Especially when it came to memories that didn't just rock the boat but freaking capsized it.

Hunter shook his head, refocusing on the doc's question. "I guess it'd be a six when I move my arm. A seven if I try to lift something heavy."

"Hmm." Doc Sanders scribbled something in Hunter's chart, her expression softening even though she looked no less serious. "Then you're in more than 'a little' discomfort. You want to tell me how you hurt it?"

"The pain's not so bad." The joint in question ached at Hunter's verbal hopscotch around the truth, and, fuck it. He threw in the towel. "I was hauling bales of hay with Owen, and I lost my balance on the edge of the hayloft. I managed to catch myself before I fell all the way over, but the force torqued my shoulder pretty hard. The pain isn't as bad now, but my arm is still sore. It's the same one I hurt in high school, so . . ."

Doc Sanders nodded, the end of her neat ponytail swinging over the shoulder of her doctor's coat. "I remember."

"You do?" Surprise prickled through Hunter's chest beneath the faded-green gown he'd put on over his jeans.

The doc dished up a wry grin. "Not too many of my patients tear a rotator cuff on the winning touchdown in a high school football championship game, Hunter. Plus, if you recall, I assessed your injury on the way to the hospital. So, yes. I remember."

"Oh, right." Leave it to Doc Sanders to be able to dial up the details. The woman was whip smart. It also probably didn't hurt that she'd been a local for twenty years and Hunter's doctor for just as many.

Speaking of hurt . . . Time to get that all clear so he could go back to what mattered. Owen hadn't just been spouting off about how much needed done this week. "This pain isn't near as bad as when I tore my rotator cuff, though. And I didn't fall on my arm or anything like I did back then."

Okay, so the grab to save his ass today hadn't tickled, but he was well enough acquainted with manual labor to know this shouldn't be a big deal. Hauling bales of hay—or farm equipment or fertilizer or feed or any of a dozen other things—was all part of the daily checklist at Cross Creek. He could handle a little soreness.

"Rotator cuffs are tricky business," said Doc Sanders. "Let's start by taking a look at yours and seeing what we've got."

Her fingers traveled over Hunter's chest, shoulder, and arm in a careful clinical assessment. The contact wasn't so bad, and he could even handle the gentle pressure she applied when she got to the muscles and tendons on the back of his shoulder, proper. But as soon as she asked him to lift his arm and move it side to side, the pain jackhammered back through him hard enough to push a hiss through his teeth.

"So what do you think?" Hunter asked, his pulse picking up speed at the seriousness coloring Doc Sanders's expression.

"What I think is you're not going to like this. But without X-rays and an MRI, there's no way of knowing what we're dealing with here."

A cold sweat popped over Hunter's brow. "The injury is that bad?"

"It *might* be," she qualified. "Sometimes, damage to a rotator cuff is caused by one specific incident that can be easily pinpointed."

"Like when I tore mine in high school." Getting body slammed by an all-star defensive back with his arm fully extended had definitely been a specific incident. At least Hunter had gotten the arm with the ball over the goal line first. Not that the touchdown had mattered much when he'd had to spend eight months on the sidelines at the farm.

Doc Sanders nodded, taking a step back on the gray-and-white linoleum. "Exactly. But other times, we see what's called degenerative damage. The cause is usually repetitive stress over time. All it takes to aggravate that sort of damage is one wrong move, even a small one."

Ah hell. "Like grabbing on to the edge of a hayloft."

"I'm afraid so," she said, her expression backing up the truth in her words. "Listen, Hunter, we don't know anything for sure right now other than the fact that your shoulder needs to be looked at more closely. There's a possibility your pain is being caused by run-of-the-mill muscle strain. But with you already having suffered a full-thickness tear once before, and the fact that manual labor is a big part of your daily activity . . . I have to send you to the orthopedist in Camden Valley to find out what we're dealing with."

Hunter scraped in a deep breath. Held it. Forced himself to stay calm, composed. Steady. "Worst-case scenario." At Doc Sanders's obvious hesitation, he added, "I can handle it, Doc. But I need to know."

Slowly, she nodded, and her answer knifed through him harder than any pain his shoulder could dream of working up.

"Worst case is that your rotator cuff is torn, which would put you out of commission on the farm. Indefinitely."

CHAPTER TWO

Emerson Montgomery straightened the boxes of elastic bandages on the shelf in front of her for the thousandth time that hour. Turning to survey the one-room physical therapy office tucked in the back of Millhaven's medical center—aka Doc Sanders's family practice—she surveyed her new digs in search of something to keep her occupied. She'd already rearranged the rolls of athletic tape, wiped down the questionably sturdy portable massage table—along with the geriatric treadmill and recumbent bike over by the far wall—and organized the mismatched hand weights and resistance tubing she'd dug out of the storage closet.

She was still an hour shy of lunch on her first day at work, and she'd officially run out of things to do. Beautiful.

Now she had nothing but time to dwell on the fact that in the last two weeks, she'd lost a job she'd loved, a boyfriend she hadn't, and the ability to keep the one vow that had saved her life twelve years ago.

She was back in Millhaven.

Emerson blew out an exhale, trying to ignore the stiffness in her knees that made her wonder if her synovial fluid had been replaced with expired Elmer's glue. She knew she should be happy Doc Sanders had been willing to hire her to do supplemental physical therapy, especially when the fifteen job inquiries Emerson had made before her last-ditch call to the doctor had yielded fifteen positions requiring sixty hours a week, with fifty-nine of them on her feet. Under normal circumstances, Emerson would've pounced on any of those employment opportunities before returning to Millhaven. Hell, under *normal* circumstances, she'd have never left her high-powered, higher-energy job as one of the top physical therapists for the Super Bowl Champion Las Vegas Lightning in the first place. Of course, everything she'd known about normal had been blasted into bits five weeks ago.

And if there was one thing Emerson knew by heart, it was that once you broke something into enough pieces, your chances of putting it back together amounted to jack with a side of shit.

The door connecting the physical therapy room and the hallway leading to Doc Sanders's office space swung open with a squeak, and the woman in question poked her head past the threshold.

"Hi, Emerson." She swept a hand toward the PT room in an unspoken request for entry. Emerson nodded, sending a handful of bright-red hair tumbling out of the loose, low ponytail at her nape.

"Hey, yes, sure. Come on in Doc . . . tor Sanders," she said, awkwardly tacking on the more formal address. But the woman was her boss, an MD whom she respected greatly, and at any rate, more than a decade had passed since Emerson had left Millhaven. She was an adult now, a professional. Accomplished. Capable.

Even if her pretense for coming back home was a complete and utter lie.

"Emerson, please," Doc Sanders said, her smile conveying amusement over admonition. "I know with all your experience, you're probably used to different protocol with physicians, but call me Doc. No one in Millhaven has called me Doctor in . . . well, ever. And quite frankly, it makes me feel kind of stodgy."

Emerson dipped her chin, half out of deference and half to hide her smile. While all of the doctors on the Lightning's payroll had been top-of-their-field talented, they'd also sported enough arrogance to sink a submarine, making sure everyone down to the ball boys knew their status as MDs. Even though she'd technically earned the title of "Doctor" along with her PhD five years ago, she never used it, preferring to go by her first name like all the other physical therapists at the Lightning. True, she'd been the only one of the bunch with the varsity letters after her name, but the title meant nothing if she wasn't good enough to back it up hands-on. Plus, she'd always felt something heavy and uncomfortable in her chest on the rare occasion anyone called her Dr. Montgomery. She turned around every time, looking for her father.

Don't go there, girl. Head up. Eyes forward.

Emerson cleared her throat, stamping out the thoughts of both her father and her lost job as she kept the smile tacked to her face. "You got it, Doc. How are things in the office?"

"Not so bad for a Monday, although I could've done without Timmy Abernathy throwing up on my shoes."

"Gah." Emerson grimaced. Broken bones and ruptured tendons she could handle, no sweat. But stomach woes. No, thank you. "Sorry you've had a rough morning."

"Eh." Doc Sanders lifted one white-coated shoulder. "Timmy feels worse than I do, and I had an extra pair of cross-trainers in my gym bag. At any rate, I've got a patient for you, so I thought I'd pop over to see if you have an opening today."

Emerson thought of her schedule, complete with the tumbleweeds blowing through its wide-open spaces, and bit back the urge to laugh with both excitement and irony. "I'm sure I can fit someone in. What's the injury?"

"Rotator cuff. X-rays and MRI are complete, and Dr. Norris, the orthopedist in Camden Valley, ordered PT. But the patient is local, so I figured if you could take him, it'd be a win-win."

"Of course." An odd sensation plucked up Emerson's spine at the long-buried memory of a blue-eyed high school boy with his arm in a sling and a smile that could melt her like butter in a cast-iron skillet. "Um, my schedule is pretty flexible. What time did he want to come in?"

"Actually, he's a little anxious to get started, so he came directly here from the ortho's office . . ."

Doc Sanders turned toward the hallway leading to her waiting room, where a figure had appeared in the doorframe. Emerson blinked, trying to get her brain to reconcile the free-flowing confusion between the boy in her memory and the man standing in front of her. The gray-blue eyes were the same, although a tiny bit more weathered around the edges, and weirdly, the sling was also a match. But the person staring back at her was a *man*, with rough edges and sex appeal for days, full of hard angles and harder muscles under his jeans and T-shirt . . .

Hunter Cross.

Emerson stood with her feet anchored to the linoleum, unable to move or speak or even breathe. For the smallest scrap of a second, she tumbled back in time, her heart pounding so hard beneath her crisp white button-down that surely the traitorous thing would jump right out of her chest.

A blanket of stars littering the August sky . . . the warm weight of Hunter's varsity jacket wrapped around her shoulders . . . the warmer fit of his mouth on hers as the breeze carried his whispers, full of hope . . . "Don't go to New York. Stay with me, Em. Marry me and stay here in Millhaven where we'll always have this, just you and me . . ."

"Emerson? What . . . what the hell are you doing here?"

The deeper, definitely more rugged-around-the-edges version of his voice tipped the scales of her realization all the way into the present. She needed to say something, she knew, but her mouth had gone so dry that she'd have better luck rocketing to the moon in a paper airplane right now.

"I work here," Emerson finally managed, the truth of the words—of what they *meant*—delivering her back to reality with a hard snap. She hadn't returned to Millhaven for a jaunt down memory lane. Hell, she'd come back only when her process of elimination had dead-ended in total despair. She was here for one thing, and one thing only. To bury herself in as much work as her body would allow. Even if her first client probably hated her guts.

Check that. Hunter had probably moved on ages ago and didn't care one whit about her.

She sure hadn't given him any reason to when she'd turned down his marriage proposal and left town without a backward glance.

"You work here." Hunter's lips parted, his shock going for round two. "As in, you're back in Millhaven permanently?"

Regaining her composure (or, okay, *most* of it), she nodded. "I'm providing physical therapy for some of Doc Sanders's patients."

As if on cue, the doctor stepped toward the door, her Nikes squeaking softly over the aging linoleum. "Since you two seem to remember each other, I'll leave you to discuss the particulars. Thanks for your help, Emerson. Hope you heal quickly, Hunter."

They murmured a pair of thank-yous to Doc Sanders, although neither of them moved their eyes to watch her slip quietly down the hall. Emerson had no doubt the woman knew they'd remember each other—more than a decade might have passed since Emerson had clapped eyes on Hunter, but they'd spent their entire senior year glued at the hip *and* the lips. In a town as small as Millhaven, Doc Sanders would've had as much luck forgetting her own name as the fact that Emerson and Hunter had once been crazy about each other.

Although from the absolutely unreadable look on his still hand-some-as-hell face, if Hunter remembered, it wasn't fondly.

"Well," Hunter said as he finally broke the silence. "Can't say I ever expected to see you in Millhaven again. You were awful hell-bent on getting out of Dodge twelve years ago."

She knew she deserved them, but his words made a direct hit to her solar plexus all the same. "I was."

His brows lifted slightly, the only betrayal of his emotions. "I had no idea you were moving back to town."

"I just got in over the weekend," she said, selecting each syllable with care in order to give up as little information as possible about her return. If leaving the past behind was her number one goal, staying under the radar was a close second. Still, the fact that Hunter clearly hadn't heard she was back was a minor miracle considering the fortitude of Millhaven's small-town grapevine.

Then again, Emerson had barely been on the East Coast for a day and a half, and the only people who had known she'd planned to return were Doc Sanders, who detested gossip, and her parents, who were as unthrilled about the fallout from her move back to Millhaven as Emerson was to be here. Not that she'd told them the real reason she'd quit her job . . . or the truth behind why her star running back ex-boyfriend had quit *her*.

Head up, eyes forward.

She cleared her throat, straightening every millimeter of her five-foot-six frame despite the thudding ache it sent down the length of her spine. "Anyway, yes. I'm here in town permanently."

"Welcome back." Hunter's expression had grown perfectly polite, as if only twelve days had passed instead of the twelve years since they'd last seen each other, and Emerson's cheeks burned. She'd been so caught up in the spin cycle surrounding her move that the possibility of running into Hunter so soon hadn't been on her radar.

But she'd known she would see him, and she'd known it would hurt. Just like she'd known without a shred of doubt that he was still in Millhaven. He'd certainly made no secret of his desire to stay in the small Virginia town every day for the rest of his life. And, of course, despite his chilly reception, he'd probably long since gotten over her leaving after high school.

Even if the fact that she couldn't possibly have stayed had broken her heart.

"Thank you," she said stiffly, stuffing the past back where it belonged. "You look great. Shoulder notwithstanding."

"And you look like you've been busy over the last twelve years. *Doctor* Montgomery."

The slight emphasis on her technical title accompanied an equally slight lift of Hunter's chestnut-colored brows, and both made Emerson take a step back. She might not wear her title like a crown, or, okay, even care for the formal address, but she was still good at her job. She knew how to take care of people and help them heal, that was for damn sure.

"I got my doctorate in physical therapy five years ago from Swarington University. I may not be an MD like Doc Sanders, but I'm a licensed physical therapist with a concentrated specialty in sports medicine."

"I don't know," he said, scanning the painted cinderblock walls with a cool, ice-blue stare. "That sure sounds well and good, but there are no credentials up there. Am I supposed to just trust you?"

Emerson's pulse pressed hard at her throat. She'd left Millhaven for a reason, and it had been a damned good one. But that reason had been the one thing she'd never been able to tell him, the only thing she couldn't possibly have confessed, so now she had no choice but to say, "I guess I can see why you wouldn't want to take me at my word. My license and my degrees are currently in a moving van somewhere between here and Las Vegas. But I can promise I'm still more than qualified to treat you."

"Actually, I know all about your qualifications." Hunter regarded her from beneath the brim of his faded navy-blue baseball cap, but God, his expression was still indecipherable.

"You do."

Hunter met both the challenge and the disbelief in her voice head-on. "First of all, Doc Sanders never would have hired you if you weren't really legit. Secondly, you seem to forget how we operate around here. When the homecoming-queen-slash-valedictorian-slash-class president gets a handful of degrees from the most high-brow university in the nation, then a fancy job with a Super Bowl–winning football team, people in Millhaven tend to talk. A *lot*."

Emerson slid a deep breath into her lungs at the laundry list of her senior year accomplishments. Not that she'd chosen any of them. "I remember exactly how you operate around here," she said, smiling even though she had to work for it. "If Molly Mae so much as cuts someone's bangs crooked down at the Hair Lair, people in Millhaven tend to talk."

"Guess you've got us small-towners pegged just right, after all. So, what brings you all the way back to our humble little spot on the map, anyway?"

She fought the nervous fidget building in her veins. Nope. No chance in hell was she putting her toes in that pond. Especially not with Hunter Cross, no matter how many sexy muscles time had managed to chisel over his body.

From the look of things, time had been one busy bitch.

"I came back here to work. Which I suspect is what brought you in to see me." She gestured to his shoulder, praying the redirect would stick.

Score one for subterfuge. Hunter took a step forward, reluctantly offering up the manila file folder in his free hand. "It's how I got hurt, yeah. Owen and I were hauling hay bales last week, and I lost my balance in the loft."

Emerson's heart twisted against her rib cage, but she smoothed her expression into neutral as she took the folder and placed it on the slim stretch of counter space in front of her. "Did you fall on your shoulder?"

"No." He punctuated the word with a single shake of his head. "I caught myself one-handed going over the side."

"Whoa. No wonder your rotator cuff is pissed." Emerson propped the folder open, flipping through the orthopedist's notes and the X-ray and MRI printouts in a clinical assessment. "Looks like you got lucky."

Hunter's brows winged upward. With his free hand, he gestured to the navy-blue canvas holding his right arm flush to his T-shirt. "You call this lucky?"

"Your shoulder strain is moderate," she admitted, giving Dr. Norris's notes one last look before closing the folder to meet Hunter's are-you-kidding-me stare. "But there's no tear to the muscles or tendons, not even a partial. Considering you hung, what"—she paused to measure him with a glance—"a hundred and ninety pounds on a network of tendons meant to hold your bones in place rather than support your body weight, and that you've previously suffered a full-thickness tear in the same rotator cuff, yes. With luck like that, I think you should be playing the lottery."

Hunter paused, although the frown tugging at the edges of his ridiculously full mouth didn't budge. "One ninety-five. And I guess we'll just have to agree to disagree, because from where I sit, not being able to lift anything heavier than a bottle of water is far from lucky. Especially in summer."

"It's only halfway through June," Emerson pointed out. "If you follow doctor's orders and rehab your shoulder properly, you should be able to return to light lifting at Cross Creek in about four weeks."

"Are you implying that you think I won't play by the rules, Dr. Montgomery?" Hunter's eyes flashed more gray than blue, one corner of his mouth lifting just enough to bring out the dimple it had taken Emerson a full six months to block from her brain.

She scooped a breath all the way from her breastbone to her belly. The Hunter she'd known hadn't been a rule breaker—rocking the boat had just never been his way. But he had been dedicated to the farm above all else, a devotion that had clearly grown even stronger in the twelve years that had passed. As badly as Emerson needed to drown herself in work right now, she wasn't about to waste her time if he wasn't going to take his rehab seriously.

"I'm not implying anything, *Mr.* Cross." The formality hit its mark, unfolding his stance to its full six-two. "I'm flat out saying it's imperative for you to stay within the parameters set by your orthopedist if you want to regain full mobility and the muscular functionality required by your profession."

"In plain English for the country boy?" Hunter's expression revealed nothing, his tone a slow drawl that slid over her like honey. But he wasn't stupid, and neither was she. Emerson read the implication threaded deep within his voice as clear as a 160-foot jumbotron. The last thing she needed was yet another reminder she'd escaped everything that had smothered her in Millhaven—even at the cost of her heart—only to have no choice but to leave the job she'd loved to return as an outsider.

"I can get you back on the farm in good working order, Hunter, but if you want that shoulder to heal up right, you're going to have to trust me and do exactly what I tell you. Now are you okay with that, or should we just call it a day?"

CHAPTER THREE

For a gut-crushing second, Hunter thought Emerson would boot his ass out of the makeshift therapy room set up in the back of Doc Sanders's office, and God dammit, why had his cucumber-cool composure chosen *now* to pull a Houdini? Okay, so he'd probably have been less shocked to be face-to-face with Clint frickin' Eastwood than Emerson Montgomery, and yeah, the last time Hunter had seen her, she'd been stomping a mudhole in his heart. But twelve years had passed since the day she'd climbed into the BMW her father had given her for graduation and driven off to the most prestigious college in the United States. Caring about her, and all the impulsive, high-level emotions that had once gone with the thought of her, was just plain stupid. What he'd had with Emerson wasn't just the past—it was ancient history.

Christ, how had time only made her more gorgeous?

"So what you're saying is that if I want my shoulder to heal so I can get back to the farm, I have to trust you."

"The sessions won't work if you don't, so, yes," Emerson said, crossing her arms over her chest. "You're going to have to trust me."

Hunter's gut twisted, the word "no" forming hot and fast on his lips. Twelve years might have dropped off the calendar, but a hundred years wouldn't change the fact that she'd smashed his trust right along with his heart when she'd turned down his marriage proposal and abruptly left town. He'd been head over boot heels insane for her, and while proposing at eighteen might seem like an act of pure puppy love to some, Hunter had known differently. Or at least, he *thought* he had, and wasn't that all the more reason to let loose with that "no."

But, dammit, he couldn't make himself say it. As much as he hated the reality of his situation in the here and now, Dr. Norris had been crystal clear that physical therapy wasn't optional if Hunter wanted to return to the farm in one piece. The farm was what mattered now—belonging there was the only thing he could trust. Which meant he didn't just need to suck it up and follow the rules of rehabbing his shoulder to get back in working order.

Emerson was literally the only game in town. If he wanted his nice, simple life back, he needed *her*.

"Look, Hunter—" she started, but he cut her off with a shake of his head.

"You'd be willing to help me? If, you know, I do what you tell me and promise not to mess with my shoulder." He might not like the fact that he needed Emerson—in fact, he pretty much hated the crap out of it. But the last five days had been stressful enough. No way was he going to let this woman come out of the woodwork and rock the composure he needed in order to get back to the farm.

He'd forgotten her once. He could damn well stick to forgetting her again.

Emerson paused. "Are you willing to follow the therapy protocol?"

"Yeah. I guess. Yeah." He jammed his free thumb through the belt loop on his Wranglers, the tension in his chest unraveling by just a sliver as she tilted her head in a slow nod.

"Then of course I'll help you," she said, wiping a wayward strand of flame-red hair from her field of vision to tuck it primly behind her ear. "It's my job. I meant what I said when I told you I'm good at it."

Right. Figured she'd do the all-business thing. Fuck, with her mile-long list of expensive degrees and highbrow accomplishments, why not? "I guess you're the boss, then. So where do we start?"

Emerson gestured to the tiny therapy room. "Assessment. Now that I've seen your injury on paper, I'll need to examine your shoulder and do some tests to determine where you are in terms of pain threshold and mobility. Then we can get started on your first therapy session."

"You want to do all of that today?" His chin lifted, his surprise going for a double when a tiny smile crossed Emerson's lips.

"Don't you?"

Hell if she didn't have a point. "I'd do the whole four weeks of PT today if I could."

"You can't," she said, turning to get down to business. "I'm sure you remember from the last time you hurt your shoulder that rehabilitation is a marathon, not a sprint."

"I remember lots of things, actually." The words were out before Hunter could cage them, and Emerson's bright-red ballet slipper–looking shoes slapped to a halt as she swung to face him. His chest kicked with a healthy dose of *way to let it go, asshole*, but he still didn't drop his stare.

He did remember. He remembered busting his ass all summer long after his senior year of high school to save for a ring. He remembered sitting in the bed of his truck, just him and her and a billion stars, and asking her to be his wife. To stay with him in Millhaven forever.

And he definitely remembered her answer.

Emerson folded her arms over the front of her flawlessly pressed blouse, standing still for just another minute before continuing toward the exam table by the far wall. "So can you tell me what you're taking to manage the pain in your shoulder?"

Hunter followed her to the exam table, accepting her obvious bid to change the subject. The faster they got through this, the faster he'd be back at Cross Creek, where he belonged. "Dr. Norris gave me a prescription for some painkillers, but so far, I'm doing okay with ibu-profen." Not that he'd been able to get much sleep in the five days since he'd gone ass over teakettle. Every time he tried to roll over, his shoulder felt like it was chock-full of fire ants, just waiting for an excuse to swarm.

Emerson nodded. "That's good. You might want to fill that pre-scription just so you've got something stronger on hand if you need it, though. Once we start therapy, you'll probably be pretty sore."

"I'm already pretty sore," he mumbled. The exam table gave up more creaks and groans than a haunted house at midnight as Hunter settled his weight on the dark-red vinyl cushion and dangled his legs over the side, and Emerson lifted a brow.

"Let's see if we can't fix that a little." She pointed to his sling in a wordless request. He nodded, gingerly ducking out of the canvas and handing it over.

"Go ahead and lift your arm in front of you as high as you can," she said, repeating the request five different times at as many different angles while his shoulder grew more and more indignant.

"How is this fixing things, exactly?" Hunter asked, a thin sheen of perspiration warming his forehead from the pain rattling down the back of his shoulder.

"For starters, it's showing me that you need to ditch your sling."

"Really?" Huh. That *was* decent news.

Emerson's aquamarine stare didn't move from his shoulder, and damn, she took her job capital *S* seriously. "Don't get too excited, cow-boy. Losing the sling doesn't mean you're in great shape; in fact, it's quite the opposite. Your file says you fell five days ago. Has your shoulder been immobilized this whole time?"

"Yeah," Hunter said, the look on Emerson's pretty face blotting out the flicker of hope sparking behind his sternum. "Dr. Norris said he wanted to play it safe until he knew for sure there was no tear. Why, is that bad?"

"Yes and no. Erring on the side of caution is a good standard of care for someone with a repeat injury."

"But . . ." he led, and she didn't hesitate to fill in the blank.

"With the extra two days in there for the weekend, the immobility has locked up your shoulder pretty tightly. When was the last time you took that ibuprofen?"

He slid a glance at the clock on the wall, doing a quick count back. "This morning. Five hours ago, I guess."

"Mmm." Emerson took a handful of steps to a set of nearby storage shelves, pressing up to her toes to grab first one item, then another, from a set of medical supply boxes. Before completing the trip back to the exam table, she stooped down low in front of a mini fridge, but her movements slammed to an awkward halt with her fingers just shy of the handle.

"Emerson?" Hunter's pulse knocked a warning rhythm against his throat. "Are you okay?"

"I'm perfectly fine." As quickly as she'd paused, she began moving again, opening the fridge and unearthing a bottle of water with such ease that he felt pretty stupid for even asking the question.

Of course she was fine. Her demeanor was practically bulletproof.

Emerson retraced her steps back to the exam table, handing over the bottle of water and a single-dose packet of ibuprofen. "We've got our work cut out for us, but we should be able to get that shoulder at least a little looser today."

"Okay." Cracking open the water bottle, he threw back the ibuprofen, mostly because Emerson's expression told him in no uncertain terms that, if he didn't, she'd give him what for and why not 'til the sun went down. She stepped in front of the exam table, so close that just a few scant inches kept the outside of her thigh from brushing against his denim-covered knee, and Hunter slipped a covert glance over her while she readied the other supplies she'd grabbed from the shelf.

Emerson had been pretty back in high school, her fiery hair and quietly determined personality setting her apart from most of the other girls in their class. But the last twelve years had turned pretty on its ear, filling her with confidence and curves and all sorts of things Hunter couldn't help but notice now that she was within arm's reach.

Capable hands, with long fingers and neatly kept nails, slender forearms showcasing lean muscles leading up to the shirtsleeves she'd rolled to just below her elbows. Long, copper-colored hair that smelled like the honeysuckle he and Eli always had to cut back from the fence separating Cross Creek's wildflower garden from the yard of the main house . . . skin the shade of fresh cream that Hunter knew for a fact flushed pink whenever she—

"Ready to start?" Emerson's voice fast-tracked him right back to reality, and Christ, had he shredded his sanity along with his shoulder? She'd already crushed his pride once before by leaving Millhaven *and* him in her wake; plus, as of this second, she was his physical therapist. She held his livelihood in her hands, literally and figuratively. Thinking about her in any manner other than purely professional headlined the list of Worst Ideas in the Entire Fucking Galaxy.

He needed his calm, and he needed it right now.

"Yep. Absolutely." Hunter shifted his weight on the exam table, calling up a double dose of easy-does-it in order to buckle down on his brewing hard-on. Emerson activated the portable heat pack in her hands with a quick squeeze, and he exhaled in a burst of relief when she placed the gel-filled plastic on the back of his arm over his T-shirt.

"Ah." The sound was more groan than an actual word, but, helllllll yeah, Hunter didn't care. "That feels good."

Emerson blinked, just once before she gestured to the heat pack, moving her fingers after he reached across his body to hold the thing in place with his good hand. "Well, don't get used to it," she said, clearing her throat. "The increased blood flow will help everything unwind, which is what we want right now. But once it does, ice is going to be your best friend to reduce all this swelling."

Reaching for her pile of supplies, she plucked a thickly rolled ACE bandage from the exam table. She freed the end of the stretchy cotton with an efficient tug, her fingers pressing firmly against his as she began to secure the heat pack into place, and every last one of his muscles went on involuntary lockdown at the skin-on-skin contact.

"I'm sorry." Emerson froze, her shock-widened stare lifting to meet his from less than a foot away. "Did I hurt you?"

"No." Hunter's shoulder throbbed, doing its level best to keep time with his hammering pulse. How the hell had he forgotten that physical therapy was pretty much synonymous with physical contact, and a whole lot of it?

The question must've broadcast over his face in HD, because a frown commandeered Emerson's features, lickety-split. "You said you were okay with me treating you."

The slight flick of her glance toward the spot where their fingers still touched told Hunter she knew all too well why he'd flinched, and screw this. The past was the past. What he needed now was to patch up his shoulder, period.

"I'm fine," he said, willing his muscles to surrender their death grip and fixing her with a steady stare that backed up the sentiment. "Just let me know when I can let go of this thing."

"Okay," she finally answered, winding the ACE bandage over his chest and shoulder until the heat pack was secured snugly into place. "There. All set for now."

"Wow." Hunter turned from side to side, surprised to find that the bandage didn't budge but also wasn't so tight as to feel uncomfortable or hinder his movement. "You're pretty good at that."

Emerson's laugh caught him completely off guard, the sound unnervingly sexy and sweet all at once. "Considering that's one of the easier job requirements, I'd hope so."

God. She'd spent five years conditioning multimillion-dollar athletes. Of course she could wrap his shoulder with ease. "Sorry." Hunter dropped his chin in sheepish apology. "It's just that when I'd treat my shoulder in high school, I'd either lose the bag of ice in two seconds flat, or I'd feel like a walking tourniquet."

"Let me guess," Emerson said, and although the smile had left her lips, traces of it still hung in her voice. "Eli did the first bandage job, and Owen did the latter."

For the first time since he'd banana-peeled out of the hayloft, he considered a genuine laugh of his own. "Aw, look. You can take the girl out of the small town, but not the small town out of the girl."

"Oh, come on," she argued, albeit without the heat he knew she was capable of. "Anyone who's ever met your brothers could peg that one from a mile out. Anyway, you'll be doing this a lot in the coming weeks. I can show you the best technique to get an ice pack in place. That way it'll be easier for . . . um." She stopped short, blushing a ridiculously enticing shade of pink before soldiering on. "Whoever's wrapping your shoulder now."

A beat of deafeningly awkward silence followed, then another, before Hunter gave up a silent *fuck it* and forked over the truth. "Still Eli or Owen," he said, biting back a grunt as Emerson lifted his arm to the side. Jesus, his shoulder felt like it had been spray starched and set out in the afternoon sun.

"Really?" Her cinnamon-stick lashes fanned upward, betraying her surprise. "You didn't marry some sweet local girl like Jenny Hostetler or Candy Thompson?"

He pulled back far enough to make the exam table issue another ominous creak. "Oh, so now you're interested in talking weddings."

"It was just a question," she said, and the flush on her face told him it was one she hadn't intended to let out.

Don't be a dick. Do not be a dick. Don't . . . "Are you fishing for information?" he asked, and okay, then. Looked like he'd take Being a Dick for two hundred.

"I'm making polite conversation," Emerson corrected, releasing his arm back to his side.

"About my marital status."

"We can talk about the weather if you'd prefer."

"No," Hunter said, addressing both her suggestion and her question at once. He'd buried the past a long time ago. Over. Said. Done. If she wanted to go for the group share in the here and now, far be it for him to say no.

"I never got married. Candy and her sister moved to Camden Valley to open a bakery, and Jenny Hostetler married Mike Porter a couple years after we graduated. They have two kids and another one on the way."

Emerson lifted his arm again, and again, his shoulder cranked down on the movement. "Wait . . . Moonpie Porter, who ate all those dessert cakes on a dare in the sixth grade? Are you serious?"

"As a heart attack," he said, working up an expression to match the assertion. "Although I doubt Jenny calls him Moonpie."

"Everyone calls him Moonpie."

"Not everything around here is the same as it used to be."

Her fingers stuttered over his shoulder, and although the hitch lasted less than a second, Hunter felt it all the same. "Duly noted." A tiny crease appeared between her brows, erasing the ease that had softened her expression not ten seconds earlier. "God, your shoulder really doesn't want to let go. Let's try this."

She sidestepped to his left, angling her body so that her right hip pressed flush against the inside of his left knee. Flattening her palm over his sternum, Emerson splayed her fingers over the center of his chest. "Go ahead and lean forward until your good shoulder rests on mine.

Your injured arm should hang over the side of the table, and you can let it gently swing free for a minute like a pendulum."

"You want me to lean on you?" Hunter paused. He had to have a good sixty pounds on her in body weight, not to mention the eight-inch height differential that wasn't helped by his current position on the exam table.

But Emerson didn't hesitate. "We can't let your shoulder lock up any tighter, and this is the best way to allow gravity to loosen you up. The table will support the bulk of your body weight, but I can handle the rest. So to answer your question, yes. I want you to lean on me."

Hunter blew out a breath. He wanted to lean on her about as much as he wanted a tax audit right now—if the brush with her fingers had nearly fried his motherboard, a full-contact body lean was likely to send his idiot brain around the bend. But he'd promised to do what she told him to, and, to be honest, letting his arm swing free for a minute did sound pretty freaking appealing.

Even if he did have to trust Emerson in order to make that happen.

"Okay, fine. No sweat." He scooted to the edge of the exam table, placing his left shoulder against her right. Her right hand stayed firm against his breastbone, and he hinged forward, carefully and cautiously.

Nothing.

He shifted his weight, flattening his right palm on the table beside him for support. Again, he took a breath, inching forward at an awkward angle until the muscles in his back tightened in protest.

Again, nothing.

"Hunter." Emerson's voice vibrated against the thin cotton where his T-shirt met her shoulder. "I know you're out of your comfort zone, and that you're not thrilled about any of this, but I also know your shoulder has to be killing you, so, please. Do me a favor. Stop holding back so I can help you, here."

For a second, he nearly balked. Of *course* he was out of his goddamn comfort zone. He'd been benched for a solid month at Cross Creek, his shoulder was as tangled up and twisted as old Mrs. Ellersby's knitting, and he had to rely on the woman who'd once blown his heart to bits to get himself right again. But then he inhaled, the fresh floral scent of Emerson's hair going all the way into his lungs, and his shoulder shocked the hell out of him by beginning to unwind.

For the smallest part of a second, Hunter tried to fight the sensation. His traitorous body won out, though, pure muscle memory destroying the caution pumping down from his brain, and slowly, unwittingly, he released his weight against her body. Emerson held him up, her hand, her shoulder, her torso all warm, solid support. He melted into her, his breaths round and belly deep, pressing closer until his left arm dangled loosely over the side of the exam table.

Holy shit, the relief was enough to make him groan.

"There you go. Keep leaning," she murmured, her voice steady and calm, smooth as warm butter on bread. "Good. Now let your arm swing, nice and easy."

Hunter was powerless to do anything other than comply, the muscles on the back of his shoulder relinquishing another layer of their death grip. Letting his lids drift shut, he metered his breathing, releasing more and more tension from his body with every round of inhale/exhale. Finally, Emerson shifted her weight, carefully easing him back upright on the exam table.

"God, that was . . ." *Incredible. Mind-scrambling. Hot as sin.* Seriously, what was *wrong* with him?

Hunter straightened his spine and reset his shoulders, his brain finally kicking back into gear. "Uh, nice. Feels like it worked," he finished lamely. "I don't think I've ever done that stretch before."

"Oh." Emerson blinked once, then once more before turning to scoop up his chart from a nearby ledge. "You probably haven't, since I'm pretty sure I made this version up. It's a variation of leaning against a doorframe with your good shoulder. Same principle of letting gravity loosen the musculature, only this way tends to be more comfortable for the rest of the upper body, so you're better able to relax your arm."

Huh. Hell if that wasn't a half step from brilliant. "And you just made it up?"

"Sure." One corner of her mouth lifted along with her shoulders. "After working with a handful of all-star quarterbacks, you tend to have a few tricks up your sleeve."

The mention of her job—or former job, he guessed—brought him the rest of the way back to reality. "Speaking of which, what does your star running back boyfriend think of your relocation?"

Emerson tensed, and helllllooooo, sore spot. "You know about Lance?"

"Small town," he reminded her. Lance Devlin had been the Las Vegas Lightning's team MVP for the last three years, and as far as Hunter could tell from the press, the guy had been a douche bag for pretty much his entire adult life. While Devlin's relationship with Emerson wasn't too widely publicized in the media—certainly the work of some tireless PR rep, seeing as how they'd worked for the same team and all—it had been prime fodder for the Millhaven gossip mill ever since they'd started seeing each other about a year ago. But now she was here. And Devlin definitely wasn't.

At least there was no love lost for Hunter on that second part.

"So no wedding bells for you, either? Is that why you came home?"

A flash of vulnerability appeared in her bright-blue gaze, there and then gone. "I already told you, I came back to Millhaven to work. I'd prefer not to discuss my personal life during our sessions."

Hunter's heart kicked a hot burst of you've-got-to-be-kidding-me against his ribs. "But my personal life is fair play?"

"Actually, it's not," she said. "We've got a lot of ground to cover in the next four weeks to get you well again, and I am your physical therapist. All things considered, we should just concentrate on your shoulder."

Hunter opened his mouth, an argument locked and loaded on his tongue. But his boat had already been rocked enough this week, and truly, healing up as fast as possible was his number one goal. Once he did that, he'd be able to get back to the farm—hell, get back to *normal*. Without Emerson Montgomery or his busted shoulder messing up his status quo.

"You know what? That sounds perfect," Hunter said.

If Emerson wanted just business, that's exactly what he'd give her.

CHAPTER FOUR

Emerson lowered herself to the creaky, fake-leather office chair behind the particleboard table masquerading as the physical therapy center's front desk, trying to decide which part of her body ached the most. Her knees had been the blue-ribbon winner for the last handful of days, although now that she'd finally made it the eight hours to quitting time, her lower back was throwing down the gauntlet from beneath her black dress pants.

Don't forget your heart. Because it's kind of a contender, too.

Emerson sat up straight, stilling her urge to fidget and tamping down on the unease that had set up shop behind her breastbone. Okay, so running into Hunter here at the PT center this morning had done a number on her in the surprise department, and yes, *maybe* the solid, unexpected warmth of his body as he'd leaned on her to release his shoulder strain had brought back heated memories she'd thought were long gone. But he was her patient—her only patient—and Emerson hadn't come back to Millhaven to get sappy or reminisce. She couldn't let herself think of how steady Hunter had felt, or how he'd been the only person she'd ever been tempted to confide in. And she definitely couldn't dwell on how close his mouth had been to hers when he'd given her that same smoldering stare that had always stolen the breath directly from her lungs.

No. She had a practice to build. People to take care of. Things to forget.

Starting with Hunter Cross's firm, sexy mouth.

Finding her feet, she snuffed out the emotions sparking through her chest—and fine, maybe a few of her other parts—once and for all. Hunter might've been the only person she'd treated, but today still felt like it had lasted for weeks. She was more than ready to put her crazy emotions behind her and escape to the four walls of her tiny apartment to snuggle up with a glass full of merlot and a really good book.

Except she didn't even have furniture in her apartment, let alone any real food or wine. If anything other than a granola bar or leftover Chinese takeout from Camden Valley was going to pass Emerson's lips tonight, she was going to have to stop and buy it on the way back to her place.

She shouldered her purse and closed up shop, making a beeline for her BMW. Regaining the lay of the land hadn't been too tough, partly because she'd grown up in Millhaven, but mostly because the small town hadn't changed a lick in her absence. The two-lane road acting as the main artery through downtown—aptly named Town Street—still connected all the essential points in Millhaven. The clapboard building housing Doc Sanders's office, the fire station, the Hair Lair (aka Gossip Central), Clementine's Diner, the Corner Market grocery store . . . God, everything was exactly as it had been when Emerson had driven down Town Street twelve years ago, swearing she would never, ever set foot in Millhaven again.

On second thought, there might not be enough wine for this.

Emerson pulled into a parking space in front of the Corner Market, closing her eyes against the sunlight slanting in past her windshield. Returning to Millhaven wasn't ideal. Hell, she'd exhausted every other alternative, to the point of exhausting herself. But there were no other options, and Emerson needed to face the facts.

Millhaven was what she had. Time to make the best of it and move on.

Head up. Eyes forward.

Her ballet flats shushed over the brick-paved sidewalk as she walked the dozen or so steps toward the Corner Market's glass double doors. Both side windows were emblazoned with red-and-white posters advertising this weekend's Watermelon Festival, prompting a tiny, unexpected smile over her lips. She hadn't thought of the annual start-of-summer celebration in ages. Still, she wasn't surprised the tradition was going strong. Not much seemed to change around here.

And hell if *that* wasn't way more curse than blessing.

Grabbing a cart from the row by the doors, Emerson kicked her creaky legs into motion, giving herself a crash course on the Corner Market's layout with one long glance. Although the grocery store was maybe an eighth of the size of the gourmet mega center she had frequented in Las Vegas, she couldn't deny the charm in the wood-plank floors and cute little chalkboards posted over various items spilling from repurposed baskets and barrels. Add to it the fact that she had to travel ten aisles rather than a hundred and ten in order to grab everything she needed to fill her fridge for an entire week? Yeah, today was finally looking up.

"Jesus, Mary, and all the saints! Emerson Montgomery, is that *you?*"

Or not.

She looked up, her heart dropping to a spot somewhere around her aching kneecaps as she connected the platinum blonde in front of her with the cheerleading captain in her memory. While Emerson had known her return to Millhaven would light up the small-town grapevine like bonfire kindling in the summertime, running into Amber Cassidy right out of the gate was one hell of a way to spark those flames.

If gossiping were an Olympic event, the woman's face would be on Wheaties boxes nationwide.

"Hi, Amber. It's been a long time," Emerson said, working up a polite smile. Maybe the last twelve years had mellowed her out.

Amber's smile in return was caught somewhere between the Cheshire cat and a toothpaste commercial, and crap, there went Emerson's hopes for mellowness of any kind.

"Look at you, still so *modest*," Amber drawled, her inch-long hot-pink nails flashing in an aren't-you-cute gesture. "Girl, it's been twelve *years*, and you're keepin' company with the hottest football player in the *en-tire* NFL! And here you are, finally visiting home. How *exciting*."

Emerson's palms went slick over the cart handle in her grasp, but she might as well rip off the Band-Aid and get right to the sting. "Actually, I'm back in town for good. I moved from Las Vegas over the weekend."

Amber's mouth formed a frosted purple *O*. "You're back in Millhaven *permanently*? Is Lance here with you?" She smoothed a hand over her sequin-edged halter top and second-skin jeans, swiveling her gaze over the Corner Market as if Lance might materialize from behind the doughnut display and start offering autographs.

"No." *Stick to the facts, girl. Head up, eyes forward.* "Lance is still in Las Vegas. We're spending some time apart."

"Oh." Amber's eyes flickered with disappointment before suddenly going as round as a pair of pennies. "Oh my *gravy*, does Hunter know you're back?"

"Yes," Emerson said, trying not to wince at how loud and fast she'd answered. But it was bad enough that her name was about to land on the lips of every gossip in town. Adding Hunter to the mix would only make the whispers and stares harder to field, and truly, all she wanted to do was blend in and move on. "I ran into Hunter this morning."

"*Did* you." No less than a thousand pounds of implication hung in Amber's non-question, and, okay, yeah, Emerson had reached her limit.

"It was great to see you again, Amber, but I'm so sorry, I've got to run." She might've reached her little white lie quotient for the month between both parts of the sentence, but sweet God, cutting the conversation short was worth whatever penance she'd have to endure from Amber and the gossip mill.

"Oh, *right*. I bet you're *super* busy getting settled." The corners of Amber's flawlessly lipsticked mouth lifted in another shot of innuendo. "Well, you be sure to come on in to the Hair Lair real soon, Emerson. Mollie Mae and I can tame those curls for you, no problem, and I'm dyin' to hear all about Las Vegas. *And* Lance."

Not wanting to set a personal record for the sheer number of lies told in less than a minute, Emerson simply nodded and waved as she hightailed her way through the produce section. She made quick work of the handful of aisles in her path, grabbing the bare bones of what she needed before making a hasty retreat from the Corner Market. Her back, which had already been fairly indignant with the amount of time she'd spent upright today, creaked out a protest as she loaded her groceries into the back of her car, then again as she climbed into the front of her trusty BMW. God, between Hunter Cross's sexy scowls and Amber's full-on inquisition, this day couldn't possibly get any worse.

At least until she got to her apartment and saw her mother standing on the threshold.

"Mom?" Emerson jerked to an inelegant halt on the sidewalk, but not before two apples escaped from the grocery bag in her hand and a muttered curse followed suit past her lips.

One perfectly slender auburn brow raised, and just like that, the last twelve years of her life evaporated. "I understand you're used to working for a football team, Emerson, but must you swear? It's so unladylike."

Emerson let loose a string of mental f-bombs before slapping a too-tight smile over her face. Arguing with Elizabeth "Bitsy" Wellington Montgomery just wasn't worth the energy. Not that she had any to spare.

She bent to reclaim the renegade apples from the three-by-three square of concrete serving as her threshold before flipping her keys into her suddenly damp palm. *Stupid involuntary physiological response.* "Sorry. I wasn't expecting to see you here."

"Yes, well. I have some time before I have to go to Camden Valley for this evening's board meeting at the hospital, and there's something I'd like to discuss with you."

Emerson's heartbeat picked up the pace. Her chest twisted and squeezed with an old, hauntingly familiar sensation, but she scraped in a breath to temper it. She hadn't had a panic attack in years, dammit. Backsliding now—in front of her mother, no less—was simply not on her menu of options.

"You could've called," Emerson said with unerring calm, opening the front door to usher her mother inside her apartment. "It would've saved you a trip."

This time, the eyebrow raise was accompanied by a disdainful frown, both of which called Emerson's bluff. "It also would've allowed you the opportunity to avoid the conversation," her mother said. "Since you've been doing that for the last two weeks, your father and I thought it was time to take a different approach."

Seriously? Her father was the only man alive who could guilt a person without even being present.

Emerson shifted her weight from one foot to the other to burn off the last of the unease still threatening to send her vitals into red alert. "And how is Dad?"

"Darling, you're fidgeting. And if you'd bother to come to the house, you'd see he's quite well," her mother said, the words as crisp and tart as the Granny Smith apple Emerson had just put back in her bag. "You, on the other hand, are still dodging the topic."

Emerson stopped moving, midshift. Breathed in. Counted her heartbeats. *Thump*-thump. *Thump*-thump. *Thump* . . . "I've been telling you this since I made the decision to leave Las Vegas a couple of weeks ago. I'm not avoiding anything, Mom. There's just nothing to say."

"Sweetheart, please. You up and quit your job as a medical professional for one of the most lucrative and well-established sports organizations in the United States and ended a relationship that could've become a lovely marriage to a very auspicious young man, all out of the blue. There's plenty to say. You're simply not saying it."

Emerson's knuckles went sheet white over the handle of the grocery bag looped over her palm, but she forced herself to walk calmly into the kitchen and lift it to the counter without fanfare. She needed a different channel for this conversation, and fast. "I thought you and Dad would be happy I'm back in Millhaven."

"That's not fair." Her mother followed her, running a hand over her classic Chanel sheath in her equally classic nervous tell. "Of course we're pleased to see you, but you're impulsively turning your back on successful endeavors. Your father and I are concerned."

Translation: Your father and I are concerned about how this looks. God, her parents hadn't changed a bit. Too bad for them, Emerson had; namely, she'd grown a backbone.

One she intended to keep, even if she *had* broken the vow she'd made to herself twelve years ago and come back to Millhaven.

"There's nothing to be concerned about. I'm simply here to work with Doc Sanders. I'm not turning my back on anything," she said, but her mother met the words with a noise that was as close as she'd ever get to a scoff.

"I beg to differ." After a pause, she asked, "Is this about Lance? Did he have an indiscretion?"

Emerson's urge to laugh was strong, but she caught the sound between her teeth. Lance's only love affair was the one he'd recently started with himself. He wasn't a bad guy, necessarily—he didn't kick puppies or blow past little old ladies on the highway with his middle finger held high, and he'd been attentive and sweet, especially in the beginning. But the hotter his career had grown, the more Emerson had come to realize nothing would ever matter to Lance as much as Lance. She just wished she'd grasped the magnitude of his self-absorption sooner and saved them both the trouble. "No, Mom. That's not why we broke up."

"Alright." Another pause. "Did the Lightning decide they no longer required your services?"

Of course her mother had a tidy euphemism for being shit-canned. Nothing unpleasant or imperfect ever got an out-loud mention from Team Montgomery. "No. I resigned from my position on the training staff."

Her mother's lips thinned into a line of frustration. "And may I ask why?"

"I just needed a change of pace," Emerson said, because it was the only truth she could stick to that would keep her suit of armor in place and intact.

Unfortunately, her mother knew exactly where to slide the barbs to make said armor about as effective as a string bikini. "If you needed a change of pace, you could've taken a vacation, or even a leave of absence. But quitting? Moving across the country? It's just so *permanent*, Emerson."

Just like that, something deep in her belly snapped. "Believe me. I know how permanent this is. But it's done, and nothing I can do will change it."

"Oh, darling, don't be so dramatic. I'm sure if we—"

"Was there something else you needed, Mom?" Emerson's cheeks flushed in time with her quickening pulse. Okay, so she hadn't meant to be quite so terse, and she was certain she'd regret giving her mother the verbal stiff-arm. The woman made Miss Manners look like an epic rookie. But standing her ground was the only way Emerson would survive. No way was she lifting the lid on this conversation and putting a spotlight on why she'd come back to Millhaven. Not with her mother. Not with anyone.

Nothing she could do would change the truth. Her only option was to forget it and move the hell on.

Her mother straightened as if she'd been starched on the spot. "Well, then. No. I suppose not." She removed her car keys from her purse, her words chilly and her head held high. "I'll just show myself out."

Emerson waited for the squeak of the door hinges and the controlled thump signaling her mother's departure a second later before releasing the breath holding her lungs hostage.

"Awesome. Good talk, Mom," she said, slumping against the narrow stretch of wall space dividing her kitchen from the rest of the apartment's living area. Logically, she'd known her parents would react to the circumstances of her return in exactly this manner, questioning everything right down to the moving service she'd chosen to slow-boat her furniture and most of her belongings back to town, then trying to pressure her to do better, faster, more.

But Emerson held a master's degree in disappointment, especially where Dr. Bradford Montgomery, chief of surgery at Camden Valley Hospital, and his lovely wife Bitsy—who just happened to be the president of the hospital's board of trustees, thank you very much—were concerned. Her father may have had meager beginnings, growing up as the son of a farmhand and an elementary-school teacher, but he'd always aimed for the very top of the pile, and set every last one of his expectations for her even higher.

If Emerson's parents were let down by her change in locale and her disintegrated relationship, telling them the real reason she was back in Millhaven would win her a gold medal in the Defective Daughter Olympics.

Which was all the reason she needed to keep her head up, her eyes forward, and the truth buried deep.

Emerson yawned and blinked back the relentless early-morning sunshine spearing past the blinds in her bedroom, cursing the very nature of inflatable mattresses. Her spine felt as if someone had snuck in and replaced it with a rusty corkscrew overnight, and she turned to her side on the floppy, makeshift bed to try to release some of the triple-knot tension.

Nope. No go. God, she'd give her left arm and her latest paycheck for a hot tub—no, a ninety-minute massage right now.

Sure would be nice to have someone put their capable hands in all the right places . . .

Unrepentant and unexpected heat pooled between her thighs, turning her half-sleepy state into all want. Between Lance's militant training schedule and her overwhelming fatigue, remembering the last time she'd found pleasure between the sheets was pretty much a statistical impossibility. Then her relationship with Lance had abruptly become past tense, and Lord knew the last thing she needed while she'd waded through the shit storm of leaving Las Vegas was for another man to fall into her life.

A couple of down and dirty orgasms to satisfy her drowsy state of arousal, though? Now *those* wouldn't hurt.

Emerson pressed her legs together, the warmth from the covers and the friction of her panties over bare skin waking her better than any alarm clock. Her eyes drifted shut, her heart beating faster as her breasts grew heavy, her nipples tight. Sucking in a breath, she shifted, reaching beneath the powder-blue blanket for the hem of her nightshirt. Up the soft cotton went, brushing the sensitive skin of her thighs, her hips, her belly, until the only thing between her fingers and her aching sex was a swath of satin and lace.

Oh God, it had been so long since she'd let herself feel this good. Pushing the damp material aside, she canted her hips slowly forward in search of more contact. Emerson slipped her fingers upward, shocks of undiluted pleasure sparking all the way through her as she delved into the slick heat of her folds.

More. *More.* She needed more.

Eyes squeezed tight, she stroked faster, imagining a pair of wide, callused hands on her needy body. Not hands hardened by agility drills or the guidance of thousand-dollar-an-hour personal trainers, uh-uh. The hands in Emerson's imagination were strong from the kind of work done with sleeves rolled up, with dirt and sweat and good, old-fashioned exertion.

Hard. Strong. Hot. Touching her in all the right places, as if they knew every inch of where she needed them most.

There. Ohhhhh, she needed them right . . . there.

A moan tore past her lips, a powerful climax brightening deep between her legs, and Emerson twisted onto her back in order to—

White-hot pain shot from the base of her spine all the way down both legs, carving out a vicious path of numbness and tingling that doused her desire in an instant.

"Ow! Oh, ow." The pain nailed Emerson into place, tears pricking the backs of her eyelids like tiny, scalpel-sharp daggers. She scraped a ragged inhale, then another into her lungs, metering her breath until the pain coalesced into a dull, thudding ache. Frustration burned in her chest, tightening around each of her ribs like a steel band. Had she seriously been fantasizing about mind-scrambling sex with a rough and tumble man? Was she insane? She couldn't even get *herself* off painlessly, for God's sake.

And here Emerson had thought she'd already hit all the benchmarks for being a complete failure. But the thought of being with a man, any man, ranked right up there with sprouting wings and learning how to fly.

Emerson flung the blanket from her body, welcoming the shock of cool air as she pushed herself off the mattress and into the bathroom. She was a smart woman, logical and well trained. There was no sense not admitting the facts.

Multiple sclerosis was going to make having a normal life impossible. The best thing she could do for herself was change her expectations and move the hell on.

CHAPTER FIVE

Hunter leaned against the top rail of rough-hewn horse fence behind him, his eyes on the sunrise even though his mind was conservatively a trillion miles away. His shoulder had come up with a whole new definition of sore over the past four days of physical therapy, making even limited work difficult and sleep downright impossible. In theory, Hunter got the whole "use it or lose it" aspect of rehabbing an injury like his. He didn't mind some blood, sweat, and tears—literal or figurative—if it meant grabbing his goal of returning to the farm. But the twelve years that had ticked by since his last round of PT, plus all the daily wear and tear that had gone with them, was making this second go-round a whole lot more challenging.

Add in the near-constant arguing his brothers had thrown down and the "just the facts, ma'am" nature of the four sessions he'd had with Emerson this week? Yeah, Hunter had his toes on the edge of batshit crazy.

"Don't be an idiot," he muttered, his breath scattering the steam from his coffee as he raised the mug to his mouth for a long draw. Emerson had made it clear as the summer sky above him that she wanted to keep things strictly on the level, and, in truth, doing just that made sense. She'd been gone for over a decade, and while he hadn't done the first-comes-love-then-comes-marriage thing with anyone else, Hunter definitely hadn't sat around pining for her return, either. He'd gotten over Emerson's leaving ages ago.

Not that he'd had a choice in the matter.

"Hey." His brother's voice floated over his shoulder, fast-tracking Hunter back to reality. Approaching from the side of the main house, Owen covered the grassy space, leaning both palms against the top rail of the fence and gesturing to the field in front of them with a lift of his chin. "I thought you had three more weeks on desk duty. What're you doing out here?"

Hunter blew out a slow exhale. Might as well come out with the truth. There wasn't much point in lying, and anyway, even if he tried, his brother would know he was chock-full of shit.

"Honestly? I don't know. But my eyes popped open at o'dark-thirty just like always, and staying in bed seemed kind of pointless if I wasn't gonna sleep. So here I am."

"Ah." The short response was pretty much par for the course from Owen. The guy was as frugal with his words as their other brother Eli was loose with 'em. "Dad and I just finished breakfast. We'd have made room at the table if we'd known you were out here."

"It's all good." Hunter waved Owen off with ease he had to work for. He'd been awake with plenty of time to make the six a.m. family breakfast where the four of them planned their daily work schedules together. But talking work was kind of pointless when he couldn't do any, and as much as Hunter had wanted to keep to his routine, hearing the rest of them talk shop fucking stung. "You said breakfast was you and Pop. What about Eli?"

Owen's irritation escaped by way of a snort. "What do you think?"

Dammit. Eli didn't have the best relationship with timeliness, especially in the morning. "I'm sure he has a good reason for running behind."

"I'm sure he doesn't," Owen said, letting a minute tick by before shaking his head on the subject. "Your shoulder feeling any better?"

Ah hell, Owen was batting a thousand with all the hard topics this morning. "I'm doing everything I'm supposed to," Hunter said, cherry-picking his words in order to stick with the path of least resistance.

Owen opened his mouth, presumably to throw the bullshit flag on Hunter's verbal evasion, but his words stopped short at the bang of the screen door and the thump of work boots on the porch boards behind them.

Owen's auto frown sent a fresh twist through Hunter's gut, but he kept his expression as laid back as possible. He was getting way too used to doing double duty as a referee between his brothers lately. Hopefully, they'd cut him a break by actually keeping things civil this time.

"Morning, Eli," Hunter said after a beat, aiming the words at a bleary-eyed, sleep-rumpled version of his younger brother approaching from the side yard of the main house.

"Morning," Eli replied into his coffee mug, although the drowsy murmur suggested he might as well still be hogging the covers and snoring like a lumberjack.

"Nice of you to join us." Owen sent a pointed stare at the sky, where the brightening shades of pink and orange signaled a good six thirty a.m.

But Eli met the obvious censure in Owen's voice with a slow smile that was just as challenging. "My pleasure." He hung on to Owen's stare just long enough to hammer home the unspoken *kiss my ass* in his tone, and Christ, Hunter so wasn't in the mood for this.

"Thanks for helping me out in the south barn yesterday," he said to Eli. Maybe the mention of the two hours Eli had spent hauling around feed and equipment while Hunter had done nothing but make nice, neat check marks on their inventory lists would knock Owen's irritation down a rung.

Not today, big man. His older brother's frown refused to let up. "You don't have to cover for him, Hunt," Owen said. "His actions speak for themselves."

A muscle ticked in Eli's clean-shaven jaw as he looked at Hunter with a humorless laugh. "And *his* actions are always perfect, of course. Our brother here is so flawless, his shit is nothing but roses and pure gold."

"Look, you guys—" Hunter tried, but Owen lifted one palm with a noise of disgust.

"No, you know what? Let's not sugarcoat this. He's always thought working the farm is a joke, rolling out of bed whenever the spirit moves him, doing the bare minimum to scrape by while you and Dad and I bust our asses day in and day out. I get that you're trying to be the peacekeeper, Hunter." Owen took a step back on the grass, his frame rigid, limbs locked beneath the denim and cotton covering them. "But I'm just about out of slack for someone who doesn't give a rat's ass about anything other than himself. If you need me, I'll be in the cornfields with Dad. *Working.*"

Eli waited until the sound of Owen's footsteps turned into the soft rumble of his truck engine, watching the taillights fade up the dirt path before lifting his shoulders in a shrug. "Looks like he's got me all figured out."

Whether it was his lack of sleep or his brimming frustration with the matter at hand, Hunter couldn't be sure, but something made an uncharacteristic thread of anger tug at his belly. "You've gotta admit, you didn't really help matters by oversleeping."

"Guess not," Eli said after a heartbeat's worth of a pause. "Anyhow, I'd better find something to do before Mr. Stick Up His Ass strokes out over tomorrow's Watermelon Festival." He turned toward the barn adjacent to the main house, making it exactly two paces before Hunter's voice brought his movements to a halt.

"Whoa." Hunter's gaze raked over the cluster of angry red scratches showing on Eli's triceps from beneath the sleeve of his T-shirt. "What'd you do to your arm?"

Eli angled his chin to examine the injury in question with the same expression he'd use to watch soybeans germinate. "Ah, it's nothin' but a thing. I was working on the fence out by the perimeter of the east field after I helped you in the barn yesterday, and I got a little personal with the rough edge of one of the wood posts."

Wait . . . "You repaired the fence out in the east field after you hauled all that stuff around the barn yesterday afternoon?" Hunter asked, his thoughts clicking together like magnets. Mending fences was the most boring grunt work the farm could offer up. The one in question had been halfway to falling down for weeks, and that was before a nasty storm a few days ago had knocked down a handful of sections completely.

"Dad mentioned the thing was in bad shape, and he had both hands full with prep for the festival, so yeah," Eli said.

"How many of the busted sections did you get to?"

One shoulder rose halfway. "All of 'em."

What the *hell*. "Jesus, Eli. That must've taken you 'til sundown."

Eli's truck had disappeared shortly after they'd finished in the barn. Hunter—like Owen, and even their father—had just assumed he'd called it quits for the day.

"A little before," Eli said. "But, really, the scratches are no big deal."

Hunter shook his head. "Forget the scratches. Why didn't you say something to Owen just now?" After hauling equipment all over the barn *and* repairing the fence? Even Paul flipping Bunyan would need a little extra shut-eye.

"Because it doesn't matter. Owen's gonna believe what he wants. He always has." Eli's words arrived with nothing more than honesty, hanging between them in the morning air for just a second before he boomeranged the subject. "Meant to ask—how's your shoulder feeling?"

"It's okay." Hunter was halfway through a shrug to match Eli's before he realized the movement fell into the Very Bad Plan category. Pain streaked across the back of his upper arm and neck, digging in hard enough to make his wince inevitable.

"Yeah, you look like it." Mischief lit bright blue in his brother's eyes, spreading to a smirk Hunter knew all too well. "Hey, speaking of which, I didn't know you were doing your physical therapy with Emerson Montgomery."

"Ummm." Hunter drew out the word in a caution-laden question. "Who told you that?"

"Have you looked at Facebook at all this week?" Eli held up his iPhone, the backlit screen glinting in the morning sunlight. "Amber Cassidy apparently ran into Emerson at the Corner Market a few days ago and posted all about it. I overheard a couple of the guys at the farming co-op talking about her when I ran over there yesterday for some fencing supplies, saying how she's working for Doc Sanders now. With her area of expertise, it wasn't tough to figure that one and one probably equaled the two of you doin' PT together."

Great. No wonder Amber and Mollie Mae had been looking at him sideways when he'd walked past the Hair Lair to get to his truck after his therapy session yesterday. Between those two and Billy Masterson down at the co-op, more than half the town probably knew Emerson was back in Millhaven by now. Along with the fact that Hunter had seen her. "Emerson's the only physical therapist in Millhaven, so yeah. I'm doing my PT with her. But it's really not a big deal."

His brother shot him a look as if he'd just asked why someone would choose to breathe air instead of apple butter. "Is your ass on crooked? According to Amber, the woman came back from Las Vegas clear out of the blue, and word around the campfire at the co-op is that she's hotter than an August afternoon. I'm half tempted to bust something in *my* shoulder just to get her hands on me."

Something unexpected and sharp turned over in Hunter's chest, sizzling a straight path out of his mouth. "Keep talking," Hunter said past clenched teeth, "and I'll be happy to help you out with getting banged up."

Eli's dark-gold brows winged upward, and shit. *Shit.* If Hunter couldn't keep his own cool around his brothers, then they sure as hell weren't going to keep theirs. "Sorry," he mumbled. "Guess being on restricted duty is starting to get to me."

"No worries, brother. I was just being flip. I didn't mean to overstep my bounds." Eli readjusted the brim of his red baseball hat, but not before Hunter caught the genuine remorse in his younger brother's normally cocky expression.

He forced his good shoulder into a shrug, although his usually easy-to-find nonchalance took effort. But the truth was, he had no claim to Emerson, no matter how in love with her he'd once been or how hard her leaving had smarted. Hell, for all intents and purposes, he didn't even know her now. "That's past tense by over a decade. Don't worry about it."

But Eli's half-cocked grin didn't make a repeat appearance. "I know you really used to dig her. You cool with her being back?"

"Yep." Okay, so "cool" might not be the first word Hunter would use to describe the way he felt about Emerson's return to Millhaven, but for Chrissake, all this high-intensity stuff was making him twitch. Emerson was back in town. Hunter needed her in order to rehab his shoulder. It was as simple as that.

Fortunately, Eli was about as comfy talking Deep Thoughts as Hunter was, and he went for a full-throttle subject swap. "If anyone can get you patched up quick, I bet Emerson can," he said hopefully. "She always was really smart. Except for dating What's His Name, that running back."

"Lance Devlin?" A bitter-burnt taste filled Hunter's mouth, and damn, whoever had made the coffee this morning needed to lighten the load with the grounds.

Eli pulled a face only a mother could love, and even then, only at a fifty-fifty shot. "I don't care how many yards he racks up in a season. If that guy was an ice cream flavor, he'd be pralines and dick."

A tiny smile tempted the corners of Hunter's mouth, but he kept the gesture in check. Emerson had gone all close to the vest the minute he'd mentioned Lance the other day. She didn't seem the type to come home after twelve long years just to lick her wounds over a breakup, even from a high-profile dick—uh, football player. While Hunter suspected there was a whole lot more to Emerson's return to Millhaven than un-dating Lance Devlin, she was clearly still touchy about the situation. The fact that she and Lance had called it quits shouldn't make him happy.

Oh, who the hell was he kidding? This was a guy who'd recently told the media, "There might not be an 'I' in team, but there sure is a 'me.'"

Emerson deserved better.

"Yeah. I guess I'd better get to the books," Hunter said, ungracefully closing the conversation. But hell, between his gimpy shoulder and his brothers' propensity for acting like the farm was some sort of no-holds-barred cage match, Hunter's status quo had taken enough of a whack this week. Throwing thoughts of Emerson Montgomery and her newly single relationship status on top of all that?

Fuel, meet flame. Better to snuff his feelings out now and move on with the business of healing so nothing exploded, at Cross Creek *or* in his personal life.

Hunter exchanged a quick "see ya later" with Eli, downing the last of his now-cold coffee as he headed to the main house. Stopping in the kitchen just long enough for a refill, he headed for the main-level bedroom his father had converted into an office about fifteen years ago. He grabbed a handheld radio from the charger out of habit before his stomach clenched with the realization that he really didn't need the thing since he'd be parked inside all morning. Still, Hunter clipped the radio to the belt loop of his wash-faded Wranglers anyway as he turned to survey the room in front of him.

A large, *L*-shaped walnut desk claimed center stage on the old red-and-tan area rug spread over the floorboards, its surface covered by a hulking desktop computer and haphazard stacks of papers and file folders. Three metal file cabinets stood sentry in the left-hand corner of the room, the sunlight filtering in from the windows on the opposite wall illuminating the dents and dings in each one. The only thing in the room that made Hunter even consider a smile was the roly-poly black-and-white mutt happily snoring away at the foot of the desk.

"You're busted, old girl." Hunter placed his coffee next to the computer monitor, bending to scratch Lucy behind the ears. "You gonna keep me from going around the bend today? I sure could use the help."

There was a four-way tie among the Cross men for who hated bookkeeping the most, and their old man's aversion to technology didn't smooth the process. But, come on. They were farmers, not number crunchers. Give Hunter complex soil compositions or planting time-tables any day of the week and twice on Sunday, and he'd balance 'em on a blade of Kentucky bluegrass. Spreadsheets and accounting software and maximizing marketing trends via social media?

The thought alone was enough to give him the fucking shakes.

Still, the work needed to be done, and as much as he'd rather have a prostate exam than manage the books, Hunter wasn't about to sit back and play tiddlywinks just because he was injured. Parking himself firmly in the Windsor-back chair his father had liberated from the dining room over a decade ago, he dug into the closest pile of papers.

Three hours, two cups of coffee, and one giant neck cramp later, Hunter was actually filled with relief at the idea of heading into town for his PT session with Emerson.

Emerson, who spoke to him only about his standards of care and the hotter-than-usual weather they seemed to be having. Emerson, whose pretty, ocean-colored eyes flashed with something he couldn't quite label but that jabbed at his gut all the same. Emerson, whose hands felt way better on him than they should.

On second thought, maybe the damned bookkeeping would be less stressful.

Hunter quickly traded his jeans and work boots for a pair of basketball shorts and cross-trainers, plucking the keys to his F-250 from the table in the front hall and heading for his truck. He kept his windows rolled down, even though it was hotter than hell's doorstep outside, hoping the fresh air would kick his unease to the curb on the short drive into town. But all the weather did was dampen his T-shirt with perspiration, not to mention remind him of everything he'd been missing for the last week straight while he rode the pine down at Cross Creek.

So much for losing his craptastic mood. Now Hunter was hacked off *and* sweaty, and if the pain cranking through the back of his shoulder was any indication, no closer to healing his way back into action than he had been at the start of this week. Biting down on his irritation, he slid out of the truck, moving past Doc Sanders's front office to push his way through the door to the physical therapy room.

"Wow," Emerson said, looking up from behind the scuffed fake wood veneer of the reception desk. "Tough morning?"

"No. Everything's great." The default springboarded past Hunter's lips, although the untruth pinched like a son of a bitch. "Yeah, maybe," he recanted.

"Are you in pain?" A crease of genuine worry formed between her cinnamon-colored brows, but Hunter was quick to shake his head.

"No, nothing like that. I mean, my shoulder's still pretty sore, but . . ." Remembering their just-business agreement, he started to jam his feelings of frustration back into his rib cage.

But, funny, they flat out refused to go. "I guess I'm not used to sitting on the sidelines at Cross Creek. This morning's just been pretty rough, is all."

"Ah." Emerson rolled up the sleeves of her light-blue blouse, waving him past the desk. "Well, let's take a look at your sore spots and see what we're dealing with in that shoulder."

Right. Just business. Surely she had an exercise or three in her bottomless arsenal of ways to torture him.

Hunter crossed the threshold of the reception desk, holding still and trying to breathe through the ache while she pressed and prodded his shoulder over his T-shirt.

"Hmm. You're pretty locked up today. You haven't been doing any lifting, have you?"

"Nothing other than an inventory clipboard and the desk chair in the office," he said, the reminder filling him with a fresh shot of exasperation.

Her fingers stilled on his rotator cuff, a soft "aha" floating over his shoulder.

"Is something wrong?" His pulse thumped faster in his veins. His day—hell, his entire week—had been bad enough, thank you very much. A setback with this injury would obliterate the last shreds of his usually stalwart calm.

"I'm pretty sure I found the source of your problem. Good news is, it should be an easy fix once we get started." Emerson looked up at him, her smile professional and polite. But now that they were separated by less than an arm's length, Hunter could see the shadows beneath her eyes that she'd done her best to cover, along with the tiny worry lines etched on her pretty face.

But it was the flicker of pure vulnerability, so out of place in the capable, confident stare she'd worn all week, that popped him right in the chest.

"Emerson, are you okay?"

His mouth launched the question before his brain even knew it would fully form, and although the part of him that didn't go borrowing trouble wished for a rewind, a deeper part of him prickled in sudden concern.

"I'm fine," she said, her expression growing so smooth that he had to wonder if he'd just been projecting his own fatigue onto her. "How about you? Are you ready for our session?"

Hunter's worry screeched to a halt on his tongue. He might not have as much cocky charm as his brother Eli, but he knew better than to tell a woman she looked tired—hell, he might as well plaster himself with four-foot signs that read, "Kick Me in the Junk." Anyhow, Emerson looked fine now, albeit serious, and the way she felt was really none of his business.

"As ready as I'll ever be, I guess." He shook off the last of the odd feeling and followed her over the linoleum.

"Good. We can start with a few minutes of warm-up on the arm bike." She moved farther into the therapy room before adding, "I'm glad you're following doctor's orders. But as far as hating the sidelines goes, you're preaching to the pulpit."

Huh. Can't say he'd been expecting *that*. But anything was better than small-talking their way through the weather report. What the hell. He'd bite. "Am I really?"

Emerson turned to deliver a look of brows-up surprise over one shoulder. "Does that honestly shock you?"

"A little, yeah. Not that you don't have a serious work ethic." Hell, she'd nearly been the end of him this week with all of her relentless exercises and mobility stretches. "But you just left a job with the hottest football team in the NFL to come back to a town that's barely on the map, let alone the sidelines."

The curiosity was out before Hunter could trap it, and he stopped short in front of the makeshift exercise area. Emerson had made it clear that sharing wasn't on her to-do list, and he wasn't really sure he wanted to get all "Kumbaya" with her, anyway. He really should just shut his yap and drop the topic. "Sorry. I'm—"

"Right."

His pulse stuttered along with his words. "I . . . what?"

"You're right," she said softly, although her expression remained unrattled and unchanged as she motioned for him to sit on the recumbent bike. "My life was a lot faster paced in Las Vegas. But just because I'm back in Millhaven doesn't mean I want to kick up my feet and rest on my laurels."

A question formed in Hunter's brain, and shit. If he was going to break the just-business barrier, he might as well go all in. "What does it mean?"

She paused. "It means I needed a change. But lucky for your shoulder, I'm still here to work hard." Emerson dropped her chin to adjust the hand pegs she'd attached to the upper part of the bike, a swath of hair breaking free from the low ponytail at her nape to cover her eyes. "So Owen and Eli are at each other's throats, huh?"

"Yeah." Okay, so she was obviously shuffling the subject, but even talking about his brothers' bickering was better than sticking to canned pleasantries like *nice weather we're having* and *how's your shoulder pain on a scale of one to ten?* "Not a huge deal, really. Just today's version of an argument that's about a decade old."

"Wow. That doesn't seem like no huge deal."

Hunter went to shrug, and shit, sooner or later he was going to remember that the move was a bad idea *before* he did it. "I'm sure you remember they've always had totally different personalities, and nothing there has changed. Which is cool in general," he said, leaning forward in the seat to curl his fingers over the hard plastic pegs in front of him.

"But difficult when you're trying to run a business," Emerson finished. She motioned for him to start pedaling with his arms, but her attention didn't stray from the conversation.

So Hunter kept talking. "Yeah, and lately, things are only getting worse. We had a rough spring at the farm, and a rough winter before that—lots of bad weather and a few missed predictions on soil compositions, so we lost some livestock and the crops are weaker than usual."

"I'm sorry."

The words were simple, a standard-issue response Hunter might expect from any well-meaning person in passing conversation. But something in Emerson's voice told him she wasn't just saying them to show off her impeccable manners, and hell if that didn't make him continue to flap his trap.

"There's a ton of work to be done if we want to rebound," he admitted slowly. "And even though he'd rather be skinned alive than admit it, my father isn't able to do as much as he used to."

"Oh." A flicker moved through her stare, softening her expression. "How is your dad?"

"He's okay. Tough," Hunter added, although he couldn't deny that between the unpredictable weather and the bone-wearying manual labor that inherently went with running a farm, the last few years had done their best to wear his old man out. "Still up with the roosters every day, trying to work circles around the rest of us."

A puff of laughter crossed Emerson's lips. "Guess you come by that whole hating-the-sidelines thing pretty honest."

He knew he shouldn't mess with her, but God, she'd been so buttoned up all week, it was too good to pass up.

"Does that honestly shock you?" he asked, unable to keep one corner of his mouth from lifting into a half smile as he recycled her words from a few minutes earlier.

How about that—she smiled back. "I suppose not. You did balance working on the farm with school and football practice when you were barely eighteen. Not exactly something a guy can pull off if he lacks ambition."

"Spoken like a woman who managed to carve out a four-point-oh GPA while waving from the homecoming float," Hunter said. He waited out Emerson's silence by continuing his rhythm with the arm bicycle, his shoulder not pleased with the exertion, but not quite as pissed as it could've been.

Finally, just when he figured he'd exhausted his supply of personal conversation with her, she tilted her chin in a wordless *fair enough*. "Okay, so we both still hate the sidelines. But you had the chance for a faster pace, too. You were scouted by some of the best colleges on the East Coast. Even with that rotator cuff injury senior year, you still could've landed one of a half-dozen scholarships, yet you stayed here, anyway."

Okay, now she had him in the surprise department. Hunter had never made any bones about his desire to spend his entire life in Millhaven. Sure, he'd liked playing football. But he loved the farm, from breath to balls. Always had.

"Did you really think I wouldn't?" he asked.

Emerson didn't say no, but the curiosity in her eyes didn't relent, either. "You said it yourself. Millhaven's barely on the map, let alone the sidelines. Haven't you ever wondered what if?"

Hunter paused, letting all the layers of her question sink in. "What if what?"

"I guess . . . what might've happened if you'd left for something bigger."

His heart sped up. "You're forgetting the most important part of the equation."

"Which is?"

"For me, running the farm with my brothers isn't sitting on the sidelines. It's not just where I want to be. It's where I've always belonged. As far as I'm concerned . . . there *is* nothing bigger."

"I didn't forget," Emerson whispered. For a second, she stood beside him, her eyes wide and her expression wide open, and all of a sudden, Hunter's pounding heartbeat had nothing to do with the exercise.

He opened his mouth—to say what, exactly, he had no freaking clue. But then she took a step back, the look on her face growing impenetrable once again, and his chance to say anything disappeared like mist at sunrise.

CHAPTER SIX

Emerson took a step back on the floor tiles, absolutely convinced she'd lost her faculties. Okay, so there had been a method to her madness when she'd bypassed her strictly business chitchat with Hunter at the start of their session. Emotional stress had direct physiological impact on a lot of injuries, and it never made them heal faster. The way Hunter's shoulder had knotted up at the mere mention of being out of action at the farm told her all she needed to know about the source of the tightness in his shoulder. Emerson had started their conversation in an effort to get him to relax, knowing it would loosen some of his tension and therefore help him heal.

She hadn't realized that lowering Hunter's stress would also lower her guard until it had been too late.

Emerson tucked her hair behind her ear, strong-arming her pulse back out of the stratosphere. The past was over, her decisions made no matter how much her memories stung. Right now she had a job to do, and her only client was in pain. Which meant the tension in Hunter's muscles and tendons absolutely had to go.

There was only one surefire way to make that happen, and it damn sure wasn't confessing how she'd come within a thin thread of telling him the truth about her family life and begging him to go with her when she'd left for college.

"So tell me more about how the farm runs now," Emerson said.

Hunter's chin popped up with the force of his surprise. "You want to talk about daily operations at Cross Creek?"

"If you'd like, sure." She realized a beat too late that he might not want to talk to her at all—she *had* been pretty adamant about keeping things on the straight and narrow this week, and he probably wanted to get personal with her about as much as he wanted a colonoscopy. But then his shoulders loosened just slightly beneath the white cotton of his T-shirt, the small but genuine smile spreading over his face telling her she'd hit pay dirt.

"Some things at Cross Creek are the same as they've always been," he said, his shoulders dropping even farther from his neck as he rolled through the motions on the hand bicycle. "We're still the biggest family-run farm in the Shenandoah. Corn, soybeans, seasonal crops, livestock, although we hired a separate manager for the sheep and cattle about seven years ago."

Interest sparked in Emerson's mind, so strong she couldn't resist. "Whatever happened to that brown Jersey cow? The one your brother begged your dad to keep in the barn with the horses by the henhouse?"

"Clarabelle?" Hunter's laugh was all warmth and rumble. "She's getting a little long in the tooth, but she's still around. All eleven hundred pounds of her. And before you ask, yes. Eli still treats her like a puppy. Going on fourteen years old, and that old cow has got the nicest stall in the horse barn. Blankets in the winter, the whole nine yards."

Now it was Emerson's turn to laugh. "Sounds like a lot of things really are the same."

"Not everything," he countered. "Although most of our livestock and crops are still sold to distributors, in today's market, a farm the size of Cross Creek needs multiple streams of revenue in order to stay in the black."

"I'm afraid you're losing me a little." Human bodies, she could fix no problem. She'd even worked with some moderately high-tech imaging and record-keeping systems when she'd been with the Lightning. But running a business with all those moving parts—and one that had to do with things like managing crops and livestock at that? Yeah, that was waaaay out of Emerson's league.

But if Hunter minded her cluelessness, he didn't let it show. "Think of it like covering all the bases. Yes, we do most of our business selling our agriculture to companies that process it for different uses. But there's more than one way for us to utilize our resources to make money."

"So you're not just selling corn and soybeans and cattle to distributors anymore," she said, and he lifted an index finger from one of the bike pedals to gesture that she'd caught on.

"Exactly. We sell produce to a few local grocery stores and restaurants, and we dipped our feet in the agritourism pond a few years ago."

"Agri-what?" Emerson's brows lifted as her brain went for a full spin. She'd always known farming was more than seed/feed/sow, but, wow, she'd missed a lot in the last twelve years.

Hunter, however, hadn't missed a single step. "It's just a fancy way of saying we added a few things to bring people out to the farm, proper. We've got some pick-your-own fields for smaller seasonal crops like strawberries, apples, and pumpkins, and we started a community-supported agriculture program so people can buy produce direct. We're also trying out some specialty market stuff in the greenhouses year-round. That's sort of been Owen's baby for the last couple of years."

Just like that, Emerson's interest tripled. "Specialty market stuff, huh? Like what?"

"You name it, we've tried it. A bunch of different kinds of squash, root veggies, asparagus, some herbs and greens. About twenty varieties of heirloom tomatoes. The list goes on and on."

"Wow. Those tomatoes sound delicious," she said, her stomach seconding the motion with a slightly embarrassing and very toothy rumble.

Hunter arched a chestnut-colored brow. "And your stomach sounds empty."

"Not exactly." Most of the time she was too busy for breakfast—or at least, she used to be—and the meds her new neurologist had started her on a few days ago were wreaking havoc on her stomach, besides. But just because she wasn't a breakfast person didn't mean she wasn't a coffee person.

Emerson's stomach growled again at the thought, and, okay, she was *definitely* a coffee person.

As if he'd suddenly sprouted brain-reading superpowers, Hunter said, "Coffee doesn't count."

"Are you insane? Coffee always counts. It's practically its own food group."

The corners of his lips edged up against the dark stubble on his jaw, shaping his firm, full mouth with just a hint of a smile. "I assure you, I'm perfectly sane. I also farm for a living, so there's pretty much nothing you can say or do to convince me that meals involve anything other than fresh food. Did you seriously not have any breakfast this morning?"

"I told you." Emerson tried on her very best stern expression, but holy cow, that sexy little smile of his was making it tough to stick. "I had coffee."

"Mmm. I'm bringing you some of those tomatoes on Monday."

"Oh no." Emerson motioned him off the recumbent bike and pled her case at the same time. Yes, the tomatoes sounded amazing, but she'd meant to get him talking to relax his shoulder, not take advantage by way of her pantry. "That's really nice of you, but—"

"But nothing. Do you still love BLTs?"

Her lips parted in surprise, but she was powerless to say anything other than, "Yes."

He followed her to the exercise stations she'd set up for him earlier this week, his muscles flexing beneath the snug cotton of his T-shirt as he gripped the handle on the resistance tubing looped around the weight rack. "Then I insist. If you won't eat breakfast, the least I can do is aim for lunch."

Emerson nearly argued. But Hunter wasn't the only one with a great memory. His laid-back charisma didn't fool her one bit. She'd bet he could still be stubborn as hell when he set his mind to fixing something, and she knew all too well how to choose her battles. Plus, she'd spent the last few years living on quickie meals she could throw down the hatch between therapy sessions and whatever she could order on the fly at various airports and hotels, and Hunter hadn't been off the mark about her love for a really good BLT.

"With an offer like that, I suppose I can't refuse." She guided him through a mobility exercise, although their conversation didn't skip a step when they returned to the topic a minute later. "Hey, does the county still run that farmers' market outside of Camden Valley every Saturday?"

"May through October, with the exception of the day of the Watermelon Festival," he confirmed. His movements were nice and fluid, and Emerson pressed a *gotcha* smile between her lips as she listened to him continue. "The farmers' market is actually another great source of revenue. Cross Creek has one of the busiest tents there."

"Considering the new crops you've been growing, that's not too surprising."

"The whole event has gotten pretty popular, actually. They had to move the event to the pavilion by the town park about three years ago to accommodate all the vendors."

Whoa. "The one by the old train yard?" That place was huge.

"Yes, ma'am. One and the same."

Hunter's voice—and his smile—held just enough sexy Southern charm to remind Emerson that getting personal with him was a very bad idea. But even though he probably didn't realize it, he'd already made more progress today than all four of their other sessions combined. No way could she clam up on him now.

Emerson smiled back, working up a little charm of her own. "Isn't 'ma'am' for old ladies, Mr. Cross?"

He lowered the resistance tubing, stepping close enough for Emerson to catch the double whammy of woodsy, masculine soap and the felony-grade dimple peeking through the stubble on his left cheek. "No, ma'am."

Hunter's gaze traveled a slow, hot path from her eyes to her mouth, then back up before he added, "It most definitely is not."

Oh. *God.* Suddenly, she felt far from being old. As for any ladylike tendencies?

Yeah, those had just gone up in flames. Along with her cheeks.

And maybe her panties.

Emerson looked up, her pulse beating hard and fast against her throat. She opened her mouth to say something—at this point, *anything* to distract her from the dizzying heat of his nearness would do.

But then Hunter stepped back, his expression perfectly polite as he moved on to the next exercise with the resistance tubing. "Sorry. I didn't mean to make you uncomfortable. Calling women 'ma'am' is one of those small-town habits, I guess. Anyway, the farmers' market is what put the idea in Owen's head to try all the specialty items."

Emerson dipped her chin toward Hunter's chart in an effort to hide the still-raging heat on her face. Of course he'd just been letting his manners show. How could she have forgotten that everyone with an XX chromosome got the "ma'am" treatment in Millhaven?

"That makes sense," she managed, refocusing on the subject at hand. "You, ah, don't need as much quantity for the market or the CSA as you would for a deal with a distributor, right?"

"Right." He stretched his arm across the front of his T-shirt, holding it steady with his opposite palm. "With the greenhouses, we have the ability to plant year-round. Plus, we can get kind of creative since we're growing those crops on a much smaller scale, then we can gauge trends over the course of a season and plant accordingly in the fields for the next year if something really takes off."

Huh. Low risk, high reward. Hell if she didn't know all the words to *that* song. "Sounds like a win-win."

Hunter nodded, letting go of the stretch and rolling his shoulder in a gentle circle before answering. "Yeah, when the climate and the soil cooperate. Owen's goal is to open a permanent shop on site at Cross Creek so we can fulfill the demand for those items more than just twice a week with the farmers' market and the community share program."

"Wow." Masking her surprise would've been impossible, so Emerson didn't bother trying. "That would be a big source of income for you guys, right?"

"It would if we could make it go," he qualified. "But building even a small retail store takes a ton of money and manpower. Between the bad weather this year and now me being hurt, we're really tight on both."

The flicker of raw emotion in his stare lasted for less than a second, but it sent a sharp tug through Emerson's chest all the same.

Cross Creek really was everything to Hunter. He didn't just love his job. He *needed* it.

And, oh, she knew just how that felt.

"You've made some great progress this week, Hunter. Look"—she motioned for him to lift his injured arm in front of him, extending her own hand above shoulder height to give him something to aim for, and well, well, would you look at that—"your range of motion is better than it's been all week. See?"

Hunter's brows climbed in obvious surprise. "But my shoulder was totally jammed up when we started our session. I thought I'd managed to make it worse somehow."

Emerson guided his hand back to his side, unable to keep her wry smile in check. "I hate to break it to you, but that tension had more to do with your head than your arm."

"Sorry, I don't follow," he said, and his expression backed up the sentiment.

"I'm not saying this is some sort of miracle cure, or even a cure by itself at all. You've still got to do three more weeks of therapy in order to safely heal. But your body's musculature takes cues from the rest of you," she said, moving past the weight rack to grab the four-foot wooden pole propped in the corner, then retracing her steps to the spot where Hunter stood. "So when you're stressed mentally, your body responds in kind. But when your mind is relaxed . . ."

She dropped the pole between Hunter's hands, waiting until he flattened a palm over each end before gesturing him into a stretch to prove her point.

Yessss. "Your body relaxes, too."

"Holy—" The rest of his words fell prey to his shocked exhale, and he held the markedly improved stretch for a few beats, just like she'd taught him. "That's incredible. How did you know that's what the problem was?"

"You mean aside from the fact that your muscles went tighter than a snare drum as soon as you mentioned being on the sidelines at the farm?" Okay, so teasing him might not be strictly professional, but damn, it still felt good.

Hearing Hunter's laugh in response? Even better.

"Touché, Dr. Montgomery. You clearly know your stuff."

His use of the formal address sent her shoulders into an involuntary vise grip around her neck. Hunter's gaze narrowed over the movement, and shit. So much for feeling good.

But no amount of casual conversation could segue into her admitting that the only people who ever called her "doctor" were her parents, as if the use of her title would somehow add to her value and they could pass her off as something she wasn't.

"Right." Emerson controlled her voice, smoothing the words over her quickening heartbeat. "Well, I guess we'd better continue with your session."

She straightened, her knees suddenly aching in time with her lower back. The three hours she'd spent driving to her new neurologist's office all the way out in Lockridge two days ago hadn't done her joints any favors, but no way could she risk seeing a specialist in Camden Valley. God, she should've known that escaping her father's shadow was going to be a full-time job now that she was back in Millhaven.

Emerson gestured to the portable massage table, and although Hunter's smile didn't budge, his body didn't, either.

"Looks like I'm not the only one with mental stress."

Knowing he'd seen the hitch in her shoulders and that he'd never buy it if she said she was fine, Emerson went for option number two: deflection. "Maybe, but you *are* the only one with a therapy session right now."

Of course he didn't bite. "This session might have my name on it, but we're both here." Hunter lowered one end of the pole to the floor, leaning against the other just as easy as you please, and dammit, eyes that blue should seriously come with some kind of warning label.

"You want to talk about it?" he asked. "I mean, I am sort of a captive audience, and you said it yourself. Relaxation does a body good."

The ache in her back twisted and throbbed. Listening to Hunter talk about Cross Creek was one thing, a thing that had gone a long way toward helping him get through today's therapy session. But listening was in a whole different universe from talking, and airing out her personal life was a far cry from a little back and forth for the greater good. Letting anyone in wasn't part of the plan to work hard and move on.

Letting Hunter in, with that rugged smile and those ice-blue eyes that had always tempted her to let down her titanium-reinforced guard?

That was downright dangerous. Because if Emerson started talking to him, she might not stop until every last secret was out on the table. And she could not, under any circumstances, allow that to happen. No one could know she was sick. Damaged. Defective. No one.

No matter how crushingly heavy the weight of her recent diagnosis was.

Head up. Eyes forward. Just work.

"I'm fine," she said, turning toward the portable massage table and ordering the rest of his session in her head. External rotation exercises, posterior deltoid static stretches, pressure point massage . . . yeah, they'd be good to go.

At least, they would be, if Hunter stopped pinning her with that X-ray vision stare. "Are you sure? Because I really don't—"

"Thanks for the offer, but I really am fine," Emerson said, dialing up every last ounce of her resolve along with a courteous smile. They'd made a ton of progress today. She didn't want to lose that momentum. "Your shoulder looks strong enough for some new exercises. Why don't you get comfortable on the table and we'll give some lateral raises a try."

Hunter looked at her for what had to be the longest minute of her entire thirty years, and, please, please, all she wanted was to be able to do her job, to help him heal.

To bury herself in the one thing she had left.

Finally, he dropped his eyes and lowered his body to the exam table. "Lateral raises it is. You're the boss."

CHAPTER SEVEN

Hunter rocked back on the heels of his farm-dusty work boots, taking in the early-morning view of Town Street with equal shots of excitement and unease. He'd been up since before daybreak, which for a Saturday in June wasn't necessarily news. But Millhaven's Fifty-Sixth Annual Watermelon Festival kept today from being any run-of-the-mill Saturday, just like Hunter's shoulder injury was keeping him from being able to fully relax. With the workout his comfort zone had gotten over the last week, it was the eighth wonder of the world the damn thing hadn't detonated. Still, even though he'd been put on restrictive duty for working the festivities, the sights and the sounds and the anticipation brewing in front of him right now made *not* smiling pretty much a statistical impossibility.

Every year for the Watermelon Festival, the two-lane thoroughfare of Town Street was closed off to through traffic, allowing everyone in Millhaven to gather along its path to set up tents and tables to showcase their wares. The whole "watermelon" part of the festival had grown more symbolic than literal over time, although Owen and their father had loaded a dozen crates of hothouse Queen of Hearts and another ten of Sugar Babies into their produce truck at the whip crack of dawn. It had wiped out their supply damn near completely—watermelons were a tough grow in smaller greenhouses, and the ones they had infield wouldn't be ready for harvest for a couple more weeks—but for this, it was worth the pain in the pants. The Watermelon Festival was a celebration of the impending summer, with everything from horseshoe competitions to pie-eating contests to old Harley Martin serving up pulled-pork barbecue out of a drum smoker that'd been around since Methuselah.

The event wasn't just a draw for revenue, although the fact that people came from all over the Shenandoah to enjoy the festivities didn't hurt. To Hunter, the Watermelon Festival was more like a chance for everyone to show off what made the town special. Mrs. Ellersby's hand-sewn quilts, the Baker's Dozen's fresh-canned jams and jellies and even fresher-baked cakes and cookies, the detailed truck tours the fire department gave to every wide-eyed kid who came asking—every last contribution made the festival as unique as a fingerprint and as warm as the handshake that went with it.

Millhaven might not qualify as the big time, or okay, even have a fast-food restaurant within a thirty-mile radius, but damn, Hunter loved this town.

"Well, aren't you just standing there looking pretty as a prom queen," came a voice from over his shoulder, and he put a sardonic edge to his smile as he (barely) bit back the urge to give his little brother a single-fingered salute.

"Not me. That falls square under the heading of Your Job." While Hunter liked to think he wasn't terrible to look at, Eli had always gotten far more play with the opposite sex than him and Owen combined. A cocky smile, some flirty innuendo, and bam. Eli had someone's panties in his pocket. The asshole.

Of course, Eli just laughed. "Don't hate me because I'm beautiful. Where do you want these, Boss Man?" He used his chin to gesture to the wooden crates full of collards and spinach stacked three high in his grasp.

Hunter held on to his smile, although suddenly, it was a stretch. "Come on, now. Don't add being in charge of you to my résumé. That's a full-time job all by itself, brother."

"Please." Eli snorted without losing his grin. "Half the time, *I'm* not even in charge of me. But don't worry. I know you're not all hat and no cattle, Hunt. The clipboard's temporary. Once you ditch it in a few weeks, I'll try bossing you around the farm."

"Believe me, I'd pass this thing over with a hallelujah if my shoulder would let me." Hunter held up the old-school brown clipboard between his fingers before sending his gaze back to the trio of oversized canopy tents Owen and their father had finished putting together just a few minutes ago.

"All the greens are going to go over here, so I guess just set them down in the middle tent 'til we get the rest of the tables unloaded and good to go," he said, double-checking the schematic he'd drawn up last night with the reality of the setup on the street in front of him. His fingers itched like crazy to take the triple-stacked crates out of Eli's hands and move them himself—shit, they weren't *that* heavy—but he burned the energy on adjusting his baseball hat and bending down to give Lucy a scratch behind the ears instead. He'd ended the week on a high note in physical therapy. Pushing his luck would be stupid, no matter how tempting.

Haven't you ever wondered what if?

Speaking of pushing his luck.

Not to mention tempting.

"Whoa." Eli stopped short, lowering the crates to the asphalt with a thunk as his brows winged up toward his hairline. "That's a helluva face. You feelin' okay?"

"Yup." The auto answer shoveled past Hunter's lips, but Christ, the sentiment behind it still sat in his chest like a wad of cold rubber cement. No matter what she'd said at the end of their session yesterday, Emerson wasn't fine.

And no matter how much he knew he should, Hunter couldn't forget the look on her face when she'd lied.

Eli measured him for a minute before throwing a thumb into the belt loop of his Wranglers. "Tell you what," he said, his voice all lazy drawl. "We got here before nearly any of the other vendors, so we're ahead of the game. Why don't we take a break for a quick spin up the street to see what we can see."

"I don't know." Hunter eyed the filled-to-the-gills box truck. "There's a lot of work to be done here. Owen packed up two dozen crates of specialty produce alone, and that was even before the regular stuff like corn and greens." He gestured around Town Street. "We've got one of the biggest tents at the festival."

"We also have a buttload of time on our side," Eli said with a patented grin. "I'm not saying we should skip out entirely, but come on, dude. If I plan on kicking Greyson Whittaker's ass from here to the moon in Clementine Parker's pie-eating contest—and trust me, that is *so* in my game plan for today—I've gotta build my appetite."

Hunter squinted at the sky, measuring the time by the sunlight and shadows. "I guess there won't be *too* much left to do after we get these crates unloaded," he said, cracking a grin that sent his pulse back into business-as-usual territory. "Okay, why not?"

"Excellent." Eli slapped his hands together, but Hunter pointed the clipboard at him in a *not so fast* motion.

"We still have to get the greens done. And don't forget about the heirloom tomatoes, either. We ended up with a ton, so I figured we'd put 'em up front so Owen can brag like a proud papa."

"Greens and tomatoes. You got it, Boss Man."

This time, Hunter did give Eli the finger, although his laughter probably made it a tough sell. Really, he should be happier than a pig in a puddle that he'd made progress in PT this week, just like he *definitely* knew he should leave Emerson Montgomery in the past where she belonged. He might've found the way she'd brazenly ditched her just-business demeanor to ask him about the farm kind of sexy, and the way she'd laughed and really listened to his answers? Sexier still.

But she'd lied through her pretty pearly whites when she'd said she was fine, and shit, wasn't that just one more reason not to trust her? Emerson wasn't just playing her personal life close to the vest. She was *hiding* something, and her stubborn refusal to not only tell him what was wrong so he could try to return the favor and help her, but to admit that her world was anything other than all systems go was sending him around the fucking bend.

Even if her expertise as a therapist was helping him heal.

Hunter shook his head, sliding his thoughts back to the sunny stretch of asphalt in front of him. Working with Emerson was his ticket back to business as usual on Cross Creek's front lines, which meant pissing her off with nosy pushback was definitely not in his best interest. His bullshit detector might've detonated when she'd claimed she was fine, but she'd backed up the claim for the rest of their session. Yeah, he was still certain she was hiding something, but she was nothing if not iron willed. If she didn't want to open up to him, he couldn't make her.

Just like he hadn't been able to make her want to stay in Millhaven with him twelve years ago.

Sliding back into the sort of effortless conversation he and Emerson used to lose hours and hours on might've been all too easy, but as enticing as their back and forth had felt, he'd do well to remember the past. While he'd once known her well enough to decipher her in less than a glance, now Emerson was guarded. Tougher. Wary.

Yet still beautiful enough to knock the breath directly out of his lungs.

Keep it simple, stupid. Only a few weeks left and you'll be back to normal. Rehab your shoulder and let the rest go.

◆ ◆ ◆

It took all of ninety minutes after she got out of bed for Emerson to go batshit crazy. Even with fewer hours and the scaled-back intensity of her workweek, she'd been exhausted enough to barely pick her way through some canned soup and half an episode of *Supernatural* on Netflix before falling into bed at a whopping seven thirty last night. Her eleven-hour stay in dreamland—coupled with the facts that she'd recovered from that hellacious drive to Lockridge and her furniture had finally arrived from Vegas a few days ago—had gone miles toward killing some of the ache in both her back and her knees.

Too bad her extended snooze also left her wide awake and crawling the walls at the ungodly hour of eight o'clock on a Saturday morning. And the more time she had to dwell on her current situation, the harder it would be to ignore the elephant-sized reality of her week. The thirty-five hours she'd put in at the PT center had yielded one client, and even then, he'd come to her only out of the sheerest of necessities.

How was she supposed to drown herself in work if there was no work to be done?

Nope. Not going there. Stilling the nervous energy that had made her start to fidget, Emerson smoothed a hand over her nightshirt and turned to survey the dingy walls of the dollhouse-sized apartment around her. She just needed a distraction to get her through the weekend—even the next few hours would be good—and then she could get back to building her client base first thing Monday morning. Trouble was, she'd been so focused on her career over the last few years that free time had been way more theory than practice, and what little time she had taken off had been spent completing continuing-ed courses or volunteering at the Lightning's various fitness outreach camps.

But, come on. She was smart and resourceful—she had a PhD, for Pete's sake. Surely she could come up with something to keep her occupied when she wasn't at the therapy center with Doc Sanders. Something that wasn't breakfast (she'd managed to eat half a piece of toast with her coffee an hour ago), TV (110 channels of infomercials.

Ugh), or trying to cover up the fact that while furniture made life a boatload more comfortable in terms of functionality, it somehow didn't make her apartment any more homey or appealing.

Shit. Three strikes and she was definitely out.

Just as Emerson finished her shower and get-ready-for-the-day routine, which killed a whole forty minutes, even though she had nothing to actually get ready *for*, her cell phone buzzed its way across the chipped Formica of her kitchen counter. Her heart thumped faster beneath her pale-pink T-shirt, then plummeted all the way to the waistband of her denim capris at the sight of the name and number flashing up at her from the display on her caller ID.

She might be desperate for something to do, but she wasn't masochistic. A conversation with her mother would send what little sanity Emerson had left into immediate extinction right now.

Her phone dinged a minute later, signaling a voice mail and tripping her warning sensors into high alert. Bitsy hated voice mail, to the point that she rarely left messages for anyone that weren't going to be "appropriately handled" by a living, breathing human. Chances were sky high her sanity was about to take that hit even without the actual mother-daughter airtime.

"Sweetheart, it's your mother calling. I do hope you're not still in bed at this hour." The pause in the recording gave Emerson just enough time to lock her molars together, and wheee, they were off to an awesome start. *"At any rate, I'm headed into Camden Valley for some work on the hospital's annual fund-raiser gala. I thought it would be in your best interest to come with me so you can meet some of the hospital staff. They have a wonderful orthopedics department, and certainly Dr. Norris would consider having you on board as a favor to your father. I'll stop by your apartment on my way through town to see if you're available to make the trip."*

Emerson's cell phone hit the counter with a clatter, her pulse going full-on Rocket Man in her veins. Twelve years might have passed since she'd left town, but dammit, her parents hadn't changed one iota. She might not have a schedule full of clients (or, okay, more than one client) but she already had a job she was damned good at, in a field she loved. Even if she *did* have the desire to go to medical school at age thirty to become an orthopedic surgeon—which she didn't—her multiple sclerosis would make getting through even an inch of the grueling residency a virtual impossibility.

Which was problematic as shit, since that was surely where her parents had set their sights, and she had absolutely zero intention of telling them about her diagnosis. Now her mother would be here in T minus—Emerson turned to look at the clock on the stove behind her—shit! Twelve minutes and counting for a trip to Camden Valley that would surely boast . . . well, a whole lot of boasting. Not to mention a metric ton of the pressure and panic she'd managed to keep at bay for the last twelve years by staying far enough away for her parents not to be able to wield their influence on her life.

She had to get out of here. *Now.*

Scooping her purse from the counter, she fast-tracked her feet into a pair of sandals and out the door. A quick drive around town to avoid her mother was a bit on the cowardly side, sure, but desperate times called for desperate measures.

And Emerson was definitely. Completely. Painfully. Desperate.

Thankfully, she didn't have a ton of time to dwell on that sad little nugget of truth. She dug her keys from the bottom of her purse, locking her front door with a swift flick of her wrist. Turning on her heel, she hustled over the sidewalk leading to the parking lot, fully intent on getting out of Dodge as fast as humanly possible . . .

And ran smack into a petite, pixie-faced blonde carrying two plastic bins packed full of bubble bath.

"Whoa!" the blonde squeaked, shifting to the toes of her navy-blue sneakers as she fought to keep both her balance and her grip on the bins. Emerson's hands shot out to steady the process, her cheeks flushing in chagrin.

"I'm so sorry. I wasn't looking where I was going. Are you alright?"

"I'm A-okay. No worries," the blonde said, her smile marking the words as the truth. "To be honest, I was hoping to run into you. Just not, you know"—her ponytail slid over one shoulder as she gestured toward the bins to indicate their near miss—"literally."

Emerson blinked, the unease in her belly becoming genuine surprise as her brain paired the voice with its owner. "Daisy? Daisy Halstead?"

"Yep, it's me. Well, I guess I'm Daisy Bradford now, although not for much longer." The woman shook her head as if to dismiss the words, lowering the bins to the pavement beside her to pull Emerson into an unexpected hug. "Seriously, I'm so glad to see you, Emerson! It's been, what, since the summer after high school? Of course you look fantastic."

"Oh! Um, thanks. You look great, too," Emerson said, a small smile finding its way to her lips. While the academic and extracurricular schedule set in stone by her parents had given her little choice but to keep her classmates at arm's length during most of high school, Daisy had been the closest thing she'd had to a true girlfriend. At least, Daisy had been the only girl at Millhaven High who hadn't whispered behind Emerson's back about her being too smart or too pretty or too stuck up for her own good.

Daisy's laugh jarred Emerson back to the here and now of the sun-strewn sidewalk. "I don't know about great," she said, running a hand first over her plain gray tank top, then her fraying cutoffs. "But I suppose I'm lucky enough to be getting by. I'd heard you were back in town and living out this way."

Just like that, Emerson's unease came winging back in all its glory. "Let me guess. Amber Cassidy?"

"She still has the market cornered on gossip," Daisy agreed with a sheepish nod. "I try not to buy into it too much, but she can be kind of hard to miss. Especially when the news is, um. A big deal."

Of course. God, she couldn't blend in any less. "Yeah. I definitely got that impression. Anyway, I'm sorry for nearly bowling you over."

Emerson sent a covert gaze over the faded asphalt of the apartment complex's parking area, which blessedly held no signs of her mother's Mercedes. At least for the moment.

Daisy shook her head to cancel out the apology. "I was rushing, too, so we're even. Preparing for this Watermelon Festival has been making me crazy, and it doesn't help that I'm cutting it really close on time."

"Oh, right. The Watermelon Festival." Between last night's exhaustion and this morning's evasive maneuvering, she'd forgotten all about today's festivities.

"Isn't that where you're headed?" Daisy asked, sending a pointed glance at the keys in Emerson's hand. As far as most folks in Millhaven were concerned, the only good excuse for not attending the start-of-summer festival was if your pulse went missing. Even then, it depended on for how long. But Emerson had left over a decade ago, and the chance that she'd fit back in as a local now was way more none than slim.

"No, actually, I . . ." Emerson's brain spun in search of a good answer, but screw it. Even though the truth stung, it was still the truth. "To be honest, I don't really have a destination in mind. I just wanted to get out of my apartment for a while. I'm kind of dodging my mother."

"Oh. *Oh.*" Daisy's green eyes did the round-and-wide routine, but Emerson had to hand it to her. Despite the curiosity running rampant on her face, Daisy didn't press for more details. "Well, if you're looking for an escape, I sure could use some help at the festival since I'm already running late," Daisy said, smoothing over the conversational pothole with a kind smile. "I mean, I'm just selling my new handmade soaps and beauty products, so it might not be the most exciting thing going, but—"

"It's perfect. I'd love to be your assistant," Emerson said with an enthusiastic nod. Helping Daisy out sounded kind of fun, plus it would keep her busy *and* get her out of Bitsy's crosshairs. Talk about a win trifecta.

"Great." Daisy's smile slid into a grin. "These are my last two boxes. We can get them all loaded up and I'll give you a quick primer on the Fresh As A Daisy products on the way to town."

"Lead the way. I'm all yours."

Emerson wrapped her fingers around the bin on the top of the stack, taking care to use her leg muscles as she lifted so her back wouldn't squall in protest. Daisy's little red SUV was fewer than a dozen steps away, and between them, they made quick work of loading the bins next to the six identical ones and the pair of small card tables in the back. Fresh scents of lavender and lemongrass filled the truck's interior, but rather than being overwhelming or too perfumey, they smelled comforting, like fresh-cut flowers and laundry on a line.

"So you make all of these products yourself?" Emerson asked, settling into the passenger seat and gesturing over her shoulder as Daisy pulled out of the parking lot and headed toward town.

"Soap, bubble bath, body scrub, and massage oil. I'm also working on lotions and face masks, but the lotions in particular can be trickier, so I don't have too many different scents yet." Daisy paused for a self-deprecating laugh. "I bet homemade beauty products sound kind of silly to you, what with your being a big-time physical therapist and everything."

But Emerson shook her head, adamant. "Not at all. A lot of studies show that aromatherapy can be incredibly effective with patients doing physical rehab, especially when it's accompanied by massage therapy. I actually took an intensive class in alternative healing practices last year to explore the subject more in depth. The physiological effects are fascinating, and—"

Daisy blinked at her from the driver's seat, and Christ on a cracker, Emerson needed to get out more. Her first friend outing in who knew how long, and she was going to bore the poor woman straight to death.

"I'm sorry," Emerson said, sliding a hand over the back of her neck to try to disperse the warmth that had bloomed there. "I've been pretty focused on work lately."

"I never would have guessed." Daisy tacked just enough humor to the words to put Emerson right back at ease. "Still, that's really interesting. I mean, the aromatherapy part," she added with a little shudder. "I don't imagine the broken-bones or torn-ligaments part of your job is too much fun."

Girlfriend definitely had a point. "I've seen some pretty terrible injuries," Emerson agreed. "But even for the most devastating conditions, there are usually lots of therapy options to help people adjust and heal. Getting my clients as functional and healthy as possible is worth all the training and hard work."

"Do you think you could send me the links to some of those aromatherapy studies?" Daisy asked, her tone edging higher with excitement. "I just started Fresh As A Daisy a few months ago and I've been kind of lasered in on production, trying to get the recipes and formulas just right. But I'd love to learn more about the positive benefits people might get from the essential oils used in the products."

Emerson's laugh snuck up on her, but she let it out all the same. Daisy definitely didn't have to twist her arm to talk shop. "Of course. I've got a bunch of studies bookmarked on my laptop, along with all my course notes from last year. I'm happy to share them."

They filled the rest of the car ride and the following half hour of unloading and setup with back and forth about Daisy's new business and Emerson's knowledge of alternative medicine. Finally, after the last bar of orange blossom and shea butter soap had been set carefully beneath the shade of the cheery yellow canopy tent Daisy had brought from home, Emerson took a step back to survey their display.

"Wow. Everything looks great, Daisy," she said, taking a big inhale as she brushed her fingers over the slightly rough texture of the sea salt soap. "And it smells even better. I bet you'll do a ton of business today."

"I really hope so." Daisy sent a dubious glance at the milling, pre-festival crowd and the brightly colored tents now covering Town Street like confetti on New Year's Eve. "My husband"—she paused, pressing her lips together as she reset her words—"ex-husband, didn't really think starting my own business was a good idea, so thanks for helping me out today."

Emerson's gut squeezed, but she hung on tight to her smile. She hadn't recognized the last name Daisy had offered up earlier, so she knew the guy almost certainly wasn't local. Judging by the look on her friend's face right now, she wanted to drop the rest of the topic like a red-hot potato, so Emerson said, "Well, I think Fresh As A Daisy is a fantastic idea. In fact, if we can round up a few willing participants later, I don't mind offering five-minute therapeutic hand massages to go with your soothing lavender-chamomile lotion."

Daisy let out a soft laugh, and bingo, mission accomplished. "Okay, but only as long as I get the first one."

"Deal." Ignoring the snap, crackle, and pop in her knees, Emerson bent to grab two water bottles from the cooler they'd tucked under one of the card tables beneath their tent. If the sheen of moisture on her brow was any indicator, Mother Nature was hell-bent on following through with the weather report's promise of a scorcher today. The symptoms of her MS didn't tend to play nicely with the heat. She'd have to be really careful to hydrate and stay off her feet so her legs didn't give out.

Don't think about it. Not even a little bit.

"So." Emerson handed over one water bottle, toasting Daisy with the other. "Now that we've got a few minutes to relax before the festival kicks off, why don't you catch me up on what's been happening in town?"

"I can," her friend said, although her expression remained clouded in doubt. "But you just spent the last few years jet-setting all over the

US with a crazy-famous football team. Do you really want to talk about what everyone in Millhaven has been up to since high school?"

"I know Vegas is pretty far from here." Although Emerson wasn't about to say so, the lifestyle, both in Las Vegas and with the Lightning, was light-years away from Millhaven's sleepy, small-town vibe. "But, I promise, I was really just doing my job. Anyway," she continued with a shrug, "everyone in town knows all about me. It seems only fair that I get the dish on them in return."

Daisy gave her a look that read *good point*. "Okay, let's see. The Bar is still the best place to hang out around here"—at Emerson's brow lift, Daisy corrected herself—"okay, the *only* place to hang out, unless you're at a bonfire or you head into Camden Valley. Amber's working with Mollie Mae over at the Hair Lair now, and they're like two apples on a branch. Kelsey Whittaker rounds out the bunch, although she's Kelsey Lambert now."

Not surprising. Kelsey had staked her claim on Brad Lambert on the playground in the fifth grade, at about the same time she and Amber had become BFFs.

"What about the Baker's Dozen? Do they still come to the festival?" Emerson asked, trying to squelch the memory of her run-in with Amber. The group of thirteen ladies had been baking up a category-5 hurricane since Emerson had been in elementary school. God, she hoped they were still at it.

As if to second her chocolate-covered thoughts, Daisy gave her belly an appreciative rub over the gray cotton of her tank top. "A few of the members passed the torch to their daughters, and the group decided to embrace gender equality when Edith Lewis's son turned out to have mad pastry skills, but they're going strong as ever. Still make oatmeal cookies as thick and soft as a pillow."

"Oh yum." Emerson grinned and made a mental note to find their tent and stuff herself silly before the day was over. "Those are my favorite."

"Girl. That's not even the half of it for killer food," Daisy said, casually waving a hand through the humid air. "Every Saturday, Harley Martin still sets up shop over by the firehouse and serves the best barbecue in the Valley from that ancient old drum smoker of his."

Okay, someone needed to call Pavlov because now her mouth was just plain watering. "The one he welded together out of scrap metal in the nineteen seventies?"

The thing could be part Studebaker for all Emerson cared. Harley's pulled-pork sandwiches were the stuff of legends.

"The very same," Daisy said. "And speaking of the same, even though old man Whittaker will argue otherwise, the hands-down best place to get fresh produce around here is still Cross Creek Farm."

Emerson's heart did an involuntary two-step against her breastbone, and whew, the weather was getting downright ridiculous already. "Good to know," she said, taking a long swig from her bottle of water.

Daisy continued, her tennis shoes scuffing softly against the curb as she leaned in closer and dropped her voice to a near whisper. "Yeah, that rivalry between the two farms is still alive and kicking harder than the Rockettes. It's mostly a lot of smack talk between Eli Cross and Greyson Whittaker. They like to duke it out for the title of Baddest Boy in Millhaven, but to tell the truth, I'm pretty sure it's a dead heat. Owen's still serious enough to keep Eli in check and out of trouble, although every once in a blue moon Owen and Sheriff Atlee get a mind to throw back a few beers and close down The Bar."

Daisy's cheeks pinked at the mention of the sheriff, but Emerson had to slap a mental "File for Later" sign over her curiosity as she rewound. Processed. Dropped her jaw in shock.

"Wait. Lane Atlee is Millhaven's sheriff? Tall guy, body like a prize-fighter, attitude to match, Lane Atlee?" He and Owen had been the same year in high school, two ahead of her and Daisy, although admittedly, Lane's attendance was sparse at best. She'd have been less surprised to hear he'd become a ballerina than Millhaven's top boy in blue.

"Mmhmm." Daisy cleared her throat, her flush downgrading to nearly normal. "Carl Barker retired six years ago, and Deputy Hutchinson was only two years behind him. Lane surprised everyone by deciding to go to the police academy in Camden Valley so he could run for sheriff."

"Huh," Emerson finally managed. "Can't say I saw that one coming."

Something she couldn't quite pin down shifted in Daisy's expression, her friend's smile growing too forced, too fast. "Funny you should say that. You *have* seen Hunter Cross since you've been back, right?"

"Yeeeeeah," Emerson said, half acknowledgment, half question. Talk about a weird segue. Plus, Daisy had to already know the answer since Amber had likely told everyone in the county by now. "Why?"

Daisy's smile didn't move a millimeter as she whispered through her teeth, "Because he's about eight feet to your left and coming in hot."

CHAPTER EIGHT

Hunter was less than a dozen steps away from Emerson before he realized this was a bad idea. He was at the Watermelon Festival to relax a little and work a lot, and the flash-bang going on in his rib cage right now wasn't going to help turn either of those into reality. But best he could tell, Emerson had slept, eaten, and breathed work all week, without so much as a baby toe off the caution path. To unexpectedly see her standing there, talking with Daisy Halstead in the middle of the Watermelon Festival and looking as casual and gorgeous as ever? Yeah, that lit him up like a Fourth of July firecracker.

Hopefully his knee-jerk curiosity wasn't about to blow up in his face.

"Hey," Eli said, confusion creasing his forehead into a *V* at Hunter's rapid swerve in direction. "What are you . . . oh shit. Is that—?"

"Yup."

Eli whistled under his breath, but God bless him, he kept up stride for stride. "Gotta hand it to you. You sure can pick 'em. Hey, ladies!" His brother's smile increased by about forty watts as the last of the asphalt between the two of them and Daisy's tent became history. "Great day for a Watermelon Festival, don't you think?"

"Oh, hey, Eli! Hey, Hunter. I sure do," Daisy said, fixing them both with a genuine smile that reminded Hunter why he'd always liked her. "It's my first time as a vendor, and Emerson was nice enough to say she'd be my assistant today."

"Really?" Hunter's surprise slipped out before he could trap it, the emotion going for broke as Emerson laughed in reply.

"Yes, really. I do leave work on occasion." She paused, clearly catching the doubt that had to be plastered to his face, then added, "Okay. I do now. But I ran into Daisy a little while ago in front of my apartment and helping her out seemed like a great chance for us to catch up."

"Well, it sure is good to see you back in town, Emerson," Eli said, and oh no. What the hell was he doing, giving her that aw-shucks smile? "I didn't know you were renting a place at the Twin Pines."

At Emerson's puzzled expression, Daisy chimed in. "Eli lives on the other side of the building, over in 16B."

"Ah," she said with a nod. "4A."

Hunter borrowed the puzzled expression that Emerson had just gotten rid of. "You're not staying with your parents until something else opens up?" While the place wasn't a complete rattrap, the Twin Pines could hardly be what she was used to, and her parents had a private carriage house right on their property.

"Yeah, no." She shook her head hard for emphasis. "That definitely wouldn't work out."

The swift delivery combined with her adamant tone to create a whole lot of ooookay then, and Eli swooped in to smooth it over with another charming grin.

"Well, I for one don't mind having you as a neighbor, and I think it's right nice of you to help Daisy out with her business like that."

Emerson's smile in return was so pretty, Hunter's trademark calm threatened a complete labor strike. "It's been fun so far, and the products look amazing," she said. "I'm happy to do whatever I can."

"Actually"—Daisy brightened, splitting an excited gaze between him and Eli—"Emerson was just saying she'd offer up a therapeutic hand massage to anyone willing to try my lavender-chamomile lotion. Either of you boys willing to find your softer side? This stuff isn't just for women, and it works great on smoothing out calluses."

She lifted a bottle emblazoned with the letters "LC" off the table beside her, and Emerson's ocean-blue eyes went as round as her mouth.

"Oh, I'm sure Eli and Hunter don't want to—"

"I'm game," Eli said, shifting on his broken-in Red Wings to take a step closer to Emerson.

Hunter's pulse kicked hard against his rib cage. "No, you're not."

Despite the ruckus going on in his chest, his words came out as slow and easy as a Sunday morning, and although they stopped Eli's movement, his brother's grin stayed put.

"Lavender and chamomile sound kinda nice. Sure, I am."

"No," Hunter repeated, neither his smile nor the rest of him letting up. "You're not."

Okay, so he had no claim to Emerson whatsoever, and considering how seriously she took her job, a hand massage right here in front of God and everybody was bound to be harmless. But good behavior wasn't one of Eli's talents, and even though Hunter knew his brother had a code of honor lurking someplace beneath his cocky exterior, he wasn't about to choose now to test the boundaries of where the freaking thing began.

Even if that meant testing the boundaries of where his composure ended.

"Okay, then," Eli said, holding up his hands in surrender for just a second before gesturing toward Emerson. "Guess you get to be the one to give it a go. I always knew you had a softer side."

Hunter's breath jammed in his lungs, and he realized too late what Eli had done. But backpedaling now was out of the question, and anyway, he'd been doing PT with Emerson all week. He could handle a little hand massage, no problem.

The fact that he didn't *want* to backpedal, even if he probably should? Yeah. He'd deal with that later.

Hunter shot Eli a split-second look that promised murder, or at the very least a solid ass kicking later, before turning toward Emerson. "Looks like I'm your guinea pig."

She took the lotion from Daisy, who turned to answer Eli's question about the sandalwood soap at the other end of the tent, both of them moving out of earshot.

"Your brother's still a troublemaker, I see." Emerson pinned the words with enough of a smile that Hunter's smile in return slipped out with ease.

"Yeah, it's at the top of his résumé. But, really, we can skip the massage if you want." As much as Hunter didn't mind the one on one, he wasn't about to make her uneasy in order to get it.

"Therapeutic massage is part of my job, remember?" Emerson freed the lid from the bottle with a soft pop, squeezing a dime-sized amount of lotion into one palm. "Plus, we've done nearly half a dozen of them this week on your shoulder."

"Not in the middle of Town Street."

Just like that, she froze, her cautious demeanor slamming back into place like a set of two-ton doors. "I'm sorry. I didn't mean to make you uncomfortable. I only offered—"

"I'm not uncomfortable," Hunter said, mostly because it was the truth, but also because, dammit, he wanted that smile of hers back. "I know you want to help Daisy with her business. All I meant was that people will probably talk."

Emerson laughed, soft and yet matter-of-fact. "They started talking the minute I got back, and I doubt they'll stop anytime soon. The reality is, I live here now, and you and I are going to run into each other. Seems like turning that into a big deal is only feeding the fire."

And wasn't *that* a hell of a good point. "Okay then," Hunter said, extending his arms toward her. "I guess my hands are in your hands."

"Great." Emerson pressed her palms together, rubbing her fingers back and forth just like she did before the massage therapy they did at the end of his sessions. "So are you having a nice festival so far?"

"Awfully formal, aren't you?" The teasing was out before he could trap it, and shit, could he put her any further on the spot? "Sorry, I just meant—"

"I know what you meant," Emerson said, reaching for his hands. Closing her fingers around one wrist, she pressed her thumbs into the heel of his palm, rotating them in slow circles. "And I guess you're right. It's just a little weird to be back in Millhaven as an outsider."

"You're not an outsider." She'd been born and raised here, for Chrissake. Now, that asshat Daisy had met in Camden Valley and married a few years ago? *He* was an outsider.

Emerson seemed unconvinced. "I've been gone for twelve years, Hunter."

"So now you're back. Sure, some things have changed a little." Twelve years wasn't twelve minutes. Nothing stayed exactly the same, even in small towns. "But that still doesn't make you an outsider."

She lowered her chin, a tendril of hair dropping over her gaze in a copper-colored curtain as she concentrated her touch on the spot between his thumb and forefinger, and damn, how could he feel one little touch all the way up his arm?

Emerson spoke without looking up. "Not even if I'm one of the things that's changed?"

"You haven't changed that much."

Okay, so the reply was bolder than his norm. But despite whatever she was guarding, the words felt as obvious as the bright-yellow canopy tent over their heads.

What's more, Emerson didn't argue. "Neither have you. You still like to fix things, don't you? Keep the status quo."

For a second, Hunter was tempted to call her out on the subtle shift in focus, but since that'd probably kill the conversation in six syllables or fewer, he said, "I still like things simple, sure. I live on a farm. I don't want to fix you, though, if that's what you're getting at. I think you're fine just as you are."

Her laugh was all amusement. "But you don't even know me anymore."

"Bet I do." Okay, so he was borderline flirting with her now, but that relaxed, wide-open smile she'd been wearing when he'd first seen her talking to Daisy had found its way back over her face, and Hunter felt too damned good to listen to reason and stop.

"It's been twelve years," Emerson tried again. Too bad for her, she wasn't the only stubborn kid on the block.

"Uh-huh. You still hate mayonnaise."

She scrunched up her nose, and even with frown lines bracketing both her mouth and her forehead, she looked cuter than anyone had a right to. "That's a given. I've hated that stuff since birth, and I'll hate it 'til I go in the ground. Anyway, mustard's better."

"Okay." He paused while she seamlessly transferred her touch from his right hand to his left, the crisp, fresh scent of lavender filling the space between them. "Something tougher, then. Let's see. I bet you still have that dog-eared copy of *Pride and Prejudice* on your bedside table even though you know more than half the book by heart."

"That's not too surprising," she said after a pause. "*Pride and Prejudice* is my favorite book."

"Uh-huh. Even money says it's sandwiched between two romance novels."

Emerson's blush had her dead to rights. "So I still like a good happily ever after." The doubt in her eyes remained, and okay. Guess he'd have to go all in.

Hunter tilted his head. "I bet you make a charitable donation every year, but not to a big organization. You pick something small, where the people really need the help."

Her hands hitched over his, and ha! He had her. "I may make a contribution to the local food pantry in Las Vegas every winter," she said. "But those volunteer-run places get so much less donation money than you'd think. Every dollar helps."

He measured her with a thoughtful glance, hoping like hell that his triumphant smile wasn't popping through too much. "See? Not so different after all."

"Just because you made a couple lucky guesses doesn't mean I'm the same girl you went to high school with."

The slow, deliberate pressure she was sweeping over the tops of his knuckles put him at a tactical disadvantage—holy hell, her hands felt good on his—but he wasn't about to scale back now, even if she seemed more pragmatic than pissy. "And just because you've been gone for a while doesn't mean you're an outsider in your own hometown."

Emerson lifted her chin to move the hair from her eyes, the sassy smile on her lips sending yet another slap shot against his sternum. "Some of my favorite things include indie movies and sushi, Hunter. At the very least, I'm pretty sure that puts me outside the norm here in Millhaven."

Whoa. She might have you there, chief. "Okay," he conceded. "So I wouldn't know an indie movie if it jumped up and bit me, and you already know that around here, we call sushi 'bait.'"

She lifted her brows into victory formation, but uh-uh, he wasn't ready to go down just yet. Although Emerson hadn't completely shed her air of caution, she was a hell of a lot more at ease than he'd seen her since she'd been home.

And calm composure be damned, Hunter wanted to show her what he saw.

"Still, I bet you fit in better than you think," he said.

She shook her head as she slid her fingers over the work-made calluses on his thumb. "I'm gossip fodder, Hunter. In fact, I bet Amber Cassidy is probably itching to tell the entire universe that we're holding hands right now."

Emerson's eyes darted to his left like a lightning strike, and sure enough, Amber was doing some high-grade whispering into Kelsey Lambert's ear across the sunny pavement of Town Street.

But Hunter didn't care. He curled his fingers around Emerson's without so much as a nanosecond's hesitation, pulling her close enough that their forearms touched, warm skin on skin.

"Then I guess she'll come damn near close to hives when she sees us having lunch together later."

"What?" Emerson's breath coasted over his cheek in a puff of hot surprise, but again, he didn't hesitate.

"Look, beating around the bush isn't really my style. I like things simple, so I'm gonna cut right to the truth. You said you think you're an outsider here, but I disagree, and I'd like the chance to prove you wrong."

"You want me to go to lunch with you to prove that I still fit in after being gone all this time?"

Ah hell. Maybe taking the no-bullshit approach wasn't the very best idea he'd ever sprouted. But he'd already let the words fly.

Now it was time to take action and back them up.

"I want to show you that you're not too far from home. So what do you say? Are you going to let me give it my best shot, or not?"

"I've got to hand it to you, brother. You are one lucky bastard."

Fifteen minutes had passed since Hunter and Eli had walked away from Daisy's tent, yet neither Hunter's shit-eating grin nor Eli's merciless ribbing had let up, even for a minute.

"Who, me?" Hunter asked, hooking a thumb in the direction of his chest. "I don't know what you're talking about. You got the exact same treatment I did, hand massage and all."

Fair being fair, Emerson had corralled Eli for his turn with his lavender-scented softer side as soon as she'd finished Hunter's hand massage. Of course, that'd been after she'd agreed to meet Hunter at Cross Creek's tent during her lunch break in three hours.

Okay, fine. He really *was* a lucky bastard.

Eli held up his hands, flipping them from palms to knuckles, then back again. "I told you the lotion sounded kinda nice. That lavender smells relaxing, and the chamomile . . . anyway." He returned to the topic just in time to head off the gigantic raft of shit Hunter had been thiiiiis close to heaping on him. "You know exactly what I'm talking about, you sly dog. You're going on a date with Emerson Montgomery."

Hunter's boots tripped to a graceless halt. "It's not a date," he said, his smile evaporating and his heartbeat working out a solid *hey now* beneath his white T-shirt. Sure, he and Emerson had flirted a little, and maybe asking her to meet him later had been a touch more impulsive than his usual MO. There was certainly no way he could deny that she was sexier now than ever—for Chrissake, he wasn't blind, dead, or stupid. But walking around the Watermelon Festival for an hour to reacquaint her with the town was still a far cry from a date.

Sexy or not, Emerson had turned his heart into finger paint once. He couldn't let that happen again.

Eli's expression said he wasn't buying Hunter's veto, but at least his brother had the wherewithal to keep his thoughts on the matter to himself. "Whatever you say, man."

"Good, because I say it's not a date."

Hunter pulled in a slow, steady breath, nailing his calm back into place. He and Eli retraced their steps over Town Street, walking past the multicolored tables and tents now packing the thoroughfare with no room to spare. *Shit.* They'd been gone longer than Hunter had realized or intended.

"We're gonna have to haul balls to get back with enough time to finish setting up," he said. Eli lifted one shoulder but nodded in agreement and picked up the pace. Two minutes of solid hoofing it had them back at Cross Creek's tent, where Owen and their father looked to be setting out the last few crates of watermelons and summer squash.

"Hey, there you are. I tried both of your cell phones." Sure enough, the words had barely crossed Owen's lips when both Hunter and Eli's back pockets chirped with incoming text messages. The spotty-on-a-good-day cell service they got out here in the sticks was pretty much the only thing Hunter *didn't* love about Millhaven. Hell, two steps in any given direction could turn even the fanciest cell phone into a sleek silver paperweight.

Eli shook his head, sliding his phone from his banged-up Wranglers to silence it with a quick tap. "That's service in the boonies for you."

"We could've used your help hauling all the rest of these crates. Where'd you run off to, anyway?" Owen asked, his chin lifting a few inches as Eli sauntered by him to grab a bottle of water from the cooler by the cash box. "And what's that smell?"

"Ah, it's Daisy Halstead's new lavender and chamomile hand lotion," Eli said, his brows waggling beneath his faded red baseball hat. "Free hand massages to anyone who gives it a try. I'm totally going back later for seconds."

A muscle in Owen's jaw hardened beneath his dark stubble. "Seriously? We're three minutes from the start of the Watermelon Festival, and instead of working like you're supposed to, you're wandering around hitting on Daisy Halstead? She's one of the nicest people in Millhaven, for Chrissake."

"I wasn't hitting on her, and I got plenty unloaded before Hunter and I left." Eli's demeanor turned as subarctic as his voice. "Anyway, what's that supposed to mean? A *nice* girl's too good for a guy like me?"

Hunter's gut formed a knot, and he stepped in to fill the space between his brothers. "We were just blowing off a little steam and checking out the other vendors, O. If anything, this is my fault." He'd been the one to beeline for Daisy's tent in the first place.

"No, it's not," Owen said. "You were in charge of the schematics and inventory, and both of those got done. That's more than I can say for Eli's share."

Confusion trickled past Hunter's unease, and wait . . . "Eli, didn't you unload all the greens before we left?"

He jammed a thumb through his belt loop, his silence extending for just a beat too long. "Most of 'em. I figured I'd just do the rest when we got back, but I didn't realize we had so much inventory from the greenhouse. Or that we'd cut it so close to the start of the festival."

Hunter cursed under his breath—*dammit*, he should've double-checked the inventory list to be sure the work had been done—but Owen cut him off with a curt shake of his head.

"You're hurt, Hunt. No one's blaming you for not being able to haul these crates around. But it doesn't take a rocket scientist to figure out that we need all the hands we can get around here, and instead, Eli's got his own agenda. As freaking usual."

Although he knew his brother didn't intend any guilt, the reminder of his injury peppered Hunter's chest full of holes. Before he could recover—and before Eli could pop off with the angry retort clearly brewing in his mouth—Owen shook his head in disgust.

"Just forget it. I'm tired of trying to get you to take the farm seriously, Eli. You're going to do whatever you want no matter what anyone says, and there's slack that needs picked up. I'm unloading the last of these crates." Owen's boot heel scraped in a hard turn over the pavement as he pivoted toward the box truck parked adjacent to the tent and walked away.

"You could use a good hand massage. Along with a serious ass kicking. I would've gotten everything off the truck just fine," Eli muttered under his breath. Shoulders bunched and brimming with tension, he threw his half-empty water bottle into their plastic trash bin with a curse. "Screw this. He wants the work? He's got it. I'm taking Lucy for a walk. Call me if you need me, Dad."

Uncharacteristic impulses flared in Hunter's chest. He turned to haul Eli back and remind him that, A) he knew damn well they'd need him since now they were behind schedule and everyone and his mother would be at the festival today, and B) calling him when they did would probably be about as useful as a trap door on a frigging canoe with cell service being what it was, but his father stopped him cold.

"Let him go, Hunt," he said, his gravelly voice low and quiet. "He'll burn it off and be back quick enough."

Hunter watched Eli clip Lucy's old red leash to her even older collar before stomping off in the opposite direction from Owen and the truck, and truly, Hunter didn't know how much longer he could hold the two of them off before shit turned into World War III.

"Well, that was fun," he said, releasing a slow exhale as he looked at his father. He wasn't surprised his old man had remained quiet during the exchange. Letting the three of them duke out their grievances on their own was simply his way. Hunter supposed there were worse things to inherit than the desire not to rock the boat.

"Your brothers have been fixin' to throw down for a while now," his father agreed, a small frown traveling over his sun-weathered face. "My guess is they'll get to it soon enough."

Now it was Hunter's turn to mutter under his breath. "That's what I'm afraid of."

His father looked at him from beneath the brim of the caramel-colored Stetson he damn near never took off. His eyes flashed with steely gray concern Hunter recognized all too well, but the emotion disappeared quickly, replaced by quiet calm as he straightened the wooden crate full of pickling cucumbers on the table at his hip. "How's that shoulder treatin' ya?"

Not wanting to linger on the current topic, anyway, Hunter dropped a glance at the offending joint, rolling it gently beneath his T-shirt before answering with the truth. "Best day yet, actually. The physical therapy seems to be working."

His dad lifted one salt-and-pepper brow, just enough for Hunter to notice. "Sounds like you're in good hands."

"Three weeks and I'll be better than new," he said, trying like hell to dodge the thought of who those hands belonged to and this morning's impulsive reminder of how warm and sweet they'd felt on his skin. He had enough on his freaking plate as it was. "For now, guess we'd better get ready to sell some produce."

Hunter and his father lapsed into comfortable silence, both of them working up a sweat as they finished the last-minute prep for the festival. The simplicity of the food in front of him smoothed the raw edges of Hunter's nerves—round, jewel-green Sugar Baby watermelons, velvety bunches of sweet-scented basil, satiny, fat tomatoes, and brightly ruffled butter lettuce. Sunlight speared down from overhead, tag-teaming Hunter in a vicious combination of heat and humidity despite the limited shade from their canopy tent, and man, the weather had been brutal lately.

"I don't usually mind a little heat, but it's getting to be an inferno out here," he said, swiping an arm over the moisture already fully formed on his brow and reaching down to palm a pair of water bottles from the battered cooler. "Even my sweat is starting to sweat."

His father's chuckle was largely unapologetic. "Headed for ninety-six, according to the gal on the radio this mornin'. Looks like this season's gonna bring us all sorts of surprises."

"I think I've had all the surprises I need this season," Hunter said, passing one of the water bottles over to his father before pouring the contents of the second into the bowl they'd brought from home for Lucy.

"Thanks," his father said after draining half the bottle in one go. "Guess I could've used that more than I thought."

A thread of worry uncurled in Hunter's gut, but he knew better than to state it flat out. Time to rely on his laid-back smile. "Yeah, well, take it easy, would you? You end up with heat exhaustion and you'll never hear the end of it from Owen."

"Bah. It's gonna take a helluva lot more than a little heat to do me in." His father gave up a nothing-doing grin identical to Hunter's, just a slow flash of his teeth. "Now what do you say we get a little work done, here?"

His father took another long draw from his water bottle, and although Hunter knew it was probably more for his benefit than to quench the old man's thirst, he'd take whatever he could to get this day back to normal.

"I say that sounds like a damn good plan."

CHAPTER NINE

Emerson straightened the display of lilac body scrub six times in twenty minutes before Daisy flat out busted her.

"Girl. That is some righteous fidgeting you've got going on over there. If you're not careful, you're liable to rearrange a hole in the tablecloth."

"What? I'm not . . ." Oh hell. Insulting the intelligence of the only friend she had right now was an epically bad plan. "Sorry," Emerson said, dropping her hands to her sides. "Guess I've got a little nervous energy to burn."

Daisy's blond brows snapped together in obvious confusion. "Over the body scrub?"

A laugh barged past Emerson's lips, scattering her nerves on exit. "No. I told Hunter I'd meet him on my lunch break."

"The lunch break you're taking in five minutes?" Daisy asked, mouthing the word "whoa" a second later. "Hunter and Eli headed back to their tent three hours ago. How come you didn't say anything?"

"I knew you had a lot on your mind with the festival. Plus, it's not a big deal."

Her friend sent a pointed glance at the containers of body scrub, all of them lined up with mathematical precision. "Pretty sure the table-cloth would say otherwise. So I take it you and the football guy are no longer a thing?" Daisy stopped short, her cheeks flushing. "I'm sorry. That was just about the nosiest question ever."

"No, it's okay," Emerson said. She might not want to fork over a complete tell-all of her personal life, but at least this she could freely admit. "Lance and I broke up when I decided to leave Las Vegas, yes. But it was amicable."

At least, as amicable as a breakup could be when one party was diagnosed with a debilitating disease and the other had a career that was taking off like the space shuttle. The part of her that housed her pride had wanted to be furious when Lance had gently suggested they separate less than two weeks after her diagnosis. But, really, who was she kidding? Multiple sclerosis was forever, and even though she'd liked him well enough while they'd dated, she'd always known Lance *wasn't* forever.

"How about what's going on between you and Hunter?" Daisy asked, bringing Emerson back to the present with a small smile. "Is that amicable, too?"

Emerson's chin snapped up. "There's nothing going on between me and Hunter."

"But there could be, right?"

"I don't think so." First of all, she was his physical therapist—not that she could say that to Daisy, or would even if it didn't violate his privacy six ways to Sunday. Secondly, the last thing Emerson needed was a distraction, not even a blue-eyed, broad-shouldered, charming-as-hell one.

She was here to work. To get on with her life. To forget.

And dammit, when Hunter had wrapped his fingers around hers, all she'd been able to do was remember.

"Y'all were once quite the thing. Are you sure?" Daisy asked gently. But Emerson's new normal couldn't include old pasts. Both her heart and her body would make damn sure of that.

"Positive. I guess I'm just not used to being back in the town spotlight after twelve years. I'm sure it'll pass."

"Hmm." A flicker of doubt moved over Daisy's face, but thankfully, she didn't put it to words. "Well, lucky for you, those twelve years are in the rearview, and the only thing in front of you is today. Go. Have a nice lunch break. And don't come back for at least an hour, you hear?"

Emerson hesitated, sending a look around the tent and the steady stream of festivalgoers on Town Street beyond. "Promise you'll call me if things get busy?"

"Not on your life," Daisy said with a laugh. "Your cell phone's not too likely to do you much good around here, anyway. I'll give rain checks for your hand massages, don't worry. Now scoot before I deliver you to the Cross Creek tent myself."

"Okay. Okay, okay!" Emerson added with a grin as Daisy waved her hands to shoo her from the tent. "I'll be back in an hour."

Tamping down the nerves still jangling in her belly, she kicked her feet into motion, moving up the street. So her conversation with Hunter this morning had been a little flirty. They were both adults, and while not a little bit of time had passed since they'd been a couple, they certainly weren't *total* strangers. He'd taken her virginity, for God's sake—not that she hadn't been offering it up at the time. How difficult could a quick spin around the Watermelon Festival really be?

And then Emerson caught sight of him from across Town Street, and sweet baby Jesus, Hunter Cross was gorgeous.

Her breath slapped to a stop at the same time her pulse sped way up. Hunter was standing about fifteen feet away beneath Cross Creek's triple-wide vibrant red canopy tent, which all things considered, was normal enough. Turned to the side so his profile was showing, he focused his gaze first on the clipboard in his hands, then on the produce on the table next to him. Although the task seemed run of the mill, even boring, maybe, something about his movements spoke of pure ease, from the reverence in his eyes as he leaned in to check the wooden crates full of ripe green watermelons to the look on his face when he threw his head back and laughed at whatever his brother Owen had just said. The tension that had claimed Hunter's muscles all week in the PT center was nowhere to be found, replaced by a fluidity and calm that Emerson couldn't cultivate through any treatment or exercise, and oh God, he simply looked . . .

Like he belonged.

Emerson forced her feet forward at the same moment Hunter turned and saw her, his eyes going round with recognition and surprise.

But before either of them could speak, a fat, dark blur darted from beneath the canopy, beelining directly for Emerson and parking its big, wiggling self smack at her feet.

"Oh my God." Her brain raced, and her heart along with it, but no. It couldn't be. "Is this . . . ?" She met Hunter's stare for a fleeting second, catching his nod before kneeling down to greet the exuberant dog with a laugh. "Lucy, you pretty girl! The last time I saw you, you were only a puppy."

"She never did lose the mentality. Obviously," Hunter said, taking a few steps forward to lean one hip against a stack of sturdy wooden crates. A handful more seconds passed while Emerson gave Lucy a healthy round of praise and scratches behind the ears—jeez, she was still the sweetest thing. Then a whistle sounded off from beneath the tent, sharp and quick, causing Lucy to stop mid-preen and hightail her way back under the shade.

"Oh." Emerson straightened and smoothed a hand over her T-shirt, her eyes following Lucy to the bustling activity beneath Cross Creek's oversized canopies. "I'm sorry," she said, taking a step toward Hunter. "You guys look really busy. If you need to stick around, I totally understand."

He opened his mouth, but before he could free a single word, an all-too-familiar time-roughened voice came from behind him to stop her argument.

"Emerson Montgomery. Is that you, darlin'?"

She blinked, an involuntary smile bubbling up from the bottom of her chest. Hunter's father might look a bit more worn around the edges than the last time she'd seen him, but Lord, his smile was still as warm and smooth as butterscotch. "Yes, sir, it's me. How are you, Mr. Cross?"

He took the hand she extended and embraced it warmly in both of his. "As good as an old man can be. Sorry about Lucy here." He gestured down to the bona fide mutt sitting by his boots, still wagging her tail in a clear bid for attention. "I'd teach her some manners, but you know what they say about old dogs."

"Oh, no worries. I don't mind a bit," Emerson said, reaching down to give Lucy one more pat on the head.

Mr. Cross gestured to Hunter, who was still leaning against the crates and listening just as easy as he pleased. "Hunter mentioned you were back in town and workin' with the doc. Welcome home."

The warmth blooming behind her breastbone took her by complete surprise, but still she said, "Thank you. I'm happy to be working with Doc Sanders."

Mr. Cross tipped his timeworn Stetson at her. "We sure are grateful you're takin' good care of Hunter's shoulder."

"Thanks, but he deserves some credit, too. He's been working really hard."

Hunter's brows popped, outing his surprise. "You're the expert. All I'm doing is following the plan so I can get back to work."

Mr. Cross gave a rusty chuckle, lifting his chin toward the thoroughfare of Town Street. "Well, I won't keep you two from catchin' up. Hunt, you take your time. Emerson, it sure was nice to see you."

"You sure you're good here with Owen and Eli?" Hunter asked, sending a curl of guilt through Emerson's belly.

"I don't want to keep you from work," she said, but his father waved off her concern with a lift of one work-callused hand.

"Don't make me fire him, now." A wink slipped flawlessly over his warm gray gaze. "We'll be just fine here, don't you worry. And make sure you come up and see us in the strawberry fields, you hear? We'll see to it you get the best of the picking."

Emerson's stomach perked up and took notice, right along with her taste buds. Strawberries were her absolute favorite. She could probably eat a pound of them without so much as slowing down, maybe even two if they were fresh. "That's awfully kind. Thank you."

"Ah, it's my pleasure."

"I'll be back in an hour," Hunter said, waiting for his father to amble back under the tent with Lucy on his heels before gesturing toward the milling crowd on Town Street. "So what do you say? You ready to get back in the swing of things, small-town girl?"

Although keeping her laughter in check was a total no-go, she still wasn't about to cave completely. "Don't push your luck, hotshot."

"Wouldn't dream of it," Hunter said, although the smile tugging at his lips said otherwise.

Emerson blocked out the sudden shock of heat between her hips, forcing her feet to do the one-after-the-other thing while she inhaled to a count of five. *Head up. Eyes forward. Focus.* "Your father's still as nice as ever."

"He still flirts with all the pretty girls," Hunter corrected. "Believe me, you'd change your tune if you had to harvest corn with the man in the middle of August."

"You say that as if you hate harvesting corn. Somehow, I'm not sure I believe that."

He paused to squint at her through the overbright sunlight, finally lifting one shoulder beneath the white cotton of his T-shirt. "Fair enough. I love my job, even when it's tough. But you're not really a stranger to that concept, are you?"

She lifted her hands in concession. No point denying the obvious. "Guilty as charged."

"Nah," Hunter said, his boots keeping time with the soft clack-clack-clack of her sandals on the pavement. "If you're meant for something, the last thing you should feel about it is guilt."

"You think I'm meant for my job?" The urge to let her jaw drop in shock was strong, but he didn't skip so much as a step or a breath.

"Yeah. Don't you?"

"Oh, I know I'm meant for my job." That wasn't the no-brainer part of the equation. "I guess I'm just surprised that *you* think so. We've only been working together for a week."

"True," Hunter said slowly. "But this isn't my first rodeo with this shoulder. You know all sorts of exercises and tricks that I've never done before, and I'm already feeling worlds better. I guess I'm just calling it like I see it."

"Buttering me up won't get you out of working hard for the next three weeks, you know." She arched a brow at him, all show, and he laughed in return.

"Duly noted. So how are things going at the physical therapy center now that you've had a week to settle in?"

Ugh. Emerson tried to brazen her way through a smile, but the sudden pinch in her chest made it a tough go. "A little slow," she admitted, and screw it. She couldn't violate anyone's privacy when there was no one's privacy to violate. "You're kind of my only client right now."

"Really?" Hunter's chocolate-brown lashes fanned upward to frame his obvious shock.

Unable to resist, she pulled a page from his playbook. "Small town," she said. "In truth, I figured building a client base might be tough going at first. I ended up spending most of this week getting the center organized."

Not that *that* would last much longer. The place was only so big, and even with the supplemental equipment she and the doc had ordered this week, nearly everything had found a place to belong. Well, except for Emerson, anyway.

Hunter's brows gathered beneath the brim of his faded blue baseball hat, his eyes skimming the crowd around them. "With all the people doing manual labor on the farms out this way, I'm surprised you don't have more folks coming in for treatment."

"Doc Sanders and I have talked about me working with some of her patients on preventive care," Emerson said. "People with past injuries or chronic conditions like arthritis and degenerative joint damage can be a lot less likely to experience complications if they engage in regular therapeutic exercise."

"So you want to try to nip their pain in the bud, huh? Seems smart."

"In theory, sure." As far as Emerson was concerned, the only thing better than helping a client heal was keeping their pain from happening in the first place. "Concept and reality don't always play nicely, though. Everyone in Millhaven trusts Doc to take care of them."

Realization flared in Hunter's eyes as he finished her sentence. "But they don't trust you yet."

She nodded, forcing a breath past the tightness in her chest. "Exactly. Most people haven't even stopped staring when I stop at the Corner Market for coffee creamer. As far as they're concerned, I'm on the outside looking in."

Cutting her teeth as a brand-new therapist five years ago had been difficult enough, and she'd been part of a busy practice in New York at the time. Flying solo to gain the faith of the people in the small town she'd left behind?

Definitely more of an uphill battle than she'd expected, even with Doc Sanders's help.

For a minute, Hunter didn't say anything, just walked comfortably next to her as they moved past people browsing at nearby tents and waiting in line for everything from funnel cake to kettle corn. "You keep saying you're an outsider, but I'm not sure I'm convinced."

"And you keep saying I fit right in," Emerson pointed out. "But I'm not convinced of that, either."

"Okay." Hunter dished up a lazy smile, and God, how could one tiny dimple still be her Kryptonite after twelve freaking years? "Just remember, you asked for it."

Not waiting for her to answer, he scooped up her hand to guide her through the crowd. The gesture was so simple, so natural and easy, that by the time the surprise had slipped through her system, Emerson had already wrapped her fingers around his. Heat rippled up from the asphalt, and even though the temperature had to be close to record breaking, the buzz of excitement in the air relaxed her. Kids darted from tent to tent, their lips stained red from snow cones and their faces lit with sheer bliss, and even the adults running after them looked laid back and happy.

Emerson recognized a handful of people in the crowd, her smile coming easier and easier as many of them smiled first. Sure, a few folks (okay . . . most of them) went wide-eyed as she and Hunter passed by, and yes, some eyebrows (specifically, Mollie Mae's and Kelsey Lambert's) winged upward at the sight of their interlaced fingers. But the sights and the sounds and the smells reminded Emerson of all the best parts of Millhaven, to the point that she couldn't deny the truth even as it surprised her.

She'd missed this town.

The unmistakably smoky scent of barbecue filled the air, sending a prickle of anticipation down Emerson's spine. "Oh, low blow," she said, although her laughter refused to let the sentiment stick. "You're going to entice me into feeling at home with Harley Martin's barbecue?"

Hunter looked at her as if she'd taken leave of every last one of her senses. "Uh, yeah. For starters. There's even a new addition to the menu that I think you're going to like."

He led the way from the main drag to the narrow stretch of grass in front of the firehouse, where a line of people at least ten deep stood waiting to be served. Harley's daughter Michelle, who had been a year ahead of Emerson in school but looked as if she'd barely aged a nano-second, stood next to her father. The two of them worked in tandem to serve up pulled-pork sandwiches along with heaping portions of coleslaw and cups of what appeared to be potato salad, and despite her aversion to all things mayonnaise, suddenly Emerson couldn't remember the last time she'd been so darn hungry.

"Hey, there, what can I . . . oh my word." Michelle's tongs hit the serving counter built into the food warmer in front of her with a metallic clack. "Emerson Montgomery! I heard you were back in town. And all the way from Las Vegas!"

A hard shot of heat swept over Emerson's cheeks at the attention, but she still managed a smile. "Hi, Michelle. It's nice to see you."

"Aren't you still as polite as ever." Michelle's genuine laugh marked the words as a compliment, and she turned toward her father, who was manning the gigantic steel drum smoker a few paces away. "Pop, look who's here."

Harley looked up, his silvery beard parting to accommodate his grin. "Well, I'll be! Emerson Montgomery. Last time we saw you, you weren't but fresh outta high school, girl. Glad to see you came to your senses and moved back home."

Nope. Not touching that one. "And I'm glad to see you're still making the best barbecue in the continental US," Emerson said, every breath of it the truth despite the dodge in topic. She'd traveled from coast to coast with the Lightning, sampling barbecue everywhere from the Carolinas to Kansas City to Texas. Harley's had always won the blue ribbon in her mind, hands down.

"Still smart." Harley pointed his tongs at her before tipping his graying head at Michelle. "Make sure this girl gets extra servings, now. Gotta remind her we do things right 'round here."

"I'm happy to," Michelle said. "You want the works, right, Emerson?"

Although she wasn't sold on the idea of potato salad, which had to be the new addition Hunter had mentioned, since Emerson was already happily familiar with both Harley's pulled pork and his secret-recipe honey-mustard coleslaw, she didn't want to be rude. "Sure. That sounds great."

Michelle paused to slide her glance to the side. "I take it you want the whole shebang, too, Hunter? With drinks for both of you?"

"Yes, ma'am." He caught Emerson's eye, his raised brow reading a seven out of ten on the I Told You So scale, but at least he didn't gloat out loud. Yet.

"You got it. Two loaded sandwiches with potato salad and sweet tea, coming right up."

Michelle's hands moved in a blur over the food service containers in front of her, filling two red-and-white cardboard meal baskets with a pair of coleslaw-topped pulled-pork sandwiches and hefty scoops of red-skinned potato salad. Emerson's stomach let out a growl just shy of embarrassing as her mouth watered and excitement swelled in her chest, and she barely made it all the way through the checkout line before her smile got the best of her.

"Okay, so that wasn't too awkward. Also, this sandwich smells as incredible as ever," she admitted, sipping her tea and following Hunter to a wooden picnic table shaded by a nearby red oak. Still, she wasn't about to go down easy. "But one person doesn't count."

The edges of his mouth kicked up in mischief, and it looked like Hunter wasn't about to tap out, either. "Oh, I beg to differ. I think the right person counts an awful lot."

Emerson stilled, a bolt of sweet, hot need arrowing all the way through her. But as quickly as it had arrived, Hunter's smirk disappeared without a trace, leaving her to wonder if she'd conjured the gesture from nothing more than thin summer air and the desire still pumping in her veins.

"Anyway," he continued, placing a small stack of napkins between them on the silvery, weatherworn table boards. "Michelle and Harley are two people, and they were both happy to see you back in town."

"You cheated. They're two of the nicest people in Millhaven." She picked up the plastic fork Michelle had tucked into her meal basket, pointing the tines at him for added emphasis. "And quite possibly the entire state of Virginia, besides. Of course they'd make me feel welcome."

Hunter laughed, toasting her with his sweet tea. "Nice try. Still counts."

"Hmph." Emerson speared a forkful of potato salad from the sturdy cardboard container nestled next to her sandwich, forgoing a smart answer in favor of taking a small, obligatory bite. But then anything she'd meant to say—hell, anything she'd meant to even think or do or be—fell prey to the flavors having an all-out riot in her mouth.

"Mmm, holy *God*, this is . . ." She let the rest of her sentence go, closing her lips along with her eyes to savor every nuance. Rather than loading his potato salad up with tons of heavy mayonnaise and standard-procedure celery, Harley had opted for taste over tradition. The tangy-sweet flavors of smoke and honey danced over Emerson's palate in a burst of surprise, smoothed out by the mellow taste of olive oil and the bite of fresh black pepper. Something slightly crunchy—wait, were those fresh corn kernels? Ah, genius!—hit her senses as she continued to chew, and two more forkfuls went into her mouth and down the hatch before she finally came up for air.

"This isn't potato salad. It's a metaphysical event." Emerson moved her fork through the mixture, taking a closer look at the small wedges of red-skinned potatoes, the pretty pop of bi-color sweet corn, and the fresh bright-green parsley in her cup. "When did Harley come up with this recipe?"

"Five, maybe six years ago." Hunter picked up his fork, digging into his own potato salad with a grin. "He started with fries, but then he decided he wanted the real down-home experience. Mayo doesn't keep too well in hot weather, so he got a little creative. And opportunistic, I guess, because that's his homemade honey barbecue sauce in there, along with a bunch of other ingredients he guards like a national secret."

Emerson took another bite, the smooth, smoky goodness exploding on her tongue. "As long as he doesn't stop making it, and I do mean ever, I won't complain."

"I thought you might like it."

"Because there's no mayonnaise?" Her instinct to keep her guard up took yet another direct hit in the face of Hunter's easy smile.

"Because it's off the chain." He paused, his dimple flashing even deeper, and yep, her guard was toast. "Okay, and also maybe because there's no mayonnaise." He lifted his sandwich, waiting until they'd each taken a few bites before continuing. "I know you're not a fan of breakfast, but seriously. Don't you eat?"

"Not really." The answer flew out before Emerson had any idea she'd let it, and her cheeks flushed at the admission. "I mean, obviously, I eat enough to survive. But I guess it's been awhile since I really enjoyed a meal."

"That's a shame," he said with nothing but kindness in his tone. She prayed he wouldn't follow up by asking her why not—there really was no subtle way to say that between the upheaval of the career she loved and the heavy cocktail of meds she was still getting used to, her appetite had pretty much gone on an extended sabbatical.

Thankfully, he didn't. They ate in comfortable quiet, punctuated by Emerson's inevitable food appreciation noises (she tried to restrain herself, she really did, but the honey-mustard coleslaw was as ridiculous as the juicy, butter-soft pulled pork it was piled upon, and she was only human, after all.) The thick umbrella of leaves overhead offered just enough cover to keep the heat at bay, and Emerson turned her face up toward the dappled sunlight as she popped the last bite of potato salad into her mouth.

"You might not want to wait so long next time before you indulge," Hunter said, folding his burnished forearms over the table with a crooked, sexy smile. "It looks pretty good on you."

A soft laugh bubbled up from her chest, and God, he'd always known exactly how to put her at ease. "Thanks."

"I'm just speaking the truth, the same way I was when I said you still belong here."

Warmth that had nothing to do with the weather flooded Emerson's body, and all at once, she realized how close he was. The way their knees barely brushed beneath the tabletop, the light sprinkling of stubble covering the angle of his jaw, the slight smudge of barbecue sauce at the corner of his wickedly full lips.

The way she wanted to open up to him without thought.

"Thank you. I mean, not just for lunch." Ugh, so maybe a *little* bit of thought would've been a decent idea. "But, you know. For letting me help you with your shoulder. And making me feel at home."

But rather than put her on the spot with some stilted or Hallmark-worthy response, Hunter just grinned. "Is this the part where I get to say I told you so? Because, truly, I've been waiting awful patiently, and—"

"Oh my God, fine!" Emerson caved, letting her laughter have its way with her. "You were right. I may have been gone for a while, but I'm not a total stranger."

"In that case, welcome home, Emerson."

Hunter shifted forward, one hand braced on the table in front of him, the other brushing over her forearm. Heart pounding, she leaned in to meet him out of pure instinct, knowing that he was going to kiss her and, as crazy and impulsive and dangerous as it was, she was going to let him.

But then the familiar sound of a throat clearing from over her shoulder sent ice water through Emerson's veins, chilling her in spite of the record-breaking temperature and freezing her in place.

No. No, no, no. It couldn't be . . . it wasn't . . .

"Well. Isn't this quite the surprise? Hello, sweetheart. It's been awhile."

Her pulse fluttered dangerously fast, and she struggled to swallow her spiraling panic in slow, hard gulps. She wasn't ready. She hadn't expected this.

She had to strong-arm her emotions. Right. Now.

Emerson straightened, and every last ounce of her free-flowing ease disappeared like a flame in a rainstorm as she turned around to face the man standing behind her.

"Hello, Dad."

CHAPTER TEN

Hunter couldn't tell what was more gut-punching, that he'd gone from all systems go to all systems *no* in five seconds flat, or that every trace of the wide-open happiness that had brightened Emerson's pretty face those same five seconds ago had done a complete vanishing act at the sight of her father.

Holy shit, had Hunter seriously been about to kiss her? In the middle of the Watermelon Festival? With her old man right there behind her?

Yes on all counts. Christ, he hadn't even thought twice.

Or maybe he hadn't thought at all.

"Dr. Montgomery." Hunter scrambled to stand up. The manners he'd been ingrained with pretty much since birth had him reflexively extending his hand, realizing only after Emerson's father pinned him with a chilly blue stare that his fingers were smudged with barbecue sauce.

Shit. *Shit.* Hunter fumbled for a napkin to take care of the offending mess, but the moment was gone.

"Hunter," Dr. Montgomery said, clipped and crisp. His shoulders were rigid beneath his light-blue button-down shirt, as if someone had aligned them with a level and a T-square, and not even a hint of moisture appeared on his forehead despite the unrepentant heat. "Are you having a nice time at the festival?"

The formality landed in Hunter's ears with the same oddness as when Emerson had asked him that very question this morning. Then again, her parents had always given staid and serious a run for its hard-earned cash. "Actually, I am. Emerson and I were just catching up."

"So I see."

Tension thick enough to clog the already-humid air threaded around all three of them for a breath, then two, until finally, Emerson broke it.

"I didn't know you were coming to the festival today. I thought you'd be at the hospital, working on the gala with Mom," she said, finding her feet to stand stiffly in front of her father. Funny, Hunter had never thought they looked very much alike, but hell if they weren't nailing the exact same stance right now.

Her father raised a brow ever so slightly toward his impeccably neat hairline. "With all your time away from Millhaven, you must not remember. The Watermelon Festival is an important town event. Of course I'm here. One of us needed to make an appearance."

"Right. Appearances," Emerson said, the front of her T-shirt lifting with a controlled inhale. "How could I have forgotten?"

"Speaking of which, we haven't seen you at the house. I'd been under the impression you were still busy getting settled, but it seems you've got time on your hands after all."

The pointed glance he split between the two of them tempted Hunter's pulse to pump faster in his veins, but Emerson's expression remained perfectly cool, so he kept his in check, too.

She nodded, just one quick lift and lowering of her chin. "A little."

"Perhaps you'd consider a visit then, if you're at loose ends," her father said. "There are a few things your mother and I think it's important to discuss with you now that you'll be in town permanently."

Emerson began to fidget, just like she always used to when she was nervous or upset, and okay, this had officially gotten weird. True, she'd never been really affectionate or close with her parents in the past—at least not in the way he and his brothers were tight with their father—but the tension running between Emerson and her old man right now was seriously off the charts.

"Mom mentioned that the other day," she said. "I think she and I covered things pretty well."

"I'm sure you do."

Before Hunter could decipher whether his tone was meant to be cordial or condescending, Emerson's father took a step back, gesturing to the shaded picnic area around them. "Well, I won't keep you any longer. I'm certain we'll see you at the house for that discussion soon, Emerson. Do enjoy your afternoon."

He turned on the heel of one polished loafer, the grass swallowing the sounds of his brisk footsteps as he walked a straight line away from them, and Hunter could barely wait until Dr. Montgomery was out of earshot before his confusion got the best of his mouth.

"Is something wrong between you and your father?"

"Not at all. Everything's perfectly fine," Emerson said, but her smile was tacked on and too tight for the words to be anything other than a lie. "Thanks for lunch, but you know, I really should get back to helping Daisy out. She asked me for some research on the uses of aromatherapy in alternative healing practices, and—"

"Emerson, stop," Hunter said, surprise pinging through his belly when she actually did. But that same vulnerability that had flashed in her eyes yesterday was back full throttle, and this time he'd be damned if he'd play it safe.

"Everything isn't fine, and as helpful as I'm sure Daisy will find that research, she can't do much with it in the middle of the Watermelon Festival. So do you want to do me a favor and tell me what the hell just happened here?"

◆ ◆ ◆

Emerson opened her mouth to dodge the topic by default. She shouldn't even be flirting with Hunter, let alone consider blabbing to him about the out-and-out panic attack she'd just dodged at being unexpectedly thrown back under the microscope of parental disdain. But even though she'd gone out of her way to hide the crushing pressure her parents had put her under in high school, he was no stranger to Emerson's stilted and stuffy family dynamic. Plus, standing there in the face of his surprisingly bold, no-bullshit question, she couldn't deny the truth.

Her answer wasn't no.

"Do you remember yesterday during your PT session, when you said it looked like you weren't the only one hauling around mental stress?"

Hunter's chin lifted first in surprise, then in a nod. "Yeah."

"Well, you weren't wrong," she said, and funny, the words didn't burn on exit like she'd expected them to. "It's just that you called me Dr. Montgomery, and whenever I hear the formal address, I think of my father."

A pause opened up between them, but only for a second. "You say that like the comparison is a bad thing."

"And you say that like there actually *is* a comparison."

Hunter's brows lowered into a *V* over his steely blue gaze. "Isn't there?"

"That's"—Emerson stopped, her stomach going low and tight with tangled energy as her eyes traveled over the moderately crowded picnic area—"where things get a little complicated."

"Okay," he said. But instead of elaborating or giving her the full-court press with a bunch of annoying questions, he simply rounded the picnic table to cup a hand beneath her elbow.

The move was so easy, so not what she expected, that her nerves smoothed right out in favor of her surprise. "Where are we going?"

"It's no secret that I love this town." Hunter squeezed her arm, just the slightest warm pressure of his callused fingers on her skin. "But right now, I think we could stand to see a quieter part of it. Come on."

Turning toward Town Street, Hunter guided her to the main drag. But instead of retracing their steps to go back in the heavily populated direction they'd come, he cut a path down one of the small side streets next to the firehouse, leading away from the crowd. The movement—coupled with the breathing room it created—knocked Emerson's unease down another notch, and she gave in to the steady thump-thump-thump of both her heartbeat and her footsteps.

"So where were we . . . ah right. Complicated," Hunter said, as if the topic were anything but. "I know you two haven't ever been particularly close, but you really don't think there's a comparison between you and your father?"

Although her veins pumped with enough irony to fill a cast-iron bathtub, she answered with a matter-of-fact, "Not quite."

"But you both went into medicine." He lifted a hand, staving off the argument brewing on her lips. "I know you've got different training, and you obviously have different specialties. Still, you both help people when they're hurt. How is there no correlation there?"

Her chest tightened and twisted, begging her to buckle down on the conversation. But then she caught Hunter's expression, so wide open and unassuming, and the words just slid out.

"Technically, we have the same title. But when your father is the chief of surgery at the biggest hospital in four counties and you decide more than halfway through college that you want to get a PhD in physical therapy instead of following in his MD-shaped footsteps? Let's just say not all 'doctors' are created equal. Especially as far as my parents are concerned."

"Okay," Hunter said, his boots shushing over the grass as they traded the sunny side street for one of the shaded footpaths winding around the perimeter of nearby Willow Park. "So you didn't become a surgeon. You're still clearly a damned good physical therapist. No way your mom and dad aren't proud of the work you do."

The look on his face was so genuine, Emerson felt a little guilty for the tart laugh that barged past her lips in response. God, she'd forgotten how much she'd kept hidden from him in high school, and how different their family dynamics really were. Hunter's father had always been equal-opportunity proud of him, from football to the farm. Her parents, on the other hand, had been a lot more choosy with their expectations, and they'd made them Waterford Crystal clear.

Nothing but the best, no exceptions.

Anything less was unacceptable.

And oh, how her chosen profession had fallen just as short as the rest of her.

"My parents started grooming me for medical school when I was still in *middle* school, remember? The possibility that I wouldn't want to become a surgeon like my father never even occurred to them. Hell, it didn't occur to me, either, until I was up to my waist in the pre-med program in college." As stifled as she'd felt by her parents' constant pressure to succeed, Emerson had never hated the idea of making a career in medicine. Putting a pecking order on which fields were more worthy of respect? Now *that*, she'd hated in spades.

"I was a little surprised to hear you'd decided against being a surgeon," Hunter admitted. "What made you change your mind?"

Emerson smiled. Finally, an easy question. "I took a sports medicine class in my junior year at Swarington. It was part of the premed track, geared mostly toward students with an interest in orthopedic surgery. I signed up because the class was mandatory, but after three weeks, I was hooked. I knew I didn't want to just do the surgery to repair a patient's injury. I wanted to be part of the process, from start to finish. I wanted to help people really heal."

"And your father was less than thrilled with your choice to go into physical therapy instead of becoming a surgeon like him." There was no question in Hunter's words, which worked out great since he was dead freaking accurate.

"That's one way of putting it," Emerson said. Her father had been a lot of things when she'd told him she wanted to switch her major from premed to sports medicine. Proud hadn't even made the top one hundred.

Furious? Frustrated? Highly disappointed? Now those were headliners.

Taking a handful more steps down the semi-secluded footpath, Hunter gestured to a park bench, sliding in next to her as she nodded and sat down. "I guess it was pretty obvious they wanted you to go to medical school. But being disappointed with your choice not to become a surgeon is still a far cry from being disappointed with *you*."

Emerson's heart kicked against her breastbone, which was stupid, really. She'd had nearly a decade to face facts, and a lifetime's worth of work-faster-be-smarter-do-better to back them up.

Chasing good enough was a waste of time.

"Not to my parents, it's not. My father may have been raised in a small town and had to work his way through community college in Camden Valley, but he always wanted the best, the biggest, and the brightest, no matter what."

"So how come he came back to Millhaven after medical school?" Hunter asked, his expression changing as he backtracked. "Don't get me wrong—I obviously love living here. But we're hardly big or bright. Your mom is from Richmond. Why not stay there, or head to a big city like Washington, DC? Hell, if he wanted the biggest and brightest, as a surgeon he could've gone anywhere."

The question was legitimate, and one that had crossed Emerson's mind no fewer than a hundred times before she'd left Millhaven herself. After all, her father had met her mother while doing his residency in Richmond, and she'd been an administrative assistant at the hospital there.

"I asked him that once, right before I went to college," Emerson said. "He told me that in big cities, great surgeons are a dime for a baker's dozen. Being part of a crowd—even a distinguished one—wasn't good enough for him. He wanted to be the best, so that's exactly what he did. He came back here and became chief of surgery at Camden Valley hospital faster than anyone before him."

She knew, because her father had made it plain as her name during that conversation that his record was her yardstick, and he fully expected her to come home after medical school and break it.

And that was the moment she'd realized that if she didn't leave Millhaven forever, she'd never escape the pressure of her parents' expectations.

Hunter's gaze flicked to the path in front of them, moving over the bright-green fields beyond the scattering of trees holding their bench in the shade. "Definitely sounds ambitious."

"I don't think ambition is a bad thing when it comes to doing what you love," Emerson said, and it was the truth. After all, there had been no shortage of high expectations in her PhD program, and she'd happily worked hard in order to meet every single one, no panic attacks in sight. "But for as long as I can remember, my parents have expected me to live up to *their* standards, their way, no matter what. Valedictorian, homecoming queen, early admission to Swarington." The list was as long as her leg, and those were barely the highlights.

"Wait . . ." A muscle tightened in Hunter's jaw, pulling ever so slightly beneath the sprinkling of stubble on his skin. "Didn't you want to do all those things in high school?"

"Whether or not I wanted them didn't matter. It was the best or nothing. My parents made that perfectly clear."

"Jesus, Emerson." Hunter turned toward her, his knee sliding against hers in a warm brush of denim on denim. "How come you never said anything? I mean, I always knew they wanted big things for you, but I had no idea the pressure was so bad. That must have been a hell of a load to carry."

The thread of remorse whisking through his eyes sent a pang right to the center of her chest. Of course Hunter would've wanted to fix the mess between her and her parents. His glass-half-full mentality had been one of the things she'd loved about him the most.

Too bad it didn't apply when the glass was broken to start with.

"For a long time, I thought if I worked hard enough, eventually my parents would be happy. Piano recitals, science fair competitions—God, I even took cotillion classes without complaining." She laughed, because it was too late to cry over all her spent effort. "But there was always something else to win or earn or do, and none of it was ever good enough. And if I wasn't good enough for my own parents, I thought . . ."

Emerson stopped, biting her lip hard enough to sting. But she'd already loosened the story, and anyway, she couldn't change the past. What would it hurt to tell Hunter the truth?

"I started having panic attacks. Really bad ones, where my heart raced so fast and it was so hard to breathe, I nearly passed out."

"Are you serious?" Hunter asked, his voice gravely matching the word in question. "The pressure was making you sick, literally, and you never said anything?"

"I know it doesn't make much sense now," she said. "But I kept the pressure to myself for so long that after a while, it felt like a secret. I thought if I told you the truth about not being able to meet my parents' expectations, then maybe you'd think I wasn't good enough for you, either. I was afraid to let you see all of me. That you might think I was weak because I couldn't handle the pressure."

For a minute, Hunter sat perfectly still. "Are you kidding? I was crazy about you."

Her pulse pitched, knocking the words right out of her mouth. "I know." God, that had been half the reason she'd gotten into her car and driven away in the first place. "But between football and working on the farm, you were always so easygoing and confident and strong. I was scared to admit that I wasn't, too, especially since you thought I was."

"Still. If the pressure was bad enough to trigger panic attacks, you should have told me."

He spoke without judgment, although the flash of gray in his stare betrayed the emotion beneath his calm, and Emerson didn't think, just answered.

"Maybe. But it only would've made things more difficult in the end when I had to—"

Hunter's head snapped up. "When you had to what?"

Emerson's heart slammed in her chest, silencing her all too late, and dammit, she had defenses for a *reason*. But impulsive or not, she'd let the past out.

And dangerous or not, Hunter deserved to know all of it.

"When I had to leave Millhaven. I didn't go to New York because I wanted to, Hunter. I went because I didn't have a choice. But what I really wanted was you."

CHAPTER ELEVEN

Hunter tried as hard as he possibly could to process Emerson's words. Failed. Tried again.

Nope. No fucking way that was happening.

"I'm sorry," he said, and okay, at least that was accurate. "I don't understand."

"I never wanted to leave Millhaven. I love it here. I loved . . . you." Her smile was completely bittersweet, the corners of her pretty, peach-colored mouth turning up just enough to keep his pulse jacked sky high.

"But that's not what you said," Hunter managed, hating the sting in his tone even though he felt every inch of it. Thousands of nights had come and gone since the one when he'd asked her to stay in Millhaven and marry him, but he'd never lose her answer from his memory.

I can't stay. I have to go to New York, and I'm not coming back. I'm sorry, but this is for the best . . .

"I know what I said." Emerson dropped her chin, her hair tumbling over her gaze, and the sweet, heady scent of honeysuckle took a potshot at his chest. "The night before you asked me to marry you, I told my father I wanted to go to community college in Camden Valley instead of going to Swarington."

Hunter knew he should feel the warm, wooden bench slats beneath him, or hear the leaves over his head rustling in the soft summer breeze. But his brain spun too hard and his heart spun too fast for him to process anything other than the bombshell Emerson had just dropped square in the lap of his well-worn Wranglers. "You . . . what?"

"I wanted to stay," Emerson said, her voice soft but sure. "I'd been thinking about it for weeks, trying to come up with a way to make my parents understand. I didn't want to skip college," she clarified. "But I also didn't want to go to New York. God, I never even chose Swarington in the first place. The university had been hand-picked for me, just like everything else."

Dozens of questions dusted up in Hunter's mind, each of them trying to make the trip past his shock and out of his mouth. Any idiot on two legs could see Emerson's need to get the story out, though—Christ, the look on her face alone was enough to crush him—so as much as it took effort, he bit his tongue and let her keep talking.

"I planned out my argument to the letter," she said. "Which classes I'd take in Camden Valley, how I could supplement the curriculum by earning extra credits from the state university online, places that might be willing to let me do internships in the summer. I'd even gone to the head of admissions at the community college and gotten a letter of acceptance."

Even in the face of his uncut shock, Hunter had to huff out a tiny laugh. All that smart, savvy strategy sounded like her. "And then what happened?"

"The only thing left to do was tell my parents I wasn't going to New York." Emerson's fingers knotted in her lap, knuckles pale white against the navy-blue denim hugging her hips. "I thought if I told them together, they'd present a united front and I'd never have a chance at making them understand my choice to stay. So I waited until my mother had a board meeting at the hospital."

Whoa. "You told your father first?"

"Part of it was circumstance," she said over a nod. "He was home and she wasn't. But then . . ."

She stopped, her mouth pressing into a thin, flat line, and adrenaline peppered Hunter's gut full of holes.

"Em?" The shortened version of her name, the one only he had used throughout high school, rolled from his mouth unbidden. She blinked at the single syllable, her gaze growing stronger as she returned to the story.

"Part of me was glad it was him. My father grew up here. He knew what it was like to love Millhaven, to belong in the town. Plus, he'd gone to the community college in Camden Valley himself. I knew he'd be harder to convince, but I thought maybe, just maybe, he'd understand."

Hunter thought of the man they'd run into, with his set-in-granite jawline and his shrewd, icy stare, and the adrenaline in his gut slid into dread. "So you told him you didn't want to go to New York."

"I did." A joyless smile crossed her lips, lasting for only a second before she said, "I knew he'd be mad, and that we'd probably argue. I did. But my father didn't argue with me. What he did was worse."

"Worse how?" A ripple of something dark and nameless sent Hunter's hands into fists at his sides, but Emerson was quick to defuse it.

"He's not the type to yell or lose his cool. In fact, as weird as it sounds, I almost wish he had."

Hunter took a deep breath and tried to force his brain around what she'd said, coming up woefully short. "I don't follow. Why would you want your father to blow his stack?"

Her pause stretched into silence. Just when Hunter was about to press his luck, patience be damned, she said, "Because if he'd yelled and carried on, then maybe later I'd have been able to blame what he said on the heat of the moment and tell myself he didn't really mean it. But he did."

A glint of raw emotion whisked through her eyes, then Hunter's chest, but Emerson pushed forward, as if she wanted nothing more than to keep talking before she lost her nerve.

"He told me he'd worked too hard to get me into Swarington, and all that time and money wouldn't go to waste just because I was weak and I thought I'd be a little homesick. Turns out, my father not only went to medical school with a member of the school's board of trustees, but he also made a sizable donation three days before my early-acceptance letter arrived."

"Holy shit," Hunter breathed. He'd always found Emerson's father kind of stiff and standoffish, but stooping to bribery? That was a whole new flavor of belly-in-the-dirt.

"My father said I was just being foolish and emotional, that I had no idea what I really wanted. But he was perfectly clear," Emerson said. "What *he* wanted was more important, anyway, and staying here—God, going anywhere other than New York and becoming a doctor and living my life exactly how he saw fit just wasn't good enough. And that was when I knew. Leaving Millhaven for good was the only way I would ever escape the pressure of my parents ruling the rest of my life, and going to Swarington was the only chance I'd ever have to get out."

Her voice, which had stayed characteristically steady until now, wavered as she added, "And breaking your heart was the only way I could guarantee you'd be happy."

"I wasn't happy," Hunter argued, low and quick. Fuck, he'd been so miserable and miserable to be around after Emerson had left Millhaven, even his brothers had cut a wide berth around him for weeks. "Jesus, Em. The stress must have been . . . dammit, I wish you'd told me."

"Don't you see? I couldn't have."

A sudden spurt of anger filled his veins. They'd been in love with each other—he'd freaking *proposed*. He got that she'd felt insecure in the face of the pressure, and her hesitation to confide in him made sense now that he understood how crushing that pressure had been. But how could she not have trusted him with something so huge? "I could have helped," he insisted.

Emerson steeled her spine, her shoulder blades hitting the back of the bench with a soft thump. Of course, he should've known better than to think she'd let go of her moxie entirely, even in a vulnerable moment. "There is no fixing my parents' opinion of me, Hunter, especially since I chose physical therapy over med school. You just saw that for yourself. Anyway, what would you have done if you'd known that leaving was my only option?"

"We could've figured something out. Hell, Emerson, even if you couldn't have stayed, I could have . . ."

As if all the dots had connected like stars in a constellation, the fragmented pieces of the past that he'd once thought had nothing to do with each other—hell, with anything—fell into sharp, startling focus.

"You left the way you did so I wouldn't go with you."

The barely-there smile ghosting over her mouth answered him before she spoke a word. "You belong here. This town, the farm, your family. I wanted to be with you, Hunter. But I couldn't stay. I knew that if I told you why, you'd want to come with me. Just like I knew that if you'd left, you'd have been miserable."

Hunter's heart twisted, his rib cage going tight. "I already told you, I was pretty miserable here."

Remorse covered Emerson's face in a deep flush. "I'm sorry. Hurting you was the hardest thing I've ever done. But I knew that eventually, you'd get over the heartbreak of our relationship ending. If you'd lost your livelihood by leaving Cross Creek behind, I didn't think you'd ever recover, and I just couldn't do that to you. So that's why I left."

He sat for a minute, inhaling deep breaths of slow summer sunshine that felt completely at odds with the emotions pumping through his chest and veins and mind. Everything about his past tilted and tumbled into a new light, and finally, he turned toward Emerson with a nod.

"I suppose that makes sense," Hunter said, brushing his fingers over her forearm to keep hold of the conversation for a minute longer. "I'm not saying it's not going to take me awhile to really let the truth sink in, or that I like it. I still wish you'd told me what was going on between you and your parents."

He paused, unable to really even wrap his head around what her father had said and done. The man was her father, for Chrissake. Her *family*. "But just because I don't like what happened doesn't mean I don't understand why you left."

"I never wanted to hurt you," she whispered. "I didn't even want to go."

"I believe you," he said, because there was no point in denying that her leaving had hurt. But there was also no purpose in dragging out a past that was behind them. "We were eighteen years old. Young and impulsive. I mean, I even proposed. Not that I didn't mean it, but . . . well, it was twelve years ago, and we can't change what happened now."

Emerson nodded tentatively. "That's true. The only thing we can do now is move forward."

"Forward sounds good to me."

Hunter's heart kicked, each beat thumping against his ears. But they'd lost an awful lot of time to things not said. Bold or not, he'd be damned if he'd hold back now. "Do you remember the other day? When you asked if I've ever wondered what if?"

Emerson's eyes darkened in the muted sunlight, but she didn't lift her stare from his. "Yes."

"I might not have ever thought about leaving Millhaven, but I've definitely wondered what if. A lot."

"You have?"

"Mmhmm." Hunter knew the words were brash, but suddenly, he didn't care. While his brain might be throwing caution flags up, down, and sideways, the deeper, more primal part of him remembered everything about her—how her chest fit perfectly against his, the way she managed to look so wicked and still so sweet when she came undone—and he added the slightest slow pressure to his grasp on her forearm, stroking her skin with his thumb. "I'm even wondering what if right now. Like what if"—he paused, but just long enough to fully face her on the bench, letting his opposite hand trail up the outside of her arm—"you let me get closer to you."

She leaned in, her pulse darting under the pad of his thumb. "Like this?"

Her denim-covered thigh slid against his as she eliminated even more of the space between their bodies, and fuuuuuck, she was *really* good at the what if game.

"Yeah. Like that." Hunter's fingers traveled higher, leaving the semi-safety of her shoulder for the bare skin where her collarbone met her neck. "So what if I touched you right"—he found the sweet, sensitive spot right below her earlobe that had always made her sigh—"here? Would you like it?"

"Yes." Emerson's sigh had grown exponentially sexier over time, and the soft, lusty sound shot straight to his cock, daring him to get even bolder.

"How about"—his forefinger slid over the slope of her cheekbone, desire spiking through his blood when he reached the tiny indent over her top lip and stroked—"here?"

"Hunter," she whispered, her breath hot on his hand, and just like that, he was done waiting. He'd wanted his mouth on hers for twelve goddamn years. He might be light-years away from playing it safe right now, but he didn't even want to wait another twelve seconds.

He just wanted her.

Closing nearly all the distance between them, Hunter lowered his fingers, replacing them with his lips just a scant inch from hers. "And what if you let me kiss you?"

"That's not going to happen."

Fingers of dread laddered up his spine, freezing him to a full stop. "It's not?" Oh shit, had he somehow misread her?

But rather than pulling away, Emerson leaned in farther, her mouth curving into a smile that could halt the earth on its axis. "No. Because I'm going to kiss you first."

She slanted her mouth up to his, turning the sliver of space that had separated them to dust. The enticing scent of honeysuckle filled Hunter's senses as he breathed her in past his surprise, and every last detail hit him with vivid clarity.

The softness of her lips, still shaped by her smile. The pressure of her fingers, tightening over his T-shirt where the cotton covered the waistband of his jeans. The husky sound in the back of her throat that said they were about to make up for lost time.

Oh *hell* yes.

Hunter pressed forward to deepen the kiss. With a single glide of his tongue, he tested the seam at the juncture of Emerson's lips, fighting back a groan when she opened for him and darted her tongue forward. He pushed into the heat of her mouth, searching and sweeping and taking, and she met every one of his movements with equal intensity.

"Jesus, Em," Hunter said, breaking from her lips to slide a kiss to the side of her jaw. How on earth could she taste so sinful and so sweet all at the same time? "You feel so damn good."

He hooked his hand beneath her chin to hold her close, returning his attention to her mouth. She kissed him back, slipping her tongue over his again and again, and, okay, yeah, his composure was pretty much a foregone conclusion.

"You feel good, too," Emerson murmured, edging her teeth along the sensitive skin of his lower lip just enough to make him want to scream. Hunter was vaguely aware that they were outside, and although the shaded, tree-lined footpath around Willow Park wasn't quite the same as the wide-open public of Town Street, they were still far from behind closed doors.

But right now, he was far from caring. Curling his fingertips into the soft angle where Emerson's jaw met her neck, he thrust again with his tongue, sucking and tasting and relearning every nuance of her mouth. He dove in deep, kissing her as if he'd die if he didn't, pulling her even closer against him with no regard for time or place, fully intent on leaving his mouth on hers until they both forgot their names . . .

And then a pair of voices, too close to be avoided, ricocheted him right back to reality.

Hunter and Emerson flew to opposite sides of the bench just as a young couple came chattering around the bend in the path, both of them seeming surprised at the sight of anyone nearby.

"Oh! This is kind of a lucky break," said the guy, his shock fading into a friendly smile in two blinks. "We're looking for Willow Park. We overheard some local folks talking about it and figured we'd have a picnic." He held up a bag printed with Harley's name and logo on the side, and Hunter nodded farther down the path, thanking God that his hard-on had done a cease and desist at the sound of company.

Company that had been the only thing keeping him from impulsively acting on said hard-on until he and Emerson were both good and sweaty and spent right here on a park bench, and holy shit, was he insane?

Hunter cleared his throat, forcing his voice to its most neutral setting. "You're not too far off. Just keep following the path here for another couple hundred yards. You'll end up at the east end of the park."

"Thanks," said the girl holding the guy's hand, and man, they couldn't be more than eighteen. She looked up at her boyfriend, her smile spanning ear to ear as they moved down the footpath. By the time they'd moved out of earshot, Hunter's calm had found its way back into place.

And apparently, so had Emerson's guard.

"I'm sorry," she said, smoothing a hand over the front of her T-shirt and straightening the already-straight hem. "I shouldn't have gotten so carried away."

"Why not?" *Way to blurt it out there, Casanova.* Hunter shook his head at his utter lack of finesse and tried again. "I mean, yeah, we got pretty caught up together, and a park bench in the middle of the day probably isn't the best place for that. But we are consenting adults. Why shouldn't we get a little carried away?"

Emerson blinked, her shoulders losing a fraction of the tension holding them tight. "Because I'm your physical therapist, for one."

Legit under the right circumstances, he supposed. Still . . . "That's temporary. Plus, we've known each other way longer than the week you've been my physical therapist, and we're not at the therapy center right now."

"No," she said slowly. "But we will be on Monday."

"And everything will be business as usual when we are. I know you're not going to treat me differently at the PT center just because we kissed." Hunter paused, nudging her gently with an elbow. "Are you?"

"Of course not." Emerson's chin hiked up, but the tiny smile winding over her mouth said she heard his teasing tone of voice loud and clear.

Hunter took the ball and ran like hell. "I mean, it *was* a really good kiss," he said, fixing her with half a grin and all the charm he could work up. "Maybe you should go just a little easier on me with those resistance tube exercises."

"If I go easy on you, even a little, you won't heal as fast or as well," she pointed out, although her expression didn't match the sternness of the words. After a second, she added, "It was a really good kiss, wasn't it?"

"One of my best, if I do say so myself."

"Oh my God, you're terrible!" Emerson said over a peal of laughter, and Hunter arched a brow, unable to resist.

"Not according to you. Okay, okay!" He held up his hands in concession as she flashed him an indignant stare. Man, she was still feisty when she wanted to be. "But come on, Em. We kissed. There's no sense turning it into a headline."

She nodded, sending a wistful gaze to the thick canopy of leaves over their heads. "No one else has ever called me that, you know."

His chest panged with something that felt oddly proprietary. "Does it bother you?"

"No. I just . . . you need to know I'm not looking for anything serious. I really am here in Millhaven to focus on work."

Hunter opened his mouth, fully intent on asking her exactly why she'd come home when she had so much bad family history here. But the truth of it was, however understandable her motivations for leaving were now, Emerson *had* still hurt him in the past.

Trusting her completely was going to take time, and as sexy as their kiss had been, he didn't want anything serious, either. Jumping into anything with her—including a conversation about why she'd suddenly come back to Millhaven—would only rock the boat.

"Tell you what," Hunter said, extending a hand in her direction. "How about we put everything else behind us and just go one day at a time?"

She smiled, wrapping her fingers around his for a handshake that meant business. "Head up, eyes forward sounds perfect to me."

CHAPTER TWELVE

Emerson's body might have been perched in the rickety old chair at the front desk of the physical therapy center, but her mind was no less than a billion miles away. Or maybe it was just twelve miles, up Town Street and past Pete Hitchcock's poultry farm, on a sprawling lot of land she'd be able to find in the dark, even after all this time.

Less than two days had passed since her unexpected, oh-so-steamy encounter with Hunter Cross, but one thing was for damn sure. Despite her very best efforts—and maybe-probably-definitely a pair of very, *very* cold showers—ever since he'd walked her back to Daisy's tent at the Watermelon Festival on Saturday, Emerson had been completely unable to get Hunter out of her brain.

Have you ever wondered what if . . .

She sat up straight, the desk chair giving up a hearty squeal of protest at her sudden shift. She couldn't deny that their kiss had felt mind-scramblingly good, better even than all the other times Hunter had kissed her in the past. But she'd come back to Millhaven to work hard and move forward with her life. She had so many other things to worry about, namely the wide-open spaces in her appointment book and the fact that, sooner or later, she was going to have to face her parents in a showdown she didn't want or need.

She couldn't afford a distraction. Not even one that came in a sexy, Wrangler-wearing, sweet-talking, slow-kissing package.

Oh God, this morning's shower hadn't been cold enough.

"Excuse me. Emerson?" came a soft voice from the doorway leading back to Doc Sanders's waiting room. "I apologize for not having an appointment, but Nurse Kelley said I should come on back."

The heat in Emerson's veins turned to surprise in an instant, her brain whirling in an attempt to play catch-up with the reality around her. "Mrs. Ellersby?" The sweet old woman had lived in Millhaven since the day she'd been born there nearly seven decades ago. "Sure, of course. What can I do for you?"

"Well, it might be silly," she said, her bespectacled gaze growing wary. "I know you're used to working with all those famous football players. They must get hurt real serious all the time."

"Sometimes." Emerson nodded, proceeding with care. "But if you're having discomfort, that's not silly at all. Do you want to come in and tell me about it? I might be able to help."

Mrs. Ellersby crossed the threshold into the PT center, taking the seat Emerson offered beside her at the reception desk. "My hands have been giving me fits lately," the older woman said. "I've had arthritis for about ten years now, and sometimes I get the old aches and pains when snow's coming or I knit too much. But for the last few weeks, these babies have just been hurting something fierce."

She flexed her fingers, wincing slightly at the movement, and Emerson's heart gave up a tug at the same time her brain began to process.

"I'm sorry to hear that. Joint pain can be pretty debilitating." She sure had been cozying up with *that* reality lately. "Do you see a rheumatologist for your arthritis?"

The cluck of Mrs. Ellersby's tongue answered the question before she even spoke. "Oh, sugar. Seems a bit silly to haul my bones all the way to Camden Valley just to have the doctor there poke me and prod me and tell me I'm old as dirt. I used to go in the beginning, but Doc Sanders keeps me in good with my medicine now, and usually, the pain's not so bad."

"But lately that's changed," Emerson said, waiting until the woman nodded before adding, "Can you think of anything out of the ordinary that might have caused the increase in pain? Any kind of injury at all?"

"Not that I can think of, although I did crochet a whole bucketload of doilies to sell at the Watermelon Festival."

No wonder the poor woman's joints were hurting. "That would probably do it. Have you talked to Doc Sanders yet to see what she thinks?"

Mrs. Ellersby's head shake sent a ripple of surprise up Emerson's spine. "No. Michelle Martin told me you were doing those hand massages over at Daisy Halstead's tent at the Watermelon Festival, and then Hunter Cross was just bragging up a storm yesterday morning at Clementine's Diner, sayin' how much you've helped him with his shoulder. So I figured I'd come here first to ask you."

"Hunter told you about his physical therapy?" Shock knocked the question right out of her mouth. Maybe Emerson had misunderstood the woman. No way had she meant—

"Why, yes he did, hand to God," Mrs. Ellersby said. "I went to Clementine's after church for some coffee and a slice of pie, and he was sitting in the next booth over, having breakfast with his brother Owen and Sheriff Atlee. I made mention of my pain to Cate McAllister—poor, sweet girl, she's waiting tables at the diner now—and wouldn't you know, Hunter overheard us. He was so sweet to tell me all about you two working together. Talked you right up, he did."

Emerson's face flushed all the way to her temples. "That was very nice of him." While she could think of a dozen different words to substitute for "nice," all of them would have to wait for now. "Here's what I'd like to do, Mrs. Ellersby. I think you should make an appointment with Doc Sanders just to make sure she thinks this is a flare-up of your arthritis and not something different causing your pain. If she does, I can put you on my schedule for some maintenance therapy as soon as you're ready, okay?"

"You make it sound so easy." The older woman smiled up at her, clearly relieved, and Emerson couldn't help but smile back.

"I don't know about easy. Maintenance therapy takes a lot of patience. But let's see if we can't get you feeling better."

Finding her feet, she ushered Mrs. Ellersby down the hall to Doc Sanders's waiting room to give Nurse Kelley the lowdown, and on a stroke of pure luck, the doctor had an opening later that morning.

"If Doc Sanders thinks you'll benefit from a few sessions on my side of the fence, feel free to have her bring you right on over here after your appointment. We can get started with your therapy today, if you'd like," Emerson said.

"Oh dear! Thank you so much. That's right nice of you to be so quick about it."

Emerson smiled, placing a gentle squeeze over the older woman's shoulder. "That's all part of my job, Mrs. Ellersby. The quicker we take care of that pain, the better, right?"

Emerson walked Mrs. Ellersby to the front door, retracing her steps back to the physical therapy office. She checked the clock on the wall, realizing with a start that she had about only sixty seconds before Hunter was due to arrive for their session. Her faithful Keurig Mini didn't need longer than that to crank out a ten-ounce cup of heaven, though, and her stomach did an up-and-at-'em beneath her light-gray swing pants at the thought.

"Hello, coffee. Come to Momma."

Her knees made their displeasure known as she bent down to grab a coffee pod from the storage cabinet adjacent to her desk, sending streaks of pain up to her hips and down both legs. Ugh, with the exception of some gentle stretches and a handful of trips to her kitchen for what little food she'd found appetizing, she'd spent most of yesterday couch bound, trying to make a preemptive strike on any exhaustion the workweek might bring. Starting out in pain was far from a good sign.

Suck it up, girl. Head up, eyes forward.

The masculine rumble of a throat being cleared hooked Emerson on a straight path back to the present, and she swung around, her heart hopscotching all the way up her rib cage. "Oh jeez! I didn't see you there."

Of course, Hunter looked just as calm, cool, and gorgeous as ever, his dark-blue T-shirt hugging every hard plane and angle on his upper body. "Sorry. Didn't mean to interrupt your breakfast."

He jutted his chin at the coffeemaker, which had just made its final gurgle and beeped out the doneness of this morning's nth cup of earthy, caffeinated goodness.

"You're not interrupting. You have an appointment," she reminded him. Scooping up her mug, she snuck a quick sip, letting the coffee soothe her jangling pulse.

"Right." He tipped his head at her with a slow smile that said he remembered their kiss just as much as she did, and yeah, so much for her pulse slowing down. "Before we get to business, I should probably give you these. After all, I owe you some tomatoes."

Emerson noticed, just a beat too late, the half-bushel basket slung over Hunter's tanned forearm. Satiny, fat tomatoes peeked from the brim, surrounded by an oversized bunch of brightly ruffled butter lettuce, and her mouth went from zero to watering in about three seconds flat.

"You don't owe me anything," she said, and oh my God, was that a pint of strawberries next to the lettuce?

"Okay." He handed over the basket in spite of her protest, as easy as a Sunday sunrise. "Then how about this. I really wanted to give you another good meal. So I'm afraid you're stuck with the whole lot of those tomatoes, and a few other extras, besides. Just think of it as helping Cross Creek out with a little quality control."

Emerson blew out a breath, but she knew when she'd been beat. Plus—*hello*—strawberries.

"Thank you." She smiled and tucked the basket safely onto her desk, waving Hunter back to the center of the therapy room and forcing her lady bits back to business as usual. No matter how sexy their kisses had been, she and Hunter needed to stay on the level here at the therapy center.

Speaking of the therapy center . . . "Between growing these beautiful tomatoes and putting in a good word for me around town, you've been pretty busy since I last saw you," she said.

Hunter's cross-trainers squeaked to a stop on the linoleum, his dimple making an appearance to accent his sheepish grin. "I take it Mrs. Ellersby dropped by."

"Right before you got here," Emerson confirmed, gesturing to the arm bike. She waited until Hunter sat down and started to pedal his way through his warm-up before she added, "You told her about your physical therapy on purpose in order to boost my business, didn't you?"

"I overheard her telling Cate McAllister that her hands were bothering her. Seemed like it might fall under your umbrella of expertise, so I may have mentioned our sessions."

The glint in his eyes marked the words for the dial-down they were, and she raised a brow in answer.

"I believe the word Mrs. Ellersby used was 'bragged.'"

Although Hunter laughed, he didn't give in. "It's not my fault you're working wonders on my shoulder. You have no one to blame but yourself for being good at your job, you know."

"You're the one doing the work," Emerson pointed out, and she laughed back without realizing she would. "I suppose that makes us both to blame."

Hunter pedaled through a few revolutions on the arm bike, his shoulders loosening a fraction more with each move. "Fair enough. But for the record, I didn't tell her anything that wasn't one hundred percent true. I think you're a great physical therapist, Emerson."

Her heart squeezed in undisguised goodness, and she smiled in thanks. "And I think you're still great at trying to fix things."

"Not everything," he said, and just like that, both his expression and his shoulders filled with tension.

Whoa. "Is something wrong at the farm?"

"Not wrong, I guess, just . . . well, yeah. Maybe wrong is a good word for it."

The temptation to push pulsed through Emerson's brain. Hunter wouldn't heal with his muscles wound tighter than a Salvation Army drum, and he looked downright miserable at the mention of trouble at Cross Creek. But he'd given her breathing room the other day when she'd needed to talk. The least she could do now was return the favor.

"I don't mind listening, if you want an ear to bend." Despite the concern burning a hole in her belly and the questions burning a hole in her mind, Emerson simply took a step back. The arm bike clacked out a soft rhythm as Hunter pedaled, and after a minute, he looked up to meet her gaze.

"Do you remember the other day, when I told you my brothers are fixin' to throw down?" he asked, waiting out her nod before continuing. "Let's just say they get one step closer every day."

"I take it you didn't have a smooth morning at the farm," Emerson said. She might not have any siblings to use as a barometer for this kind of thing, but constant friction between brothers didn't seem normal. Especially for a family like the Crosses, who had always been so tight-knit in the past.

"This morning, the morning of the Watermelon Festival, every morning last week. Take your pick. They've all been rough." Hunter punctuated the words with a heavy exhale. "No matter what I do, I can't seem to get Owen and Eli to talk to each other without a bunch of shit slinging. Even the small stuff is a huge deal lately. It's like living with a pair of powder kegs."

Emerson turned the facts over in her mind, an idea swirling and taking root. "Are they only arguing about work? Or is there something deeper there?" Now *that* was the sort of family tension in which she was sadly well versed.

"At first, I thought it was just their personalities clashing over how to get things done, and they'd learn to work around it," Hunter said, his muscles flexing and releasing as he continued his warm-up. "But now, I'm not so sure. They've been fighting like this for months, and they're both so pissed off at each other all the time. The tension is wearing everyone thin."

That did sound pretty tedious. "What does your father have to say about the two of them arguing?" she asked.

"He's not really the sort to put his foot down and tell them to get over it. My mother was always the disciplinarian, wrangling us boys and getting us to act right." A flicker of emotion whisked through Hunter's stare, jabbing Emerson right in the breastbone, but the calmness didn't waver from his voice. "I don't know what started this mess. But whatever's going on between Owen and Eli feels a whole lot bigger than something they can fix by throwing a couple of punches and then dusting themselves off to shake hands."

Emerson bit back the urge to question the whole trial-by-testosterone method of problem-solving. She was more for the I-call-bullshit approach, herself. "So why don't you, then?"

"What, call them out on things? I'm not really the sort, either," Hunter said truthfully. "Plus, they've both got their heels dug in so hard, I don't think it would do any good. Owen is convinced that Eli doesn't take working at Cross Creek seriously, and I've gotta say, Eli earns the bad rap a lot of the time by blowing things off. But then Owen comes down on him like a pallet of bricks even when Eli does work hard, and no one wins."

"So they've got to figure out how to get their shit together on their own."

"Either that or one of them is liable to murder the other."

A small laugh tempted Emerson's lips, until she caught Hunter's expression. Eyes steely beneath the fringe of his lashes. Mouth pressed into a grim line. Muscles taut beneath his T-shirt.

Her pulse tripped in surprise. "You think they won't be able to fix this?"

Hunter's pause extended into silence for a handful of heartbeats. "Here lately, I wouldn't be surprised."

Realization hit Emerson with all the subtlety of a Mack Truck on a downhill grade, her words flying on a nonstop trip from her heart to her mouth. "And that's why you don't want to push them to air everything out. Because you think if whatever this is comes to a head, your brothers will shut down instead of making amends."

Hunter stopped pedaling, his body rigid against the black vinyl seat rest of the arm bike. His face was as serious as she'd ever seen it, the tiny lines around his eyes etched deep in worry and sadness, and oh hell, she'd said she would listen, not put a giant, shining spotlight on all the stress in his life.

"You know what, forget I said anything. We don't—"

"Yeah." His voice was just a low rumble of sound. "I am worried Owen and Eli won't get right with each other if they have it out. If it were just me worrying, I wouldn't care so much. But my old man . . . I can tell all the arguing is wearing on him. We're already tapped out at Cross Creek with money being tight, the weather being unpredict-able, and me being sidelined. If my brothers have a blowout on top of that . . ."

The rest of Hunter's sentence hung in the air unfinished. Emerson took a step forward, moving before her neurons had fully gotten the message to go. Her heart begged her to comfort him, and not just to help his body heal. But offering up a bunch of canned platitudes about how things had a way of working out and everything would be okay seemed stupid—Emerson knew firsthand that they were bullshit, and what's more, she knew Hunter wouldn't believe her even if she tried. So she said the only thing she could think of. The only thing that made sense.

"I'm so sorry, Hunter. I know how much you want to get back to the farm to try and get things back on track."

"Thanks." He lifted his eyes, his gaze holding tightly to hers. "I haven't really aired any of this out with anyone, so, yeah. Thanks."

"Sure." Emerson stood fixed to the floor tiles with her eyes on Hunter's and her heart in her windpipe for another second before forcing herself into a soft smile. "I know I promised to get you back in working order as soon as possible, but if you'd rather skip today's session, I understand. We can make it up tomorrow."

A slow half grin spread over Hunter's face, his shoulders beginning to loosen their vise grip around his neck. "Are you kidding? I came to work. Plus, I thought you said you weren't going to give me any preferential treatment."

The reminder of their kiss flooded back through her, lingering in all sorts of spots, and she turned to grab a small hand weight from the rack behind her, grateful for the opportunity to hide the sudden flush of heat on her face surely translating to a blush. Working up her best game face, Emerson moved back toward Hunter, dropping the weight into his palm.

"Just remember, you asked for it. Let's start with lateral raises, since I seem to remember how much you love them."

The rest of their session passed with a healthy combination of hard work and casual conversation. Hunter gave her the highlights of things that had happened in Millhaven since she'd been gone—classmates who had gotten married, divorced, started local businesses, or in rare instances, moved away from town. A chill ran the length of Emerson's spine when he relayed the awful story of the car crash that had killed their classmate, Brian McAllister, and his nine-year-old daughter. Brian and his high school sweetheart, Cate, had been two years ahead of them in school, but Emerson remembered them both.

The story was thankfully Hunter's only sad piece of news. Although a few things surprised her (after thirty years of old-fashioned chicken farming, Pete Hitchcock had gone into business with a high-end poultry integrator and made a mint), most didn't (Mollie Mae was on husband number three, Kelsey Lambert was on baby number three, and Amber Cassidy was on hair color number thirty-three.) By the time she and Hunter had done their last series of assisted stretches, Emerson felt as at ease as he looked.

"Okay. Let's get you two ibuprofen before your electrical stim therapy, since we stepped up your game a little today." She threw Hunter a grin before crossing to the far side of the room, bending to grab a bottle of water from the mini fridge so he could hydrate and swallow the pills. Her muscles seized as she tried to stand, pain knifing through her lower back in a hot twist, and her free hand shot out to cover the pain before she could stop herself.

"Emerson?" Hunter was beside her in less time than it took to exhale, and how the hell had he moved so fast? "Are you okay?"

"I . . . of course. I'm fine." God, the lie slid out so easily, the words well-oiled and automatic.

But at the sound of them, he narrowed his stormy blue stare. "You don't look okay." His eyes dropped pointedly to the hand she'd splayed over her lower back, and dammit. How had she been so sloppy?

Emerson steeled both her resolve and her body. While she might be okay sharing her stilted family dynamic and even a few sizzling kisses with Hunter, a full-on personal reveal wasn't going to happen. It wasn't as if she could subtly come out with, *oh, don't mind me and my inability to stay properly upright. What's a little MS-induced nerve damage among friends?*

The truth was, they weren't just friends. She was his physical therapist. Charged with his care and his healing.

How could he expect her to be good enough to manage his pain if she couldn't even handle her own?

"Oh, this?" Emerson sent the briefest of glances over her shoulder, removing her fingers and offering up the bottle of water in her opposite hand. "It's nothing. Silly, actually. I was unpacking the last of the boxes in my apartment last night and I must've strained a muscle."

Although Hunter took the bottle of water, he kept his eyes locked on hers. "You look like you're in pain."

This is your new normal. Get used to it. "Just a little bit achy. That's all."

"Did you put any heat on it?"

"No," she admitted. "But really, it's not a big deal."

Between the frown bracketing his mouth and the crease in his forehead, Hunter's expression broadcast his disagreement in HD. "You're always telling me heat helps, right? Improved circulation to the site of the injury and all that?"

"Well, yes." Dammit. How come none of her other patients ever remembered their standards of care so well? "But this doesn't even qualify as an injury, and anyway, I didn't have any heat packs at home." Dammit again, why was she still talking about this?

"So why don't you take a bath to relax your muscles?" At the shock bursting over her face and parting her lips, Hunter added, "It's on one of those checklist sheets you gave me—you know, with all the suggestions for things you can try for alternative pain relief."

Emerson couldn't tell if she should be irritated or impressed. "Wow. You really are taking your therapy seriously."

"I promised you I would."

His lifted brows told her in no uncertain terms that she hadn't dodged the subject, and screw it. Just because she'd already copped to being a little sore didn't mean she had to go full disclosure over why. Plus, Hunter clearly wasn't going to let her off the hook until she assured him she was fine.

"I suppose a bath might help alleviate my soreness, but I don't have a tub at my place." Her stall shower was as fun sized as the rest of her apartment.

"I do," Hunter said, as easily as if he'd been remarking about a stick of gum and not a place where people typically got very, very naked.

Heat sparked, hard and insistent, between Emerson's legs, and great, she'd bypassed being a little hot and bothered and landed smack in the lap of stark raving horny. "You do?"

"Mmhmm. It's one of those big claw-footed, cast-iron deals. When we were building my cottage, the contractor said the tub would add 'rustic charm' to the place, whatever that means. I'll be honest—I've never used the thing, myself. But you're more than welcome to give it a test run if you want."

Her laugh came out in a shocked chirp. "You want to loan me your bathtub?"

"Why not?" he asked. "You don't have one of your own, and a soak would make you feel better, right?"

"Yes." Emerson cursed her malfunctioning brain-to-mouth filter the second the word crossed her lips. Spending time with Hunter here at the PT center was one thing—hell, even the time they'd shared at the Watermelon Festival was okay. But going to his house, to take a *bath*, of all things? That had no place in her new normal, no matter how much she wanted it.

Oh God, part of her really. Really. Wanted it.

"But I really couldn't," she said, her resolve waning even as the words slipped out.

"Sure you could." The corners of Hunter's mouth lifted in the slightest suggestion of a smile. "You just don't want to."

"I don't want to intrude," Emerson argued, but dammit, his laughter was contagious.

"Uh-huh. Whatever you say, Em."

Hunter's personal nickname for her—and the way it dropped so easily from his lips—sent a shot of something she couldn't quite name through her blood. "Oh, come on. Would you really be okay with me crashing your bathtub?"

He gave up half a shrug, the lift and release of his shoulder outlining his muscles beneath the snug navy-blue cotton of his T-shirt. "Why not? We're smart, sensible adults. I'd give you all the privacy you wanted, of course."

For a hot, dark second, Emerson was tempted to tell him she didn't want any privacy at all. That what she really wanted was him, wet and soap slicked and no holds barred.

But instead, she said, "I'll think about it," and he stepped in to meet the words.

"I really hope you do."

CHAPTER THIRTEEN

Emerson eyeballed the half-gallon bottle of vodka on Daisy's kitchen table with a little bit of curiosity and a whole lot of skepticism.

"You do know it's a Wednesday night, right?" she asked, but Daisy just laughed in return.

"It's not for drinking, although I guess we could snag a shot or two if the spirit moved us." She adjusted the blue-and-white bandana keeping her pair of braids at bay, pointing to the row of empty plastic containers next to the sink. "But most of the vodka will be sacrificed for the cause."

Emerson peered at the four-ounce tubs, her brows popping. "You're going to make vodka-scented bath scrub?"

"Facial mask," Daisy corrected with a grin. "But yep. I thought if I mixed the vodka with some other invigorating scents, then added sea salt as an exfoliator, the mask would make a great wake-up call. So far I've got peppermint and grapefruit on the agenda."

"Make it coffee and I'll be your customer for life." God, Emerson could use a good wake-up call. Seven thirty in the evening midweek and she was already fighting back exhaustion.

Daisy's green eyes lit up, her smile growing with excitement. "That is a *great* idea," she crowed, moving toward the notepad next to the keg of vodka to scribble down a few notes. "In the meantime, do you want to see if this new sage-and-jasmine body lotion makes you feel sexy as it softens your skin? I want to use it as part of my sensual scents line, and aphrodisiacs sell like hotcakes, baby."

Without thinking, Emerson huffed out a laugh. "Pretty sure I've got all I can handle in that department."

The cold showers that had become a part of her daily routine were doing nothing for her back pain *or* her overactive libido. But no matter what she did, she couldn't erase the memory of Hunter's sexy, suggestive smile from her mind, or the truth of the matter from her gut.

She wanted him, and not just for his bathtub.

Emerson registered Daisy's complete silence just a second too late, the brows-up surprise that went with it a second later, and dammit, she really needed to keep her lips on lockdown.

Before she could protest, Daisy's hands were on the vodka, pouring two neat shots into juice glasses, then pressing one into Emerson's palm. "That's a story."

But after that she didn't elaborate, didn't push with a bunch of nosy questions or stare at Emerson with that greedy, tell-all look Amber Cassidy always had glued to her face whenever Emerson walked within a fifty-foot radius of the Hair Lair, and God help her, the words just flew out.

"I'm not sure it's a story." She took a sip from her glass, the vodka burning a path of courage to her belly. "Hunter and I may have, um, kissed a little at the Watermelon Festival. For fifteen minutes. Without stopping."

Daisy's grin was all mischief. "Oh my God, how was it?"

"On a scale of one to ten?" Emerson asked, her own laughter blindsiding her as it escaped. "The whole thing was pretty much a twenty-seven."

"Girl, good for you!" Daisy toasted her with her juice glass, pausing to throw back the contents with a quick shiver. "So why is that more sexiness than you can handle? It was just kissing, right?"

Emerson frowned. They'd been on a park bench. Not that it had stopped her from tasting him like a seven-course meal, complete with happy noises, but that was beside the point. Sort of. "Yes."

"And you like him?"

"Yes," Emerson said, because anything else would've been a raging lie.

"And you're both single, not to mention wildly attracted to each other," Daisy prompted.

"Yes." Heat crept over the back of Emerson's neck, but still, she added, "And yes."

She took a minute to relay the *Reader's Digest* version of the conversation she and Hunter had shared on Monday, complete with the offer to use his bathtub and her I'll-think-about-it reply, and Daisy gave up a knowing nod.

"I'd say that's a big yes in the attracted-to-each-other department. So what's holding you back, exactly?" she asked, her gaze going soft in the glare of the kitchen lights. "Are you worried it'll be weird because of the past?"

"I don't know. Not really," Emerson amended. She took another sip of vodka, even though the liquor twisted in her empty stomach. "It's just that I'm starting a brand-new physical therapy practice, and I'm still trying to deal with my overbearing parents." She'd finally had to bite the bullet and agree to Sunday dinner at their house after her mother had ambushed her with another drive-by yesterday. "I'm not sure starting a relationship on top of that is the best idea."

"Sweet pea." Daisy took the glass out of Emerson's hand, replacing it with a warm squeeze of her fingers. "While Hunter is definitely a stand-up guy, I'm not entirely certain a relationship is what's on his mind right now, if you know what I mean. But if you're into each other, a little *non*-relationship might not be the worst thing in the world."

Emerson's mouth went desert dry. The no-strings-attached route had flickered enticingly through her mind no fewer than a thousand times over the last two days. While she believed Hunter wouldn't push the invitation to use his bathtub if she declined, just like she knew he'd make good on his promise to give her privacy even if she did take him up on his offer, she was also certain that if she made a move, he'd make one back. Her mind was on board with that—after all, they were adults, and they *weren't* strangers—and her libido? Holy crap, it wasn't so much on board as it was the commander of the whole damn starfleet. But there was a third player in the equation, one that could cancel out her mind and even her amped-up libido in less than a blink.

Her body had failed her in so many ways. What if, despite what the rest of her might want, her body didn't let her forget she had MS?

And what if . . . what if for just one night, it did?

Emerson's pulse thrummed harder in her veins, but she squared her shoulders and said, "You know what, Daisy, I do know what you mean. And you're absolutely right."

"I am?" Her friend's lashes arced wide to frame the surprise in her eyes, but Emerson's certainty and her smile grew stronger with each passing second.

"You are. In fact, I'd love to buy some of this sage-and-jasmine body lotion, along with some of your best foaming body wash. I've got a bath to take."

Hunter stood on the threshold to his cottage, half hard and half convinced he was out of his fucking mind. But after Emerson had told him at the end of yesterday's PT session that she'd like to take him up on the offer to borrow his bathtub, then let her eyes linger on his mouth for the span of at least three heartbeats before smiling and walking away, he couldn't deny the truth.

Business as usual was killing him. Despite the fact that he knew he should be calm and cool and rational, what he wanted was to recklessly turn business into pleasure with Emerson.

Hard. Fast. And right now.

Hunter ran a palm down the front of his freshly washed jeans, working up a smile as he reached for the doorknob. It was Saturday afternoon, for Chrissake. Barely three o'clock. He could back up his perfectly innocent offer to let Emerson borrow his bathtub by acting like a gentleman and not a Neanderthal. No problem.

As soon as he opened the door, all bets for gallant behavior were unequivocally off.

"Hey," he managed, but only just. Emerson stood on his porch, her eyes shaded with one hand, the slim muscles in her shoulder flexing into a long, graceful line. The overabundance of June sunlight turned her long black-and-white skirt just sheer enough to outline the shape of her legs through the fabric, creating a silhouette that fueled both his quickening pulse and his wicked imagination. Her copper-colored hair spilled over her shoulders in a soft waterfall of waves, and her smile tumbled over her mouth just as easily.

Hunter swallowed. Then did it again for good measure.

Yeah. His status quo had been completely obliterated.

"Hey," she said, that smile that was already making him want to kiss her reaching all the way up to her eyes as she shifted her weight over the porch boards. "I really appreciate you letting me come over on a Saturday. I hope I'm not taking you away from work."

She gestured over her shoulder, to the tidy bright-green rows of corn and soybeans flanking either side of his cottage past the fence lines, but Hunter shook his head to reassure her.

"Nah. I clocked my weekend hours this morning." At least being on restricted duty had one tiny perk. Everything he'd been physically able to accomplish had fit into the time span of about four hours. Normally Saturdays held a full workload of a good eight to ten, depending on the season. "Is your back feeling any better?"

Emerson let him usher her over the threshold, out of the oppressive summer heat. "A little. I took some over-the-counter anti-inflammatories, and I've been careful not to mess with any more boxes. But I've got to admit, I'm looking forward to a good, long soak to get me all the way back to normal."

Images of Emerson, flushed pink from a steamy bath and oh-so naked, formed a naughty slideshow in his mind, and seriously, had every last rational part of his brain been on a leave of absence when he'd offered her his bathtub?

Pretty much, yeah. But *damn*, asking her had felt good.

And hearing her say yes had felt even better.

Hunter nodded, thumping the door gently shut behind her and himself back to reality. "Well, I can take you upstairs if you want. I mean"—his chin winged up as he heard the innuendo in his words, too late—"to show you where the bathroom is, and everything." Christ, could he fumble this any harder?

But Emerson just let out a soft laugh. "I know what you meant." Adjusting her brown leather bag over her shoulder, she followed him into the cottage and up the sun-filled stairwell. "I'm not kicking you out of the only bathroom in the house, am I?"

Focus, dumbass. He might want her, but he also wanted her to feel comfortable. "Not at all. There's a guest bath up here and a powder room on the main level, so you've got the space in the master bath to yourself for as long as you'd like."

Hunter led the way down the upstairs hall toward his bedroom, which he'd made triple sure didn't look like a stand-in for the pigsty over at Whittaker Hollow, his boots coming to a stop on the floorboards when they reached the master bathroom.

"Here we go. One great, big bathtub, at your service."

Emerson's eyes went wide, and she slipped past him to fully enter the room. "Oh, wow. This is about as far as it gets from the bathroom in my apartment." She lowered her bag to an out-of-the-way spot by the vanity, extending her arms out slightly as she turned a full circle over the sand-colored bathroom tiles. "Seriously. It's *gorgeous.*"

A pang unfurled low in Hunter's belly as he watched Emerson take in the room. Letting his gaze follow hers, his eyes moved over the marble-topped vanity, the oiled bronze light fixture over the mirror behind it, the circular window set just below the gabled line of the ceiling that was too high for anyone to see inside yet large enough to fill the room with soft, golden sunlight.

He returned his stare to hers as her eyes traveled the length of the wheat-brown walls, then the plain white molding framing both the door behind them as well as the one off to the side, keeping the toilet private. Even though he'd never used the bathtub, Hunter had to admit that the fixture really did make the room, with its curved, glossy edges and sturdy feet finished with the same oiled bronze as the faucets and the light over the vanity.

Of course, his appreciation for the cast-iron monster tripled when Emerson caught sight of it with a sigh.

"All I did was paint, really. The builder did the rest. But I'm glad you like it," Hunter said, taking a step back despite the fact that every part of him save his conscience was strongly vetoing the maneuver. "The towels on the bar here are all clean, and there's soap and shampoo on the counter there if you'd like to borrow some. I'll be downstairs if you need anything else."

Yep. You'll be downstairs fending off the world's biggest hard-on. And she'll be up here. Warm. Wet. And naked in your bathtub.

Emerson fixed him with a smile as sweet and slow as butter over warm bread, and Good Christ, he hadn't thought this through even a little bit.

"You know, I've been thinking." She stepped toward him, her skirt rustling and swaying around her ankles. "It seems a shame you've never used your own bathtub."

Every part of Hunter froze except his heartbeat. "Guess I'm more of a shower guy."

"Most guys are," Emerson said, stopping only when there was less than a foot of space between their bodies. "Still. It's an easy fix, right?"

"I do live here. I guess I could use the tub anytime I wanted to."

Emerson's pupils dilated in the soft sunlight, but her aquamarine gaze didn't waver as she leaned in even closer. "Like right now, for example."

Surprise winged through him, followed by a hard shot of heat. "But you're going to be in here."

"I am." Her hands found his waist, fingers skimming the top edge of his jeans with a light, lazy touch, and his cock stirred just from the proximity. "You could stay with me," she whispered. "Two birds, one stone, and all."

Yes, yes, yes, came the chant from above his neck and below his belt, and it took every ounce of restraint in the universe for him to grate out, "Are you sure that's what you want?"

"Do you think I'd ask if I wasn't?" Emerson's mouth tilted into a smile, and he reached up to swipe his thumb over the curve of her peach-colored mouth, satisfaction spearing through him as she shuddered in response.

"No. But just to be clear, if I stay in here with you, you're not getting what you came for."

Emerson's smile grew wicked in a way Hunter had never seen before, her tongue darting out in a sexy, torturous glide over his skin. "Oh yes, I am. All you have to do is give it to me."

Hunter's heart pounded, his cock painfully hard against the fly of his jeans. Staying in here with her was impulsive and crazy and all the things he knew he should avoid like a forty-pound land mine. She'd broken his heart once. The only way to keep himself safe was to *play* it safe.

He brought his mouth down on hers without thinking twice.

CHAPTER FOURTEEN

Hunter kissed her hard enough to make her lips ache and her legs consider giving out, and Emerson nearly moaned in relief. Hunger pulsed through his touch like wildfire, traveling from his fingers all the way to her core, and even though the strength of the kiss bordered on pleasure/pain, all she could think was *more*.

"Hunter." His name rolled a path past her lips to fill the heated air around them, and he responded with a sound she felt under her skin.

"I'm sorry," he said, cupping her neck to pull her in for another bone-melting kiss before she could make her confusion form words.

"For what?"

He pulled back to pin her with a steel-blue stare that was all certainty. "For delaying the bath I promised. But I've waited twelve years to have you back in my bed, Em. I'm not waiting anymore."

In one swift move, Hunter wrapped both arms around the back of her rib cage, pulling her tight against his body. Sensations slammed into Emerson from so many directions that, for a split second, she could barely process them all. Hunter's firm, full mouth coaxing her lips open to glide his tongue over hers. The press of his chest on the thin layers of fabric between his muscles and her aching nipples. The suggestive friction of his erection, low and hard over her belly, and oh God, she didn't want to wait, either.

"Your bed sounds good. Go."

They moved in a combination of deep kisses and laughter and tangled limbs, back over the threshold of Hunter's bedroom. His simple, masculine bed sat in all its king-sized glory in the middle of the space, and Emerson found herself thanking God and every saint she could think of that they'd been only a dozen steps away.

"Yes," she whispered. Wasting no time, she kicked off her sandals. She reached out to slide her fingers beneath his T-shirt and lift it up, wanting more, wanting everything, hard and fast and now, now, now before her body could betray her.

But Hunter stepped out of her grasp, capturing both wrists with his work-roughened fingers. "Not yet."

Emerson's heart pounded, the ache between her legs following along with the rhythm. "What do you mean?"

"I mean not yet." His eyes glittered with an edgy intensity all new to her, and her breath caught in her lungs.

"Hunter, please. You just said you don't want to wait." Her face flushed. She hadn't felt this good in so long—hell, she might not have *ever* been so desperate for an orgasm. She needed to be naked, the sooner, the better. "Please take me to bed."

The smile lifting one corner of his mouth hardened her nipples to tight peaks behind her sheer white top. "Just because I want you in my bed right now doesn't mean I want to rush through being here." Dropping her wrists, he hooked a finger beneath her chin, letting his mouth hover just over hers. "You want me to do more than kiss you?"

Emerson shivered in anticipation, biting back the moan in her reply. "Yes."

"Do you want me to undress you?" At the sound of the hitch in her breath, Hunter's eyes flared. "Put my hands on you? My mouth?" He angled his lips even closer, his promise-filled words making her panties go damp as he asked, "Do you want me to spread your legs and bury myself inside you until we both lose our minds?"

Need raced through Emerson's body, humming beneath her skin. Oh God, she was already losing her mind. "Yes. Please, *yes*."

But rather than strip her naked and skip to the end of the list the way her brain and body were demanding, Hunter just smiled.

"I want that, too. But not yet," he said, quelling the protest building in the back of her throat. "I've waited twelve years for this. To remember where you blush." He traced a line from the soft spot beneath her chin to the hollow between her collarbones, her skin prickling with a flush beneath his fingers. "To relearn how you sound."

His touch drifted lower, coming to a stop on the bare skin at the deep *V* of her shirt, and this time, Emerson couldn't hold back her moan. "Hunter."

A dark edge filled both his smile and his stare as he brought his lips down on hers in a hot, suggestive sweep. "To remember how you feel and how you taste. So no matter how bad you want to rush, I'm taking my time with you. Starting right now."

Sending his arms around her shoulders, Hunter brought their bodies flush. He kissed her slowly, exploring her mouth with his lips and teeth and tongue, and as much as Emerson wanted to stay one step ahead of her traitorous body, slowing down felt too good to resist. She knotted her fingers in Hunter's hair, meeting some of his movements while surrendering to others. Deep strokes of their tongues played off soft licks, soft licks leading to the sweet sting of her bottom lip between his teeth, and finally, she pulled back on a gasp.

"Okay," Emerson said, stealing one last taste of his firm, full mouth. "You win. Kissing is underrated."

A low, sexy laugh rumbled up from his chest. "I've only just started kissing you. But now it's not your mouth I want."

Uncut desire ribboned through her as Hunter's hands found the buttons on her shirt, freeing the halves of sheer cotton with a few economical twists of his wrist. Her bra was just as thin as the blouse he was currently sliding off her shoulders and the skirt that quickly followed, and for a stark second, the desire to cover up the body that could betray her at any second took hold.

But Hunter's eyes followed his fingers over her skin, his expression so colored with desire, that moving—hell, even breathing properly—wasn't an option.

A low oath slipped past his lips. "Jesus, Em. You are . . ."

He trailed off to scrub a hand over his mouth, and in that moment, she realized how much he wanted her, too. The tautness of his muscles, the ridge of his cock pressing hard against his jeans, the flash of hunger turning his stare a dark, stormy blue. All of it combined to make Emerson feel beautiful and bold.

She lifted her chin, squaring her shoulders to let him look at her. Although the blinds on his bedroom windows were closed, the ample sunlight behind them easily illuminated the room. Her heart thrummed faster as Hunter took her in with a slow stare, sliding his fingers over the thin satin straps at her shoulders. Without a word, his hands met at the swell between her breasts, unfastening the front closure of her bra and guiding her back over the bed.

He tugged his T-shirt over his head, fitting himself next to her across the center of the mattress. In a clear reaffirmation of his promise not to rush, he slanted a slow kiss over her mouth, lingering just long enough to build a whimper in her throat before sending the kiss down the line of her jaw. His path traveled lower, stubble rasping against the sensitive column of her neck, then the flat plane where her shoulder gave way to her chest, and another shot of need bloomed low and hot in her core.

"Hunter." Emerson barely recognized that the gravel-and-velvet murmur belonged to her voice, and she arched up at the same moment he dropped to part his lips over one aching nipple.

"*Ah.*" The wordless sound burst out of her on a cry. Her back bowed to follow it, curving the edges of Hunter's mouth into a smile, but he didn't slow his movements. Tightening his lips, he circled his tongue around the hard peak trapped there, and the wet friction was enough to make her pulse hammer even faster. He sucked and swirled and licked, angling over her for better access and bracing one palm wide over the comforter in the spot just beside her head. Slick heat built, steady and demanding between her legs, and Emerson realized the truth all at once.

Her body wouldn't betray her. Being with Hunter just this once was hers for the taking.

And fast, slow, and everything in between, she wanted *all* of it.

Emerson's hand reached out of its own free will to discover his hip, wrapping around the denim in a tight grasp. His breathing changed just a fraction, letting her know he felt her hand on him, and the effect dared her to be even more brazen. Releasing her grip, she let her hand travel lower, relishing both his moan and his faster ministrations on her breast as she closed her fingers over the hard line of his cock.

"Emerson." The word was all warning, and grated against her sensitive skin.

But she continued to stroke. "Turnabout is fair play. Plus"—she paused, making a round-trip circuit from root to tip and back again over his jeans—"I'll go slow if you want. But, trust me, Hunter, you're not the only one who's only just started."

He pulled her nipple all the way past his lips, kissing her hotly before sliding his attention to her other breast, and Emerson followed his lead. She freed the button and zipper on Hunter's jeans, moving from a light touch to firm intention. His cock jumped against her palm as she slipped her hand between the denim and his boxer briefs to stroke him faster, and he parted from her nipple to capture her hand with a groan and a curse.

"Not yet."

"But—"

The look on his face, so full of die-hard certainty, stole the breath right from her lungs. "There's one more place I haven't tasted yet. Now come here and let me remind you how underrated kissing *really* is."

Hunter moved before Emerson could blink or breathe. He found his feet, turning to face the spot where she lay across the short side of the bed. Taking barely a second to shuck his boots and jeans, he leaned back over her body, curling his palms around her hips to slide her legs over the side of the bed.

"I used to think about you like this." He parted her knees and knelt on the floor between them, his breath nearly as hot as his gaze as both raked over her thighs.

"I thought about you, too," Emerson admitted. After she'd left, she'd spent so many nights lost in memories. She'd touch herself until she cried out, imagining that the hand between her legs belonged to him instead.

Hunter dragged a finger up one inner thigh, drawing a shiver over her skin. "And now here you are. Hot. Wet. Exactly like I remembered."

A reminder of how deceptively different her body really was now kicked at the back of her mind, but she shut it out in favor of his touch, so close to the place where she ached for it most.

"So pretty," he said, moving his hand to the seam of her body, stroking softly. Emerson bucked against the slide of his fingers, crying out when he circled her clit over the damp cotton of her panties. Hooking his thumbs around the material at her hips, Hunter tugged downward, exposing the last bit of her covered skin. "So perfect."

The want building deep inside of Emerson's core became the background for the slam of her heart. She levered up to her forearms, and the sight in front of her sent the breath from her body in a gasp. She'd been too preoccupied before to notice the full-length mirror on the wall by the bathroom door. But now, faced with the unexpected reflection of Hunter's muscular shoulders angled between her thighs, she couldn't do anything but stare.

His sun-burnished skin was a direct, sexy contrast to her cream-colored legs, and she widened them out of pure instinct. He pressed his shoulders beneath her thighs, increasing their contact, and Emerson lost herself in the sight of the two of them wrapped together so intimately. Heat and need pumped through her even harder as Hunter lowered his mouth to her sex with a long, slow sweep of his tongue.

In the mirror, she watched herself tremble and moan. "Oh . . . God. Please don't stop."

And in the mirror, Hunter didn't. Curling his arms around her thighs from beneath her, he flattened both palms over her hips, pressing her wide as he pleasured her with his mouth. Emerson watched their reflection, completely entranced. Every flick of his tongue sent sparks through her belly, and she chased each sensation with a pump of her hips. The body in the mirror was strong and sensual, skin flushed pink with arousal, and yes—*yes*—that body was hers, meeting every sinful glide of Hunter's mouth and wanting even more.

"Damn, I've missed how you taste," he whispered, slipping higher to swirl his tongue over her clit. Release built between her legs, tempting her to thrust even faster against his lips and tongue. Splaying the fingers of her left hand over the comforter, she pushed herself nearly to sitting, knotting her right hand through Hunter's hair to hold him close between her legs.

The image in the mirror was wicked and beautiful, and the sight of their intimate connection snapped the last thread of Emerson's control. Her orgasm surged up from deep inside, replacing all of her senses with wave after wave of pure pleasure. Hunter worked her through each one, softening the movements of his mouth until, finally, her mind and body returned to one another.

"Come here." She pulled him close, letting her shoulders fall back over the mattress.

Pressing a kiss to her neck, then another to the space just below her ear, he chuffed out a small laugh. "You're even more beautiful than I remember, you know that?"

"So are you," Emerson said, reaching between their bodies to run her hand up the corded muscle of Hunter's thigh. "Will you let me show *you* now?"

His heavy, want-filled exhale was answer enough. She trailed her fingers over his hip, above the waistband of his boxer briefs, making her way to the flat plane of his abdomen. Hunter's muscles were lean, work hardened and strong in a way they hadn't been twelve years ago, and now that he was on top of her, dividing the cradle of her hips with his frame, Emerson could make them all out in mouthwatering detail.

Her hand moved over his warm skin, the thin line of hair arrowing from his navel to the waistband of his boxer briefs crisp beneath her touch. She sent her fingers lower still, slipping past the cotton and closing them around his cock.

"Em." The word broke from Hunter's throat on a low sound. His eyes squeezed shut, and he began to thrust against the circle of her fist, slowly at first. Need rebuilt in Emerson's body, quickly pulsing through her veins, and she canted up to meet his thrusts with her hips as well as her hand.

They moved together in rhythm until both of them were left breathing in short, needful bursts. A thought made its way past the lust-fueled haze in her mind, and as much as she wanted nothing more than to take Hunter's boxer briefs all the way off and have him inside her right this second, that thought was too important to ignore.

"I need . . ." *So many things, so many things.* "My bag."

His eyes opened, but Emerson didn't wait long enough for him to stop his motions.

"I have condoms in my bag," she said, and the confusion on Hunter's face slid into a mischievous smile.

"Why, Miss Montgomery." His drawl was pure honey, and God, she wanted to come from the sound of it alone. "Did you come over here today to seduce me?"

"I sure did, Mr. Cross." She put on the sultriest expression she could muster, although current circumstances didn't make it tough. "Now are you going to go get those condoms so I can finish the job, or am I going to have to take charge here?"

Hunter's gaze glinted, but he slipped from her body just far enough to reach his bedside table drawer. "You can take charge next time. In fact, I have a feeling I'll like that very much. But I'm prepared, too, and today, you're mine."

He took a condom out of the drawer, pausing for just the briefest of moments to take off his boxer briefs and tear past the foil. Returning to the bed, he guided her lengthwise along the comforter, centering himself between her legs.

Emerson opened for him without a second thought. Hunter slid his cock along her folds, and she lifted her hips in search of more. Slowly, he pushed inside, stretching her with delicious pressure, inch by inch, until they were completely joined.

"Holy . . . God, you feel so good." His murmur spilled over her shoulder as he leaned in to cover her body, drawing his hips back and returning them just hard enough to make her clit throb. Hunter felt familiar and brand-new all at once, the warm cedar smell of his skin, the delicious friction of his stubble where her ear met her neck. Emerson's lips parted over his shoulder, her teeth grazing the hard line of muscle there, and he thrust deeper without increasing his pace.

"Yes. Oh *yes*." The handful of sounds was all she could manage past the pleasure coming at her from all sides. Her heart pounded, nipples tightening to beaded points from the slide of Hunter's chest on hers. He held her close, whispering all sorts of things in her ear that made her move faster, begging him deeper inside. Balancing his weight between his forearms and knees, he pumped his hips to fill her over and over, and she let out a high-pitched cry as a powerful climax blindsided her.

"That's it. Come for me. I'm right here with you, baby," Hunter whispered in her ear.

And he was. He rode out her orgasm until her cries became moans, then her moans turned to soft, breathy sighs. But he never stopped moving, never put space between their sweat-slicked skin, and before she could process the command from her brain, her body moved of its own volition.

Emerson knotted one leg around Hunter's waist, pushing with both arms to roll him beneath her. Surprise claimed his expression, but she pressed two fingers over his mouth in reassurance.

"And I'm right here, too. Please, Hunter. I know you're holding back." She tipped her hips to let him fill her to the hilt, his groan proving her words. "I want you to let go. Let me make you feel good. Let me in."

The intensity returned to his stare, and Emerson's breath caught in her throat. He reached out, palms shaping her waist, fingers gripping her tight. Finding a rhythm with his hands, Hunter rocked her back and forth, his cock hitting some sweet, hidden spot deep inside of her, and she reached down to grab his wrists, urging him faster.

"Hunter." Emerson widened her knees, rolling the cradle of her hips tight against his body. Oh God, she'd never seen him so intense. "Take me, please. Just like that."

"So pretty. So perfect," he grated, continuing to thrust. The pressure between her legs toed the line between ecstasy and ache. She turned her nails into his wrists, bucking into him as he guided her forward again and again, and his muscles grew taut. His back arched off the bed, leaving no daylight between them, and with a few more movements, he shuddered beneath her, coming with a shout.

Dazed, Emerson slid over Hunter's body, belly to belly, chest to chest. Tucking her cheek to his shoulder, she waited out the slam of her heartbeat and the rise and fall of his ragged breath. After a period of time she couldn't gauge, he gently lifted her to separate their bodies, taking a brief minute to slip to the adjacent bathroom. When he returned, she braced herself for reality to crash in, to remind her that this had been casual, a one-time thing, that her happiness with Hunter had to stay in the past and she'd run out of time to escape her damaged body.

But it never happened, so instead, she curled up in Hunter's arms.

CHAPTER FIFTEEN

Hunter lay back against his bedsheets, his body completely relaxed while his brain spun at sixteen thousand miles a minute. Less than two hours had passed since he and Emerson had crawled under the covers and settled against each other in the same spot he'd slept last night, last week—shit, for the last decade since the cottage had been built. Today, however, the composure he'd relied on for those ten years had been hairpinned into a full one-eighty, because he'd recklessly shared said bedsheets with a woman who—if you'd asked him three short weeks ago—he'd have sworn he'd never lay eyes on again.

And not only had Emerson blown his fucking mind both in bed and out, but the only thing Hunter could think of was how badly he wanted to part her legs and sink into her slick heat again and again.

He shifted slightly, not wanting to disturb Emerson from the nap she'd drifted into about ninety minutes ago. In truth, he hadn't been entirely sure what to expect when he'd returned to the bedroom after they'd had sex. But she'd slipped back into his arms so easily, her warm, soft body fitting right against his, that he'd just pulled her in close under the covers. She'd fallen asleep not soon after, her body going loose and her breathing changing along with the patterns of sunlight over the floorboards. While Hunter had closed his eyes for a few minutes along with her, he'd spent most of the last hour wide awake and tangled in thought.

Yes, Emerson had changed since the last time she'd been in his bed, and yes again, even though she'd opened up to him about her parents, she still carried a tough brand of caution and a weariness in her eyes that plucked at his warning flags. But she was also the same, with her limitless laugh and that flawless combination of sweetness and sass that never failed to trip every last one of his switches. Hunter's *what if* was right here in front of him, asleep in his arms, for Chrissake, and it was getting harder and harder to deny that he wanted to keep her there.

Slowly, she stirred against him, and he pushed back his thoughts in favor of dropping a kiss to the crown of her head. "Hey. I was starting to wonder if you were going to sleep through the whole evening," he joked, and she pulled back in surprise.

"I fell asleep?" she murmured in a husky voice, her cheeks pinking with the realization that followed her words. "I'm sorry. I didn't mean to, but sometimes I . . . I guess I was just tired."

He shrugged, his bare shoulders sliding against the pillow beneath them. "I don't mind. I dozed off for a little while there, too."

"Wait." Emerson blinked, propping herself up to her elbows to swing her still-sleepy gaze around the room. "What time is it?"

Damn good question, actually. Hunter turned to grab a look at the clock on his bedside table. "Mmmm, nearly six," he said, the words chased quickly by a mental slap upside the head. "Shit."

"What's the matter?"

His pulse pushed faster, and he tugged a rough hand through his hair. Dammit, how could he have lost track of that much time?

Gorgeous redhead, best sex of your life . . . ring any bells, dumbass?

Hunter cleared his throat, working up a smile. "Nothing's wrong. My father and brothers and I normally have supper together on Saturdays after all the work is done—you know, to break down the week at the farm and spend a little time together. I just have to call over to the house to tell my Pop I can't make it, that's all."

"No, no." Emerson sat up and started rummaging for her clothes. "I overstayed my welcome by falling asleep. Just give me a minute to grab my things, and—"

"You didn't overstay anything." Okay, so interrupting her skirted the boundaries of bad manners, but come on. He wasn't about to boot her out the door, especially after they'd just spent the better part of three hours naked in his bed.

Fuck, he wanted to turn those three hours into an all-nighter.

But Emerson hadn't called back the search party for her clothes. "Really, it's fine." God *damn* she'd gotten her bra and panties on with speed that bordered on the preternatural. "I wouldn't dream of keeping you from a family dinner."

Although she seemed oddly embarrassed at having crashed out for a catnap, her tone was still devoid of drama, as if she'd feel genuine remorse for keeping him from the meatloaf and mashed potatoes special Owen was probably slapping together right now in their old man's kitchen.

Hunter slid out of bed, quickly tugging on his boxer briefs before clasping his fingers around her wrist, mid-button. "Then don't. Come with me instead."

"You want me to go with you? To your father's house," she added, confirming with, "for family dinner."

Emerson looked as shocked as he felt that he'd uttered the words, but still, he didn't backpedal. Asking her might be impulsive, but it also felt right.

"Look, I know we agreed we'd take things easy. What was it you said?" He replayed their conversation on the park bench in his mind, snagging the words a second later. "Head up, eyes forward, right?"

"Yeah." She nodded, her expression telling him he'd been spot on in gauging her reason for hedging on supper and rushing out the door.

Reality was, Hunter got where she was coming from. He didn't want to dive into anything, either.

But he also didn't want to let her go.

Taking a step toward her, he said, "Then let's do that. You've been to probably a hundred suppers at my Pop's place. They're about as formal as a football game, and it's not as if you're a stranger."

Emerson lifted her chin, her aquamarine stare going wide. "That's true," she said, and Hunter took the opening and ran.

"I'm sure my father and Owen and Eli would be happy to see you." Hell, maybe his brothers would actually cut their crap for a night if Emerson were there with them.

"I'd be happy to see them, too." Her pause lasted for only a second before she shook her head to cancel it out. "Your family isn't expecting me, though. I can't just show up."

Now this part, Hunter could definitely argue with ease. He supposed there were families out there who stood on that sort of formality, but his sure as hell wasn't one of them. "Sure you can. We always make plenty to go around. Anyway, you think it's perfectly normal to drink your breakfast. Even Owen's meatloaf is bound to be better than a meal you don't chew."

One copper-colored brow arched up, and man, that fire in her eyes revved him all the way up. "Do not mock my love for coffee," she warned, sliding a hand to her hip.

"I'll make sure you get a cup after supper." He leaned in for a bold taste of her mouth. "Come on, what do you say, small-town girl? Care to stick around?"

She kissed him back, and Hunter felt a smile edge over her lips. "Make it two cups of coffee and you've got yourself a deal, hotshot."

They finished getting dressed with a handful of quick movements, and he went downstairs to give Emerson some privacy to freshen up in the bathroom. Ten minutes had her back down the steps, her mussed hair combed into pretty waves and some lip gloss–type stuff turning her pretty, bow-shaped mouth the color of ripe peaches. The hot twinge in Hunter's gut arrowed due south at the thought of those lips forming his name, begging him not to stop as he kissed between her legs hard and fast and deep enough to make her come.

Yeah. They needed to go before they didn't.

He pried his thoughts away from Emerson's sheer, sinful mouth, leading the way through the front door and over the whitewashed porch boards. A wall of late-day heat and humidity hit him like a brick, and he flipped the keys to his truck in his palm.

"Normally I'd suggest we walk since it's not that far," he said, gesturing up the packed dirt path leading toward the main house at the heart of the property. "But it's been hotter than hell's furnace lately. The trip might melt us both."

Relief flickered over Emerson's face, even stronger than he'd expect for getting a pass on an easy half-mile hop skip. "Driving sounds nice," she said, following him to his F-250. "You guys must do a ton of walking around here on any given day."

He swiveled his gaze over the cornfields growing tall and green on either side of his cottage, unable to cage his smile. "We get in our fair share of stompin' around. We have a few ATVs that we use for the longer hauls, and in a pinch, we'll cover the distance by truck if we've got to move hay or fertilizer or feed."

Hunter spent the two-minute drive to the main house reacquainting her with Cross Creek, pointing out the grove of apple trees and the greenhouses off in the distance, then the dirt road leading to the back half of their property where they did all their cattle farming. Emerson rolled down her window, her stare rounding with surprise beneath the shade of her hand as her line of sight caught on the old hay barn on the hill.

"Oh my God, that barn is still there," she said, and the smile spreading over her face was contagious.

"Sure is. Come to think of it, that's actually where I busted up my shoulder."

The irony tagged Hunter right in the sternum. In high school, he and Emerson had snuck off to the hayloft in that barn with a blanket and a whole lot of bad intentions more times than he could count. "I could give you a tour later. You know, for old time's sake. The view of the moon from the hayloft is still pretty great."

"The view." She laughed, a tart, sexy sound. "Do women really fall for that?"

Too easy. Hunter tried on his best grin as he pulled in front of the main house and parked his truck between Eli's and Owen's. "You did."

But instead of getting indignant, Emerson shocked the hell out of him by leaning over the console and putting those perfect, peach-colored lips on his. "And so did you. Or did you really think I went up there with you all those nights expecting an astronomy lesson?"

"Touché," he said, holding up his hands in concession. Of course she'd been smart enough to see through his flimsy line. Just like of course he'd never told her she'd been the only woman he'd ever taken to the hayloft, before or since.

"Don't you mean 'cliché'?" she asked, laughing as she brushed her mouth over his one more time.

Hunter kissed her back—he wasn't a dolt, for God's sake—but only for a minute before pulling back to slide out of the driver's seat. Ducking around the back of the truck to open Emerson's door, he surreptitiously swiped a hand over his mouth to remove the evidence of their kiss. His brothers would give him a boulder-sized ration of shit if he walked into Saturday supper with sparkly pink lip gloss on his face, no matter that the prettiest woman in the county had put it there.

Not that the ear-to-ear grin on his face wasn't going to be a dead freaking giveaway that he and Emerson had done a whole lot more than kiss.

"Are you sure this is really okay?" she murmured as he guided her out of the passenger seat, the quick hit of uncertainty in her voice delivering Hunter back to the here and now of the farm.

"Absolutely. I just hope you're hungry."

Their footsteps echoed softly on the neatly kept path between the driveway and the main house, then the sun-warmed porch boards on the threshold. Hunter's heart thumped a little faster (oh, who was he kidding? A hell of a lot faster) as he turned the doorknob, but he tacked a business-as-usual smile to his kisser and led the way into the house.

"Hey. Sorry I'm a little late," Hunter called out, walking a path from the foyer toward the back of the house. The clatter of kitchen noise—combined with the rumble of voices and the hearty scents of meatloaf and gravy—told him he'd missed most of supper prep, and the cocky smile Eli delivered from behind the butcher-block island as Hunter put the hallway behind him served as confirmation.

"It's about time!" Eli said, pointing the wooden salad spoon in his hand to the spot where Hunter stood in the kitchen's entryway. "Did you get lost, you slack-ass, or did you—whoa."

The spoon hit the counter with a wood-on-wood clack. His brother gaped like a largemouth bass coming fresh off the line, which would've been Facebook material if it hadn't made Emerson stiffen next to Hunter on the floorboards. Thankfully, Eli was slicker than owl snot, and he recovered his grin in short order.

"Hey, Emerson! 'Scuse my language. I didn't know you'd be joining us for dinner, or I'd have minded a little better."

"That's okay," she said, the sound of her voice making Hunter's father pause halfway through washing his hands and Owen's head snap up from where he stood in front of the old white enamel cooktop. "I know I'm joining you last minute. I don't mean to intrude."

"No such thing." Eli got the protest out before Hunter could, and he made a mental note to buy his brother a round at The Bar next Friday night. "There's always enough to feed a platoon around here.

Plus, Owen's meatloaf will be a whole lot more bearable with you at the table."

Owen rolled his eyes, although whether it was at Eli's insult or his sweet-talking charm, Hunter couldn't be sure. Still, he smiled at Emerson as he said, "We've always got room for an extra at supper. It's nice to see you, Emerson."

His old man turned off the faucet, gesturing her into the kitchen with a tilt of his salt-and-pepper head. "Come on in, darlin'. You're always welcome here."

"Thanks." She smiled, the tension in her shoulders easing even though she shot Hunter a covert, sassy look when he murmured a teasing I-told-you-so under his breath. "How can I help with dinner?"

"You're a guest," Owen said, but she shook her head, a headstrong glint flashing in her eyes even though she kept her genuine smile in place.

"And I came to eat. I don't mind putting in a little work for it."

His father's rusty chuckle filled the kitchen from over by the sink. "You've got us there. Guess we've gotta put you to work, then."

"I've got tomatoes and peppers that could use chopping for this salad," Eli offered, gesturing to the butcher block.

"Done." Emerson moved to the sink to wash her hands, fitting in just as seamlessly as Hunter had promised she would. Funny, seeing her there laughing and starting to chop vegetables at the counter next to Eli sent a ripple through Hunter's gut, anyway.

Ignoring both the weird feeling and the knowing stares both of his brothers winged at him over Emerson's head, he said, "Guess I'll set the table, then."

Hunter stepped his way to the cupboard by the oven, counting off five blue-and-white plates before grabbing silverware from the drawer below to match. They all moved around one another with ease, alternating between putting the finishing touches on supper and talking about Cross Creek's operations for the week. His father and brothers hadn't made nearly as much progress as they'd wanted on the farm due to the stifling heat, and a solid fifteen days had passed since any part of the Valley had seen a single drop of rain. Dammit, if this heat wave kept up, the next two weeks were going to drag on even slower than the first two Hunter had spent on the sidelines.

"I should be able to take care of getting the CSA orders filled and ready for pickup this week," he offered as soon as they'd gathered around the table and his father had finished saying grace. The task might not require a lot of physical effort or expertise, but at least it was something.

Owen let out a breath, slow and heavy. "There aren't too many, unfortunately. We've been way low on orders, especially for June. Thank God for the Watermelon Festival last week, or I'd have ended up with crates worth of produce from the greenhouse that went to rot."

"Really?" Emerson sent an apologetic look first to Owen, then to Hunter before adding, "I'm sorry. It's just that the food is so pretty, not to mention delicious. I guess I'm just surprised to hear you say you'd have to toss so much."

"We have more leeway with crops like corn and soybeans—feed corn in particular. But moving perishables is a lot tougher. It's literally feast or famine sometimes, depending on supply and demand," Hunter said, passing the platter of meatloaf in her direction.

Owen filled his water glass to the brim, nodding in agreement. "We sell some of our produce to Clementine's Diner, and even more to the Corner Market every week, but the timing is tricky. Even a couple of days can make or break summer produce, and sometimes things just don't make it to the farmers' market or the CSA. This heat sure isn't doing us any favors in keeping things from spoiling fast, either."

His father lifted his chin. "Haven't seen a June this hot since you boys were in school," he said. "Weather like this'll make even the best of things go pear shaped."

Fatigue carved deeper wrinkles than usual at the corners of his old man's eyes as he spoke, sending yet another jab of worry deep between Hunter's ribs.

If the concern in Emerson's gaze was anything to go by, he wasn't the only one who noticed, either. "So what you need is to bring in more people to buy direct on a daily basis," she said, and Eli's laugh carried a whole lot less humor than usual.

"That plus a break in the weather, a dozen extra farmhands, and a million bucks in revenue to build something better than a roadside stand for those daily visitors ought to be a good start."

In an instant, Hunter's spine snapped to full attention against the ladder back of his chair. "Eli."

The warning rumbled from his throat, half growl and all pissed off, and Owen fixed their younger brother with a subarctic stare to match. Even their father sent a frown of disapproval in Eli's direction, but Emerson put one hand on Hunter's forearm, waving off the tension in the room with the other.

"No, it's okay. I can understand Eli's frustration. You all care about Cross Creek. Struggling to do a job you love is . . ." She paused, lining up her silverware with surgical precision. "Well, I'd imagine that's difficult."

Ah hell. Of course Emerson knew firsthand how hard it was to resuscitate a career she was passionate about. Not that he was going to out her in the middle of his father's kitchen—or anywhere else, for that matter.

Eli nodded at her in quiet apology, and Hunter let go of his irritation. For now. "It's not easy on any of us, no," he admitted.

Emerson put a big scoop of salad on her plate, her head tipped in thought. "I know having a roadside stand is less than ideal, but it's better than nothing, right?"

"If we could move enough inventory to justify paying someone to rotate stock and take money, it would be," Owen said. "Farm to table has been one of our biggest goals ever since we built the greenhouses, but we don't even get enough folks in the pick-your-own fields to open those more than a day or two a week, even at the height of the season."

"Back to bringing in more people, then. Hmmm." She tapped a finger against her lips, a deep *V* forming in the center of her brow. "This might be a stupid question, but have you thought about using social media to increase your reach?"

"In theory, sure. In practice . . ." Hunter paused, looking around the table at his father and brothers before admitting, "Not really. I mean, we've got a website and a Facebook page just like every other business on the planet, but other than that, we've been juggling so many bigger things with day-to-day operations that finding the time to expand our marketing has been kind of tough."

"And digging up the cash to hire someone with the know-how is even harder," Owen said.

"Don't even get me started on finding someone with decent enough skills to write the copy for things like newsletters and ads," Hunter added. "Although the freelance writer Eli found to do the stuff for the website wasn't bad."

Eli shrugged and remained weirdly quiet, but at least he wasn't getting mouthy again. God, he'd been so hot and cold lately.

"I used to hang out with one of the marketing directors for the Lightning," Emerson said slowly, as if her thoughts were forming out loud. "She was in charge of getting the word out for their outreach programs—updating social media pages and growing digital newsletter lists for their sports camps, things like that. I helped her with some of the basics from time to time when she'd get slammed. If you want, I could take a look at what you've got in place."

Jaw, meet floor. "You want to help with Cross Creek's marketing?"

"I don't really know how much help I'd be, but business is kind of light down at the PT center right now." Sadness flickered through her gaze, so fast that if Hunter hadn't known the circumstances, he'd have dismissed it. "I have the time, and I don't mind looking to see if any of what I learned from my friend might work for Cross Creek."

Owen hesitated, his expression caught between excitement and apology. "We don't really have the budget right now to pay you like we would a freelancer."

"Oh." Emerson got through three saucer-wide blinks before her words caught up with the rest of her. "*Oh.* God, that's okay. I wouldn't expect you to pay me at all. I have a little experience, but I'm not a marketing expert by any means."

Hunter's father didn't go the stubborn route too often, but when he did, it was an all-in affair. "Work's work," he said, both his tone and his stare brooking no argument. "It deserves fair pay."

Emerson answered by gesturing to the plate in front of her. "How about we barter?"

"Barter," his father repeated with a lift of his salt-and-pepper brows, and she nodded, spearing a fat, juicy wedge of tomato with the tines of her fork.

"Yes, sir. See, I'm not sure if Hunter told you this or not, but I've got a particular fondness for these tomatoes. Oh, and your strawberries. And I might also have a tiny addiction to your butter lettuce." She held up her thumb and her forefinger to measure less than an inch of daylight, her sheepish smile completely genuine and even more beautiful. "Since I'm willing to bet the rest of your produce is just as good, I'd like to make a deal with you. I'll do a little marketing recon for Cross Creek, and in exchange, you can compensate me with surplus from your greenhouse. Does that sound fair?"

Oh, she's good. What's more, Emerson's offer to help was a damned good idea.

"Gotta admit, it wouldn't hurt to have someone with fresh eyes take a look at things," Hunter said, a glimmer of hope pumping through his veins.

"Anything's better than the nothing we're doing now," Eli chimed in, ignoring Owen's glare in response. "I think having Emerson help is a great plan."

"Your call, Dad," Owen said, but despite his obvious irritation at Eli's words, his tone made it clear that he was on board with Emerson's offer.

For a minute, their old man said nothing. Then a slow smile broke over his face. "Well, then. I suppose that settles that. But I hope you like your vegetables, darlin', because we'll make sure you've got your share and then some."

Emerson extended her hand, her own smile turning into a grin. "You've got yourself a deal, Mr. Cross."

They spent the rest of the meal talking about marketing, with Emerson asking all sorts of questions that proved why having her help was a top-shelf idea. Finally, after their brains were full of ideas and their stomachs were full of food, Emerson and his brothers tidied the kitchen as much as their old man would allow. Eli ducked out with a cocky "see y'all later," although he'd been unusually reserved during their supper conversation with Emerson. Better than him picking a fight with Owen, Hunter supposed, and the rest of them exchanged quick pleasantries before parting ways on the dusk-covered porch.

"It's really nice of you to offer to help around here," Hunter said, lacing his fingers through hers as he led the way to the passenger side of his truck.

Her squeeze in return felt better than it should. "It's really nice of you to let me. My workload is starting to pick up a little at the PT center now that Mrs. Ellersby and one or two other clients have scheduled appointments, but I want to stay as busy as possible."

"You really do hate the sidelines, huh?" His boots crunched to a stop over the gravel, the low hum of cricket song floating through the air in its place, and Emerson leaned back against the door of his truck with her skirt swishing around her ankles.

"Head up, eyes forward," she reminded him. Her fingers tightened around his, the softness of her skin belying the strength he knew she was capable of. Hell if there weren't two sides to her, one fierce and full of mettle, the other vulnerable, hiding behind the shadows in her eyes.

And as much as he knew it would send his smooth-sailing reality into uncharted territory, Hunter wanted both.

"Don't go home tonight," he said, stepping in to slide his lips over hers.

Emerson kissed him back, melting against his touch even as she gripped him tight. "Pretty bold words for a man who likes things simple."

"I don't stand on a whole lot of pretense, remember?" He shifted back, but only far enough to capture her gaze in the waning daylight. "The only time I've ever been impulsive was when I asked you to marry me, Em. With how that turned out, I'd always thought not taking the slow-and-steady road was just a bad idea, but I was wrong."

She froze beneath his touch, cinnamon-stick lashes framing her wide-eyed stare, and Hunter barreled on before she could protest—or worse yet, pull away. "I'm not saying I want to dive into something serious. We're different now, I get that. But being with you feels good, and impulsive or not, I don't want you to go just yet."

For a breath, then two, the only thing he could hear was the press of his pulse against his eardrums. Then Emerson's mouth was back on his, and his heart beat faster for a whole new set of reasons.

"I don't want to go, either. After all, I never did get that bath I came for. Now let's head back to your place and find out if there's room in your tub for two."

CHAPTER SIXTEEN

Emerson dropped her bag on the Lego-sized threshold of her apartment, her joints as rusty as forty-year-old barbed wire, but her smile making up for it in spades. Spending the night (and the morning. And lunchtime. And the better part of the afternoon) in Hunter's bed hadn't yielded much by way of rest. Still, she couldn't deny that it *had* yielded something even better, something she hadn't felt in far too long.

For the first time since she'd been diagnosed with multiple sclerosis nearly two months ago, Emerson felt normal.

No, strike that. Despite the weariness in her body and the stiffness in her bones, she felt freaking spectacular.

Kicking off her sandals, she padded over the threadbare carpet, heading toward her bathroom. She had less than an hour to get ready for the Sunday dinner she'd promised to attend at her parents' house, and the reminder took a swipe at her blissed-out mood. While Emerson could think of approximately sixteen thousand things she'd rather do than offer herself up for an evening of tag-team parental disdain, she also knew she couldn't avoid her mother and father indefinitely. Certainly, the dinner would sting. But Emerson had known that coming back to Millhaven would mean facing their chagrin from time to time. Just because she didn't like that reality didn't mean she couldn't handle it. She wasn't the same scared teenager she'd been twelve years ago.

At least her parents were in the dark about the *real* reason she'd left Las Vegas. Knowing their already-imperfect daughter had MS would only send their desire to control her life into a tailspin, not to mention deepen their belief that she'd never live up to their standards. After all, she'd already disappointed them by following her heart into physical therapy, then again by leaving her job with the Lightning. If they discovered her body was spoiled goods on top of that?

The letdown might just break her.

Emerson inhaled, slowly and deeply, bracing her hands on the cool faux-marble vanity top. She'd spent the last twenty-four hours moving on with her life, happy for the first time in God knew how long. She couldn't let the thought of her parents' disappointment put a wrecking ball to her good mood.

As long as no one found out she had MS, she could deal with the rest, just like she'd planned. She'd work as hard as she could, fill her extra time helping Daisy with her business and Hunter at Cross Creek, and everything would be fine.

She would be fine. Head up, eyes forward.

Secret buried. No matter how heavy the truth was.

Pulling back the flimsy shower curtain, she turned the water as hot as she could bear before peeling off yesterday's skirt and sleeveless blouse. Her tired muscles screamed in protest when she stepped into the spray a minute later, but still, Emerson smiled at the cause of her fatigue. On the surface, she knew the fact that she'd spent so much time with Hunter should make her wary. Hell, she hadn't even intended to let her body betray her into falling asleep next to him for that highly embarrassing post-coital nap, let alone staying at Cross Creek for the better part of the weekend. But Emerson's knee-jerk caution had fallen silent in the face of Hunter's nothing-doing calm, to the point that she couldn't deny the truth.

She liked him. She trusted him. And she'd wanted to stay with him last night, even before he'd asked. A weekend full of hot sex (oh God, the sex had been so. Very. Hot) was a whole lot different from picking out china patterns—and Hunter seemed as happy as she was to stick with the former.

And he'd broken in his bathtub with her to prove it.

"Oh." Her throaty murmur escaped before she even knew it would form. Hypnotic heat flooded her belly at the memory, and Emerson let it spill all the way through her before giving the shower knob a heavy nudge toward the cold side. As tempting as it might be to let her thoughts drift back to her steamy night with Hunter, she was going to need every bit of her game face for this dinner.

With efficient movements, she finished her shower and dried off. A Sunday meal at the Montgomery estate was nothing less than a formal affair, and even though she hadn't attended one in over a decade, Emerson still knew exactly how to dress the part. A tasteful black sheath dress, a single strand of ribbon-bound pearls, and a pair of kitten heels later, she was nearly presentable by Bitsy's standards.

Wrangling her riotous curls into a sleek knot at her nape took more time and energy than Emerson had to spare, but she finally managed to put the finishing touches on her hair and makeup and hustle herself out the door. The drive to her parents' house was as short as it was scenic, and she made it all the way to the winding drive of the sprawling two-story colonial before her dread made a comeback.

Head up. Eyes forward. In a couple of hours, you'll be home in bed with a pint of Ben & Jerry's.

Leaving the comfort of her air-conditioned car behind, she slid out of the driver's seat and set her sights on the house where she'd grown up. Stepping precisely over the stamped stone walkway, she reached for the doorbell, letting her gaze travel over the expanse of the flawlessly swept threshold. A pair of large, regal-looking urn planters flanked the front door, overflowing with classic red and white geraniums and professionally placed foliage annuals, pretty in a *don't touch* sort of way. They were a perfect match for the rest of the landscaping, along with the glossy white trim and gleaming brass accents adorning the bricks on the front of the house. Although small updates had been made here and there in her absence, everything about the scene in front of her was just as magazine worthy as Emerson had expected it would be.

Including her mother.

"Sweetheart." Bitsy's sweeping head-to-toe appraisal held enough scrutiny to rival most police investigations. "Do come in out of that awful heat. Look, you've already begun to glow."

"It was ninety-five degrees today." Emerson slipped the words past her clenched smile. It'd be a hell of a lot more troubling if she *didn't* sweat a little in weather like this.

Her mother lifted her brows in a nonverbal translation of *I fail to see your point.* "Yes, well. You know where the powder room is."

"I'm fine, Mom," she said, her feet purposely not budging over the foyer's marble floor. The trip up the sycamore-shaded walkway hadn't been a triathlon, for God's sake, and as hot as today had been, the sun was already halfway to setting.

Of course, the tiny defiance encouraged her mother to swoop in for another pass. "I see. You must be anxious to have a good dinner, then. Haven't you been eating over at that apartment of yours? You look practically anemic, darling."

Now *that* one made a direct hit. Despite last night's delicious meal at Cross Creek, Emerson's new meds were messing with her system enough to render her appetite useless. On the rare occasion she did work up any actual hunger, she was full after four bites. The drugs had clearly managed to pale her face enough to outline the fatigue beneath her eyes like a beacon, though, and dammit, she was going to have to buy some better concealer.

"Thanks, Mom. You look lovely."

To her surprise, her mother's graceful posture hitched. "I didn't mean . . ." Her mouth pressed into the slightest frown before her expression defaulted back to chilly neutrality. "Why don't we join your father in the living room for a drink? I know he's anxious to see you."

For the life of her, Emerson couldn't picture her iron-fisted father anxious even if the world were about to implode, but the sooner they started this charade, the better. "Sounds great," she said.

Her mother's spine was so straight, her gait so poised and polished, that by the time Emerson had followed her down the hall to the formal living room, she was convinced the hiccup had been a figment of her imagination. Barely anything in the living room had changed, from the elaborate crown molding and the built-in floor-to-ceiling bookshelves to the matching Queen Anne sofa and love seat. Her father sat by the fireplace in his favorite wingback chair, and the sight loosened a memory from deep in Emerson's brain.

"Daddy, I can't remember all the bones in the wrist." The nine-year-old version of herself frowned in her mind's eye, sticking her arm out with a sigh. "The names are too long. I'll never learn them."

Her father took off his reading glasses and closed the medical journal he'd been reading, setting both aside. "What's this word, 'never'? You can do anything, my smart girl. Come on over here. Your daddy will get you all sorted out . . ."

". . . Emerson?" The lift of her mother's voice that clearly indicated a question brought her tumbling back to reality, and Emerson did her best to cover her racing heartbeat at the long-forgotten memory.

"I'm sorry, Mom. I must not have heard you." Lame, but considering the circumstances, it was all she had.

"I asked what you'd like to drink." Her mother gestured to the fully stocked side bar in the living room, and God, she couldn't afford not to pay attention to everything her parents said tonight. How could she have lost her focus so easily?

And more importantly, where the hell had that memory come from?

"Just water for me, please. I've got to work tomorrow."

Her mother poured a highball glass full of ice water and a tumbler with just enough of her father's favorite single malt Scotch to be socially acceptable, delivering both drinks before sitting primly on the sofa. Emerson took the love seat, grateful for the opportunity to give her legs and back a much-needed rest, but her father barely waited until she was settled before cutting right to the chase.

"Your mother and I are certainly glad you managed to find the time to join us. Now that all three of us are finally together, we've got several things to discuss."

Emerson's palms grew slick, and she tightened her fingers on the crystal in her grasp in a supreme effort not to fidget. "Such as?"

Although his voice remained low, her father's icy-blue stare offered no quarter. "I believe we can all stop pretending here, Emerson. For some reason you're refusing to disclose, you've taken it upon yourself to upend both your personal life and your career."

"I still have friends. And a job," she added, punctuating the words with a stare of her own. *Stay cool. Stand your ground.* "I may have made some changes, but nothing's been upended."

Her mother's exasperated exhale was dangerously close to unladylike. "Darling, please. Think about how this looks. Your position with the Lightning. Your move across the country. Your father and I simply want—"

Emerson lifted her free hand, needing to put an end to this conversation before it got any worse. "I know what you want, Mom."

"I'm not certain you do," her father said, the slow finality of his tone rippling down her spine. "These changes of yours have got your mother and me deeply concerned. We think it's time to consider alternate plans."

Just like that, Emerson's warning sensors hit DEFCON One. "Alternate to what?"

"To your current job, of course." Her father straightened against the back of his chair, clearly gaining steam. "I've spoken to Dr. Norris about your qualifications and your experience with the Lightning, and he's agreed to consider making a position available for you on his staff. Of course, there would be an expectation that eventually you'd further your training to become a physician's assistant at the very least. But truly, even though you've lost some time, medical school is by no means out of the question. Becoming an MD would be a process, to be sure, but that's something Dr. Norris fully understands."

No way. No way could she have heard any of this properly. "You . . . you already spoke to Dr. Norris about this?"

Her father placed his glass on the side table at his elbow, straightening his dark-gray suit jacket with authority. "Shifting careers is a delicate process. Getting Dr. Norris's support was the first step."

"I'm sorry," Emerson said, even though she was far from apologetic, "but isn't the first step getting *my* support?"

"I asked you to accompany me to the hospital last weekend." Her mother sniffed, obviously still stung at Emerson's bob and weave on the day of the Watermelon Festival. "It would have been the perfect opportunity for you to see reason."

She scraped in a breath, her pulse beating fast enough to press against her ears in a whoosh of dark anger and white noise. "You mean it would've been the perfect opportunity for you to blindside me in front of Dr. Norris."

"The man is the head of one of the most renowned orthopedics departments in the state," her father said, censure lacing over every word. "Considering your current circumstances, one would think you'd be thrilled he'd even consider taking you on."

Brilliant. The hard-earned career that she loved had just been reduced to a pity fuck. "And what about my 'current circumstances,'"

Emerson asked, slashing air quotes around the phrase. "Did you ever stop to think I might be perfectly happy working here in Millhaven? Did it even cross your mind to ask me how my job with Doc Sanders was going before you made plans on my behalf?"

"Despite your mother's and my efforts, you haven't been here to ask."

"I'm thirty, not thirteen," she shot back, her voice pitching dangerously high. She wasn't the same wide-eyed daughter they'd bullied all the way through adolescence. "You don't get to interfere with my career just because I moved back to town."

A muscle in her father's jaw twitched, a massive show of emotion despite the barely-there move. "Getting you out of this mess you've created is hardly interfering. The chance to fix this won't last forever, Emerson, and contrary to what you seem to believe, there's nothing wrong with a father trying to help his daughter make smart decisions."

Emerson's hands trembled along with her breath, and she lost the battle to steady both. Of course her father wanted to edge his way in and try to *fix* her, to make her right according to his own standards without any regard for her own.

Damage control for the damaged. How fucking appropriate.

And wasn't that all the more reason for her to sweep her brittle, broken pieces under the rug and move the hell on.

Emerson straightened her shoulders, mirroring her father's demeanor right down to the tightly folded fingers resting squarely in his lap. "Going behind my back to engineer a career change I have no interest in making isn't help. I don't want to work for Dr. Norris, and I definitely don't want to go to medical school. I'm fine exactly where I am."

But taking no for an answer had been part of her father's repertoire only once, and he looked anything but eager to go for a repeat.

"I don't understand why you're so intent on being unreasonable," he said, each word more covered in disdain than the one before it.

"Consider your training, your pedigree—your *legacy*, for God's sake. We didn't send you to Swarington just to see you end up in the back room of Ellen Sanders's two-bit practice, taking the scraps from her appointment books. That's simply not good enough."

Emerson's heart pounded in earnest now, so hard she felt nearly dizzy. Anger collided with the deeper pang of sadness in her veins, but still, she managed to cover them both as she lifted her chin and pushed to her feet.

"Maybe not for you, but as far as I'm concerned, it's goddamn perfect. Now if you'll excuse me, I'll be heading home early. Somehow I managed to lose my appetite."

CHAPTER SEVENTEEN

Hunter sat back against his faded couch cushions with ice on his shoulder and an ear-to-ear grin on his face. Although he'd turned on the second game of a baseball doubleheader a couple hours ago, he'd be taking a flier if anyone asked him who was winning, or hell, who was even playing.

The memory of how Emerson had looked when she'd woken up next to him this morning, how they'd split the Sunday paper over breakfast but ended up ditching both for a bunch of deep kisses he could still taste on his tongue, how her hair had tumbled over his pillows in an even combination of sweet and sexy and her mouth formed a perfect smile to match?

Now *that* had his attention.

Haven't you ever wondered what if . . .

A knock sounded off against his front door, delivering Hunter back to his cottage with a swift dose of what-the-hell. Barring anything unnatural—or, okay, *very* natural, as in, of the disaster variety—Hunter, his brothers, and their father had Sundays off while a skeleton crew of farmhands cared for the livestock on the back half of Cross Creek's property. Even during daylight hours, which at this point were quickly surrendering to dusk, company on this side of the farm was rare at best.

Then again, he hadn't answered either of his brothers' texts (Owen's being *What's up with you and Emerson? And don't insult me by saying work.* And Eli's less decorous but equally nosy *Look at you with the hot girl! Call me with deets, jackass!*), so one of them had probably decided to come out to give him a proper load of good-natured ribbing.

Hunter tugged the ice pack off his shoulder and pushed to his feet. Taking the dozen or so necessary steps to cover the ground between his couch and the front door to his cottage, he broke out a smile as he braced for brotherly impact. He twisted the doorknob and tugged the door wide on its hinges, but the person standing in front of him wasn't Owen, and it also wasn't Eli.

She was, however, the last person he'd expected to see on his doorstep.

"Emerson?" Hunter blinked, half certain his eyes were playing a mischievous trick on him in the deepening shadows. It was definitely her, though, with a nervous smile on her lips and a classy black dress hugging her curves just enough to make his pulse sit up and take notice.

"Hey. I'm sorry for coming by without calling," she said, but he shook his head, waving off the idea.

"No apologies. With cell service around here, it probably wouldn't have done you any good until you were in the front yard, anyway." Hunter aimed for a neutral expression even though his head was brimming over with a three-to-one ratio of curiosity to concern. "Come on in."

"Thanks." Emerson's heels sent an elegant clack-clack-clack over the floorboards as she followed him inside, the sound stopping short as they reached the living room. "I hope I'm not interrupting anything."

"Just a whole lot of channel surfing," he said, reaching for the remote to turn off the TV. "I didn't think I'd see you until our PT session tomorrow. Not that I mind." He lifted a hand to reassure her, because, really, that dress was starting to give him some seriously impure thoughts. "But is everything alright?"

"Oh yeah, everything's great. I just . . ." A self-deprecating laugh slipped past her lips, but she didn't shy away from his gaze. "Actually, I'm full of crap. I went to dinner at my parents' house, and the whole thing was pretty much a nightmare."

Ah hell. That explained the dress. Along with all the emotions swirling in her eyes like a bright-blue storm. But if Emerson's evening had already been rough, a raft of irritating questions wouldn't improve her mood, and Hunter knew far better than to coddle her with a bunch of overblown sympathy. Even if he *did* want to help.

"That bad, huh?"

She nodded, although she didn't lower her gaze or shy away from the question. "Did I mention that 'nightmare' was kind of a euphemism? I left before the first course."

"Ouch." There was no helping his wince, or the squeeze in his gut that accompanied it. "I'd say that definitely qualifies as pretty shitty. Do you want a beer to drown your troubles?"

"Thanks, but no."

"How about some dinner?" He'd thrown back some leftovers a little while ago, but if she'd skipped out on the meal at her parents' place, she was probably hungry.

But Emerson just shook her head. "I'm okay."

Hunter paused. "You want to talk about what happened with your parents?"

"God, no."

All at once, he registered the flush riding high on her cheeks, the ever-so-slight smile shaping the bow of her mouth, and the step he took toward her was pure instinct. "Then what do you want?"

The emotion in her eyes shifted, turning into unmistakable desire. "Just you, Hunter. Right now, all I want is you."

He didn't wait, didn't think. He just moved, bending to claim Emerson's mouth with his. The sigh that escaped from her vibrated with need against his lips, and *fuck*, Hunter felt it everywhere. Cupping her face with both hands to keep her close, he coaxed her lips apart, tasting his way into her mouth. Her palms flattened over his biceps, but for only a second before she curled her fingers to clutch the edges of his T-shirt, and the sweet scrape of her nails on his skin pushed him to kiss her even harder.

Emerson met his every move. Darting her tongue past her lips, she explored his mouth, licking some spots while sucking on others. His cock throbbed, growing harder with every ministration, and she rode the sensitive skin of his lower lip with the edge of her teeth until he was sure he'd come right out of his skin.

"Emerson." Hunter tightened his fingers on the hot silk of her skin, thrusting them back into the tidy knot at her nape. Emerson's hair unraveled over her shoulders, filling the air with the sweet, heady scent of honeysuckle, and she pulled back to pin him with a glittering stare.

"Do you remember what you said to me yesterday in bed?" She paused to run two fingers over her kiss-swollen mouth, sending his breath even faster through his lungs. "About how you'd like it if I took charge?"

Wild, wicked thoughts flashed through his mind. "Yeah," Hunter grated, his legs fast-tracking toward a labor strike as he watched her index finger slide past her lips.

"Good." Emerson dropped her hand, reaching beneath her opposite arm to lower the zipper on the side of her dress. The black fabric loosened around her lean frame, and a few well-executed dips of her shoulders sent the whole thing pooling to the floorboards.

She stepped out of both the dress and her shoes, standing in front of him in the soft glow of light filtering in from the open foyer. While her dress had been tastefully pretty—downright demure, even—her bra and panties were the polar opposite, just sheer scraps of material held together by nothing more than ribbons and luck. The inky lace cradled her pale skin, surrendering to the curve of her breasts and the sweet, soft indent between her thighs, and even though Hunter knew he was staring outright, he couldn't make himself stop or look away or even blink.

Holy shit, Emerson was so gorgeous, it hurt.

Something he couldn't identify flickered through her eyes, there and then gone. Then she closed the space between them, pressing a kiss over his mouth before leading him a few steps away to the couch. Wordlessly, she reached down for the hem of his T-shirt, lifting the cotton over his head with a seamless pull.

"Did you know I watched last night when you put your mouth on me?" she asked, the question sending a bolt of shock past Hunter's want-fueled haze.

"You did?" he managed, and wasn't that just every kind of hot in the book.

Emerson nodded. "In the mirror. I watched everything. The way you kissed me. How you used your tongue to make me come."

His heart slammed against his rib cage, his cock titanium hard. "And did you like watching?"

"Yes. But that's not all I like."

Splaying her hands over her shoulders, she guided him to the couch cushions with a push, but it wasn't until she lowered her body to kneel between his knees that he put one and one together to come up with the sum of *oh fuck yes*.

"Emerson." Her name was a prayer in his mouth, sweet and needful.

She answered with a turn of her wrist, freeing the button at the top of his jeans. "Hunter."

The impulse to pleasure her rolled through his chest, warring with the want burning deep in his belly. "You're making me"—the slide of Emerson's fingers on his cock stopped the breath in his lungs, and there went his zipper—"crazy, here."

"You're making me crazy, too. But I won't hold back if you don't."

Powerless to do anything else, Hunter lifted his hips to let her lower his jeans and boxer briefs. His cock sprang free, and she captured him in one hand while wrapping the other around his waist. The friction of her fingers directly on his skin made his balls go tight and his brain go numb.

Then she replaced her fingers with her mouth, and he lost what little was left of his goddamn mind.

"Oh fuck." Hunter's breath tore from his throat on a hard exhale. Emerson's lips tilted into a smile, but she didn't slow her movements. She edged her tongue over the crown of his cock, just a feather-light swirl of hot, wet heat, and it took every last ounce of his restraint not to buck off the cushions to thrust into her mouth.

"Mmm." As if sensing his raw need for more, she circled her fingers around his length, pumping her hand in a firm glide as she kept the strokes from her tongue soft. The opposing sensations combined to send sparks through Hunter's blood, and even though part of him was tempted to close his eyes and lose himself in the feel of her working his cock with both her mouth and her hand, he didn't. Instead, he dropped his chin to fix his gaze directly on Emerson.

Flame-colored hair wild over one shoulder. Glossy pearls clasped around her neck, bound by a satiny black ribbon. Skin flushed. Lips parted. Up and down. Over. And over.

He wasn't going to make it.

"Em." There was really no delicate way to put the thought stampeding through his brain, but they were a bit past the pleasantries stage, so he said, "If you don't stop, *I'm* not going to be able to stop."

Emerson pulled back just far enough to look up, her eyes blazing dark blue. "I came here because I wanted you, Hunter. All of you. I don't want you to stop."

She parted her lips back over him before he could answer, and Hunter was lost. The pressure of her mouth and the sensual sight of her kneeling between his legs took over his senses. She sucked and stroked, bringing his restraint to the tipping point. Release drove up from the base of his spine, wicked and insistent, and he didn't fight it. Knotting his fingers in Emerson's hair, Hunter gave in, each wave of pleasure more intense than the one before it. She took all he had to give, slowly scaling back her touches until she parted from his body with a smile.

"Come here," he grated, not waiting for her to respond before pushing forward to pull her close. Emerson let out a squeak of surprise as Hunter hooked his hands around her rib cage, guiding her to standing before righting his jeans with a rough yank.

"Where are we going?" she asked, half laughter, half gasp.

But his answer was all serious. "Right"—he paused just long enough to walk her backward to the small expanse on the wall leading to the kitchen, firmly pushing her shoulders against the space—"here."

Emerson shivered, tiny goose bumps spreading over her arms. "Oh. You don't want to go upstairs?"

"No." His body might need a minute to get back on track, but his brain screamed with a deep-seated urge to make her come. He didn't want to wait, not even the thirty seconds it would take for them to get upstairs. Caging her body with his, Hunter dropped his mouth to her neck, trailing a line of open-mouthed kisses over her skin.

"Hunter." Her voice was gravel and velvet all at once, but he didn't stop the path of his lips.

"You said you wanted all of me, right?" His mouth hovered just over her breastbone, desire pumping full-bore through his body at her heavily lidded stare.

Emerson nodded. "Yes."

Hunter's heart sped even faster as he knelt in front of her, and Christ, he'd never seen anything so perfect. "Then take it." He slid his tongue up the soft line of her inner thigh for an impulsive, teasing taste. "All of it."

Her knees parted, and the wordless reply was all Hunter needed. Reaching out, he anchored one hand on Emerson's waist, using the other to palm the swell of her ass. The move brought her lace-covered sex directly into his line of sight, and he traced the seam of her body with one finger. Her moan drove him to repeat the glide, the fabric growing easily damp at the sweet spot directly between her thighs.

Want began regathering low in his belly, but still, Hunter focused on Emerson—the catch in her breath, the sexy scent of her skin so close as he worked her over the thin cover of her panties. Keeping his grip on her waist, he let his thumb drift up to stroke her clit, and the sound coming out of her throat nearly wrecked him.

"You like this?" Hunter pressed again, slow and deliberate.

"Yes. *Please*, yes."

Emerson's hair swished over her shoulders with her nod. Reaching down, she tugged at the ribbons riding each hip, and the swath of lace fell away from her body. Her stance opened freely, revealing just enough of her sex to make his cock stir. Hunter knew he should take his time, go slowly and build up her orgasm, breath by breath. But something hot and primal refused to let him, and instead, he covered her sex with a relentless push of his tongue.

"Ohhhh," Emerson moaned, tilting her hips against the spot where they joined. God, she was flawless, wet and wanting and so damn pretty that he couldn't hold back. He kissed her with brash, bold strokes of his tongue, holding nothing back. She answered his movements with eager thrusts of her hips, her gasps filling the room. Fueled by the dark, right-now urge to make her come, Hunter released her waist to bury a finger deep inside her sex.

Yes. Oh hell *yes.* The cry that crossed her lips brought him all the way back to full arousal. Still, despite the fact that his cock wanted to switch places with his mouth in the worst possible way, he didn't stop.

Emerson didn't, either. She pressed her shoulders into the wall behind her, her back bowing toward him as she chased his fingers and mouth.

"Hunter. I . . . I . . ." The wet heat of her sex tightened. Hunter swept his tongue over her, once, then once again even harder, and her tremble began from deep inside. She arched up on a moan, her body clasping his finger in waves of release. Each one turned him on even more than the one before it, and he held Emerson close until she went loose against his touch.

The need pulsing through him grew into a demand so hot, he stood just long enough to guide Emerson to the floor.

Her eyes flew wide in the dusky shadows. "You want to do this here?"

"I don't want to wait," Hunter corrected. He grabbed his wallet from the back pocket of his jeans, pausing just long enough to take out his emergency condom before letting his clothes hit the floor. Kneeling between Emerson's knees, he rolled on the condom and ran his palms over her thighs, intent on removing the slight space between them.

She beat him to the punch, though, tilting her hips forward to create a brush of intimate contact, and Hunter cut out a harsh exhale.

"Jesus, that is hot."

"It gets hotter," she said, repeating the seductive slide to angle her body right where he ached to be most. "Come find out how much."

He pushed inside of her in one swift stroke. The sweet, slick pressure of her sex gripping his cock nearly knocked the breath from his lungs. Hunter took a second to acclimate, his hands finding the flare of Emerson's hips. Shifting to his knees, he started to move, guiding her close as he thrust slowly into her. They explored different rhythms—deep and drawn out, faster and harder—and each one dared him for more. He watched her body in the soft light, her lean inner thigh muscles flexing, the press of her berry-colored nipples against the black lacy bra that still cradled her breasts. Everything about her was wide open and sensual, so perfect that he couldn't hold back.

Hunter angled forward to take her deeper, eliminating any space between them. Emerson rocked beneath him, anyway, riding his cock with want-soaked sighs, until finally she went bowstring tight on a cry. The sight of her release sent an unexpected shot of pleasure coiling up from some deep, hidden spot in his body, and it built with speed that shocked him. Hunter clutched her hips, curling his fingers into her skin in search of more. Despite the growing intensity of his movements, Emerson stayed right there with him, thrust for thrust and moan for moan, until finally, the climax whispering through him became a shout.

"Em." He came with a guttural exhale, his cock buried deep in her sex. For long seconds that might have been minutes or months or forever, as far as Hunter knew, they lay joined in a tangle of sweat-slicked limbs, with nothing between them but quiet. He left her just long enough for a quick trip to the bathroom to clean up, and when he returned, he covered her shoulders with the blanket he kept draped over the back of the couch.

"Hey. You ready for that trip upstairs now?"

Emerson's lips parted in shock. "Are you serious?"

Hunter laughed, pulling her close. She turned him on like nothing else, and he liked to think he had some moderately good stamina, but he wasn't frickin' Superman. "Very. But I was thinking more along the lines of using the bed for its primary function. For now," he added, because hey, he might be spent, but he *was* still a guy.

"Oh." Her laughter spooled around his, and man, the sound was sweet in his ears. "Well, with an offer that good, I suppose I can't refuse."

Emerson linked her fingers through his, holding on tight as he led her to bed.

CHAPTER EIGHTEEN

Emerson lay on her back, staring at the play of moonlit shadows on Hunter's ceiling. Rationally, she knew she should close her eyes and get some sleep. Although it wasn't particularly late, she *was* particularly tired, and the last two days—or more specifically, the last two nights—had put a major dent in her energy reserves. But every time she tried to drift off in the warm quiet of Hunter's room, her brain overrode her body, refusing to let her rest.

Just you, Hunter. Right now, all I want is you.

After the showdown with her parents, Emerson had carved a direct path to her car with every intention of double-scooping herself through some triple-fudge therapy. She got halfway back to her apartment when she realized she wasn't headed to her apartment at all.

She'd been on her way to Hunter's. She'd needed comfort, and what she'd wanted was him.

Emerson hadn't just wanted to sleep with him, although at first, she'd thought it had been exactly that—the urge to lose herself in something she knew would feel good, something that would make her forget. As soon as she'd seen him on the doorstep, though, with that crooked smile and those ridiculously blue eyes that had always been able to see everything about her, Emerson understood that what she wanted wasn't to get lost.

She'd wanted to be found.

"You look like you're having some pretty deep thoughts over there," Hunter said, bringing her back to the room with a whisper. "Either that or you sleep with your eyes open and I'm having a really awkward conversation with myself."

Any vulnerability she wanted to feel at the way he'd caught her so lost in thought fell prey to the laughter bubbling up from her chest.

"No, I'm awake."

"Penny for your thoughts." He shifted to his back in the shadows so their bodies were lined up side to side, and the enticing warmth of his skin against hers put another dent in Emerson's armor.

"You do realize you're not even wearing pants," she said, and okay, maybe she wasn't quite ready to lower her guard all the way.

Hunter didn't get pushy about it, but he also didn't let her slide. "I'll owe you. So what's on your mind? Are you upset about what happened at your parents' house?"

"A little." Her heart fluttered against her rib cage, and she took a deep breath, trying to tamp down the sensation. But Emerson's pulse only rushed faster, reminding her how heavy the truth was.

Head up, eyes forward. Head up . . . head up . . .

Hunter reached out, his hand finding hers under the covers. "Talk to me, Em. Tell me what's going on. Let me help you."

Her defenses gave one last kick. "You can't."

"Try me."

He tightened his grasp, his fingers so warm and safe and frighteningly good around hers, and the words shot right from her mouth. "I have multiple sclerosis."

Hunter's body tensed beside her, his head turning sharply in the shadows. "You . . . what?"

For one ridiculous second, Emerson nearly recanted. But God, she was so tired of holding it in, of holding it together, that all the emotions she'd stuffed down since her diagnosis just came rushing up from her chest.

"I have MS," she said, the words sounding small and scared in her ears, and God, wasn't that just one more reason to hate them?

"Jesus, Em." He turned to his side to fully face her in the shadows, and Emerson braced herself for the onslaught of oh-poor-broken-you that would surely follow.

Only it didn't.

Hunter kept his hand wrapped firmly around hers, although shock still took firm possession of his face. "Does it . . . are you in pain?"

She cleared her throat in a last-ditch effort to stay strong. *Keep it clinical. You can do this.* "There are a few different types of the disease. I have what's called relapsing-remitting MS, which in layman's terms means my symptoms come and go. Most days I'm just tired, but sometimes it's . . ." *Painful. Scary. Soul sucking.* "More complicated."

"Your symptoms," he said slowly, and God, of course he wouldn't know the signs and symptoms of MS. Hell, even she had blown them off for months, labeling each one as all sorts of normal-person ailments until they'd become too front and center to ignore.

"Multiple sclerosis can affect people in different ways, so there are potentially quite a few." Emerson bit her tongue to keep the laundry list of possible symptoms to herself. She might have copped to having the disease, but phrases like *tremors, slurred speech*, and the ever-sexy *bladder and bowel incontinence* just weren't on her share list. Her body was already irreparably damaged. No need for her pride to follow suit.

After all, now that Hunter knew she had a chronic illness, he probably thought she was broken enough, thanks.

Taking a deep breath, she picked through her words and continued. "Mostly, I knew something was wrong when I couldn't shake my achy legs and fatigue. I blamed it on the busy football season at first—the

Lightning went deep into the playoffs last season, and my job isn't exactly hands off. But then my legs started to tingle, too, and sometimes one would go numb without warning, and I knew there was a bigger problem. The team's neurologist did a full battery of tests including an MRI, and that's how I ended up with the official diagnosis."

"Aw hell, Em." Hunter's voice pitched low with restrained emotion. "I don't know what to say. I wish I had . . ." All at once, he froze beside her. "Your back pain has nothing to do with moving boxes, does it? God dammit, I just had you pinned to the floor downstairs."

Emerson's heart catapulted against her breastbone, and she lasered her stare to the ceiling to hide the idiot tears that had formed at his words. "I'm *fine*. The symptoms aren't exactly a party, but I can handle them. The disease isn't going to break me." Not yet, anyway. And sure as hell not in front of anybody.

"I'm sorry," he said, the rustle of movement and the rasp that followed suggesting he'd scrubbed a hand over his face. "I'm just . . . I would never hurt you."

The words caught her right in the throat, but she couldn't let her weakness show. "I know," she whispered, and oh, how she wanted to just lean into the safety net of his arms and forget everything else. "But you didn't. In fact, the only time I feel normal is when I'm with you."

For a minute, all he did was stroke his thumb over her hand, having never broken the contact between their fingers. Then he asked, "How long have you known?"

Good. More facts. Quantifiable things that had nothing to do with how small and fragile this stupid disease made her feel. "I found out officially eight weeks ago, but I've known something wasn't right for about six months. MS can take awhile to diagnose, and the Lightning's team doctor wanted to be sure."

"Wait . . ." Hunter paused, clearly clicking the truth together piece by piece. "That's why you moved back to Millhaven, isn't it? It's why you needed a change of pace."

She nodded despite her clattering pulse. "Yes. I loved my job with the Lightning and I didn't want to leave, but the workload in sports medicine is high volume, higher intensity. I learned pretty quickly that I wasn't going to be able to keep up. All the positions I could find in other practices had similar work schedules."

He let out a breath, his realization obvious even in the near dark. "Except one."

"Except one," Emerson agreed. At this point, there was no reason not to admit the whole truth about why she'd returned. "Doc Sanders thought expanding her general practice to include a therapy center would be a great help to some of her patients, and she already had the space. Coming back to Millhaven was the only chance I had to keep working while I figure out how to manage my symptoms, so that's what I did."

Hunter leaned in to brush a kiss over the crown of her head, his exhale warm in her hair. For seconds that turned into minutes, he remained quiet, until finally he said, "I may be overstepping my bounds here, but you were pretty upset about dinner with your parents. I get that you've had differences in the past, but are they really so unsupportive of you considering all of this?"

Emerson flinched. But he hadn't been wrong about her being upset over what had gone down at her parents' house, and what's more, this part of their conversation was inevitable now that she'd told him the truth about her diagnosis.

"I don't know," she said. "I haven't told them."

Hunter's shock arrived on a delayed reaction, as if she'd been speaking a foreign language and he'd needed to translate the words. "Your parents don't know you have MS?"

"No." The thought sent a shiver from the back of her neck all the way down her spine. "And I'm not telling them. I'm not telling anyone."

His surprise went for an obvious round two. "Doc Sanders doesn't know, either?"

"Nobody knows but you, and that's the way it has to stay. I might not be throwing all my personal details on the table for the whole town to see, but I never lied to you or anyone else about why I came back to Millhaven. I needed a change of pace, and I came here to work. That's exactly what I plan to do."

"So you want to just move on and forget you've got MS?"

Oh, if only. "I work in the medical field, so I know the score. Multiple sclerosis is a serious disease, and as much as I hate the diagnosis, I'm also not blowing it off. I have a neurologist in Lockridge, and we're working together to find the best course of meds to treat my symptoms and any flare-ups I might have."

Hunter paused, the moonlight peeking in past the window offering a brief glimpse of his narrowing stare. "Why are you going all the way to Lockridge? The drive must take, what? An hour and a half each way? Camden Valley is a bigger hospital, and a hell of a lot closer on top of it."

"Because my father is the chief of surgery and my mother is on the board at CVH, not to mention half a dozen hospital committees there. Yes, the specifics of my medical privacy are protected," Emerson added, because even not even the highest of Camden Valley's higher-ups outranked old Hippocrates. "But the place is teeming with people who know my parents."

She might have been gone for a while, but she still knew all too well how things worked. The docs, especially the ones with prestigious positions, all talked. It would take only one person to see her in the hospital hallways or the waiting room in neurology and make mention of it to her parents, and bam. They would be on her like a linebacker on a loose football, trying to take charge by cashing in "favors" and expressing their opinions with no regard for her own.

"Isn't Camden Valley Hospital also teeming with people who can help you, though?" Hunter asked, and his question arrived with such a surprising lack of judgment that her reply popped right out.

"CVH has an excellent reputation, yes. Maybe a little *too* excellent."

"I'm sorry," he said. "Now you've really lost me."

Emerson's stomach knotted with dread, but she didn't hold back. Turning toward him, she replayed the dinner conversation between her and her parents, complete with their renewed disdain for her career choice and her father's over-the-line discussion with Dr. Norris. The cover of near darkness in Hunter's bedroom combined with the warmth of his body so close to hers, making it all too easy to let the story spill out. Although she stuck mostly to the facts, her voice gave up a traitorous wobble when she got to her father's parting shot, and Hunter tensed beside her.

"I think your father needs to learn a thing or two about what's good enough," he bit out, each word sharp and serrated despite the low growl of his voice.

Something Emerson couldn't pin with a name turned over, deep in her belly. "So you see why I can't tell them. My parents already want to use the fact that I've moved back to Millhaven as a means of control. If they find out I have MS, they'll try to micromanage my life down to the color of my socks, and I'm already tired enough."

"Okay," Hunter said, reaching out to tuck her hair behind her ear, and she felt the comfort of his touch all the way to her toes. "I guess I can see why telling your parents would be complicated. But keeping your diagnosis a complete secret is a hell of a burden, Em. Doc Sanders is trustworthy, not to mention a medical professional, and Daisy is your friend. They might be able to help you carry some of the weight, you know?"

Panic knifed through her, making her heartbeat rattle and her breath jam against her lungs. "No," Emerson managed. God, she needed to get a handle on this and shut down the suggestion before it took root. "I can't tell anyone, Hunter. I mean it. No one."

"Emerson—"

"No." She cut his whisper to the quick. "I know you're trying to fix this, and I appreciate the sentiment. I do. But the more people who know I have MS, the greater the chances my parents could find out, and I can't take the risk, however small. Plus . . ."

Shit. *Shit*. All these unchecked emotions were seriously addling her brain.

Of course, Hunter hadn't missed her single-syllable slip. "Plus what?"

Emerson closed her eyes to add to the cover of darkness around her. "I'm starting a brand-new physical therapy practice from scratch, in a town where trust is everything. How am I supposed to convince people I'm good enough to take care of their health when my own body has failed me? No one will believe I can take care of their body if they think I can't even get mine to work right. I can't let them see this."

Hunter tensed, his muscles going tight against her skin. "It's not your fault you have MS, and it damn sure doesn't make you any less of a physical therapist," he said, adamant. "I'm walking, talking proof that you're incredible at your job."

"But not everyone will see it that way," she argued, equally hot. "Yes, despite my symptoms, I'm perfectly fine to work with clients." No matter how much she wanted to forget she had MS and move on with her life, she would never put anyone's health at risk. "But working for Doc Sanders is my only option, Hunter. I can't take a chance—*any* chance—that would jeopardize my practice here. It's all I have. If I can't convince people I'm good enough to take care of them, if I can't do what I love, then I have nothing. You have to promise not to tell anyone I have MS."

He paused for a few seconds, each of which lasted a month. "Okay. I promise not to tell anyone. But you have more than nothing."

She stared at him, wide-eyed, the intensity of his voice slicing through the dark to land in the deepest, most vulnerable part of her. "I do?"

Hunter didn't hesitate. Closing the sliver of space that remained between them, he pulled her close, brushing his lips over hers. "You do."

"Please," she whispered, unable to keep the emotion from rushing out of her chest and into her words. But God, with his arms locked around her and holding her tight, she almost believed she was normal. "Just for tonight, please don't let go."

"Don't worry. I've got you, Em. I won't let go."

As he settled against the bedsheets with her nestled in close, Emerson realized that when she was in Hunter's arms, she didn't just feel normal.

For the first time she could remember, she felt whole.

CHAPTER NINETEEN

Hunter rocked back on the heels of his Red Wings, unable to keep his smile stuffed down as he surveyed the plants in front of him in the greenhouse. Since Emerson had insisted on doing a few hours of marketing research a day for Cross Creek, his old man had insisted with equal fervor that they load her up with as much produce as she could handle. She and Hunter had established a comfortable pattern, where the two of them would complete his PT session in the morning, then she'd come by the farm at about three every afternoon and hole up in the office with him to work.

And as soon as they'd call it quits for the day, they'd go back to his cottage together, where they'd hole up for something decidedly better and not come out until morning.

He plucked a red bell pepper from the tangle of velvety vines at his hip and dropped it carefully into one of the two half-bushel baskets looped over his palm. Six days had passed since Emerson had told him she had multiple sclerosis, and for six days, they hadn't touched the topic again. The tired lines under her eyes and her sudden hitches in movement made a whole lot more sense with the knowledge, although Hunter hated her discomfort now more than ever. He got that Emerson was tough—she had been since the second he'd met her—but according to the reading he'd done online, MS could sap the energy out of even the most determined people.

The fact that Emerson also seemed hell-bent on hiding her illness as much as possible? Yeah, that couldn't be making things any less daunting for her in the stress department.

Hell if Hunter didn't hate that even more than the lines around her eyes.

The rumble of a throat being cleared dumped him right back to the humid, earthy air of the greenhouse, and his chin snapped up just in time to catch his younger brother catching *him* lost in thought.

"You'd better not let your girlfriend see you hauling that stuff around," Eli said, a grin tugging at the corners of his smart mouth as he sauntered up the row across from Hunter. "Emerson's got a pretty face, but man, I'd hate to be on the business end of her irritation, and you still have a whole week of PT to go."

Hunter's pulse thumped with a steady stream of *hey now*, and he dialed up his most casual expression to counter it. "They're half-bushel baskets, smart-ass. Each one will weigh barely ten pounds, even after I fill 'em to the top." Still, he swung a casual look-see over his surroundings to make sure Emerson hadn't detoured her way down here from the main house, because even though he'd nearly completed his PT, Eli wasn't wrong about the iron fist lurking beneath all that velvet. "And by the way, she's not my girlfriend."

"Dude." Eli's snort couldn't be labeled as anything other than a challenge. "What do we do for a living?"

Talk about a random frickin' question. But since Hunter was looking for a one-way trip off the topic, he'd bite. "We're farmers. Although you part-time as a total pain in the ass," he said, smiling to remove any sting the words might otherwise carry.

Eli's smile in return translated to a nonverbal *message received*. "Thank you. We're farmers, which means I can smell bullshit from miles away. This close?" He lifted a work-gloved finger, drawing an imaginary circle to encompass them both. "You reek, man."

"He reeks of what?" Owen asked, crossing the threshold to the greenhouse, and fucking great. The only thing worse than his brothers ganging up on each other was them joining forces to gang up on him.

"Bullshit," Eli said with a little too much glee.

"Huh." Owen's shoulders lifted slightly in surprise. "That's not your usual go-to, Hunt. What's Eli calling you on?"

Hunter tried like hell to think of soil composition ratios or changing out spare tractor parts, or anything status quo enough to keep his expression from breaking into the moronic grin that always seemed to commandeer his face whenever he thought of Emerson. But the harder he fought, the harder the urge to get toothy fought back, and to hell with it.

Hunter let the expression loose. "All I said was that Emerson's not my girlfriend."

Owen's sardonic laughter echoed around the glass-walled confines of the greenhouse. "Sorry, bro. I don't say this too often—or, okay, ever—but I've gotta go with Eli on this one."

Ignoring the dig, along with the way Eli's mouth pressed into a thin, pale line in response to it, Hunter reached out to liberate a pair of Cherokee Purple tomatoes, setting them in the basket next to the bell pepper. "I'm not saying there's nothing there, but it's casual. Emerson and I are just spending time together, seeing where things go."

"Uh-huh," Owen said, rummaging through the thick emerald-green vines snaking over the planter box in front of him, gently snapping three of the prettiest cucumbers from their moorings. "You two are totally casual. And I'm making spaghetti and meatballs for shits and giggles."

"Wait." Eli took a step back over the packed dirt, his gaze tapering in confusion at the mention of Owen's family-famous signature dish.

"I thought Hunter was the one getting laid. Who are you trying to impress?"

Owen handed over the produce and sank a thumb into the belt loop of his Wranglers. "Nobody. Hunter asked me to make it."

Both of his brothers lifted their eyebrows high enough that ignoring them wasn't an option. Sadly. "Don't lose your minds," Hunter said. "I had a hankering for Italian. That's all."

Of course he couldn't say that what he'd really wanted was to make sure Emerson ate a decent meal. She'd made mention the other day that her new preventive meds had been making her appetite all wonky, but still, she needed to eat. She definitely liked their tomatoes; plus, despite Eli's ribbing about Owen's culinary skills, their older brother's homemade sauce was off the chain. Cashing in a favor with Owen for the spaghetti and meatballs had seemed like a win-win.

Eli laughed. "Something tells me your hankering is for the redhead keeping Dad company back at the house, but whatever you say, Mr. Casual. I'll go grab some spinach and arugula for the salad, since apparently dinner's fancy."

For a second, Hunter considered jawing back. But he wanted more crap from Eli about as much as he wanted a root canal on his nuts, and what's more, he couldn't deny the bigger truth.

He *did* want Emerson. Not just in his bed, but in his life.

"Yeah, yeah," Hunter murmured, watching Eli whistle his way down the row toward the greens. He and Owen joined forces to make quick work of their last chore, and after gathering enough produce for Emerson's CSA share as well as the salad that would ride shotgun with their family dinner, the three of them started out for the main house.

Although this week's weather had offered a brief reprieve by way of two days in the high eighties rather than mid-nineties and one rain shower that lasted about as long as Hunter's morning shower, today had been another merciless scorcher. Even though the walk wasn't terribly long or terribly taxing under normal circumstances, a heavy sheen of sweat had formed beneath the brim of Hunter's baseball hat by the time his boots thumped over the back porch boards.

"Damn." Owen squinted across the sun-parched fields behind the main house. "It's so dry, pretty soon the trees are gonna start bribing the dogs."

Hunter fit just enough of a smile over his unease to keep things nice and easy. "Weather forecast is calling for rain early next week. Hopefully Mother Nature will do us a solid and make good on ending this heat wave, once and for all."

Following Owen over the laundry-room threshold, Hunter handed off the baskets of produce, exhaling in relief at the blast of cool air pumping from the vents. But then he covered the floor tiles to slide a gaze into the kitchen, and it wasn't the change in temperature sending a hard ripple up his spine.

Emerson stood at the oversized island, her hair pulled into a loose knot on the crown of her head and her laptop propped open over the butcher block. His father stood directly beside her, his sun-burnished forehead creased in concentration beneath the brim of his Stetson as she gestured to the screen. She leaned forward, pushing back a few wisps of hair that had broken free to frame her face, and her movements were so fluid, the look on her face so purely happy, that Hunter's chest tightened by default.

Of the thousand different ways he felt about her right now, casual wasn't on the list.

"Oh, hey!" Emerson looked up, her blue eyes crinkling at the edges as her smile became a grin, and dammit, if Hunter couldn't manage an inhale soon, he was liable to keel over like a fucking idiot. "I was just showing your father how Twitter works."

Eli barked out a laugh from where he stood at the kitchen sink. "Seriously?"

"Yes, seriously." She arched a brow with just enough and-I-mean-it to make Eli lift his soapy hands in concession, and her smile returned in full force. "He's a natural."

Their father's sandpaper laugh was more amusement than argument, but still, he said, "And you, darlin', have a way of spinning the truth to make it look pretty."

"No matter how I spin it, it's still the truth," Emerson said, squeezing the old man's shoulder. "But the four of you must be starving after working in all that heat today. Can I help with dinner?"

"Nope." Finally, Hunter found his wits. "In fact, if you two want to keep your tutorial going for a little while longer, you can go ahead and take a load off at the table there. Then I can just help Owen and Eli get the rest of the meal set."

Emerson opened her mouth, presumably to argue, but then her eyes flickered over the spot where his father stood beside her, and she nodded slowly. "Looks like you're not off the hook with hashtags and retweets quite yet, Mr. Cross."

"Well, then, by all means, let's get to it," his father said, moving toward the table and hooking a weathered hand beneath one of the ladder-back chairs to hold it out for her.

Hunter sent up a silent prayer of thanks that neither one of them had pushed back. After a quick wash and chop of the salad greens and a trip through the broiler for the loaf of garlic bread he'd grabbed that morning when he and Owen had manned Cross Creek's tent at the farmers' market, dinner was as ready as it was going to get, and after setting the table and gathering around it for grace, they were as ready as they were going to get to dig in.

Emerson smoothed a napkin over her lap, giving her stomach an appreciative rub over her dark-blue T-shirt. "Dinner smells fantastic, Owen. Spaghetti and meatballs are my favorite," she said, prompting a pair of grins from Hunter's brothers that told him he'd never hear the end of making the special request.

"Oh really?" Owen asked, passing her the oversized serving bowl full of pasta. "I didn't know that."

"Mmhmm," she said, smiling as she filled her plate. "I was just telling Hunter how I haven't had really good Italian food in ages. Kind of a lucky coincidence that you made it for dinner, actually."

"That *is* lucky," Eli said, covering his laughter with a poorly constructed cough, and truly, Hunter didn't know whether to laugh along with his brothers or murder the both of them in their sleep.

Thankfully, Emerson took their obvious back and forth in stride. "Well, thanks for letting me crash your dinner again."

Hunter's father handed over the salad, his smile easy despite the grueling week Hunter knew he'd had. "Ah, I told you last week, darlin'. You're always welcome at Cross Creek."

Unable to help himself, Hunter slid a covert wink in her direction, loving every second of the soft-pink flush the gesture sent over her cheeks.

"You do pretty the place up," Eli agreed, and Owen added his two cents with a nod.

"That's for sure. Plus, you're part of the crew now."

Hunter lifted a square of butter-gold garlic bread off the serving plate in front of him, a thread of excitement sparking in his belly at the mention of the work Emerson had done for Cross Creek. "Speaking of which, the four of us got fairly well caught up on operations when we were out in the south fields earlier today, so why don't you bring everyone up to speed on some of the marketing particulars you've turned up this week?"

"Okay, sure," she said. "The good news is, you've got a lot of free or low-cost options available that have virtually limitless reach. My friend turned me on to a couple of online webinars detailing the basics on how to use social media to make your business stand out, and she also suggested starting a monthly e-mail newsletter to let people know what's in season and what sort of on-site events you'll be offering, like pick-your-own crops in the summer or the corn maze in the fall."

Eli paused, a huge forkful of spaghetti halfway to his lips. "Hey, that's pretty smart. Like a regular reminder that we're out here."

"Exactly." Emerson nodded for emphasis, her hair shining red-gold in the evening sunlight still streaming in through the windows behind her. "There are services you can use to manage your lists and distribute the newsletters each month."

"The services are well within our marketing budget. I already checked," Hunter said, and Owen closed his halfway-open mouth in favor of a wry smile.

"Okay, then," he replied. "How about the webinar stuff?"

Emerson took the salad bowl from Eli, murmuring a soft "thank you" before tackling Owen's question. "The class gave some great basics on advertising. Hunter and I have already put some generic posts on Cross Creek's social media accounts, and there was an increase in the number of both hits to your website and CSA orders this week. The ins and outs of each social media site differ, but they sure seem to get the word out once you tailor things to your target audience, and they're not too difficult to navigate once you get the hang of them."

"I'm livin' proof of that," Hunter's father said with a rusty chuckle, and damn, it was good to see the worry in his old man's eyes replaced by something a hell of a lot lighter.

"Another cool thing Emerson showed me was that there are ways to schedule posts in advance," Hunter added, taking a second to dig into the mountain of spaghetti on his plate. God damn, Owen's recipe really should be declared a national treasure.

Said brother lifted his darkly stubbled chin, blinking at Emerson in obvious surprise. "So we don't have to stop during the middle of our day to go online or make the posts at weird hours?"

Emerson dipped the tines of her fork into her pasta, twirling up a small bite. "Nope. In fact, I already scheduled prime-time posts for

Monday and Tuesday to advertise the pick-your-own blueberries. Now that all the kids are out of school, you might see some more people coming in from Camden Valley to take advantage of the chance to keep their little ones busy."

"Damn, you've thought of everything," Eli said, and even though Hunter agreed one hundred percent, Emerson shook her head to the contrary.

"Not everything, I'm afraid. While regular social media posts are a good start, they're really only the tip of the iceberg. I don't mind trying to come up with some catchy taglines and scheduling all the posts, but I'm not a writer or a photographer. Unfortunately, you might have to hire someone for both if you really want to impress folks enough to draw big crowds."

Hunter leaned back in his chair, his mind turning. "We might have enough wiggle room in the budget if we can snag more CSA shares. The freelancer who did all the copy for our website was reasonable. You know her, right, Eli?"

Eli lasered his focus on his plate. "Uh-huh."

"I don't mind reaching out to her if you want," Emerson offered. "I know you're really busy with day-to-day operations."

"Nah, it's cool. You've got a lot going on, too. I can do it."

Owen's eyes narrowed just enough to send Hunter's warning bells into a full clamor. "What's her name again?"

"Who?" Eli asked, and what was with his weird duck and cover all of a sudden?

"Your freelancer," Owen said, his tone making it crystal clear that Hunter wasn't the only one who'd noticed Eli's verbal evasion.

"Alex something or other." Eli sank the side of his fork into a meatball, the metal sounding off in a hard clink as it hit the plate beneath. "I'm sure I've got her card back at my place."

Rather than taking the information at face value, though, Owen dug in even harder. "And how do you know her, exactly?"

"Owen," their father started, worry lines creasing over his forehead, but Eli set his shoulders into a rigid line and dug right back.

"I met her at a thing in Camden Valley."

"A thing." Owen shook his head, and the chances that he and Eli would dial their shit back started circling the drain. "Brilliant. That explains so much. Did you even ask for this woman's qualifications?"

"If Hunter had found her, would you be asking him the same question?" Eli shot back. "She did a decent job when we hired her before—Hunter even said so. Jesus, Owen, I'm not some screw up. I'm trying to help, just like you. Do you have to crawl down my throat every single time I turn around?"

Owen's knuckles went white over the fork in his grasp. "When you act all dodgy about something that impacts the farm? In a word, yes."

Hunter's pulse sent a steady rhythm of *get this under control* to his brain, but before he could intervene like usual, Emerson shocked the hell out of him by quietly saying, "I don't mean to interfere, and if you'd prefer, I can butt out. But you're both kind of right."

After a whole lot of raised brows and dropped jaws, Eli recovered first. "How's that?"

"Well, it's true that your freelance writer did a great job with the copy that's on your website," Emerson started, earning an *aha!* smile from Eli. "But," she continued, turning a glance toward Owen, "even though lots of freelancers work online with people they've never even met, it's still crucial to know who you're trusting your business to. So it doesn't seem unreasonable to ask about her credentials."

"We're paying her for a service, Eli," Owen said, although his voice had lost a lot of its edge. "We need to make sure she's legit."

Frustration resurfaced on Eli's face, sending another pang of unease through Hunter's gut. "I said she was. How come that's not good enough?"

Rather than shy away from his brothers' renewed bickering, Emerson dove right back in, swinging a look at Eli. "You know her, right? Personally?"

"Yeah."

"And you're sure she's qualified to do good work. That she'll come through, just like last time?"

Eli nodded. "Yeah."

Emerson's gaze traveled to Owen. "And you're happy with the work she did on the website?"

"Yes," Owen said. "I think we all are."

"Okay. So if Eli says she checks out, then you're okay with him reaching out to her again?"

Owen waited out the silence at the table for just a beat before turning toward Eli. "All this stuff Emerson's talking about has the potential to bring in a lot of business for the farm, and it's business we need. I just want to make sure we do everything by the book. That's all."

"I get it," Eli said, and Hunter could tell by his tone that he meant the words. "The freelance writer is solid. She's got a degree in English, okay? I'm sure she'd do more work for us. She's good for it, I swear."

"That's good enough for me," came their father's raspy reply, and Hunter nodded in agreement.

"Me, too," he said.

Emerson darted a tentative look at Owen, who gave up a slow nod. "Okay, then," she said, smiling first at Owen, then at Eli. "Here are a few things you might want to ask her to get the ball rolling."

They talked back and forth for the duration of the meal, the tension between Owen and Eli loosening with each passing minute. Although things never got to the amicable stage, their interaction was a little easier than usual, and finally, once the dinner plates had been cleared to the dishwasher and everyone had parted ways for the rest of the weekend, Hunter looked at Emerson with a slow smile.

"So do you want to tell me exactly how you did that?" he asked, opening the passenger door to his truck so she could step up and slide in.

"What, the marketing?" Emerson laughed, although he didn't miss her deliberate movements or the twinge of tightness moving across her face as she gingerly stepped up to the F-250's running board. "You helped me figure that out all week long, remember?"

"No, although I don't think I helped you figure it out so much as watched you make it happen." Seriously, her savvy intuition for the marketing side of Cross Creek's business was borderline freakish. "I was talking about the magic you worked between my brothers to keep them from throttling each other over dinner."

Her answer came after Hunter moved to the driver's side of the truck. "I might've put a temporary Band-Aid on tonight's argument, but I hardly think I solved anything between them. You weren't kidding about the tension there."

Eli and Owen had been snapping at each other all week, more and more frequently within Emerson's earshot. Tonight had been the worst of it, though. At least, it had been until she'd stepped in.

"Okay, so I'm sure they're not ready to hold hands and sing 'Kumbaya,' " Hunter said, because as good as Emerson was, *that* would take nothing short of a saint-sized miracle. "But you totally defused the situation between them tonight, and that's more than I've been able to do for months."

She shrugged. "All I did was point out the truth. They really are both right."

"Yeah, but getting them to see that has been damn near impossible, so thank you."

"You're welcome," she said, a smile taking over the tired shadows on her face. "I'm glad to help out any way I can. You've all been so nice to include me this week. It's definitely different from the family dynamic I'm used to."

The low rumble of the truck's engine formed a background for the blood rushing in Hunter's ears. "I take it you still haven't returned your mother's calls."

After Emerson's cell phone had blown up no fewer than four times in Hunter's presence this week—truly a notable feat considering how many cell phone dead zones there were in Millhaven—she'd finally admitted that her mother had been trying to call her ever since their nightmare dinner last weekend.

"Nope," Emerson said, her voice frosting over slightly as she turned to look out the window.

Hunter kept his words perfectly laid back, even though his gut was making him work overtime for the calm. "Hey, I was only asking. I'm not trying to give you a hard time."

She blew out a breath, shaking her head in apology. "I know, and I'm sorry. It's just . . . I knew coming back to Millhaven would be a challenge. But I thought maybe if I could get my parents to look past what they wanted and see what I'm good at, what I *love*, that they might finally understand why I chose physical therapy."

A thought pricked at the back of Hunter's mind, and he put it to words before he could backpedal. "Maybe if they knew why you came home, their feelings would change." High expectations or not, he couldn't imagine her parents would pressure her to go to medical school if they knew the truth.

"No. Look." Emerson tugged at the hem of her T-shirt, tapping the heel of her sandal against the truck's floor mat with a rapid tat-tat-tat. "I know you're trying to fix this, but my family doesn't work like yours. Your dad is proud of all three of you, but whenever my parents look at me, all they see is the choice I didn't make, and all the ones *they* want to make in order to fix my 'mistake.' Telling them I have MS isn't going to change that. In fact, it'll only make me more broken in their eyes. Then they'll never stop trying to fix me."

Hunter pulled to a stop in front of the cottage, putting the truck into park before turning to look at her, steady and unyielding. "And what do you see?"

Her eyes widened, flashing crystal blue and totally beautiful in the setting sun. "What?"

"It's a pretty cut-and-dried question." He lifted one corner of his mouth into enough of a smile to get her past her surprise. "When you look at yourself, what do you see?"

"Oh." She paused. "I guess . . . I see a physical therapist who's devoted to her job and loves helping people."

"I see her, too. But do you want to know what else I see?"

Emerson shook her head. "Hunter—"

"Wait," he said, and okay, so there was a fifty-fifty shot his brash interruption would make her shut him out or knee him in the nuts. But when luck proved to be on his side, at least for the moment, he continued. "I see a woman who's smart." Hunter picked up her hand, tracing circles over the slender arc of her wrist with his thumb. "Kind. Beautiful," he added, even though the word didn't touch her. "And far from broken. You're strong, Em." At that one, she exhaled softly, and he leaned across the console to brush a kiss over her lips. "I just hate to see you hurting."

"I know you do. And I hate the way I left things with my parents, but telling them—telling *anyone*—will only make it worse."

Unease filled Hunter's chest like a sponge being drenched to maximum capacity. But if Emerson didn't want to budge, pushing her would only knock her down. "Okay."

"Anyway, I've got everything under control. Multiple sclerosis is chronic, but with the right meds, the periods of remission between my flare-ups can last for months or even years."

"I know," he said, and her lips parted with a tiny breath of surprise. "You do?"

He nodded. "You're not the only one who's good at online research, you know."

"Why would you do that?" Emerson asked, and although her cheeks had gone significantly pink, her tone held more confusion than accusation.

"First of all, because I didn't know anything about the disease, and I wanted to be informed. Second, and more importantly, I did it because I care about you. Listen—" His heart knocked against his ribs with increasing speed, but fuck it. No matter how much this could rock the boat, it needed to be said. "I know you don't want to tell anyone you have MS, and that you want to move on. But I want you to know you don't have to do that alone. Okay?"

"You don't have to take care of me," she whispered. "I'm really fine."

Whether it was the determination in her voice or the completely vulnerable expression warring with it, Hunter had no clue. But all at once, his emotions barged right out of his mouth.

"And I'm not. I know we said head up, eyes forward, but when I look forward, all I see is you. You rehabbed my shoulder. You calmed the water between my brothers. You're spending your extra time on our family business. Come on, Em. I know you're tough, but let me help you back."

She dropped her chin to stare at their entwined fingers, and for one gut-twisting second, Hunter thought Emerson's stubborn toughness would win out.

Then she said, "I have to go into Lockridge on Wednesday. It's nothing major, just some blood tests and a check-in with my neurologist to see how the meds are working. But sometimes the drive wears me out."

"I'm still on restricted duty for another week," Hunter said, relief washing over him harder than he wanted to admit. "I'll have plenty of time to drive you to Lockridge."

"My appointment is at three forty-five. I'd love the company, but *only* if you promise we'll have our daily marketing session on the way there."

Hunter huffed out a laugh. "You drive a hard bargain. I'll tell you what. We can have our marketing session on the way to Lockridge *if* you promise to close your eyes and rest on the way back."

Now it was Emerson's turn to laugh. "Are you bargaining with me?"

He lasered his gaze on her perfect, peach-colored mouth. "I believe I am, Miss Montgomery."

The kiss she pressed over his mouth tasted flawless, and felt even better.

"You're lucky I'm in a good mood," she said, and he kissed her back with just enough suggestion to make her tremble under his touch.

"You think you're in a good mood now? Just you wait."

CHAPTER TWENTY

Emerson turned over, wrapped in the comfort of warm bedsheets. The woodsy scent of cedar filled her lungs, and she breathed deeper, wanting to hold on to every ounce of the intoxicating smell. Her body felt unnaturally light, as if she were being held close and weightlessly carried. A deep sigh drifted up from her chest, soothing her mind upon release, and she clung to the strong, solid arms curled around her.

Haven't you ever wondered what if . . . what if . . . what if . . .

Emerson jerked upright with a gasp. Pain and confusion dug in hard, fighting for the attention of her senses, and she tried desperately to take in her surroundings.

Soft, rhythmic thump-*thump* of windshield wipers. Diffused gray daylight draped over the otherwise scenic Shenandoah countryside. Unrelenting stiffness vise-gripping her back and both legs.

Right. She and Hunter were on the way back from her neurologist's office.

"Hey, easy there." Hunter's voice delivered the calm, cool steadiness she'd been coming to rely on lately, mixed with a splash of concern. "You fell asleep a little while ago. It's been a long day, so I figured you could probably use the breather."

Emerson blinked, swiping a hand over her face in an effort to clear her groggy head. "How long was I out?"

"About an hour," Hunter said, making her already achy muscles tighten.

"Really?" Dammit, they had to be nearly home by now. "I wanted to talk to you about that article I read on advertising trends in specialty food markets."

"Nope," he replied, and okay, *that* snagged her attention.

"What do you mean, 'nope'?" she asked, unable to stifle a laugh at the ear-to-ear grin spreading over his handsome face.

"Just that. We have a ton of solid marketing ideas, some of which are already working, it's been steadily raining for the last three hours, and I've got my follow-up appointment with Dr. Norris tomorrow, where I fully expect to get the green light to get back to work at full steam. So yeah, we are officially putting work on the shelf until tomorrow."

The light, carefree feeling from her dream filled Emerson's mind, and she couldn't deny that it came pretty damned close to matching her reality right now. "Okay, you win. What should we do to celebrate this fantastic turn of events?"

"Funny you should ask." Hunter lifted his brows in an exaggerated waggle, which only made her laugh go for round two. "Eli sent out a group text while you were asleep and it popped up on the dashboard. He wanted to know if we were all in for a drink. His message was, and I quote, 'Get your asses to The Bar. Owen's buying!'"

"I'll bet Owen had a thing or two to say about that," Emerson replied. His brothers had managed a bit of a truce this week according to Hunter, and even though the camaraderie was caught up in a weird, testosterone-fueled force field she was sure she'd never quite understand, it was still nice to see.

"Yeah, his response was not PG-13," Hunter confirmed, amusement sparking in his gray-blue stare. "So do you want to go have a beer or two? I wasn't sure if you'd be beat after all the hauling around you've done today."

Ugh. Emerson's stomach soured at the thought of liquor, but the celebration? Now that would make up for her killjoy of an appetite. "No, I'm up for it. Can I invite Daisy, too?"

"I don't see why not. The more the merrier." Hunter waited out Emerson's quick text message to Daisy before adding, "There aren't a whole lot of dinner options at The Bar, unless you count hot wings or nachos. We can stop at the cottage before we go out, though. There's some leftover chicken in the fridge from last night."

"Oh, I'm good." At least, she would be if she didn't think of food. Everything she'd eaten lately had tasted like a sawdust special, not to mention wreaking havoc on her stomach once it got there.

"Not to go all PSA on you, but you really should eat something," Hunter said.

Emerson's gut churned for an entirely new reason. Of course he would notice she'd been pushing her food from one end of her plate to the other this week. He'd been right next to her at every single meal.

"The preventive medication is just making me queasy," she admitted. Although part of her was tempted to clam up or change the subject—hello, unglamorous and oh-so-unattractive body betrayals—the look of pure calm on Hunter's face made it all too easy to let the truth fly. "My neurologist said it could take awhile for my body to get used to the treatment. He's hopeful the side effects will lessen over time, and obviously, if the meds keep my symptoms from turning into episodes, they're worth it."

Hunter nodded in slow agreement. "True. But it's still kind of a crummy thing to have to get used to," Hunter said, and even though his tone was completely judgment free, Emerson's pulse flared all the same.

This is still your new normal. Head up, eyes forward.

"Well, hopefully I won't have to get used to it for long," she said, putting a nail in the topic.

Thankfully, Hunter let her. "So what were you dreaming about a couple minutes ago?"

Emerson's face burned with all the heat of being flat out busted. Still, a girl (hopefully. Oh God) had her pride, so she selected her words with caution. "What makes you think I was dreaming?"

"I'm assuming you mean aside from the fact that your cheeks are the color of the strawberries I put in the CSA orders this week." He broke out enough of a grin for his dimple to make an appearance, and great God in heaven, would she *ever* find an antidote to that thing?

"Yes," she said, giving in with a wry smile. "Aside from that."

"You were kind of sighing in your sleep. I figured your head might be full of thoughts of a mile-long client list or a bushel of heirloom tomatoes or something."

Emerson's heart thumped in her ears along with the steady rhythm of the windshield wipers, but she didn't hold back the truth. "Actually, I was dreaming about you."

"Why, Miss Montgomery, you're going to make me blush," Hunter said, pausing for only a minute before her lack of a tart response seemed to register. "Wait, are you serious?"

"Mmhmm." Three weeks ago, the words would have terrified her. But somehow, sitting here in the protected comfort of Hunter's truck with the rain and her neurologist and the rest of the world outside, copping to her dream didn't seem like such a big deal.

"I dreamt that we were together and you were carrying me. Not because I was hurt or anything," Emerson rushed to add. She might be okay with fessing up to the images her unintentional snooze fest had yielded, but the last thing she needed was for him to think she was weak, especially after today's haul into Lockridge. "You were just holding me close, with one arm around my shoulders and the other behind my knees. I'm sure it sounds pretty silly." Now that she heard the whole thing out loud, she sounded like one of those sappy greeting cards gone horribly wrong.

But Hunter just looked at her with that wide-open blue stare that told her everything was going to be just fine no matter what, and she believed him before he even said a word.

"That doesn't sound silly at all."

Quiet filled the truck, interrupted only by the steady patter of rain on the windshield and the increasing press of Emerson's heart against her rib cage. They spent the rest of the ride in silence as comfortable as a warm quilt, and by the time they pulled up to The Bar and made a dash for the front entrance, everyone else had arrived and gotten comfortable.

"Hey! There you two are," Daisy called out over the din of the jukebox, lifting her nearly empty pint glass in happy salute. "We've already had a round and ordered up some wings. Where on earth have you been? Owen said you cut out from Cross Creek hours ago."

"Um." Crap. *Crap.* Emerson scrambled for a passably believable answer, but Hunter just fixed Daisy with an easy, nothing-doing smile.

"Emerson and I had some marketing stuff to take care of for Cross Creek," he said, moving around the tall rectangular table the group had taken over to do the handshake/shoulder bump thing with both of his brothers.

"Marketing stuff." Eli laughed and pushed himself back up to the padded leather seat of his barstool. "Is that what you kids are calling it these days?"

"Knock it off, Eli," Owen said, although a tiny smile poked at the corners of his mouth. "You're just jealous you didn't get to spend your afternoon with a pretty girl, too."

Eli held up his hands in concession, his blue eyes twinkling in the low light of the bar. "Too right, brother. While I love old Clarabelle, working in the barn definitely doesn't compare."

The mention of Cross Creek tickled something in the back of Emerson's brain, and she sent her gaze past their table and all the way around the moderately populated bar. "Oh. Your dad decided not to come?"

"Yeah, where is Dad?" Hunter asked, his brows furrowing just slightly in concern.

Owen tipped his head, taking a long draw off the amber-colored bottle between his fingers. "I asked him if he wanted to join us, but he said he was gonna catch up on a few things and turn in early. He said to be sure we threw one back for him, though."

Emerson exhaled a silent breath of relief. She always liked Mr. Cross's company, but it took one to know one in the exhaustion department, and while he thankfully wasn't duking it out with an illness like MS, he'd looked all too tired to her this week.

"Guess it wouldn't be polite to say no to the old man, now would it?" Hunter asked, a slow smile moving over his face. "I'm going to grab a beer. Anyone need another round?"

"With you buying?" Eli asked, raising his glass to drain the last of its contents. "Hell yes. I'm with you."

"Me, too," Daisy chimed in, palming her empty glass and sliding off her barstool to follow Eli toward the bar.

Emerson shook her head. "Just soda for me." Hopefully the bubbles would call a truce to the epic game of I Hate Your Guts that her medication had waged against her stomach.

"Okay." Hunter pulled out a nearby barstool, his hand lingering on her lower back as he ushered her onto the seat. "O, you straight?"

"I'm good for now," Owen said, holding up his half-empty beer. "Don't worry, I'll keep Emerson company."

After Hunter followed Daisy and Eli over the boot-scuffed floorboards to the bar, Owen leaned a forearm over the table across from her, piquing the hell out of her curiosity. "You know, we're really grateful for all the work you've done at Cross Creek."

"I'm happy to help," Emerson said, and meant it. "Being part of things at the farm has gone a long way toward making me feel at home. Believe me, the gratitude goes both ways."

"Still, it's an awful lot of work. Are you sure we're not keeping you from anything down at Doc Sanders's?"

"Not at all, although my schedule *has* been a lot busier this week." Her lips folded together over a smile that felt far too good to suppress at the thought of the three new clients she'd booked, plus two more she'd consulted with during their appointments with Doc Sanders. "Maybe something to do with someone down at the co-op, talking about . . . what was it? Oh right. The best hand massage this side of the Mississippi."

Owen rolled his eyes but managed a laugh all the same. "That's Eli for you, although I'm sure you're great at your job."

Surprise rippled up her spine, straightening her creaky back as it went. "But you've never seen me work."

"Don't have to," Owen said, lifting a shoulder beneath the plaid button-down he'd slung over his T-shirt. "Hunter might be more laid back than most, but I know how he feels about Cross Creek. I'm betting he wasn't exactly a prince about rehabbing his shoulder for four weeks. You got him fixed up good as new, which makes you alright in my book."

"Thanks." Emerson had been around the Cross men enough over the last few weeks to know the guy-speak version of high praise when she heard it.

"Just tellin' you what I see." Owen sent her a covert wink just as Hunter, Eli, and Daisy returned, and huh, who knew the serious brother had a flirty side?

"One soda, coming right up," Hunter said. Placing the glass in front of her, he situated himself on the barstool to her left, giving her enough breathing room to be comfortable but staying just close enough for his proximity to warm her blood. The conversation flowed as easily as the laughter and the beer, and even when Amber Cassidy came in with Kelsey and Mollie Mae to take advantage of the two-for-one ladies' night drink specials, their obvious whispers and pointed looks at Hunter's very visible closeness didn't dampen her mood.

Emerson managed to baby sip most of her soda without too much protest from her stomach, although she hadn't needed to think twice about making the I-had-a-big-lunch excuse when their server brought a giant platter of atomic hot wings to the table. All too soon, though, the drink took its toll on her mouse-sized bladder, and she carefully pushed to her feet to excuse herself.

"Oh, I'll go with you," Daisy said, looping her arm through Emerson's. Eli made the obligatory girls-going-to-the-bathroom-in-packs joke, and Daisy playfully pinched his ear as they headed toward the ladies' room at the back of the bar.

"I know there's safety in numbers," Emerson joked, ignoring her aching legs in favor of smiling at her friend. "But I'm pretty sure I've got this covered."

Daisy made a borderline impolite noise and a face to match. "Please. If anyone can handle herself, it's you." Her expression slid into something else, however, after they moved past Amber and the gossip squad, heading toward the alcove housing the restrooms and the emergency exit. "Actually, I wanted to talk to you in private."

Emerson's steps slowed, worry peppering tiny holes in her already unthrilled stomach. "Is everything okay?"

The unease whisking through Daisy's olive-green stare was a surefire precursor to nothing good. "I'm not trying to poke my nose into your business, but your mother has stopped by your place twice in the last few days."

Just like that, Emerson's good mood flatlined. "Are you serious?"

"Yes." Daisy led her to the back of the alcove, dropping her voice to a soft murmur as the bar noise faded into the background. "I've been making a lot of extra bath scrub and aromatherapy body spritz for next weekend's craft fair, and my kitchen window faces your front door, so I just happened to see her both times. I know you said things between you and your parents have been strained lately, and I wasn't even sure if I should bring it up, but . . ."

"But?" Emerson managed, and even the single syllable trembled. God, how stupid she'd been to think her parents would let this whole career change thing go after just one no from her.

"Well, she looked pretty upset," Daisy said, biting her lip. "The first time was on Friday afternoon, then she came by again this evening, right before I left to come here. I figured you'd want to know in case something's wrong."

Emerson inhaled on a five count before doubling the number for her breath out. "Thank you for telling me, but no. Nothing's wrong."

"Are you sure?"

She paused, her heart squeezing tight in her chest. While she was still too angry to speak to her parents, she *had* drafted a polite e-mail to Dr. Norris a few days after the dinner nightmare. He'd been nice enough to consider her for a position at his practice, and just because she didn't want said position didn't mean the man should get caught in the shrapnel of her family blowout. But she wasn't going to change her mind, and her parents weren't going to change theirs, no matter how many times they revisited the subject.

Now it was time to move on.

"Yes," Emerson said, capping the word with a nod. "I'm sure."

By the time she had used the ladies' room and made her way back to the table with Daisy, the wings were mostly gone and the beer along with it. For the first time since she'd started spending the night at Hunter's cottage, Emerson found herself grateful that the workday at Cross Creek started early enough to make everyone head for home after two beers. Between the ride to Lockridge and the news that her parents didn't seem to be through with their full-court press, she just wanted to fall into bed next to Hunter and turn her dream from the truck into reality.

Haven't you ever wondered what if . . .

"Hey. You've been awfully quiet over there," Hunter said, the tires crunching over the gravel drive as he pulled up to the cottage and turned off the engine. "You okay?"

"Yeah, I . . ." A humorless laugh puffed past her lips. "No. Daisy told me my mother has been to my apartment twice this week, looking for me."

His gaze winged toward hers in the near dark. "Shit, Em. Did Daisy talk to her?"

Emerson shook her head. "She saw her through the window. I can't believe I thought my parents would actually trust me to live my own life. I don't know how else to make them understand that working for Doc Sanders is what I want."

Hunter's hesitation lasted long enough to send her warning flags into a full wave. "Have you given any more thought to telling them you have MS?"

"We've been through this," she said, frustration snapping in her veins. "Telling them will do more harm than help."

"I know you think so." His voice hardened ever so slightly over the words, outlining frustration of his own. "But isn't it possible that, despite the fact that they have a crappy way of showing it, they really do want what's best for you?"

Emerson's brain sent an unexpected litany of science fair exhibits, piano recitals, homecoming floats, and graduations through her mind's eye. Although they'd chosen all of those things for her, her parents had been front and center for each one. She'd always assumed their presence had been for show, the same way her father had felt obligated to attend the Watermelon Festival. Appearances were everything when you were a Montgomery. The only thing good enough for her parents was perfection.

She missed the mark now more than ever.

"No." Emerson knew Hunter meant well, she did. But the rift between her and her parents couldn't be fixed any more than her body could miraculously heal overnight. She needed to face those facts and keeping moving on. "They want what *they* want, and it's their version of the best or nothing. That's not going to change, no matter what I tell them."

"Okay," Hunter said, and although his tone told her he disagreed, he thankfully didn't press the issue. They darted through the rain, moving over the porch boards and into the cozy warmth of the cottage.

"You hungry yet?" he asked, tipping his head toward the shadows of the kitchen.

But what she wanted wasn't in the fridge. "No. I'd really just like to go upstairs."

Nodding, he followed her over the honey-colored hardwoods, patiently keeping time with her slower-than-usual pace as she forced her feet over each achy, painful step. Emerson dragged herself through the motions of brushing her teeth and getting ready for bed, turning to reach for the oversized sleep shirt she'd hung on the hook on the back of the bathroom door.

"Shit." The hook was empty. Cursing her spacy brain, she made her way back into Hunter's bedroom, and ugh, how could she have forgotten that she'd left her nightshirt draped across the foot of the bed this morning?

Scooping up the swath of light-pink cotton, she turned to hobble her way back to the bathroom to change. But the empty bedroom and the muffled noises from down the hall told her Hunter had gone back downstairs for something, and truly, her energy was waning fast. Emerson peeled her long-sleeved T-shirt and capris from her body, reaching for the nightshirt she'd lowered back over the bed. A sound from the doorway sent her defenses into lockdown, but her body's clumsy movements made her a living embodiment of the adage *too little, too late.*

"I'm sorry," Hunter said, his blue-gray eyes glinting to back up the apology. "I ran downstairs for a glass of water. Didn't mean to startle you."

"You didn't." Emerson winced inwardly at the lie. The tight knot of her arms offered a flimsy cover for her body, and her fingers itched like mad to grab the quilt folded at the foot of the bed so she could cover up more completely. But in order to do that, she'd have to drop her arms, which would expose her nearly naked and definitely traitorous body.

She couldn't make herself move.

Hunter came all the way into the room, placing the glass of water in his hand on the nightstand beside her. "Are you cold?" he asked, reaching out to run his palms from her shoulders to her elbows.

Oh God, how could such a benign touch feel so warm and sweet and good? "No."

His hands came to a stop, cupped around her upper arms. "Then why would you want to cover up?"

Emerson's glance moved first to the lamp on the bedside table, then to the light spilling in from the bathroom, and before she could come up with an answer, realization widened his gaze.

"I've seen you naked before," he said.

"I know." Her breath turned shallow, refusing to move smoothly. God, how could she explain this without pointing it out with a neon freaking sign?

"But you don't want me to see you now."

A primal part of her brain screamed at her to dodge the conversation, to cover up, to hide.

Only she didn't. "No," Emerson whispered. "My body hurts, and it isn't . . . it's . . ."

Hunter let go of her arm to slide one finger over her mouth, stopping the flow of her words. "Your body is beautiful."

She laughed, although there was no joy in the sound. "My body is not beautiful."

"Your body is fucking gorgeous." The unyielding intensity in both his voice and his eyes froze Emerson to her spot beside the bed. Reaching down, Hunter caught her wrist in his hand, sliding his thumb over her rapidly beating pulse point. "But as beautiful as you are on the outside, you're even more stunning underneath."

She stood in shock, completely unable to do anything other than listen as he continued. "You're kind. You don't hesitate to help people," he said, dusting a fingertip over her knuckles before letting his touch travel upward. Her stomach tightened when he reached the bandage from today's earlier blood draw and the bruise blooming beneath it, but Hunter didn't so much as pause.

"You're smart. The way you tackle problems and see what's in front of you is incredible." His hands moved through the fall of her hair, sweeping over the back of her neck in hypnotic circles, and oh God, the contact was enough to make her want to cry.

"But your spirit is the most beautiful thing about you," Hunter murmured, his hands moving to the center of her chest to press carefully over her heart. "You asked me on that first day in Doc Sanders's office why I hadn't settled down and married some local girl."

Emerson managed a shaky nod. "I did."

"The real answer is that I guess I was waiting."

"For what?" she asked, and again, Hunter didn't hesitate.

"To know it was right, right here." He slid one hand from her heart to splay his fingers wide over his own chest. "To not just want somebody, but to want to be with them, even when things got bad. To not just look at somebody, but to *see* them way down deep, and know they saw me, too. I don't think I realized it until now, but what I've been waiting for is you. It's always been you. And this time, I'm not letting you slip away."

And as he guided her into his bed and wrapped his arms around her aching body to hold her tight, Emerson realized that she didn't just trust him with her secrets.

She trusted him with her heart.

CHAPTER TWENTY-ONE

Emerson rolled over, surfacing from sleep in slow degrees. A cursory body scan yielded surprisingly little pain, and even though the day was still a newborn, she'd take the lack of debilitating discomfort as a win right now. She was alone in bed, which wasn't a shock—even on restricted duty, Hunter still headed to the main house at the crack of dawn, and the bright spears of sunlight pushing past the blinds told her he'd likely been gone for a while. But he'd known Emerson didn't have a client until Mrs. Ellersby's session at noon, so he'd clearly let her sleep in rather than resetting the alarm for her as usual, and God, the catch-up rest had done wonders to soothe yesterday's aches.

That's not all that's putting you in your happy place. Unable to help herself, Emerson laughed out loud at the thought. While the mess with her parents might still need to be sorted and yesterday had been a big, fat goose egg in terms of a body win, she still couldn't deny the feeling nestled way down deep in her chest.

She was falling in love with Hunter Cross, and this time, nothing was going to tear them apart.

Emerson gave herself one last stretch before tossing back the covers and testing her limbs with her body weight. A hot shower and an even hotter cup of coffee later, her muscles and her mood were as loose as they were getting, so she headed toward Cross Creek's main house. She still had a couple of hours to kill before her appointment with Mrs. Ellersby, and Doc Sanders wouldn't hesitate to call Emerson's cell phone if she needed a consult. Squeezing in a little recon on how to build Cross Creek's newsletter list would keep her nice and busy.

She parked beside the homey two-story farmhouse, making her way up the natural stone path toward the porch. Mother Nature had rebounded quickly from yesterday's rain, and the humidity and the already-relentless heat joined forces to send a trickle of perspiration between Emerson's shoulder blades. Her legs threatened to ache as she climbed the trio of steps in front of her—heat always seemed to amplify the symptoms of her MS—but at least she'd managed to get two pieces of toast down the hatch with her coffee.

"Hello? Anyone here?" Poking her head past the front door, Emerson called into the house. Letting herself in had felt so awkward that the first few times Mr. Cross had told her to do it, she'd knocked, anyway. But the main house was barely ever occupied during the day, so after she'd realized that if she didn't let herself in, chances were high that no one else would do the job, either, she'd reluctantly thrown in the towel.

Emerson put her car keys on the front table and started to move through the house, making sure her phone was set to vibrate as she slid it into the pocket of her bright-blue dress pants. Lucy padded into the living room to greet her, the dog's nails clicking softly over the hardwoods, and Emerson leaned down to give her a scratch behind the ears.

"Hey, pretty girl. How come you're in the house today?" Ninety-nine times out of one hundred, Lucy didn't leave Mr. Cross's side. Emerson's answer came by way of a masculine throat being cleared from the entryway to the kitchen, and she shot to her feet as fast as her body would allow.

"Oh, Mr. Cross! I'm sorry, I wouldn't have barged in if I'd known you were here."

He waved her off with a quick lift of his hand, brushing the brim of his Stetson in greeting before he lowered his arm to his side. "No worries, darlin'. I just came back in from the greenhouse for a quick spell. Been right busy this morning, what with the weather bouncing back and Hunter headed into Camden Valley to see the doc."

Of course. How could she have forgotten that Hunter's follow-up appointment with Dr. Norris was this morning? "You must be glad to get him all the way back in action tomorrow."

"Thanks in no small part to you," Mr. Cross said, and Emerson took a turn with a wave of her own.

"Ah, he did the hard part. I just bossed him around."

Mr. Cross shook his head. "Somehow, I suspect there was a bit more to it than that." He paused to pull a bandana from his back pocket to mop his neck and brow, measuring her with a long glance before adding, "You're good for him. If you don't mind me sayin' so."

"Thank you," Emerson managed past her shock and the smile taking over her face without her brain's permission. "It's mutual, though. I think he's good for me, too."

"A little funny how that works, isn't it?"

Mr. Cross's gaze flickered to the small side table next to the living room sofa, coming to rest on a silver-framed photograph of a woman with long, dark hair. She was surrounded by a field of bright flowers, her smile radiating happiness and showing off a dimple that looked oddly familiar, and realization hit Emerson like a sucker punch.

"Is that Mrs. Cross?"

Hunter's father stepped into the living room, the faded blue-and-cream area rug muffling the thump of his work-bruised boots as he crossed the floor to pick up the frame with both hands. "It is, although she's probably havin' a heavenly fit at the formality," he said over a wink. "She always insisted on Rosemary. 'Miss' if folks got insistent."

"Miss Rosemary," Emerson repeated, her heart giving up a hard tug behind her breastbone. "She's beautiful."

"I think so, too."

Emerson knew very little about Hunter's mother, other than the fact that she'd died of breast cancer when he'd been only six, and while she didn't want to pry, she also didn't want to disrespect the woman's memory by shying away from the subject. "You must all miss her very much."

"Every day," he confirmed, his eyes still on the photograph. "The boys were awful young when she passed, except for Owen. Truth be told, I don't know how much they remember her."

The odd memory of sitting in her father's office popped back into her brain unbidden, so strongly that she could smell the leather-bound medical textbook he'd pulled from his bookshelf to help her learn the skeletal anatomy. "Your family is so warm and open, I'm sure they have wonderful memories of her. And you."

Mr. Cross smiled, although the gesture didn't touch his tired eyes. "Kind of you to say."

Whether it was the sadness on his face or the unspoken way she felt so easy around the man, Emerson couldn't be sure, but she heard herself reply, "I'm a bit envious, actually. I'm not on such great terms with my mom. And definitely not with my father," she added.

"That's a bit of a shame," Mr. Cross said, giving her just enough room to keep talking.

To her surprise, she answered with the unvarnished truth. "Sometimes I think so, and I wish we were closer. But my family isn't like yours. Even when the four of you have your differences, you still know each other. There aren't any pretenses, and you accept each other at face value. I've never really had that with my parents."

"Oh, darlin'. It's true that the boys and I are closer than most." Mr. Cross lowered the photo in his hands, but he didn't put the frame back in its resting place on the lace doily centered just so on the side table.

"But I promise you, each of us has got things he's hidin' behind, and even though we've got family bonds holdin' us together, ain't none of the four of us perfect."

Pain flickered over the old man's face, there and then gone. The shadows that had made themselves comfortable beneath his eyes this week stood out in stark contrast to his suddenly pale skin, and something unspoken and not-quite-right pinched in Emerson's gut.

"Mr. Cross? Are you feeling alright?"

"Right as rain," he grated, his voice far too hoarse, but before she could launch a full protest, her phone buzzed to life in her pocket, sending her damn near out of her skin.

"Oh jeez!" She retrieved the thing with a sweep of one hand. "I apologize, but I need to check this, just in case Doc Sanders needs me at the PT center."

She took a lightning-fast glance at the display. But the text message glaring over the screen wasn't from the doc.

Emerson,

Your mother has left several voice messages for you, as well as trying unsuccessfully to speak with you at your apartment. We clearly have unfinished business, which your mother and I would like to address. Please call at your earliest convenience.

Emerson's stomach took a straight trip to her suddenly throbbing knees. God, her parents were relentless. But the acorn didn't fall far from the oak as far as that particular trait was concerned, and dammit, she was going to put an end to this once and for all.

"Please excuse me, Mr. Cross. I've got to make an important—"

The rest of her words crashed to a halt in her windpipe as she lifted her head to look at Hunter's father. Now sheet white, he swayed unsteadily in his boots, a heavy sheen of sweat beading over his temples and dampening the underarms of his T-shirt.

Adrenaline spurted in Emerson's veins. "Mr. Cross?"

His chin lifted in her direction, but his gaze barely connected. "I'm . . . feelin' a little . . . tired all of a sudden," he said, and shit. *Shit*.

She forced her legs to close the space between them in two quick strides. "Okay. Let's sit down for a minute."

Moving to Mr. Cross's side, Emerson wrapped her arm around his side, her throat going desert dry as she realized he was shaking like the last leaf in a winter windstorm. She needed to get him in a stable position so she could get a better look, not to mention some freaking help. But before she could ask him if he could make it to the nearby couch, he wobbled in place, his balance teetering.

"I don't . . . my arm . . ."

Her hold tightened around him just as his knees buckled completely. Emerson's heart ricocheted against her ribs and her joints screamed in protest at having to suddenly support his body weight, but she barely registered either as she managed to get Mr. Cross clumsily to the carpet.

"Mr. Cross," she said, wrenching her voice into calmness she didn't come close to feeling. "Can you hear me?"

He slumped like dead weight in her arms, completely unmoving, and panic sliced through her with scalpel-sharp teeth.

No. This wasn't happening. Not on her watch.

Emerson guided him all the way back over the carpet, the move sending his sweat-soaked Stetson rolling over the floor and his body limp beneath her hands. *"Mr. Cross,"* she barked with all the authority she could muster, and just as she slid her fingers into the crook of his neck to check for a pulse, his eyelids fluttered.

Breathing. Thank God. "Mr. Cross, can you hear me?"

Although his eyes didn't open, he grunted in response. "Unh. Uh-huh."

"Good. I want you to lie still, okay?"

"My arm . . . hurts somethin' fierce . . ."

He made a weak grab for his left side, and dammit, she needed paramedics. *Now.* "I'm going to help you out with that. But you've got to stay with me, nice and easy."

"I'm just . . . gonna get under the covers . . . right here in bed . . ."

Fear crawled up Emerson's spine, but she mashed down on it with all her power. "Not quite yet, okay? I need you to stay awake just a few minutes longer."

Fumbling for her phone, she jabbed her finger over the emergency icon, shoving the device between her ear and shoulder as the call connected.

"Nine-one-one, what's your emergency?"

A hard shot of relief filled her lungs at the fact that the call went through. "I need an ambulance at the main house at Cross Creek Farm. It's"—she scrambled to pluck the street address from her Tilt-a-Whirl of a brain—"ah! Fourteen fifty-six Spring Street, Millhaven. I've got an adult male in distress."

"Is the injured party breathing, ma'am?" came the operator's voice, and Emerson dropped her own so as not to make Mr. Cross panic.

"Yes. He's breathing, but he lost consciousness briefly and now he's disoriented and complaining of dizziness and left arm pain." She dropped her hand to capture his wrist for a pulse check, hating the corkscrew in her gut as she added, "Pulse is tachy at one-oh-six."

"Ma'am, are you a medical professional?"

"I'm a physical therapist." She had basic emergency training, but for cripes' sake, she'd never had to *use* it.

"Okay," the operator said, her voice crackling over a sea of static. "Do you know CPR?"

No! No, no, no, she wasn't going to *need* CPR. "Yes," Emerson croaked.

"Good." More static, and dammit, she was going to lose the connection. "Do your best to keep the injured party calm and alert, ma'am. Paramedics have been dispatched and will be there very shortly."

"Thank you," Emerson said, just as the signal dropped. Lowering the now-useless phone, she framed Mr. Cross's face with her hands. "Mr. Cross, can you hear me? I need to know if you feel pain anywhere."

He blinked his eyes open, his breaths shallow and rapid. "My arm. I feel so dizzy."

"It's okay," she reassured him at the same time she begged God not to make her a liar. "I'm right here and I'm not going to leave you. Help is on the way."

"Owen . . . and Hunter and Eli," Mr. Cross wheezed, and she smoothed a hand over his clammy brow.

Calm. She had to keep him calm no matter what. "Don't you worry one bit, Mr. Cross. I'll be sure to tell them everything they need to know. But first, we need to get you all taken care of, okay? Did I tell you how much I loved that sweet corn last week? Don't tell Hunter, or he'll make fun of me, but I actually had some for breakfast the other day."

She murmured low encouragement, telling him the story of how she'd bypassed cereal and oatmeal in favor of the leftover sweet corn in Hunter's fridge. Although Mr. Cross remained weak and somewhat confused, he also stayed relatively composed, and when paramedics knocked on the door a handful of minutes later, she sprang from the floor to let them in.

"Please, hurry!" Emerson guided the pair, a man and a woman, over to Mr. Cross, repeating the same information she'd given the nine-one-one operator. She stood back while the paramedics worked, their hands moving in a rapid flurry and their words volleying in a back and forth of medical jargon that made her head hurt.

"Owen . . . Eli . . ." Mr. Cross's gravelly whisper drifted up from the spot where the paramedics tended to him, and Emerson's chin snapped up. She commanded her legs down the hall toward the office, lasering in on the small table where they kept the charging stand for the two-way radios. Three of the four slots were empty—of course, Mr. Cross was probably still wearing his on his belt—but aha! Hunter's was resting in the charger.

Emerson swiped the handheld radio, fumbling with the power button before she pressed the bright-red rectangle on the side to speak. "Owen! Eli! It's Emerson. Can you hear me?"

She pressed the two-way up to her ear as she retraced her steps back down the hall to the living room, chanting a silent chorus of *please, please, please* with every step.

"Emerson?" Owen's voice came back first, tight with concern. "What's the matter?"

"I'm at the house. Your father . . . I had to call an ambulance. Hurry, both of you. Please."

"What?" The word was all panic, and oh God, the paramedics had gotten Mr. Cross strapped to the gurney and hooked up to IVs with startling speed.

"Paramedics are here, but you need to hurry."

"I'm on the far side of the property. I'm coming as fast as I can."

Emerson sucked in a breath, turning toward the paramedics, and wait . . . how were they already moving?

"Stop!" She raced to keep up with their brisk strides, her pulse sledgehammering with every step. "You have to wait for his sons to get here."

"We can't," said the female paramedic, a brunette who looked too young to be familiar to Emerson. "Even in the rig, it's going to take us thirty minutes to get to Camden Valley Hospital. We have to go now."

Panic threatened both Emerson's heart and her brain, but she wrestled both into submission as they cleared the front door and moved into the shock of brilliant sunshine spilling over the yard. "Okay. Then let me ride with him."

"You're not next of kin," said the male paramedic, who clearly knew the Cross family.

But Emerson used that to her advantage in less than a breath. "No, but do you want to tell the Cross brothers that you let their father ride all alone to Camden Valley? I can keep him calm," she promised, nailing the paramedic with a stare.

"Plus, you're not going without me."

CHAPTER TWENTY-TWO

Hunter adjusted his faded navy-blue baseball hat against the glare of the sun, his medical clearance in one hand and the whole freaking world at his feet. Okay, so he might be leaning a little toward the sappy side with that last part, but come on. He was back in the proverbial saddle at Cross Creek, his brothers seemed to have put a moratorium on trying to knock each other's heads in, and he was in love with a beautiful woman.

On second thought, he didn't care how sappy it was. Right now, life was fucking *outstanding*.

He got four steps away from his truck when his cell phone started making an otherworldly fuss in the back pocket of his jeans. Sliding the thing free, he glanced at the screen, his brows tightening in confusion. How had he missed seven calls from his brother?

"Hello?" Maybe his phone was out of whack. After all, the hospital got the same kind of cell reception as Millhaven in general, and Dr. Norris had been nothing if not thorough. Hunter had been in the man's office for nearly an hour.

"Hunter! Thank God." Weird. Why the hell was Eli calling him from Owen's phone? "We've been trying to get ahold of you for over half an hour. Where are you?"

The heavy dose of panic in Eli's voice told him not to mince words. "In the parking lot at Camden Valley Hospital. Why?"

A rush of static garbled Eli's response, and wait. There was no way *that* could be right. "Sorry, bro. Can you repeat that? Because it sounded like you said you're on your way here."

"We are. Emerson called us from the two-way about forty minutes ago. She was up at the house with Dad and he collapsed."

The sweat on Hunter's brow turned cold, his lungs filling with fear as thick as sand. "Collapsed . . . how?"

"I don't know. Owen was in the south fields when she called, and I was down at the cattle barn getting this week's feed order straight with Jimmy. The ambulance had to leave before we could get to the house, but Emerson's with him. They should be at the hospital by now, and we're but five minutes away."

Hunter tried like hell to make sense of the words, to pull the calm that never failed him into place, but his brain, his heart, his legs all refused to budge.

This cannot be happening.

"O-okay," he finally scraped past the snarled knot of his vocal chords. Fuck, he had to get it together. He had to stay calm, to *think*. "I'm going to the ED right now to see what I can find out. I'll meet you there."

On a delayed reaction, Hunter's legs finally got the message and kicked into motion. His boots slapped over the heat-cracked sidewalk in a sloppy run, the automatic doors of the emergency department hissing open as he approached. Although a tiny voice in the back hallway of his brain called out that it was less than polite, he didn't wait for the scrubs-clad nurse on the other side of the triage desk to speak—or, hell, even look up—before he huffed out, "My father was brought in by ambulance from Millhaven. Tobias Cross. I need to see him."

The nurse looked up, her eyes kind but her stare firm. "I'm sorry, sir. We don't allow family members in the trauma rooms while patients are being assessed. But if you'll wait right here in chairs, I'll be sure to let the doctors know you've arrived."

Hunter's pulse went ballistic, panic surging in the back of his throat. "No, you don't understand. I need to see him. I need—"

"Hunter!"

The sound of Emerson's voice whipped him around on the heels of his Red Wings, his chest filling with both confusion and relief.

"Em." He reached for her just as she flung her arms around him, pulling him close. A bolt of pure emotion shot through his blood, and even though some primal, selfish part of him wanted to stop time to make this one safe moment last just a little longer, he pulled back to look at her.

"What's going on? Christ, Em, I just got off the phone with Eli, but I don't know anything other than my dad is sick, or hurt, or . . ." No. *No.* He forced himself to swallow any other possibility. "He said you were with my father in the ambulance?"

"Yes." She led him to a bank of plastic chairs in the waiting area, keeping hold of his hand as she sat beside him. "I went to the house to do a little work before heading to the PT center, and your father was there. At first, everything was fine, but then he turned pale and said he felt tired."

"God dammit." Hunter had known his father hadn't seemed quite right for the last few weeks. He should've said something. *Done* something.

Squeezing his hand, Emerson continued. "By the time I realized something was really wrong, he'd blacked out. He only lost consciousness for a few seconds," she added, likely in response to the way Hunter had just flinched. "I called nine-one-one right after that and let your brothers know what was going on after the ambulance arrived. But the paramedics said they couldn't wait for Owen and Eli, so I rode with your father instead. We came in through the ambulance bay about five minutes ago, but the doctor wouldn't let me go back with him."

Questions swarmed Hunter's brain, all of them vying for answers. "Was he awake in the ambulance?"

She nodded, the harsh overhead lighting of the waiting area illuminating the worry lines that bracketed her eyes. "For a little while, yes, but the paramedic sedated him to try to make him more comfortable."

"Okay, but awake is good, right?" he asked. If his old man was conscious, that had to be a decent sign.

"I don't know. The paramedic . . ."

Emerson trailed off, and Hunter's stomach swan-dived toward his knees. "What? Please, I need to know."

"Look, there are a lot of things this could be, Hunter, and the paramedics and doctors have to err on the side of caution." Although her bright-blue gaze never faltered, her tone fell just short of hiding her concern, and fuck, he wanted to cling to her like a life raft right now.

"What do you mean? What aren't you telling me?"

Her lips pressed together as if the words behind them tasted sour. "One of the things your father was complaining of just before he collapsed was left arm pain. Coupled with some of the other symptoms . . . the paramedic said they couldn't rule out a heart attack."

Hunter's stomach lurched, his breakfast threatening a repeat appearance. *No way. No, no, no.* "My father had a heart attack?"

"He didn't say that definitively. The doctor and nurses are giving your father all their attention to figure out what's making him sick," Emerson said. "He's in great hands."

Great hands, he thought, turning toward her with his emotions filling his chest. "He was in *your* hands. If you hadn't acted so quickly, if you hadn't been there with him—"

"But I was." Emerson cut off the path of his gut-twisting thoughts with a shake of her head. Before Hunter could work up any other questions, the automatic doors whooshed open to reveal his brothers, both looking equally wild eyed and panicked.

"Hunt!" Owen spotted him first, cutting the space between the entryway and the alcove in just a few lumbering strides. Worry lines creased hard over his forehead, his dark hair sticking up in about six different directions as if he'd been pulling on it without mercy, and Hunter returned his brother's rough embrace.

"Please tell us you know what the hell is going on," Eli said, his request as unsteady as his expression as he divided a stare between Hunter and Emerson.

Shit, he wished with all his might that he had something to offer other than the lame headshake he was currently sporting. "Nothing other than he's here and they're working on him. The nurse said she'd tell the doc we're waiting."

Emerson quietly recounted everything she'd told Hunter so his brothers could get up to speed, and while he didn't glean any new information in the retelling, the reminder that she'd been with his old man when he'd collapsed at least kept Hunter from losing every last marble in his jar. The four of them sat in stony silence, Hunter's fingers locked over Emerson's, Owen with his forearms braced across the thighs of his dirt-streaked Wranglers, and Eli prowling over the linoleum so many times Hunter was sure he'd leave a permanent footpath on the shiny tiles. Sounds rushed together to form indistinct white noise in his ears, blurring all of his thoughts until only one thing remained.

His father had to be okay. He *had* to.

Christ, he should've said something—no, he should've taken *action*, pushed his old man to take it easy when he'd first noticed his fatigue at the Watermelon Festival. If Hunter had insisted his father get more rest, or go see Doc Sanders, maybe none of this would've happened. But he'd been too afraid to rock the boat, too worried about the status fucking quo to point out his father's overexertion.

And now his father was lying in a hospital bed, possibly having a heart attack.

Please God. Don't let him die because I kept quiet. Please.

Time passed, although whether it was minutes or hours or god-damn months, Hunter had no clue. Finally, the automatic doors leading into the belly of the ED buzzed open to reveal a muscle-bound man in green scrubs, a stethoscope looped around his neck and a serious expression in his dark eyes. "Cross family?"

Hunter's pulse stuttered. "Yes," he and his brothers said in unison, the three of them and Emerson moving forward to meet the man in less than a breath.

"I'm Dr. Ortiz, and I've been working with your father. Thanks for your patience while we figured a few things out."

"So you know what's wrong? Is he okay?" Owen asked, and the doctor gave a tentative nod, gesturing them back into the alcove, presumably for some privacy from the bustling waiting area.

"Your father has had a hell of a morning," Dr. Ortiz said slowly, and Eli cut in with a frown.

"That's not a yes."

For a split second, their eyes locked, but before Hunter could step in, the doctor shook his head and took a step back.

"I know this is stressful. Although it took some doing, right now your father is stable. The good news is his initial blood work and his ECG indicate that he didn't have a heart attack."

Relief slammed into Hunter so hard, his knees nearly quit, and beside him, Emerson murmured a quiet "oh, thank God" that echoed everyone's expression.

"I've ordered a few more tests just to be sure," Dr. Ortiz qualified with a lift of his hand. "But regardless, your father's still looking at a potentially serious diagnosis. I believe he collapsed from heat exhaustion."

Hunter and his brothers bit out various curse words. They knew—they *knew* how dangerous the heat could be. How could he have missed something so obvious as his father working too hard and not hydrating enough?

From beside him, Emerson's soft exhale equated to a wordless *of course*. "The arm pain was muscular cramping," she said. "With the profuse sweating and dizziness, that makes perfect sense."

Dr. Ortiz lifted a shadowy brow. "Are you a doctor?"

"Physical therapist," she corrected. "I was with him when he collapsed."

"Well, your quick thinking might've made all the difference," Dr. Ortiz said, allowing himself a small smile before returning his gaze to Hunter and his brothers. "We're treating your father with IV fluids, and we've managed to stabilize his body temperature somewhat. He's still a bit disoriented and weak, but that should resolve as he rests. I'll be honest. He got damned lucky."

"How's that?" Eli asked, his brows shooting up in clear disbelief.

But the doctor met it head-on. "Heat exhaustion can become heat stroke in a matter of minutes, and your father looks to have been well on his way. He's not out of the woods entirely, but at least now we can see the tree line. He's fortunate he got immediate care."

"So he's going to make a full recovery?" Hope uncurled in Hunter's chest, rising up past all the other emotions churning through him, and Dr. Ortiz lifted his stubbled chin.

"As long as he responds to treatment and his chest X-ray is clear, he should be able to go home later today."

"Can we see him?" Owen asked.

"Of course. I'll have to ask that you visit in pairs, and only briefly, until he rests some more. But he's been asking for you."

"You two go," Hunter said, because really, his brothers looked about as shaky as his legs felt right now. He needed to buckle down, to find his calm, God, even just to manage these emotions and *think* clearly.

"Are you sure?" Uncertainty colored Eli's tone, and even though Hunter nodded, he didn't meet his brother's stare.

"Yeah. Absolutely."

He watched Owen and Eli disappear behind the double-wide automatic doors. Desperate to strong-arm all the feelings cranking down on his chest like an iron band, he scraped for a breath, but the attempt was flimsy at best. Dammit, he needed to keep it together. He needed to be calm, composed. He needed . . .

"Hunter."

The one word, the soft, strong voice that whispered it, broke him right down the middle, and without thinking, Hunter turned to let Emerson gather him close.

"I'm sorry. I just . . . I need . . ."

"It's okay. You don't have to say anything," she said. Her arms circled around his shoulders, her closeness filling his lungs with the scent of lavender and an overwhelming sense of safety, and he gave in. All the emotion—the fear, the confusion, the reality of what he could've lost—everything rushed up from beneath his easygoing cover, and he let go with a broken exhale.

Still, Emerson didn't waver. "I've got you," she said.

And she did.

Standing there, wrapped together in the semi-privacy of the tiny alcove, Hunter let everything wash over him in waves. His heart slammed so hard that surely Emerson could feel it against her chest, but she didn't pull back. After time that Hunter measured by breath rather than minutes, the pressure in his rib cage released, coalescing into deeper ease. He shifted his weight, but only far enough to press his forehead against hers.

"Thank you," he managed, because as lame as it was, it was the only thing he could think of to say.

Funny how she seemed to understand. "You're welcome."

They sat back down, keeping to the unstrained silence between them until Eli and Owen came back to the waiting area a few minutes later. Despite her look of hesitation, Hunter didn't think twice about reaching for Emerson's hand so she could accompany him back to the curtain area where his father lay resting, which turned out to be a damned good thing as soon as he clapped eyes on his old man.

The too-bright glare of overhead fluorescents put a spotlight on the shadows beneath his father's eyes. He looked frail, smaller somehow without the Stetson he always wore, and Christ, Hunter couldn't remember the last time he'd seen the old man without it. His gut twisted and sank as he entered the trauma room, but he tacked a smile over his kisser, anyway. "Awful lot of trouble to go through just for Jell-O," he managed, and damn, his father's rusty chuckle had never sounded so fucking good.

"Tryin' . . . to keep you on your toes," he said, exhaustion permeating the words and sending Hunter's gut on another go-round with his roiling emotions.

Calm. Cool. You can do this. "Yeah, well, it worked." He forced one boot over the other, the sharp smell of antiseptic pinching his senses as he moved closer to his father's hospital bed.

His father nodded, his face as pale as the pillow propping his head up. "A little too well, I s'pose."

Aw, hell. The last thing the old man needed was to feel guilty. He was supposed to be taking things easy, for Pete's sake. "You know us Cross men. Nothing gets done halfway."

"Still." His father lowered his gaze to his hands. "Didn't mean to worry you."

"How about you heal fast and we call it square?"

"Sounds like a deal." His old man waited out a handful of breaths—a series of rises and falls that took far too much effort, in Hunter's opinion—before he shifted his stare in Emerson's direction. "Guess I owe you a debt of gratitude, darlin'."

"Not at all," she said, and whoa, as sweet as her smile was, she clearly meant it.

For once, his father went the defiant route. "Doc says without your quick thinkin', this coulda been a whole lot worse."

"Nah. You're way too tough for that," Emerson said, her ballerina-looking shoes shushing over the linoleum as she moved closer to brush a kiss over the old man's cheek. "But if it makes you feel better, you can return the favor if I'm ever not right on my feet."

"Done."

They spent a few more minutes at his father's bedside, mostly making sure he was comfortable enough to get the rest he'd promised. Only after Hunter assured him twice that they'd take care of everything at Cross Creek did he close his eyes, and only *then* did Hunter allow himself to fully breathe.

"We'll be back in a bit to check on you," Hunter murmured, although he suspected that between the heat exhaustion and whatever the doc had put in the IV to treat it, his old man was already well on his way to la-la land. Emerson squeezed his father's hand, tucking the tissue-thin sheet around him one more time as she whispered a goodbye and headed to the door. But before Hunter could follow, his father's eyes fluttered open.

"She's a good one," he said, the sandpaper whisper low enough to keep the words from reaching Emerson's ears. "Don't let her go."

Okay, so the meds were almost certainly talking—after all, his father had about as many sentimental bones in his body as Hunter himself. Still, the rare shot of emotion whisking through his father's eyes caught him so by surprise that he answered with the truth.

"I know, and I promise. I won't."

CHAPTER TWENTY-THREE

Emerson sank against the warm, worn leather of Hunter's passenger seat, watching the last glimmers of daylight slip into shadow over the fields at Cross Creek. Her body was about as ready to tap out as her brain, both of them having been put to the test over the last ten hours. But getting the all-clear on Mr. Cross's test results, then getting him comfortably situated at home and keeping him company while Hunter and his brothers had caught up on things at the farm had been worth every ounce of her exhaustion.

"I'm glad you managed to eat something," Hunter said from beside her, his expression nearly impossible to read in the heavy dusk. He'd been unusually quiet after he'd held on to her in the vestibule in the emergency department, but then again, today hadn't come within forty miles of normal.

Emerson smiled even though he probably couldn't see it, hoping the gesture would at least touch her voice. "I had to set the lead for your father," she said, because even with the day he'd had, no way would Mr. Cross let her get away with not practicing what she preached. "I know the baked chicken and veggies were probably kind of boring for you guys, but I wanted to go easy on his stomach."

Well, that and it was one of about three things she knew how to cook for more than a party of one, but despite the fact that he had to be completely drained, Hunter was quick on the protest.

"No, no. Dinner was great." He let go of a laugh, and while the sound wasn't harsh, it also didn't hold any humor. "God, Em, are you kidding? Between you being there for my old man this morning and how you helped me and my brothers afterward, there aren't enough words to thank you for what you did for my family today."

Emerson blinked through the near darkness in the cab of the pickup. "You don't need to thank me. Of course I helped."

"But not everybody would have. I mean"—he paused, pulling up in front of the cottage but not cutting the engine—"yes, anyone would've called nine-one-one if they'd seen my father collapse. But you didn't hesitate to go with him in the ambulance, to rearrange a job that's hugely important to you in order to stay with us at the hospital. You never thought twice about caring, and not just on the surface. I don't know how to repay you for that."

A sudden burst of emotion wrapped around Hunter's words, triggering something deep inside Emerson's chest, and she loosened her feelings without thinking twice.

"But you already have," she said, turning toward him. "The four of you included me—in your family dinners, in the business you love—from the get-go. I know that may have felt normal to you, but for me, that kind of family acceptance is rare, and . . ." Emerson bit her lip, her own emotions welling up. Still, she didn't try to hide them. "I need it. It means a lot to me that I can be who I am here."

Hunter leaned across the console, pressing his mouth over hers. The kiss wasn't forceful or rough, yet for a second, Emerson couldn't move. His mouth touched hers hungrily, with a quiet, aching need she could taste, and she opened to meet it. Reaching up, she framed his face with both hands. She held him close, sliding her tongue over his, sucking his bottom lip softly as if to say *I'm here, I have you.*

And he shocked the hell out of her by giving in. The tautness in his muscles unwound, his shoulders falling away like they'd just released a breath they'd been clutching for far too long. Hunter's hands found her forearms, hot fingers curling around her skin like a brand, but she held steady. She kissed him slowly, yet with intensity, the connection of their mouths both hard enough to make her lips tingle and soft enough to convey more than physical need.

Yes. Yes, yes, yes. Emerson explored every part of him—the tip of his tongue, the divot right in the center of his ridiculously full lower lip, the edges of his mouth that were responsible for the smiles that lit her up like the brightest star in the midnight sky. She searched and swept, tested and took. Desire pushed her pulse faster, then faster again before Hunter pulled back, a rough groan in his throat.

"Will you come somewhere with me?"

"Right now?" she blurted, startled by the unexpected request.

"Yes." His touch was still firm over her arms, his breath ragged and warm as it mingled with hers. "I'm too keyed up to sleep, and I just . . . I need—"

"Yes." The word sprang past her lips before she even realized her brain had formed it. But the hunger in his tone was so raw, so needful in a way that she'd never quite seen on him, that refusing never crossed her mind. Hunter put the truck in gear, gravel popping softly beneath the tires as he guided them over the network of unpaved paths on Cross Creek's property. Two minutes later, they coasted to a stop in front of the old barn they used to sneak off to in high school, the wide, brick-red boards cloaked in the silvery shadows being thrown down by the moon hanging low on the horizon.

"You want to be at the barn?" Emerson asked, confusion whispering up her spine.

Hunter shook his head, an irony-laced smile shaping his mouth. "I want you, Em. Right now, all I need is you."

His answer was so simple, yet she felt it in even the tiniest places, pure and strong and whole. They got out of the truck without words, Hunter pausing only to grab a heavy blanket from beneath the backseat, and Emerson's brows traveled up in surprise.

"Do you always keep a blanket in your truck?"

He shook his head. "No."

"Okay." She lifted the end of the response like the question it was, and he brushed a kiss over her mouth with just enough intention to make her belly tighten and dip from the promise of it.

"I put the blanket in my truck the morning after you spent that first night with me."

Her uncut shock had to be on full display, because he continued his explanation. "I've never brought anyone to this hayloft other than you. The place just felt too"—Hunter lingered over her lips, tantalizingly close—"intimate. Too personal to share with anyone else. But I've thought about coming back here with you for weeks. God, forever. And right now, that's all I want. You and me and nothing else."

Desire buzzed through her, heady and dark. "I want you, too, Hunter. You and me and nothing else."

Hooking an arm around her waist, he led the way to the double-wide barn door. He passed off the blanket and palmed the handle, pulling the wood-planked panel along its steel track just far enough to allow them both entry. Emerson followed him into the space, giving her eyes a minute to adjust to the darkness. The barn was strictly storage for feed hay, and the fresh, damp-earth smell nearly made her laugh from the sweetness of the memories it triggered. The shapes around her grew clearer, becoming distinct objects in her field of vision, but Hunter still caught her hand, ushering her over to the ladder leading up to the loft.

"You okay to climb?" he asked, taking the blanket from her and tossing the neatly folded cotton to the floorboards above them. Although the movement held the ease of having been done no fewer than ten thousand times before with far heavier objects, a thread of tender concern hung in his words, and Emerson nodded to hammer home her certainty.

"I am." Yes, her body was tired, and yes again, her aches were far from nonexistent. But she recognized the look in Hunter's eyes, hungry and deep. He might always stay calm and cool and take care of everyone else, but right now, he needed comfort.

And she knew exactly how to give it to him.

Gripping the edges of the ladder in front of her, Emerson placed a foot on the bottom rung and started to climb. She held on tightly, the rough-hewn wood scraping slightly against her palms with each step, but her ballet flats offered enough purchase—and her legs supported her with enough strength—for her to make her way into the hayloft without stumbling.

Hunter swung his lean frame up to the floorboards beside her. "I should've known you'd brazen your way up here all on your own. Nice job, small-town girl," he said, and Emerson couldn't help her soft laugh at both the nickname and his belief in her.

"There are some things you never forget, hotshot."

"Believe me," he said, reaching out to pull her close. "I know."

She lost herself in his kiss for just a minute before he loosened his hands from her shoulders, bending down low to grab the blanket. The hayloft was large and open, spanning much of the same space as the ground level of the barn below, and although Hunter had closed the main door behind them when they'd come in from outside, the second-story window remained wide on its hinges. Bales of hay were stacked waist high in front of the glassless opening, which not only kept anyone from taking an unexpected fall, but also blocked any direct view into the loft. Moonlight still streamed in from above, though, filling the warm night air with a view so honest and pretty, Emerson's breath caught.

"Oh." She moved over the sturdy, hay-strewn floorboards to take in the night sky. Stars winked and glittered like fresh-cut diamonds over a black-velvet canvas, framing the full moon on all sides. "The view up here is so beautiful."

"It is," Hunter agreed, but when she turned her head, Emerson discovered he wasn't looking at the sky.

He was looking at her, the need in his stare so fierce that she wanted nothing more than to fill it.

Pressing to her toes, she rushed up to meet his mouth. The intensity of the connection, the soft scrape of his stubble against her skin, the salty, masculine taste of his lips parting to let her in, all of it filled Emerson with desire. But the feeling burning through her veins wasn't a strictly physical arousal, the sort that demanded clothes to be torn off and sensitive body parts touched and licked and filled. There was another level to this want, something vital and fundamental, as if they needed each other like tides need the moon, and she circled her arms tighter around Hunter's shoulders in order to deliver.

"Come here."

He let her lead him a few steps away, to the pile of loose hay where he'd unfurled the blanket, the same corner of the hayloft where they'd always hidden together. Emerson knelt down over the heavy cotton, the material sturdy enough to protect their skin yet soft enough to be comfortable, and she reached for Hunter through the shadows.

Their bodies tangled together in a combination of mouths and limbs and need. Bracing one arm around her rib cage and the other in the crook of her knees, he eased her all the way back on the blanket, turning his body so they faced each other, side to side. Emerson returned her mouth to his, tracing the firm line of his lips with her tongue until they opened to grant her access. She slid a hand over the ridge of his shoulder, heat bursting to life between her legs at the way his muscles went taut beneath her touch. Her fingers spread wider, exploring every cord and every angle from his neck to the plane of his chest, and his breath moved faster against her mouth.

"Em." The whisper fell somewhere between a plea and a prayer. Still, Emerson didn't slow her movements, the tiny tremors that her touch sent through him pushing her to make contact with all of him. Her fingers slipped lower, beneath the hem of his T-shirt, and God, his warm, smooth skin made her dizzy with want.

"Hunter." She skimmed her hand over his body, the space between them so narrow that her knuckles grazed her own chest. The contoured muscle of Hunter's abs gave way to the indent of his navel, then the crisp line of hair leading down to the button on his jeans. With want in her belly that she couldn't control, Emerson's hand traveled the length of it, eager fingers lingering for just a breath on the heated denim before dipping lower to wrap around Hunter's already-hard cock.

A low sound tore from his throat, too rough for a moan yet not quite a growl, and her pulse quickened, wicked satisfaction coursing through her at the sound.

"Let me make you feel good." Emerson stroked him over his jeans, her movements slow and full of promise. "You said you want this, just me and you. Let me take care of you, Hunter."

He thrust into the circle of her fingers once, then again before reaching down to capture her wrist. "But that's not what I want."

Surprise had her chin jerking up, adrenaline touching her heartbeat just enough to make it quicken. "Don't you want to be with me? You said—"

"Make no mistake," Hunter said, the pad of his forefinger finding her lips and pressing hard over their center. "I want you, naked and wet and screaming my name."

Oh God. The bold suggestion made Emerson's nipples pearl beneath the thin cotton of her blouse. "Then why won't you let me return the favor?"

"Because." He dragged his callused finger over her chin, the friction sending a hard, dark thrill all the way to her clit. "Don't you see? It's taking care of *you* that makes me hot. The way you moan when I touch you." Hunter paused to let his touch play just briefly in the sensitive spot behind her ear, his mouth hooking in a savage half smile as she released a honeyed sigh. "The little cries that tell me how hard you want to come. How beautiful your face is when you get there. That's what I want, Emerson. That's what turns me on. I want you to let *me* take care of *you*."

His words were pure intensity, and in that moment, Emerson was lost. Her body surrendered, melting into the blanket and molding to fit his touch. With one swift pull, he had her shirt over her head, the material fluttering away to reveal a bra that he removed just as quickly. The juncture between her thighs grew damp as Hunter continued to undress her, then himself, until the only barriers between them were her thin cotton panties and the boxer briefs clearly outlining his rock-hard erection.

"This is what I want," he whispered, so close that his breath warmed her bare skin. He lay on his side, his hand coasting over her shoulder, moving lower to shape the slope of her breast.

Emerson arched against the solid weight of his palm. Her nipples stiffened, her breasts so heavy with desire that she had to bite back the moan that wanted to drift up from her chest. Then she thought of Hunter's words, and the sound pushed past her lips, uninhibited.

His hand tightened on her breast. "You want me to touch you here?" His thumb slid dangerously close to her nipple, but she arched higher to make the connection.

"Yes. If you want me, I'm yours. All you have to do is take me."

The words seemed to break a thread stretched thin inside of him. Cupping her breast with one hand, Hunter dropped his mouth to the top of her chest. His stubble created just enough friction to tempt her to scream, the need between her legs blurring the edges between greedy pleasure and sweet pain. He darted his tongue past the edge of his mouth, sliding a hot, wet path over the curve of her breast, not stopping until he reached her nipple.

"*Oh*. God." Emerson bowed off the blanket with a desperate cry. Her eyes, which had fluttered closed, flew wide, and the sight of Hunter's glittering stare and reverent want crashed into her like a palpable force. She watched as he laved her breasts with attention, her sex growing wet as he balanced the soft ministrations of his mouth with the rougher actions of his hands. Emerson murmured her appreciation, heat blazing all the way through her with every move, and he was an expert listener, intuitive and eager to please. But the more Hunter touched her, the more she ached, her hips lifting from the warmth of the blanket in search of more.

"Please," she said, not knowing how to finish her sentence. *Please sink inside me. Please make me come. Please hold me and don't let go.*

The one word was enough, though. Hunter straightened so they were eye to eye, reaching down low to slip her panties from her hips. His boxer briefs followed seconds later, and seconds more had him sheathed in the condom he'd taken from his wallet. Bracketing Emerson's body with his hands, he parted the cradle of her hips with his lean frame, slipping his fingers along the seam of her body.

"Hunter." She widened her knees. His gaze was fixed on the spot where he stroked her, the abundant moonlight making it all too easy for him to see even her most intimate places. But she could see him in return, and the look on his face, so lost and yet found at the same time, made her want him all the more.

Hunter leaned in to kiss her, the press of his tongue in her mouth keeping time with his hand between her legs. Hot, desperate need coiled in the bottom of her belly, turning tighter with every sweep of his fingers over her sex. For a second, he broke the contact, and a whimper threatened from somewhere deep in Emerson's chest. But then he gripped his cock, angling his hips to slide the blunt head over her folds, and the whimper became a lust-drenched sigh.

"That . . . please . . . don't . . ." The broken gasps were all she could manage past the pure desire building inside of her.

Somehow, he understood. "I won't." Hunter held steady, stroking his cock back and forth just above her entrance. Her clit throbbed with every pass, her sex clenching in absolute want and, just as her climax began to unravel, he thrust between her legs to fill her to the hilt.

"*Ah.*" Emerson knotted her arms around his hips to keep him buried deep. The sudden pressure of him inside her magnified her release, drawing out her orgasm in wave after wave. Hunter gave her the lead, anchoring his hands beneath her for support as she thrust against his cock, over and over. Only when she'd ridden out every last gasp of pleasure did he start to move, and dear, sweet God, he was a sight to see.

Handsome face, drawn tight in concentration. Eyes glittering with need, locked on the spot where they joined. Sweat-sheened muscles, flexing and releasing as he pumped his hips into hers.

Emerson rocked to meet him, her heart speeding against her breastbone. Hunter's stare drifted up to meet hers, and she didn't dare look away, simply held on to his gaze while he filled her, again and again.

"Perfect. God, you're so *perfect*," he grated, his voice so rough that the words vibrated over her skin. The rhythm between them changed, growing faster and more fierce. Curling his fingers into her hips, he dragged her close, kneeling upright between her thighs. Emerson's knees butterflied outward, the soles of her feet digging into the blanket and seeking the floorboards beneath, and the heady scents of hay and sex and something masculine belonging to Hunter alone filled her lungs. He thrust into her in powerful strokes, his movements becoming sharper, more focused. His muscles quickened, and as passionate as her own orgasm had been, Emerson couldn't deny wanting Hunter's even more.

"Show me," she said, spreading her legs as wide as she could. "Please, Hunter. Come for me."

His teeth sank into his bottom lip, holding fast. With a push of his hips that left no space between them, he arched one more time with a shout. His body pressed over hers, so closely that Emerson could feel the shake and tremble of his release, and she wrapped her arms around him to gather him close.

Time passed and they separated slowly, a softer touch here, a shift of weight there. But as they dressed and silently made their way out of the hayloft, Emerson didn't need any words to know she was in love with him.

CHAPTER TWENTY-FOUR

Hunter swiveled a gaze over the picture-perfect scene in front of him, his gut filling with dread. Stupid, really, since the weather was at a steady eighty-three and sunny, his father had spent the entire weekend resting with barely any fuss, and he'd been out in Cross Creek's fields with his sleeves rolled up and his hands on the land all morning long. But despite all the good things Hunter knew should be setting his status quo at ease, his chest felt like an overused pincushion, pricked full of tiny yet insidious holes.

His father might be on the mend, but Emerson sure wasn't. She was doing her damndest to cover up the dark circles and slow movements around everyone else, but he saw the skipped meals, the weary lines around her eyes, the exhaustion she lamely blamed on the heat when they both knew so much better. Watching her in pain was bad enough—fuck, seeing Emerson hurting made him want to beat the shit out of something. But watching her deny that the pain even existed, hearing the lie in her voice every time she told him she was fine, that it would pass, that this was normal?

Now *that* was killing him.

"Damn, Hunt. I know I'm the handsome one, but that's a hell of a face you're makin'."

Eli's voice winged him directly back to the hay field they'd been busting their asses all morning to harvest, and probably just as well. Christ, he was getting downright grim, and the day was barely half over.

"Sorry," Hunter said, tacking on a smile that was mostly for show. "Guess we can't all have no cares like you."

Shit. The muscle tightening across the angle of Eli's jaw told Hunter his jibe had missed the mark by about a country mile. "Ouch. Now you're starting to sound like Owen."

"I'm sorry," Hunter said, this time with the sincerity it deserved. "I s'pose this whole Dad thing still has me a little thrown." It was a hell of a nutshell, but for now, the understatement would do.

Eli adjusted the brim of his dust-covered baseball hat, even though the thing was already perfectly straight. "No worries, brother. I get it."

Whether it was the what if that had been nagging him for the last four days or the odd emotion in Eli's stare that he couldn't quite tag, Hunter didn't know. But instead of turning back to the hay field and getting back to business as usual, he said, "Do you want to tell me what the hell is going on between you and Owen?"

Eli's face flashed with pure surprise, and for a second, Hunter thought his brother might actually answer the question with a yes.

But then he lifted a shoulder in a standard-issue carefree shrug, the shadow cast by his baseball hat covering the look in his eyes. "There's nothing going on between me and Owen."

"Bullshit. Y'all haven't been right for months," Hunter said, and huh. Looked like he was going all-in with shaking up the status quo today. Not that Eli seemed to be budging.

"Alright, fine. It's nothing I want to talk about. Look"—Eli let out a slow breath, skimming a long glance over the half-harvested field in front of them—"I get that you hate us fighting, and I appreciate you being the middleman to try and make things easier. It's just . . . fucking complicated, that's all."

Hunter's heart tapped harder in warning. "Complicated," he repeated, but in the same breath, Eli was waving him off with a cocky grin.

"Yeah, it'll be fine. I'll figure it out, just probably not today."

"Eli, if you need—"

"I'm good," his brother said, the finality in his voice killing the topic. "Anyway, it looks like we're damn near out of baling wire, and this was the last spool in the storage shed. I can jump into town to grab some from the co-op if you want to harvest the last few bales before we're tapped."

Eli turned toward the ATV they'd ridden down to the field from the main house, but Hunter stopped him with a shake of his head and a quick, "Nah. You go on and finish. I'll do the grunt job."

"You sure?" Eli's dark-blond brows popped in obvious surprise.

"Yeah," Hunter said. Damn, he was more than ready to kick this weird tension in his chest to the curb, once and for all. "You've done a month's worth of scut work along with the real stuff waiting for me to get back in the saddle, remember?"

Eli laughed, long and loud. "Your offer wouldn't have anything to do with the fact that the co-op is a stone's throw from a certain pretty redhead's physical therapy practice, would it?"

Cue up a guilty smile. Still, he had his pride (mostly . . . sort of), so he dished up a "screw you" to go along with it.

"That's a yes." Eli called after him, still laughing as Hunter aimed his boots toward the ATV and kicked himself into motion. Okay, yeah, the opportunity to stop in to see Emerson might have colored his offer just a little. But she'd spent fifteen hours in bed yesterday, and despite the fact that she'd tried like hell to tackle the cottage stairs, she'd finally given in and let him bring her dinner in his bedroom.

He was in love with her—not that he was going to pop off at the mouth about it to his brother. Sue him for wanting to make sure she was okay.

You know her. You know she's not okay.

Hunter frowned at the voice in his head. He moved with added purpose, returning to the main house to swap out the ATV for his truck, then making the fastest trip on record to the co-op for a half-dozen spools of baling wire. He parked along the red-brick sidewalk of Town Street, tossing his hand up in an obligatory wave as Amber Cassidy poked her bottle-blond head out of the Hair Lair to greet him.

"Hi, Hunter! Goin' to see *Emerson*, I take it?"

"I was in town, so I figured I'd stop by," he said. Amber was essentially harmless, but Christ above, the woman could probably gossip about wheat toast.

Case in point. "Mm*hmm*. Aren't you two just *cozy*? It's like *high school* all over again."

Hunter threw her a smile but didn't stop walking. "Yep, that's us. Totally cozy. See you later, Amber."

He ducked into Doc Sanders's office with a covert exhale. To his surprise, the doc herself was behind the reception desk, flipping through a medical journal and eating a ham-and-cheese sandwich.

"Hey, Hunter. This is a nice surprise." Pushing her glasses over the bridge of her nose, she scanned the computer screen in front of her. "You don't have an appointment. Everything okay with your shoulder?"

"Oh, uh, yes ma'am." He rolled the joint in question beneath his T-shirt as proof. "Good as new. I actually stopped in to say hi to Emerson real quick, just as long as she's not busy."

"We're taking lunch breaks. Obviously." Doc Sanders held up her sandwich with a grin, but the gesture quickly faded as she continued. "As a matter of fact, I'm glad you're here to check on her."

The back of Hunter's neck prickled, but he forced himself to stick to his nothing-doing expression. "You are?"

The doc nodded, her gray-blond brows lifting. "Yes. That bout of food poisoning seems to have done a number on her over the weekend."

He bit his tongue to keep his curse at bay. "Yeah," he finally managed, although even that was a stretch. Had Emerson's stomach really gotten that bad? And more to the point, if she *was* throwing up, how come she hadn't said anything? Dammit, he would've helped her.

Doc Sanders continued. "She said she feels well enough to work, but . . . well, frankly, she looks pretty wiped out. I was about to go check on her myself."

"No worries, Doc. I'll make sure she's all set."

Hunter pivoted toward the PT room, trying like hell to temper his slamming heartbeat with each step down the hall. The door to the therapy room was open as usual, but what he saw as he crossed the threshold was far from normal. Emerson sat huddled over her desk, her face cast downward with her forehead resting in both palms, and Hunter's stomach clenched at the sight of how clearly vulnerable she looked.

"Em?"

The squeeze in his gut hit vise-grip status as her head whipped up in surprise. "Hunter?" she gasped, blinking rapidly. "Where . . . what are you doing here?"

Her gaze was just hazy enough to make it obvious that he'd woken her, the crescent-shaped shadows beneath her eyes broadcasting that the stolen nap hadn't been nearly long enough, and something broke loose from deep in his chest.

"I'm taking you home." Okay, so the answer came out a bit bossier than he'd intended. But come the fuck on. Her MS was getting the best of her today. She was weak and exhausted. She clearly needed to rest.

Of course, he should've known better than to think she'd actually admit either of those two realities. "Don't be ridiculous," Emerson said, her spine straightening as if it were suddenly reinforced with titanium.

"I have three clients this afternoon, and they're all counting on me. Plus, I'm fine."

Nope. No way. He wasn't going to let her brazen her way out of this one, not even if it meant saying things she didn't want to hear. "You couldn't even make it down the steps for dinner last night, and you haven't eaten a proper meal in weeks. For God's sake, you had to tell Doc Sanders you had food poisoning to cover up the truth."

"Keep your voice down," she hissed, her face pinched with panic.

The need to erase her pain warred with the promise he'd made to keep her secret, and each one had a nasty uppercut. "I'm sorry," he said, pitching his voice lower without giving in. "But I know you, and I know what I see. You can try all you want to cover it up, but you are *not* fine."

Hurt glittered in her bright-blue stare, telling Hunter his words had struck true and deep. Still, Emerson hiked her chin and knotted her arms over her chest, resolute.

"Yes, I am." She notched her voice to a whisper, but what the words lacked in volume, they made up for in pure intensity. "It's true that yesterday was tough on my legs, and yes, the meds are still affecting my stomach. But I have MS, Hunter, and the disease is forever. Just because the symptoms suck doesn't mean I don't have to deal with them. They're never going away."

Just like that, the calm he'd relied on his entire life turned to dust. Something dark and fundamental and without a name forced him into motion, propelling him to cross the floor to kneel down beside her so the two of them were eye to eye.

"Then do it. *Deal* with your symptoms instead of pretending they don't exist."

Her shoulder blades hit the back of her creaky old desk chair with a thump. "Believe me, I deal with them every day."

"No, you manage them," Hunter said. "Or at least, you do your best to. Either way, it's not the same. Tell me—what would've happened if you hadn't been there for my father when he collapsed last week?"

"What does that have to do with my fatigue or my leg pain?" Her auburn brows gathered over her stare, but he pressed, desperate to make his point.

"Humor me. What would've happened?"

"I . . . things could've been worse for him, I suppose."

Hunter's grip tightened on the arm of her desk chair. "Exactly. And what's going to happen if no one's there for you?"

Emerson's laugh was all disbelief. "I'm fine. I'm certainly not going to collapse."

"You don't know that." Fear skidded through him at the thought alone. "My father didn't think he'd collapse, and multiple sclerosis is far more serious than even heat exhaustion. Jesus, Em. You don't have to be so tough, and you sure as hell don't have to hide. Not from me. I want to help you."

Hunter broke off, but dammit—*dammit*—he couldn't sit back any more. He'd done that with his father, and look where it had gotten them.

He couldn't take the risk. Not again. Not with Emerson.

"Please," he said, the word gruff with emotion. "Let me help you."

"I know you want to fix this," she whispered, her lips pressing together in a pale, unyielding line. "But there's nothing *to* fix. I just have to get used to how these new meds will affect my stomach, that's all. Plus, I'm fine."

Hunter's gut sank. She might never forgive him for what he was about to say, but he wouldn't forgive himself if he kept quiet again.

"Okay," he said, pushing to his feet and gesturing widely to the expanse of floor tiles in front of him. "Then go ahead and prove it."

Every inch of Emerson's body begged for mercy. She'd been duking it out with her exhaustion for days, not the run-of-the-mill kind of tired she'd grown accustomed to over the last six months, but the sort of debilitating fatigue that made her question the integrity of her bones. Her nausea had morphed into full-blown vomiting over the weekend, a fact that had taken a minor miracle to keep hidden from Hunter. She'd never had a relapse so severe or so painful—God, the fire in her legs bordered on savage just sitting here—but she couldn't let the worst of her MS show.

These episodes in which her symptoms got the best of her body were just something she had to tough out and get used to. They weren't going to go away. She wasn't going to magically heal. And she sure as hell wasn't going to show *anyone* this new level of broken. Not even Hunter.

If people saw the reality of her MS firsthand—if her friends saw, her boss, God, her *parents*—then they'd all know how damaged she really was.

No one would trust her. No one would think she was good enough to do her job. She'd lose everything.

She had to get out of this chair.

"You want me to prove that I'm fine?" Emerson asked, looking up at him in disbelief.

Unfortunately, budging wasn't on his agenda. "Mmhmm. A quick back and forth over the floor here ought to do the trick, don't you think? If you're as fine as you say you are, it should be a piece of cake."

In that moment, she was tempted to hate him. But she needed every ounce of her energy for other things, namely rising to the Mount Everest–sized gauntlet he'd just thrown down, so she stowed her irritation with a smile she didn't feel.

"Suit yourself." Flattening her palms over the desk in front of her, Emerson shifted her weight and pushed herself to standing. Her spine and legs joined forces to try to thwart her, but just as she had all morning, she forced them to do their job of supporting her despite the ripping pain. Hunter stood a few feet away, his hands jammed to his hips and his eyes missing nothing.

Make it good. Head up. Eyes forward.

Emerson focused on the far wall and started to walk. Hunter might be trying to prove a point, but she'd been proving herself for as long as she could remember.

She'd make it across the floor just fine. She *had* to.

She couldn't let anyone see how broken she was.

Although each step bordered on excruciating, she walked the eight-foot circuit, returning to her starting spot to look at Hunter. "See?" she said, her joints squealing and sticking like old hinges but her determination firm. "Totally fine."

"And you're going to stand by that." The lines around his eyes softened, but no. No, no. She couldn't give in.

"I know you don't understand, but . . ." Emerson paused. Dragged in a deep breath. "Yes."

"Then I guess I can't help you at all."

Hunter turned toward the door. For a second, she was paralyzed by the shock of it, her brain and her heart and her body all frozen in a state of confusion. Then everything rebooted at once, urging her into motion.

"Hunter, wait, I—"

The rest of Emerson's words jammed to a halt as her right leg went numb and buckled beneath her. Her pulse went haywire, her arms windmilling in a desperate attempt to salvage her balance. But they landed on nothing but empty space, and the floor rushed up to greet her with a rude thud.

"Emerson!" The sound of footsteps clattered across the linoleum, followed less than a second later by Hunter's voice next to her ear. "Jesus, are you okay? Let me get Doc Sanders."

"No." She managed the word forcefully enough to make him pause, thank God, and she did a quick internal scan. No overt pain, which was good, although her hip throbbed like crazy at the point of impact and her leg had graduated from numbness to a pins-and-needles-type

tingle. She shifted awkwardly against the dead weight, the coolness of the floor tiles pressing against her palms as she turned to sit on her bottom. "I'm fine."

Hunter's laugh lacked any trace of humor. "You just went ass over teakettle onto a surface that's probably subfloor over concrete."

"Thanks for pointing that out." Emerson's face flushed with the full heat of her words, and fantastic. Were there seriously *tears* forming in her eyes?

"I'm sorry," he said, his genuine tone making her threat of crying that much more imminent. "Here, first thing's first. Let's get you off the floor, okay?"

Before she could open her mouth to answer, he'd slipped one arm beneath her knees, the other wrapping firmly around her upper body as he scooped her up in one fluid movement.

"Hunter, stop. You still need to be careful with your shoulder," she said, but the intensity glinting through his stare halted the rest of her protest in its tracks.

"I don't give a shit about my shoulder."

By the time he made it the half-dozen steps to the portable massage table and lowered her gently to the cushion, Emerson had wrestled her tears into submission. The high-powered slam of her heartbeat?

Not so much.

"Are you dizzy from not eating? Does anything hurt?" Hunter moved in front of her, his eyes traveling from her disheveled ponytail to her patent-leather ballet flats with growing scrutiny, and dammit, she needed to get a handle on this situation, stat.

"I told you, I'm completely fine." She straightened the hem of her blouse, smoothing a palm over the cotton before sliding her shoulder blades in tight around her mutinous spine.

"I'm pretty sure we're past that, Em."

Think. *Think.* "I'm not feeling dizzy," she admitted, but hell if it wasn't her only win. "My legs are still . . . hurting."

Hunter didn't even blink. "Like yesterday?"

"About the same," Emerson said, although it bordered on being untrue. She'd done all the research, studied everything on paper. But she'd never had a relapse this bad before, and never once had she thought the pain or the fatigue would be so crushing.

She'd thought she'd be able to handle it. She *needed* to be able to handle it.

"Scale of one to ten." Hunter's tone softened, his fingers brushing her cheek just enough to ground her, and dammit, why did he have to remember *everything* from his PT?

She whispered, "Eight."

"Okay. I'm getting the doc."

"No!" Fear claimed her gut, clutching tight. The frown hooking at the corners of Hunter's mouth told her in no unequivocal terms that he wasn't letting her off on her own recognizance, but still, there had to be something else.

"I'll go home to rest," she said, the words wavering past the tight knot of her throat, and Hunter stepped in, his warm fingers wrapping around her traitorous, trembling hand.

"You've *been* resting. If you're in that much pain"—he paused, his throat working over a swallow, his eyes turning more gray than blue as he continued—"and you haven't been able to keep any food down because of the meds, you're probably dehydrated. I don't have to tell you how dangerous that can get. You're a smart woman. So I can get Doc Sanders or I can take you to the hospital. Those are your choices."

Emerson dropped her chin to her chest. God, she hated it, she *hated* it, but he was right. "Okay. We can go to the hospital."

The drive to Lockridge wasn't a cakewalk, but at least no one there would know her. Plus, she could lie down in the truck like she had when Hunter had taken her to her last appointment. Maybe that would give her some relief from this stupid pain.

Hunter squeezed her hand. "Okay. I'll go tell Doc Sanders you're still not feeling well and then we can go."

A thought hit her, sending a swirl of dread through her belly. "You have to promise to let me walk to your truck, though. If the doc sees you carrying me, or God, if Amber sees, everyone in town will talk."

"You're in pain," he argued, but she shook her head. She couldn't cave. Not on this.

"I'll make it."

A few minutes and some highly creative maneuvering later, they were in Hunter's truck, headed out of Millhaven. Her legs burned and throbbed from the short walk she'd forced them to make. Even though he drove with care, Emerson's stomach pitched and twisted just from the forward motion, and she closed her eyes to ward off both the nausea and the pain.

"Can I do anything for you?" Hunter asked, and she anchored onto his voice, letting the cadence soothe her.

"Mmm mmm," she managed as a wave of pain slid down her legs. Tears formed behind her closed eyelids, but when she inhaled, the scent of leather and cedar and Hunter himself countered them.

"I've got you, Em. It's going to be okay."

That voice, the rise and fall, the honesty in it. God, she wanted to believe him, but her body *hurt*.

The tears did fall then, tracking over her face past her still-closed eyes. Hunter thumbed them away one by one, murmuring quietly that she was going to be okay, and somehow, unbelievably, despite the fire tearing through her, Emerson actually believed him.

She trusted Hunter to help her. With him, she would be okay.

Breathing in and out, she focused on keeping her stomach in check, losing herself in the darkness of her closed eyes. She drifted along with the sound of his words, the heady, comforting scent of him right next to her, until a change in momentum jerked her back to her senses.

Wait . . . "Why are we slowing down?"

"We're here," Hunter said, but that couldn't be right. They hadn't been on the road long enough.

And then the sign in front of her registered, the bright-red block print pumping dread through her veins.

"CAMDEN VALLEY HOSPITAL, EMERGENCY DEPARTMENT."

"This isn't the right hospital," Emerson blurted, but he pulled up to the circular entryway to the ED, anyway.

"It was closest, and you're in pain. I'm not arguing with you." To prove it, he put the truck in park, jumping down to round the passenger side to open her door.

Every defense Emerson had wailed in warning. "I can't," she said, darting a glance at the brick-and-glass building.

Hunter didn't even stop moving. "You can."

Her legs tingled as if to agree, and she gave in with a heavy exhale. She'd been here for the better part of the day on Friday while Mr. Cross had been treated, and hadn't seen so much as a hint of her parents. Being here was far from ideal, but it was what she had.

No matter how much she hated it.

Bracing his hands around her waist, Hunter helped her out of the truck and through the sliding glass doors. Each step sent aches from her swollen feet to her furious lower back, but she took each one. When they got to the triage desk, Hunter made sure Emerson had the nurse's full attention before he slipped back outside to park his truck.

"Can I help you?" the woman asked, but all it took was one good look for her to spring from her seat and round the business end of the desk with a wheelchair.

Great. She even looked weak to strangers. "Yes, I'm . . . not feeling well," Emerson said, unable to force herself to say the real words.

If she said them out loud, they'd be real. Irreversible.

Too true to ignore.

The nurse slid an arm around Emerson's shoulder, guiding her into the wheelchair, and Emerson was too tired, too dizzy, to protest. "Let's see if I can help you with that. My name is Jackie. I'm going to take you to a curtain area to take your vitals. What's your name?"

"Emerson." The relief at surrendering her body weight, even to a wheelchair, was enough to make her sigh.

"Okay, Emerson. Did you want me to have someone bring your boyfriend back to sit with you once we're done with your assessment?"

She didn't think. Just nodded. "Yes, please." If Hunter was with her, she could do this. He'd promised she'd be okay.

And she believed him.

Jackie guided her past the automatic doors leading into the emergency department, pulling back a curtain anchored in the ceiling tiles by a shiny silver track. The area was quiet but sterile, white sheet stretched thin over the pancake-flat hospital mattress, blue gown folded into a neat square at the foot of the bed, antiseptic smell of alcohol filling her nose, and Emerson's heart thudded with the knowledge of what came next.

Jackie asked softly, "So what brings you in to the ED today?"

"I . . ." Again, the words wedged in Emerson's throat, but then her mind tumbled back, Hunter's voice right there in her ears.

I've got you. It's going to be okay.

"I have multiple sclerosis," Emerson said.

And then she started to cry.

CHAPTER TWENTY-FIVE

Never in his thirty years had Hunter had to fight so hard to stay calm. But Emerson needed him, and even though she was in enough pain to scare him fucking senseless, he was going to stay strong.

What if . . . what if . . .

Hunter's feet moved swiftly over the pavement, the question beating a foreboding pattern in his brain. His father's near miss last week had brought the grim flip side of "what if" into sharp focus. Yes, his old man was fine now, but one twist of fate, one cruel shift in another direction, and he wouldn't have been.

What if Emerson hadn't been there for his father?

And what if Hunter hadn't been there today for her?

His mouth went as dry as the asphalt beneath his boots. Multiple sclerosis was far more grave than he'd realized or she was willing to admit, and he was literally her only lifeline. She refused to tell anyone else she had the disease, refused to believe that the side effects of the meds she was on and the pain of her symptoms were anything other than normal. If he hadn't stopped by the PT center when he did, she'd have collapsed on that floor alone.

What if . . .

Hunter reached the sliding glass doors, his arms prickling at the whoosh of air conditioning on his sun-warmed skin. He needed to focus, to find a way to fix this. Once Emerson felt a little better, they could come up with a plan. Maybe she could at least tell Doc Sanders and a few other trusted people that she was sick. Lord knew she couldn't keep hiding from it like this.

The pain might end them both.

Shaking off the thought, Hunter scanned the waiting room. Both Emerson and the nurse were gone—not a bad sign, as far as he was concerned—and he turned toward the triage desk to try to finagle his way back to the curtain area to see her.

And found himself face to startled face with Emerson's father.

"Hunter." Dr. Montgomery's brows creased over a stare caught somewhere between chill and confusion. "Quite a surprise to see you out this way."

"Uh," he stuttered, and shit. *Shit*. Compared with this moment, the spot between a rock and a hard place was a luxury destination. "Yes . . . sir. That is, I wasn't planning to be here."

"One usually doesn't. Hence the 'emergency' in the name."

The corners of his mouth twitched just slightly, smoothing back into seriousness before the gesture fully registered, and in that odd, stop-time second, Hunter realized that the response hadn't been meant disrespectfully.

Had Emerson's father been making an awkward attempt to be sociable?

"At any rate." Dr. Montgomery smoothed a hand over the front of his white coat, his gaze appearing genuinely concerned. "Are you unwell? I came down for a consult, but if you need assistance, perhaps I can point you in the right direction."

Hunter's mouth opened, a fabricated answer locked and loaded on his tongue. Emerson had made him promise not to say anything—to her parents above all else—but dammit, her illness was bigger than she'd admit, and she needed *help*. Her parents had been trying to reach out to her all week. Wasn't it possible that despite their overbearing way of showing it, they actually had good intentions? There was no way they didn't love Emerson. She was their only child, for Chrissake! Dr. Montgomery was a physician, not to mention her father, her flesh and blood. Not agreeing with her career choice was a far cry from not helping her through being sick.

Screw the status quo. She *was* sick, and Hunter would rock all the boats he had to in order to ease her pain.

"Actually, I'm here with Emerson. I think the two of you need to talk."

◆ ◆ ◆

Emerson had been around enough doctors in her life to know when things were mission critical. The look on Dr. Ortiz's face right now?

Told her in no uncertain terms she wasn't going to like what he had to say.

"Okay, Ms. Montgomery. You can relax now," he said, guiding the paper-thin bedsheet back over her two-sizes-too-swollen legs to preserve the tiny shred of her dignity that remained. "I've got a couple of concerns, and unfortunately they're going to keep you here at least for a little while. The biggest is that you're pretty dehydrated."

She blew out a breath, hating the news even though it didn't surprise her. "I figured." Poor Jackie had needed three tries to get Emerson's IV into place. Considering the digestive rebellion her stomach had declared over the last two days, she'd have been shocked to her toes if she *weren't* dehydrated. "I've been trying to at least keep fluids down, but the MS meds have been making that difficult."

"Let's tackle it this way. I'd like to give you an anti-emetic for the nausea, that way we can work on getting something in your stomach once it settles. In the meantime, we'll get more IV fluids on board so your dehydration doesn't get any more dangerous."

Her shoulders sank against the mattress, but she gave up a tiny nod. "Okay."

"Good." Dr. Ortiz looped his stethoscope back around his neck, his expression telling her his laundry list of concerns had just begun. "Your pain is also obviously an issue, as is the edema in your feet and lower legs. We should be able to get both under control with rest and medication, but . . . are your MS relapses normally this severe?"

"No. I mean, I was only diagnosed about three months ago, but . . . yes. This is the worst one by far." She bit her lip at the admission, but to her surprise, the doctor didn't crank up the aw-poor-weak-you sympathy.

"It's not entirely unusual for the first few episodes after a diagnosis to be all over the place, especially if a patient is trying different treatments to manage them." He held up her electronic chart, which contained the health history she'd given Jackie as well as the mile-long list of meds her neurologist had prescribed. "Clearly, your current regimen isn't a good fit if it's going to make you nauseous enough to become dehydrated. But let's not try to drive beyond the headlights, okay? Before we do anything else, we've got to manage this relapse. Then you can work out a new medication plan with your neurologist."

Emerson dropped her chin to the chest of her hospital gown. The thought of starting fresh with new meds was enough to make her stomach pool with dread, but still, it paled in comparison with an extended hospital stay.

"Okay. Do you think I'll be able to go home today?" she asked, mentally tacking *please please please* to the end of the question. She knew she needed to rest, but the thought of doing it in a hospital, especially *this* hospital, gave her the shakes.

Dr. Ortiz pulled his cell phone, which had started buzzing like crazy, out of the pocket of his doctor's coat. "What I think is that you need to rest and rehydrate, and let us manage your pain. Then we'll see where we are. Ah." His black brows lifted toward his just-ruffled-enough hairline, and he looked at her in what seemed like surprise. "Seems there's someone who's rather impatient to see you."

For the first time in days, a smile pulled at the corners of her mouth. "Yes. It's okay with me if he comes back."

"Okay. Get some rest, and I'll have Jackie come in with a painkiller and some meds for your nausea and swelling. I'll also send your visitor back." Dr. Ortiz nodded, tucking her electronic chart under his arm as he slipped from the room. Okay, so the road in front of her was longer and studded with more land mines than she'd thought, but she could do this. She was going to be okay.

Hunter had promised. He'd said he had her back, and she believed him. Even though it went against everything she thought she'd wanted when she'd returned to Millhaven, Emerson trusted him to see all of her, to stay right there with her no matter how bad the disease got.

But when the curtain slid back a minute later, the man on the other side wasn't Hunter.

This couldn't be right.

"Dad?" The heart rate monitor beside her bed went ballistic, the numbers flashing wildly along with the rhythm in her chest. But no way—no *way* was her father, the one person she'd been desperate to hide her sickness from the most, standing there in front of her while she was having her worst relapse to date.

"Emerson," he said, and her stomach dropped with the cold realization that he was in fact *very* much in front of her, taking in her imperfections by the minute. His brows creased in obvious confusion. "Would you like to tell me exactly what's going on here?"

"No," she said, partly because it was true and partly because it was the only word she could get past the terror in her throat. How was this *happening*? She'd been in triage for all of fifteen seconds, for God's sake!

Of course, her father took her refusal as an invitation to argue. "Clearly, you're having a medical issue. I understand you're . . ." He paused, and for the briefest of seconds, an emotion Emerson couldn't identify flickered through his gaze. But then he tucked his shoulder blades around his spine, his shoulders straightening beneath his impeccably pressed doctor's coat, and the emotion disappeared. "Upset with me regarding our dinner conversation the other night. But you don't honestly mean to not ask for my help right now."

Emerson arranged her expression to show nothing but intent, despite the pain starting to radiate through her legs with every slam of her pulse. But no way was she telling him anything, even if he *had* managed to somehow stumble over her in the ED. "As a matter of fact, that is exactly what I mean to do."

The step back he took betrayed his surprise. "Don't be ridiculous. I'm the head of surgery at this hospital."

Right. As if she'd forget. But the fact that her father had seen her here was bad enough. If he knew the real reason, if he knew the truth—

"Em, your father wants to help you. Talk to him. Please."

Time extended for a heartbeat, one single thump-*thump* of time during which Emerson's brain processed. Gathered. Processed again.

And then all the air in the room vanished as Hunter's voice—God, his presence next to her *father*, of all people—smashed into her like a wrecking ball.

"You . . ." Confusion buzzed around Emerson's head for just one more second before all the dots lined up and connected with vivid, sickening clarity. "You *told* him?"

"I told him you were here," Hunter corrected, as if the semantics made some sort of a difference, and anger sailed through her, scalding her veins.

"How could you do this to me?" Her tone was high-pitched and damn near hysterical, but oh, she didn't care. She'd trusted Hunter, she'd believed him when he'd said she'd be fine, and this, *this* was what she got for her leap of faith?

He took a step toward her bed, and she had to hand it to him. The puppy dog eyes were a nice fucking touch. "I want to help you," he said, but before she could let loose with where he could shove his "help," her father stepped in.

"Emerson. Everyone here has your best interests at heart. Whatever is making you ill, I'm certain we can take care of it. I can have whatever specialists we need down here within the hour, and I'll confer with them to hire the very best caregivers. You could even move back into the house if—"

"*No.*" The word cracked from her mouth like gunfire, but she wasn't about to apologize for it. "Multiple sclerosis may be breaking my body, but I'm still perfectly capable of making my own decisions, including the ones pertaining to my healthcare. I don't need you"— she paused to jab a shaking finger at her father—"to strong-arm me into what you think is best, and I don't need *you*"—she pointed savagely at Hunter, dangerously close to losing what little cool she had left—"to try to fix me."

Her father's eyes flew wide. "Multiple sclerosis is your formal diagnosis? Are you certain?" After a few seconds, he took her glaring silence as the yes that it was. "Emerson, please, if you would just listen to reason—" he started, but she'd had enough.

"So you can tell me what to do and get the best possible spin on things while you're at it? Thanks, but I'm all set. I told you the other day I don't need your help. I haven't changed my mind."

Her icy stare at the curtain got the message across, and her father's mouth flattened into a grim line.

"I see. Then I suppose there's nothing more for us to talk about." He turned on the heels of his flawlessly polished loafers, nodding once at Hunter before leaving the curtain area.

After a breath, Hunter broke the deafening silence. "Look, I know—"

"Get out," she said, and his eyes widened like a pair of blue-gray saucers.

"What?" He blinked, and even though a dark, horrible part of her wanted to feel satisfied at the slash of hurt on his face, all she did was ache.

She'd shown him who she was, all her broken parts, and he'd betrayed her.

"Get out," Emerson repeated, manufacturing strength from God only knew where. "I don't want you here."

Hunter's startled expression gave way to something else. "You're mad, I know that."

"You know *nothing*," she spat, all the anger and fear and betrayal colliding in her chest to push the words right out of her. "You're so bound and determined to fix everything, but you don't get it, do you? This can't be fixed!" She slashed a hand through the air, the medical tape pulling at her skin as she gestured harshly at the dead weight of her legs. "*I* can't be fixed! Not by my father or any other doctors, not by you. Not by anyone! I'm broken, Hunter. I'm always going to be *broken*!"

Hunter flinched, his stare going dark beneath the overbright hospital fluorescents. "I care about you, Emerson. I know you're angry right now. Hurting." He sucked in an audible breath. "I didn't know how else to help you."

Her heart gave up a stupid, mutinous squeeze, and for a second, she nearly gave in to it. But then her legs seized in yet another all-too-painful round of This Is Your Life, and the hope behind her breastbone flickered out.

"You really want to help? Then get out, and don't come back. I've got enough damage on my own that I'm not going to recover from. I don't need you doing any more."

Hunter opened his mouth as if to argue. But then his eyes touched on the hospital bed, the IV tubes and monitors, and his shoulders fell.

"I hope you get some rest."

Only after his footsteps had faded completely did Emerson let herself cry. She thought her body had betrayed her in the worst way imaginable.

She'd had no idea that in the end, her body would be completely outdone by her heart.

CHAPTER TWENTY-SIX

Emerson rolled over in her hospital bed, wishing for all the world that she had a toothbrush. The light slipping in past the blinds told her she'd slept through the night, and although her legs were still pretty sore, she had more energy than she'd been able to muster in the last four days, easy, and her stomach seemed to have settled considerably.

Her heart? Still a train wreck, but nothing they could put in her IV was going to fix that.

Haven't you ever wondered what if...

No. *No.* She'd taken that leap of faith and it had blown up in her face. There was no more what if. Only what was.

God, what was hurt.

"Knock, knock." A familiar voice filtered in from the door, and Emerson sat up in surprise.

"Dr. Ortiz?"

The doctor poked his head past the entryway to her room. "Morning. I've got a minute before my shift starts downstairs, so I thought I'd bring you a peace offering."

Emerson waved him in, chuffing out a rusty laugh at the tray balanced in his well-muscled grasp. "Jell-O?"

"You have no idea how hard it is to snag the strawberry around here," Dr. Ortiz said, placing the tray on the rolling table beside her bed. "Anyway, I wanted to come see how you were doing. I feel bad that we had to keep you overnight. I know you didn't want to stay."

She let out a slow breath, busying herself by reaching for a spoon. "I understand. It was necessary, and I actually do feel a lot better today." She'd hated the decision, but in truth, she'd known it was the right one.

"I'm glad to hear that. Your vitals have improved a lot overnight. Once you get up and move around a bit, the neurologist on call should spring you."

Ah, at least there was one good thing. She had a lot to do once she got back on her feet, literally and figuratively. She was two sessions behind on that marketing webinar for Cross Creek, and . . .

Damn.

"Can I get you anything other than the Jell-O?" Dr. Ortiz asked, the concern in his black-coffee stare telling her she had a shitty poker face.

"Yeah, I . . ." She swallowed. Recalibrated. *Head up, eyes forward.* "I'd love to get my hands on some toiletries. That, and I'll need to figure out how to get home once the on-call doctor decides I'm good to go."

"Oh, that's easy," Dr. Ortiz said, his running shoes squeaking on the floor as he turned toward the door. "Your mother left a bag for you at the nurses' station, and your father said he'd arrange a car service if you needed a ride. Actually, he may be in the waiting room down the hall."

Emerson's jaw unhinged. "My parents know I'm up here?"

"Of course." His brows knit together over his stare. "Haven't they been in to see you? The charge nurse said they were here most of the night."

"No," she managed, confusion muffling her thoughts. "Are you sure they've been out there most of the night? *My* parents?"

Dr. Ortiz nodded. "I saw them briefly after I admitted you. We didn't discuss your health, obviously, but they didn't ask. All your father said was that you might be more comfortable in a private room if we had one and that they'd wait upstairs for you to rest. I'm sorry, I just assumed you knew they'd been here."

Emerson grabbed at a breath. Her parents trying to control things, she got. Hell, it was practically branded into the Montgomery DNA. But this felt odd, different somehow. They hadn't barged in, hadn't demanded that she listen to reason, hadn't insisted on a private room or pricey specialists. They hadn't even let her know they were there.

Her parents knew she had MS. She'd said so in the heat of the moment yesterday. She couldn't hide from the truth anymore, even if she wanted to.

And even though that truth scared the hell out of her, she didn't.

"Could you . . . could you see if my father is out in the waiting room?" she asked Dr. Ortiz, her pulse knocking against her throat. "I'd like to talk to him."

"Sure."

The brief minute between Dr. Ortiz's departure and her father's appearance at her door told Emerson her father had been right there in the waiting room, and even though his expression was as cool and unreadable as ever, his rumpled dress shirt and the shadows smudged beneath his eyes registered louder than any words.

"How are you feeling this morning?" Her father stood, stock-still in the doorway. Once, she would have taken it as a sign of his detachment. But now that she'd checked her stalwart defenses and studied him closely, Emerson realized with a start that he wasn't unaffected at all.

He had plenty of emotion. He just didn't have a clue what to do with it.

Oh God.

"Better," she whispered, realization tightening her throat. "Is Mom here, too?"

"No." A tiny thread of emotion skated over his face. "She protested, quite loudly, in fact, but I sent her home for a bit of rest."

Emerson nodded, gesturing to the chair next to her bed. "Will you sit down?"

His light-brown brows rose. "Are you sure that's what you'd like?"

Her defenses gave up a last-pass effort to make her ratchet down on the truth. But the words were past overdue, and she'd exhausted herself by keeping them inside.

She was tired of hiding. This was her reality, her life with MS, and she needed to own it, once and for all.

"It is," Emerson said, her heart pumping faster at the words. "I have multiple sclerosis, and I need to talk to you about it."

Starting at the beginning, she told him about the last six months, from the first odd twinges in her legs to her move back to Millhaven to the crushing relapse that had brought her full circle to the hospital room where they sat. Her father asked questions—most of them clinical, because emotions or not, he *was* still a doctor—but she answered each one, owning the truth about her body and her situation.

"I'm sorry I didn't tell you sooner," she said. "But I knew you and Mom were already so disappointed in me for coming back to Millhaven and leaving my job at the Lightning—God, for even becoming a physical therapist in the first place. I was afraid that if I told you I have MS, you'd just jump in and try to control things. I didn't want you to think I wasn't good enough, like you did when I was younger."

Her father looked genuinely startled. "What . . . what on earth makes you think I found you lacking when you were younger?"

And now they were both startled. "Um, you and Mom had pretty high expectations. You pushed pretty hard."

"Because we knew you were smart enough to achieve whatever you wanted," he said, his voice growing softer as he continued with, "Not because we thought you weren't good enough to do so."

Although she hated the question on the tip of her tongue, she knew she had to ask it. "Even when I chose to be a physical therapist and not a surgeon?"

"Emerson." He placed a hand on her bed, obviously struggling for words. "I apologize for my part in this rift between us. I'll admit that when you chose physical therapy over becoming an MD, I was stung. I thought it was a mistake, and frankly, I wanted you to love medicine the way I do. But expressing my emotions has never been my strong suit, and I realize I can be quite . . . stubborn."

Emerson bit her lip. "I get it from you. I didn't help matters by pushing you and Mom away."

"I realize now we had a poor way of showing it, but your mother and I really did always want what was best for you."

"I know," she said, and God, she finally did. "But I love being a physical therapist, Dad. The same way you love being a surgeon." The thought of her job made her throat tighten, but if she was going to face this, she needed to face *all* of it. "I don't know how my diagnosis is going to change my practice. I have some things to work out there. But I do know that being a physical therapist is the only thing I'm ever going to want as a career."

"I understand." Her father paused before adding, "I understand and I'm proud of you."

Emerson blinked, tears pricking at her eyelids. "You are?"

"Of course. Your mother and I have always been proud of you. You're our daughter." He reached for her hand, letting his fingers close over hers. "It's going to take time for us to repair things, I know. We've got a lot of lost time to make up for. But I love you, Emerson."

"I love you, too, Dad."

After a minute that included a few Kleenex on Emerson's part, her father gave her a small smile.

"So am I to assume that Hunter will be driving you home later today?"

Just like that, the ache in her heart returned, twisting deep. "No. I, ah. No."

Her father's forehead creased, but thank God, he skipped the Q and A. "Alright. I'm happy to take care of that. If you'd like," he tacked on.

"I would. Thank you," Emerson said, swallowing past the lump in her throat. Yes, Hunter might have thought he'd been helping her yesterday. But she'd believed him, she'd *trusted* him, and he'd gone behind her back to betray that. Plus, she had a debilitating illness, a permanent disease that was never going to let her go. There was a learning curve to taking care of herself that she hadn't even realized, let alone mastered. Expecting to have any kind of a relationship—with someone she'd told in no uncertain terms to butt the hell out of her life—was impossible.

Head up, eyes forward.

Moving on without Hunter was the only thing Emerson could do.

Hunter stood outside the hay barn, staring the damned thing down as if they were three steps away from a shootout. Although he'd volunteered for the most backbreaking tasks Cross Creek could spin up over the last twenty-four hours, the thought of setting even one toe in the barn made his gut want to head due south.

The last time he'd been here was with Emerson. And he was never going to bring her back here again.

I've got enough damage on my own that I'm not going to recover from . . . you can't fix this . . . you can't . . .

Fuck. He needed more work.

"You want to do this, or should I just keep standing here looking pretty?"

Eli's voice reality-checked Hunter right in the sternum. "Yeah, sorry." He stepped inside the barn, forcing his boots over to the spot where Eli had parked his truck by the lead-in to the hayloft. The sunny smell of fresh-mown hay made his heart flex against his ribs, but he stuffed the emotion back. Letting his feelings rule his actions had wrecked the only thing he'd ever held sacred other than the farm. No fucking way was he going anywhere other than easy-does-it ever again.

Jesus, he missed Emerson.

"Okay, I can't stand the look on your face anymore. What the hell is wrong with you?" Although his tone was ever joking, the press of Eli's work-gloved hands over his hips said Hunter wouldn't get away with dodging the question, and dammit, he supposed his brothers were going to find out about this soon enough, anyway.

"Emerson and I broke up." The words left a bitter aftertaste in his mouth. Not that he could change them.

"Shut up," Eli said, his cocky expression evaporating in less than a breath. "Are you serious?"

"Wish I wasn't." Hell, he wished for a lot of things.

Eli blew out a breath. "I thought you said she wasn't feeling well. Is that why she hasn't been by, because you guys called it quits?"

Hunter's pulse thrummed. Not knowing what else to do, he'd stuck to the food poisoning story she'd given Doc Sanders to explain yesterday's absence from the farm. "It's kind of a long story." And not one he could tell without betraying her trust even further. "Basically, she trusted me with something and I screwed it all up. I thought I was helping, but . . . I wasn't, so she told me to take off."

"And you did?" Eli's disbelief was loud and clear, but Hunter met it with a joyless laugh.

"It's what she wanted." He'd stood in the waiting room of the emergency department for over an hour before he'd finally made himself leave. Emerson had been so angry, and sticking around to argue with her would've only upset her further and kept her from the rest she'd so obviously needed. Plus, she'd made her feelings clear.

You can't fix this.

"And you're sure that's what she wanted?" Eli asked, and whoa, the question caught Hunter off guard.

"Yeah," he said, although his treasonous brain reminded him of the tiny little glimmer of hope that had flashed through her eyes before she'd told him in no uncertain terms to get out. "Anyway, I just need to keep my nose to the grindstone and work. Rocking the boat is what got me into this mess in the first place. The last thing I need to do is stir up any more shit by going to fight about it again."

"You are such a fucking idiot."

Hunter's head jacked around. "Beg pardon?"

He cut the edges of the words just enough to translate his irritation, but hell if Eli didn't back down by so much as a millimeter.

"I said you're a fucking idiot. You think rocking the boat is what got you into this? I hate to be the bearer of bad news, Hunt, but you got *yourself* into this."

"Eli," he growled, taking a step forward. Just because he'd always gone out of his way to keep the peace in their family didn't mean he was above a brotherly brawl to blow off some steam.

A fact that Eli seemed to have anticipated, because he took a step back and lifted his hands. "Oh, don't go getting all pissy. Falling for Emerson twice is probably the best thing you ever did. Or it will be once you fix it. But you're not really going to let go without a fight, are you?"

"She's angry," Hunter said, although it was an epic understatement.

"Okay. So you betrayed a confidence. You thought you were doing the right thing, didn't you?"

"Yes." As dumb as it had been, he really had believed telling her father she was there would help rather than hurt.

"And you love her, right?" Eli asked.

Hunter didn't hesitate. "Yes."

"Well, then, do those of us who have to look at your moping face a favor, would you please, and go get that woman back. For Chrissake, Hunt. Go rock the boat a little."

Hunter opened his mouth to tell Eli he was insane. Emerson was going to slam the door in his face, maybe even call Lane Atlee to come haul his ass to the pokey for showing up on her doorstep like a lunatic.

But you know what, he *was* a lunatic. He was stark, raving crazy for her, and his brother was right.

Hunter needed to do whatever it took to make her see the truth. Even if that meant taking the biggest risk of all.

"I've gotta go," he blurted, but Eli was already waving him off.

"Uh-huh. You can thank me later, Romeo."

Hunter nodded, already running toward his truck. He'd either thank Eli or he'd be calling him for bail money. Either way, this time Hunter wasn't backing down.

CHAPTER TWENTY-SEVEN

Emerson sat curled up on her sofa with a blanket around her shoulders and a stack of romance novels at her side. Her mother had made triple sure her fridge was stocked, her stomach was full (okay, as full as was feasible, because as both her father and Dr. Ortiz had pointed out, recovery from dehydration wasn't a sprint) and her new prescriptions were filled. Funny, Emerson hadn't minded the help as much as she thought she might.

But even though her belly was full and her body was well rested, her heart still hurt like a son of a bitch.

Haven't you ever wondered what if . . .

Shaking her head, she swiped a book from the top of the stack. What's done was done, and she needed to move on, heartsore or not. But before she could crack the cover and dive into some literary therapy, a knock sounded off on her door.

"Probably Daisy," she murmured. Leave it to her friend to want to check on her after their earlier phone call. Emerson padded carefully to the door, her breath lodging in her windpipe at the sight of the person on the other side of the peephole.

What if . . . what if . . .

"Hunter?" she gasped, after tugging the door wide on its hinges. He looked half crazed, his blue eyes blazing with intensity and his hair sticking up in so many directions, she'd swear he'd driven here at Mach 2 with all the windows rolled down, and great God in heaven, he was still *gorgeous*. "What are you doing here?"

For a second, he blinked, as if he were somehow shocked she'd answered the door. But then he took a step forward, his stare growing even bolder as he said, "Em. I know you're mad, and you have every right to be. In fact, you have every right to knee me in the nuts, although I really hope you don't. But the truth is, I deserve it, and I came here to apologize. I fucked up yesterday—God, I fucked up something fierce, and even though I didn't mean to betray your trust, I know I did."

Her heart launched against her ribs. "Hunter," she started, but he shook his head and barreled on.

"Wait. Please, before you kick me out of here, please let me finish. I also came to tell you you're right. I can't fix you. I can't fix you because you don't need to be fixed. You're not broken. You might have MS, but you're still perfect. You're determined and smart and every single word for beautiful that I can think of. I should have told you this already, but I love you exactly the way you are."

Emerson's chest constricted, her lips parting in pure shock. "Hunter," she said again.

But again, he shook his head. "I only have one more thing to say, but it's the most important thing of all. I do love you, Em." His eyes flashed with emotion, pure and raw and deep. "I love you so much. I've *always* loved you. I was just too afraid to rock the boat and tell you, but then I rocked too hard and betrayed your trust, and . . . I wanted to help, but I didn't. Anyway, I just wanted to come out here and tell you that. I'm so sorry I hurt you."

For a minute, Emerson couldn't speak, couldn't move, could barely breathe. Then she realized the truth with clarity she'd never forget.

This wasn't what if. This was what *was*.

Standing right in front of her, telling her he loved her, Hunter was everything.

"You didn't hurt me," she said, and the look of sheer disbelief on his face had her amending her words with a soft laugh. "Okay, you did. But you weren't wrong, Hunter. I *did* need help. I needed a lot of things. But none of them more than I need you."

"You . . . need me?"

She nodded, and of all the things in the world she'd ever said, she meant this the most. "I do."

"But what about your parents? I didn't tell anyone about your MS, but—"

"No, but I did," Emerson said, and for the first time, the truth of it didn't frighten her. "My parents, Doc Sanders, Daisy. I told all of them. Not because I had to. But because I needed to. You're right—I'm not broken. I have MS. The disease is part of my life. I can't keep hiding that."

"And you're okay?" Hunter asked, his eyes sliding over her.

She let him look, bruises and swelling and all. "I've had better days," she admitted, because her legs still felt like Goodyear rejects. "But I'm going to meet with the head of neurology at Camden Valley this week to talk to him about better long-term treatment options, and Doc Sanders and I will work out a schedule to accommodate my relapses when they occur."

"And you did all of this because I told your father you were in the ED?"

Emerson smiled, taking a step toward him. "I did all of this because you showed me that honesty was what I needed. I was just too scared of not being good enough to see that you were right."

He met her step with one of his own, bringing him within arms' reach. "You are so much more than good enough. I never should have betrayed you. I'm so sorry, Em."

"As crazy as it sounds, I'm glad you did. You did the wrong thing for the right reason, Hunter. You knew what I needed, even when I didn't." She paused, her heartbeat growing faster in her chest. "Speaking of which, my MS is going to be a lifelong fight. I'm going to do my best to manage it, but sometimes I'm going to have bad days, or even weeks."

For a second, Hunter stood in confusion, until realization widened his gray-blue eyes. "Are you asking if I can handle that?"

Emerson's breath caught, but she needed to know. "Yes. I don't ever want to be a burden, and this disease . . ."

"Is part of you," he finished. "When I told you I had you, I meant it no matter what. Taking care of you is what makes me happy. It's what I want more than anything. You'll never be a burden to me because I love you just as you are, Emerson."

"I know you love me." She closed the rest of the distance between them, circling her arms around his shoulders and letting him hold her steady. "Just like I love you."

Hunter gathered her close, scooping her up just as he had in her dream. "Well, that's a relief, because you, Miss Montgomery, are stuck with me."

"That sounds perfect to me, Mr. Cross."

And as he kissed her face and held her close, Emerson knew deep in her heart that no matter what life sent in her direction, she would always be more than good enough in his arms.

ACKNOWLEDGMENTS

This book has been a truly exciting ride, but *Crossing Hearts* would never be in y'alls hot little hands if it weren't for the following people.

Huge thanks to my fantastic agent and fellow *Supernatural* fan, Nalini Akolekar, for not even blinking when I said, "Okay, so I want to write about farmers, but bear with me for a second . . ." I am so glad to be on this journey with you. Chris Werner and Melody Guy at Montlake Publishing, thank you for believing in this series, and also for validating my penchant for gourmet ice cream. I'm so grateful for your unending support.

It's not easy for a city girl to write about life on a 750-acre farm, so on the research side, I have to thank Jennifer McQuiston for inviting me to her hometown of Elkton, Virginia, to show me the ropes (and the co-op!). Many thanks to Matt Lohr and his parents, Gary and Ellen, who were incredibly patient with my questions about family farming. Also, a big thank-you goes out to Dean and Kay Smith, who graciously allowed me to feed their sheep, raid their henhouse, and "borrow" their dog Lucy for a cameo in this book. Any mistakes made or liberties taken with the facts of farm life are all my own.

Giant hugs and bottomless martinis go out to Alyssa Alexander and Tracy Brogan, who have been with me on this crazy writer trip ever since that very first RWA conference in 2010. I am so, so proud of all we've learned and done, and am humbly grateful for your friendship.

To Robin Covington and Avery Flynn, I'm not sure if there are words for this, but you know I've got to give it a go. Your support and love borders on the astronomical, and without it, I wouldn't be able to write a single word. Thank you for all your encouragement to reinvent the wheel.

My three daughters, Reader Girl, Smarty Pants, and Tiny Dancer, thank you for putting up with Your Crazy Mommy when it's deadline time, and also for bragging to your teachers that I am a "famous author who writes about kissing." And Mr. K, thank you for putting up with Your Crazy Wife when it's deadline time, and also for bragging to your coworkers that I am a "famous author who writes about kissing." I love the four of you more than any words can say.

And lastly, to every one of you reading this book, thank you. Being an author is my dream job, but I could not do it without you. I'm so very grateful to share Hunter and Emerson's story with you, and I hope that you love it as much as I loved writing it. Happy reading, everyone!

ABOUT THE AUTHOR

Kimberly Kincaid writes contemporary romance that splits the difference between sexy and sweet. When she's not sitting cross-legged in an ancient desk chair that she calls "the Pleather Bomber," she can be found practicing crazy amounts of yoga, whipping up everything from enchiladas to éclairs in her kitchen, or curled up with her nose in a book. Kimberly is a *USA Today* bestselling author and a 2016 and 2015 RWA RITA® finalist who lives (and writes!) by the mantra "Food is love." She resides in Virginia with her wildly patient husband and their three daughters. Visit her at www.kimberlykincaid.com or on Facebook, Twitter, Pinterest, and Instagram.